VAMPIRE ACADEMY

VAMPIRE ACADEMY

RICHELLE MEAD

RAZORBILL

An Imprint of Penguin Random House

RAZORBILL

An Imprint of Penguin Random House

Penguin.com

ISBN: 978-0-448-49429-6

Printed in the United States of America

1 3 5 7 9 10 8 6 4 2

Dear Reader,

I collect ideas. They pop into my head while I'm out in the world doing ordinary things, be it shopping at the grocery store or putting in time on an exercise bike. None of these ideas instantly transforms into a story. They're fragments. One might be a cool setting. Another might be a "what if . . ." dilemma. Or maybe there's a quirky character I think would be fun to write. Eventually, I get enough ideas, and I see if I can mesh them together and make a story. Sometimes it works. Sometimes it doesn't.

Vampire Academy worked—far better than I'd ever expected. I'd fallen in love with the Romanian myth of two races of vampires, and I became obsessed with visualizing how they'd create societies within our society. I'd read countless books about kickass heroines but never about how they became that way. What did they do while they were young? How did they temper a reckless nature with doing the right thing? And of course, there was the romance piece: just a tiny flicker of an idea about a girl in love with her mentor and the fallout that ensued.

Now, ten years later, the crafting of that collection of ideas into one girl's story has created a six-book series and a spin-off that are beloved around the world. I meet readers who get Rose's tattoos. Who identify with her. Who dream with her. And the outpouring of emotion I've seen from readers like you has been more humbling and wondrous than I can explain. I never imagined I'd have the opportunity to connect with so many amazing people.

For this anniversary edition, I've included some stories I've wanted to tell that will help flesh out the events in this first book and answer questions many readers have had. How did Christian's parents turn? What was running away from St. Vladimir's like for Lissa? What did Dimitri first think of Rose? And what exactly does Rose do for fun when she's not saving the Moroi civilization?

These questions and more are addressed in the collection of stories at the end of this book. I hope readers love getting this peek into the Vampire Academy world because I've certainly loved having the chance to revisit it. Even with it and the Bloodlines series wrapped up, the characters still go on with a life of their own, thanks to the fans who keep loving them. I'm so grateful to all the readers who've stayed passionate and loyal to the series after all these years. It's made writing a joy. And who knows? Maybe there are more new adventures for Rose and the gang on some future day.

Yours,

Richelle Mead

RICHELLE MEAD

ONE

I felt her fear before I heard her screams.

Her nightmare pulsed into me, shaking me out of my own dream, which had had something to do with a beach and some hot guy rubbing suntan oil on me. Images—hers, not mine—tumbled through my mind: fire and blood, the smell of smoke, the twisted metal of a car. The pictures wrapped around me, suffocating me, until some rational part of my brain reminded me that this wasn't *my* dream.

I woke up, strands of long, dark hair sticking to my forehead.

Lissa lay in her bed, thrashing and screaming. I bolted out of mine, quickly crossing the few feet that separated us.

"Liss," I said, shaking her. "Liss, wake up."

Her screams dropped off, replaced by soft whimpers. "Andre," she moaned. "Oh God."

I helped her sit up. "Liss, you aren't there anymore. Wake up."

After a few moments, her eyes fluttered open, and in the dim lighting, I could see a flicker of consciousness start to take over. Her frantic breathing slowed, and she leaned into me, resting her head against my shoulder. I put an arm around her and ran a hand over her hair.

"It's okay," I told her gently. "Everything's okay."

"I had that dream."

"Yeah. I know."

We sat like that for several minutes, not saying anything else. When I felt her emotions calm down, I leaned over to the nightstand between our beds and turned on the lamp. It glowed dimly, but neither of us really needed much to see by. Attracted by the light, our housemate's cat, Oscar, leapt up onto the sill of the open window.

He gave me a wide berth—animals don't like dhampirs, for whatever reason—but jumped onto the bed and rubbed his head against Lissa, purring softly. Animals didn't have a problem with Moroi, and they all loved Lissa in particular. Smiling, she scratched his chin, and I felt her calm further.

"When did we last do a feeding?" I asked, studying her face. Her fair skin was paler than usual. Dark circles hung under her eyes, and there was an air of frailty about her. School had been hectic this week, and I couldn't remember the last time I'd given her blood. "It's been like . . . more than two days, hasn't it? Three? Why didn't you say anything?"

She shrugged and wouldn't meet my eyes. "You were busy. I didn't want to—"

"Screw that," I said, shifting into a better position. No wonder she seemed so weak. Oscar, not wanting me any closer, leapt down and returned to the window, where he could watch at a safe distance. "Come on. Let's do this."

"Rose—"

"Come *on*. It'll make you feel better."

I tilted my head and tossed my hair back, baring my neck. I saw her hesitate, but the sight of my neck and what it offered proved too powerful. A hungry expression crossed her face, and her lips parted slightly, exposing the fangs she normally kept hidden while living among humans. Those fangs contrasted oddly with the rest of her features. With her pretty face and pale blond hair, she looked more like an angel than a vampire.

As her teeth neared my bare skin, I felt my heart race with a mix of fear and anticipation. I always hated feeling the latter, but it was nothing I could help, a weakness I couldn't shake.

Her fangs bit into me, hard, and I cried out at the brief flare of pain. Then it faded, replaced by a wonderful, golden joy that spread through my body. It was better than any of the times I'd been drunk or high. Better than sex—or so I imagined, since I'd never done it. It was a blanket of pure, refined pleasure, wrapping me up and promising everything would be right in the world. On and on it went. The chemicals in her saliva triggered an endorphin rush, and I lost track of the world, lost track of who I was.

Then, regretfully, it was over. It had taken less than a minute.

She pulled back, wiping her hand across her lips as she studied me. "You okay?"

"I . . . yeah." I lay back on the bed, dizzy from the blood loss. "I just need to sleep it off. I'm fine."

Her pale, jade-green eyes watched me with concern. She stood up. "I'm going to get you something to eat."

My protests came awkwardly to my lips, and she left before I could get out a sentence. The buzz from her bite had lessened as soon as she broke the connection, but some of it still lingered in my veins, and I felt a goofy smile cross my lips. Turning my head, I glanced up at Oscar, still sitting in the window.

"You don't know what you're missing," I told him.

His attention was on something outside. Hunkering down into a crouch, he puffed out his jet-black fur. His tail started twitching.

My smile faded, and I forced myself to sit up. The world spun, and I waited for it to right itself before trying to stand. When I managed it, the dizziness set in again and this time refused to leave. Still, I felt okay enough to stumble to the window and peer out with Oscar. He eyed me warily, scooted over a little, and then returned to whatever had held his attention.

A warm breeze—unseasonably warm for a Portland fall—played with my hair as I leaned out. The street was dark and relatively quiet. It was three in the morning, just about the only time a college campus settled down, at least somewhat. The house in which we'd rented a room for the past eight months sat on a residential street with old, mismatched houses. Across the road, a streetlight flickered, nearly ready to burn out. It still cast enough light for me to make out the shapes of cars and buildings. In our own yard, I could see the silhouettes of trees and bushes.

And a man watching me.

I jerked back in surprise. A figure stood by a tree in the yard, about thirty feet away, where he could easily see through the window. He was close enough that I probably could have thrown something and hit him. He was certainly close enough that he could have seen what Lissa and I had just done.

The shadows covered him so well that even with my heightened sight, I couldn't make out any of his features, save for his height. He was tall. Really tall. He stood there for just a moment, barely discernible, and then stepped back, disappearing into the shadows cast by the trees on the far side of the yard. I was pretty sure I saw someone else move nearby and join him before the blackness swallowed them both.

Whoever these figures were, Oscar didn't like them. Not counting me, he usually got along with most people, growing upset only when someone posed an immediate danger. The guy outside hadn't done anything threatening to Oscar, but the cat had sensed something, something that put him on edge.

Something similar to what he always sensed in me.

Icy fear raced through me, almost—but not quite—eradicating the lovely bliss of Lissa's bite. Backing up from the window, I jerked on a pair of jeans that I found on the floor, nearly falling over in the process. Once they were on, I grabbed my coat and Lissa's, along with our wallets. Shoving my feet into the first shoes I saw, I headed out the door.

Downstairs, I found her in the cramped kitchen, rummaging through the refrigerator. One of our housemates, Jeremy, sat at the table, hand on his forehead as he stared sadly at a calculus book. Lissa regarded me with surprise.

"You shouldn't be up."

"We have to go. Now."

Her eyes widened, and then a moment later, understanding clicked in. "Are you . . . really? Are you sure?"

I nodded. I couldn't explain how I knew for sure. I just did.

Jeremy watched us curiously. "What's wrong?"

An idea came to mind. "Liss, get his car keys."

He looked back and forth between us. "What are you—"

Lissa unhesitatingly walked over to him. Her fear poured into me through our psychic bond, but there was something else too: her complete faith that I would take care of everything, that we would be safe. Like always, I hoped I was worthy of that kind of trust.

She smiled broadly and gazed directly into his eyes. For a moment, Jeremy just stared, still confused, and then I saw the thrall seize him. His eyes glazed over, and he regarded her adoringly.

"We need to borrow your car," she said in a gentle voice. "Where are your keys?"

He smiled, and I shivered. I had a high resistance to compulsion, but I could still feel its effects when it was directed at another person. That, and I'd been taught my entire life that using it was wrong. Reaching into his pocket, Jeremy handed over a set of keys hanging on a large red key chain.

"Thank you," said Lissa. "And where is it parked?"

"Down the street," he said dreamily. "At the corner. By Brown." Four blocks away.

"Thank you," she repeated, backing up. "As soon as we leave, I want you to go back to studying. Forget you ever saw us tonight."

He nodded obligingly. I got the impression he would have walked off a cliff for her right then if she'd asked. All humans were susceptible to compulsion, but Jeremy appeared weaker than most. That came in handy right now.

"Come on," I told her. "We've got to move."

We stepped outside, heading toward the corner he'd named. I was still dizzy from the bite and kept stumbling, unable to move as quickly as I wanted. Lissa had to catch hold of me a few times to stop me from falling. All the time, that anxiety rushed into me from her mind. I tried my best to ignore it; I had my own fears to deal with.

"Rose . . . what are we going to do if they catch us?" she whispered.

"They won't," I said fiercely. "I won't let them."

"But if they've found us—"

"They found us before. They didn't catch us then. We'll just drive over to the train station and go to L.A. They'll lose the trail."

I made it sound simple. I always did, even though there

was nothing simple about being on the run from the people we'd grown up with. We'd been doing it for two years, hiding wherever we could and just trying to finish high school. Our senior year had just started, and living on a college campus had seemed safe. We were so close to freedom.

She said nothing more, and I felt her faith in me surge up once more. This was the way it had always been between us. I was the one who took action, who made sure things happened— sometimes recklessly so. She was the more reasonable one, the one who thought things out and researched them extensively before acting. Both styles had their uses, but at the moment, reck- lessness was called for. We didn't have time to hesitate.

Lissa and I had been best friends ever since kindergar- ten, when our teacher had paired us together for writing lessons. Forcing five-year-olds to spell *Vasilisa Dragomir* and *Rosemarie Hathaway* was beyond cruel, and we'd—or rather, *I'd*—responded appropriately. I'd chucked my book at our teacher and called her a fascist bastard. I hadn't known what those words meant, but I'd known how to hit a mov- ing target.

Lissa and I had been inseparable ever since.

"Do you hear that?" she asked suddenly.

It took me a few seconds to pick up what her sharper senses already had. Footsteps, moving fast. I grimaced. We had two more blocks to go.

"We've got to run for it," I said, catching hold of her arm.

"But you can't—"

"Run."

It took every ounce of my willpower not to pass out on the sidewalk. My body didn't want to run after losing blood or while still metabolizing the effects of her saliva. But I ordered my muscles to stop their bitching and clung to Lissa as our feet pounded against the concrete. Normally I could have outrun her without any extra effort—particularly since she was barefoot—but tonight, she was all that held me upright.

The pursuing footsteps grew louder, closer. Black stars danced before my eyes. Ahead of us, I could make out Jeremy's green Honda. Oh God, if we could just make it—

Ten feet from the car, a man stepped directly into our path. We came to a screeching halt, and I jerked Lissa back by her arm. It was *him*, the guy I'd seen across the street watching me. He was older than us, maybe mid-twenties, and as tall as I'd figured, probably six-six or six-seven. And under different circumstances—say, when he wasn't holding up our desperate escape—I would have thought he was hot. Shoulder-length brown hair, tied back in a short ponytail. Dark brown eyes. A long brown coat—a duster, I thought it was called.

But his hotness was irrelevant now. He was only an obstacle keeping Lissa and me away from the car and our freedom. The footsteps behind us slowed, and I knew our pursuers had caught up. Off to the sides, I detected more movement, more people closing in. God. They'd sent almost a dozen guardians to retrieve us. I couldn't believe it. The queen herself didn't travel with that many.

Panicked and not entirely in control of my higher reasoning, I acted out of instinct. I pressed up to Lissa, keeping her behind me and away from the man who appeared to be the leader.

"Leave her alone," I growled. "Don't touch her."

His face was unreadable, but he held out his hands in what was apparently supposed to be some sort of calming gesture, like I was a rabid animal he was planning to sedate.

"I'm not going to—"

He took a step forward. Too close.

I attacked him, leaping out in an offensive maneuver I hadn't used in two years, not since Lissa and I had run away. The move was stupid, another reaction born of instinct and fear. And it was hopeless. He was a skilled guardian, not a novice who hadn't finished his training. He also wasn't weak and on the verge of passing out.

And man, was he fast. I'd forgotten how fast guardians could be, how they could move and strike like cobras. He knocked me off as though brushing away a fly, and his hands slammed into me and sent me backwards. I don't think he meant to strike that hard—probably just intended to keep me away—but my lack of coordination interfered with my ability to respond. Unable to catch my footing, I started to fall, heading straight toward the sidewalk at a twisted angle, hip-first. It was going to hurt. A *lot*.

Only it didn't.

Just as quickly as he'd blocked me, the man reached out and caught my arm, keeping me upright. When I'd steadied myself, I noticed he was staring at me—or, more precisely, at my neck. Still disoriented, I didn't get it right away. Then, slowly, my free hand reached up to the side of my throat and lightly touched the wound Lissa had made earlier. When I pulled my fingers back, I saw slick, dark blood on my skin. Embarrassed, I shook my hair so that it fell forward around my face. My hair was thick and long and completely covered my neck. I'd grown it out for precisely this reason.

The guy's dark eyes lingered on the now-covered bite a moment longer and then met mine. I returned his look defiantly and quickly jerked out of his hold. He let me go, though I knew he could have restrained me all night if he'd wanted. Fighting the nauseating dizziness, I backed toward Lissa again, bracing myself for another attack. Suddenly, her hand caught hold of mine. "Rose," she said quietly. "Don't."

Her words had no effect on me at first, but calming thoughts gradually began to settle in my mind, coming across through the bond. It wasn't exactly compulsion—she wouldn't use that on me—but it was effectual, as was the fact that we were hopelessly outnumbered and outclassed. Even I knew struggling would be pointless. The tension left my body, and I sagged in defeat.

Sensing my resignation, the man stepped forward, turning his attention to Lissa. His face was calm. He swept her a bow and managed to look graceful doing it, which surprised me considering his height. "My name is Dimitri Belikov," he said. I could hear a faint Russian accent. "I've come to take you back to St. Vladimir's Academy, Princess."

TWO

My hatred notwithstanding, I had to admit Dimi-tri Beli-whatever was pretty smart. After they'd carted us off to the airport to and onto the Academy's private jet, he'd taken one look at the two of us whispering and ordered us separated.

"Don't let them talk to each other," he warned the guard-ian who escorted me to the back of the plane. "Five minutes together, and they'll come up with an escape plan."

I shot him a haughty look and stormed off down the aisle. Never mind the fact we *had* been planning escape.

As it was, things didn't look good for our heroes—or heroines, rather. Once we were in the air, our odds of escape dropped further. Even supposing a miracle occurred and I did manage to take out all ten guardians, we'd sort of have a prob-lem in getting off the plane. I figured they might have para-chutes aboard somewhere, but in the unlikely event I'd be able to operate one, there was still that little issue of survival, seeing as we'd probably land somewhere in the Rocky Mountains.

No, we weren't getting off this plane until it landed in backwoods Montana. I'd have to think of something then, something that involved getting past the Academy's magical wards and ten times as many guardians. Yeah. No problem.

Although Lissa sat at the front with the Russian guy, her fear sang back to me, pounding inside my head like a hammer. My concern for her cut into my fury. They couldn't take her back *there*, not to that place. I wondered if Dimitri might have hesitated if he could feel what I did and if he knew what I knew. Probably not. He didn't care.

As it was, her emotions grew so strong that for a moment, I had the disorienting sensation of sitting in her seat—in her *skin* even. It happened sometimes, and without much warning, she'd pull me right into her head. Dimitri's tall frame sat beside me, and my hand—*her* hand—gripped a bottle of water. He leaned forward to pick up something, revealing six tiny symbols tattooed on the back of his neck: *molnija* marks. They looked like two streaks of jagged lightning crossing in an X symbol. One for each Strigoi he'd killed. Above them was a twisting line, sort of like a snake, that marked him as a guardian. The promise mark.

Blinking, I fought against her and shifted back into my own head with a grimace. I hated when that happened. Feeling Lissa's emotions was one thing, but slipping into her was something we both despised. She saw it as an invasion of privacy, so I usually didn't tell her when it happened. Neither of us could control it. It was another effect of the bond, a bond neither of us fully understood. Legends existed about psychic links between guardians and their Moroi, but the stories had never mentioned anything like this. We fumbled through it as best we could.

Near the end of the flight, Dimitri walked back to where I sat and traded places with the guardian beside me. I pointedly turned away, staring out the window absentmindedly.

Several moments of silence passed. Finally, he said, "Were you really going to attack all of us?"

I didn't answer.

"Doing that . . . protecting her like that—it was very brave." He paused. "*Stupid*, but still brave. Why did you even try it?"

I glanced over at him, brushing my hair out of my face so I could look him levelly in the eye. "Because I'm her guardian." I turned back toward the window.

After another quiet moment, he stood up and returned to the front of the jet.

When we landed, Lissa and I had no choice but to let the commandos drive us out to the Academy. Our car stopped at the gate, and our driver spoke with guards who verified we weren't Strigoi about to go off on a killing spree. After a minute, they let us pass on through the wards and up to the Academy itself. It was around sunset—the start of the vampiric day—and the campus lay wrapped in shadows.

It probably looked the same, sprawling and gothic. The Moroi were big on tradition; nothing ever changed with them. This school wasn't as old as the ones back in Europe, but it had been built in the same style. The buildings boasted elaborate, almost churchlike architecture, with high peaks and stone carvings. Wrought iron gates enclosed small gardens and doorways here and there. After living on a college campus, I had a new appreciation for just how much this place resembled a university more than a typical high school.

We were on the secondary campus, which was divided into lower and upper schools. Each was built around a large open quadrangle decorated with stone paths and enormous, century-old trees. We were going toward the upper school's quad, which had academic buildings on one side, while dhampir dormitories and the gym sat opposite. Moroi dorms sat on one of the other ends, and opposite them were the administrative buildings that also served the lower school. Younger students lived on the primary campus, farther to the west.

Around all the campuses was space, space, and more space. We were in Montana, after all, miles away from any real city. The air felt cool in my lungs and smelled of pine and wet, decaying leaves. Overgrown forests ringed the perimeters of the Academy, and during the day, you could see mountains rising up in the distance.

As we walked into the main part of the upper school, I broke from my guardian and ran up to Dimitri.

"Hey, Comrade."

He kept walking and wouldn't look at me. "You want to talk now?

"Are you taking us to Kirova?"

"*Headmistress* Kirova," he corrected. On the other side of him, Lissa shot me a look that said, *Don't start something*.

"Headmistress. Whatever. She's still a self-righteous old bit—"

My words faded as the guardians led us through a set of doors—straight into the commons. I sighed. Were these people *really* so cruel? There had to be at least a dozen ways to get to Kirova's office, and they were taking us right through the center of the commons.

And it was breakfast time.

Novice guardians—dhampirs like me—and Moroi sat together, eating and socializing, faces alight with whatever current gossip held the Academy's attention. When we entered, the loud buzz of conversation stopped instantly, like someone had flipped a switch. Hundreds of sets of eyes swiveled toward us.

I returned the stares of my former classmates with a lazy grin, trying to get a sense as to whether things had changed. Nope. Didn't seem like it. Camille Conta still looked like the prim, perfectly groomed bitch I remembered, still the self-appointed leader of the Academy's royal Moroi cliques. Off to the side, Lissa's gawky near-cousin Natalie watched with wide eyes, as innocent and naive as before.

And on the other side of the room . . . well, that was interesting. Aaron. Poor, poor Aaron, who'd no doubt had his heart broken when Lissa left. He still looked as cute as ever—maybe more so now—with those same golden looks that complemented hers so well. His eyes followed her every move. Yes. Definitely not over her. It was sad, really, because Lissa had never really been all that into him. I think she'd gone out with him simply because it seemed like the expected thing to do.

But what I found most interesting was that Aaron had

apparently found a way to pass the time without her. Beside him, holding his hand, was a Moroi girl who looked about eleven but had to be older, unless he'd become a pedophile during our absence. With plump little cheeks and blond ringlets, she looked like a porcelain doll. A very pissed off and evil porcelain doll. She gripped his hand tightly and shot Lissa a look of such burning hatred that it stunned me. What the hell was that all about? She was no one I knew. Just a jealous girlfriend, I guessed. I'd be pissed too if my guy was watching someone else like that.

Our walk of shame mercifully ended, though our new setting—Headmistress Kirova's office—didn't really improve things. The old hag looked exactly like I remembered, sharp-nosed and gray-haired. She was tall and slim, like most Moroi, and had always reminded me of a vulture. I knew her well because I'd spent a lot of time in her office.

Most of our escorts left us once Lissa and I were seated, and I felt a little less like a prisoner. Only Alberta, the captain of the school's guardians, and Dimitri stayed. They took up positions along the wall, looking stoic and terrifying, just as their job description required.

Kirova fixed her angry eyes on us and opened her mouth to begin what would no doubt be a major bitch session. A deep, gentle voice stopped her.

"Vasilisa."

Startled, I realized there was someone else in the room. I hadn't noticed. Careless for a guardian, even a novice one.

With a great deal of effort, Victor Dashkov rose from a corner chair. *Prince* Victor Dashkov. Lissa sprang up and ran to him, throwing her arms around his frail body.

"Uncle," she whispered. She sounded on the verge of tears as she tightened her grip.

With a small smile, he gently patted her back. "You have no idea how glad I am to see you safe, Vasilisa." He looked toward me. "And you too, Rose."

I nodded back, trying to hide how shocked I was. He'd been sick when we left, but this—this was *horrible*. He was Natalie's father, only about forty or so, but he looked twice that age. Pale. Withered. Hands shaking. My heart broke watching him. With all the horrible people in the world, it didn't seem fair that this guy should get a disease that was going to kill him young and ultimately keep him from becoming king.

Although not technically her uncle—the Moroi used family terms very loosely, especially the royals—Victor was a close friend of Lissa's family and had gone out of his way to help her after her parents had died. I liked him; he was the first person I was happy to see here.

Kirova let them have a few more moments and then stiffly drew Lissa back to her seat.

Time for the lecture.

It was a good one—one of Kirova's best, which was saying something. She was a master at them. I swear that was the only reason she'd gone into school administration, because

I had yet to see any evidence of her actually *liking* kids. The rant covered the usual topics: responsibility, reckless behavior, self-centeredness. . . . Bleh. I immediately found myself spacing out, alternatively pondering the logistics of escaping through the window in her office.

But when the tirade shifted to me—well, that was when I tuned back in.

"You, Miss Hathaway, broke the most sacred promise among our kind: the promise of a guardian to protect a Moroi. It is a great trust. A trust that you violated by selfishly taking the princess away from here. The Strigoi would love to finish off the Dragomirs; *you* nearly enabled them to do it."

"Rose didn't kidnap me." Lissa spoke before I could, her voice and face calm, despite her uneasy feelings. "I wanted to go. Don't blame her."

Ms. Kirova *tsk*ed at us both and paced the office, hands folded behind her narrow back.

"Miss Dragomir, you could have been the one who orchestrated the entire plan for all I know, but it was still *her* responsibility to make sure you didn't carry it out. If she'd done her duty, she would have notified someone. If she'd done her duty, she would have kept you safe."

I snapped.

"I *did* do my duty!" I shouted, jumping up from my chair. Dimitri and Alberta both flinched but left me alone since I wasn't trying to hit anyone. Yet. "I did keep her safe! I kept her safe when none of *you*"—I made a sweeping gesture around the room—"could do it. I took her away to protect her. I did what I had to do. You certainly weren't going to."

Through the bond, I felt Lissa trying to send me calming messages, again urging me not to let anger get the best of me. Too late.

Kirova stared at me, her face blank. "Miss Hathaway, forgive me if I fail to see the logic of how taking her out of a heavily guarded, magically secured environment is protecting her. Unless there's something you aren't telling us?"

I bit my lip.

"I see. Well, then. By my estimation, the only reason you left—aside from the novelty of it, no doubt—was to avoid the consequences of that horrible, destructive stunt you pulled just before your disappearance."

"No, that's not—"

"And that only makes my decision that much easier. As a Moroi, the princess must continue on here at the Academy for her own safety, but we have no such obligations to you. You will be sent away as soon as possible."

My cockiness dried up. "I . . . what?"

Lissa stood up beside me. "You can't do that! She's my guardian."

"She is no such thing, particularly since she isn't even a guardian at all. She's still a novice."

"But my parents—"

"I know what your parents wanted, God rest their souls,

but things have changed. Miss Hathaway is expendable. She doesn't deserve to be a guardian, and she will leave."

I stared at Kirova, unable to believe what I was hearing. "Where are you going to send me? To my mom in Nepal? Did she even know I was gone? Or maybe you'll send me off to my *father*?"

Her eyes narrowed at the bite in that last word. When I spoke again, my voice was so cold, I barely recognized it.

"Or maybe you're going to try to send me off to be a blood whore. Try that, and we'll be gone by the end of the day."

"Miss Hathaway," she hissed, "you are out of line."

"They have a bond." Dimitri's low, accented voice broke the heavy tension, and we all turned toward him. I think Kirova had forgotten he was there, but I hadn't. His presence was way too powerful to ignore. He still stood against the wall, looking like some sort of cowboy sentry in that ridiculous long coat of his. He looked at me, not Lissa, his dark eyes staring straight through me. "Rose knows what Vasilisa is feeling. Don't you?"

I at least had the satisfaction of seeing Kirova caught off guard as she glanced between us and Dimitri. "No . . . that's impossible. That hasn't happened in centuries."

"It's obvious," he said. "I suspected as soon as I started watching them."

Neither Lissa nor I responded, and I averted my eyes from his.

"That is a gift," murmured Victor from his corner. "A rare and wonderful thing."

"The best guardians always had that bond," added Dimitri. "In the stories."

Kirova's outrage returned. "Stories that are centuries old," she exclaimed. "Surely you aren't suggesting we let her stay at the Academy after everything she's done?"

He shrugged. "She might be wild and disrespectful, but if she has potential—"

"Wild and disrespectful?" I interrupted. "Who the hell are you anyway? Outsourced help?"

"Guardian Belikov is the princess's guardian now," said Kirova. "Her *sanctioned* guardian."

"You got cheap foreign labor to protect Lissa?"

That was pretty mean of me to say—particularly since most Moroi and their guardians were of Russian or Romanian descent—but the comment seemed cleverer at the time than it really was. And it wasn't like I was one to talk. I might have been raised in the U.S., but my parents were foreign-born. My dhampir mother was Scottish—red-haired, with a ridiculous accent—and I'd been told my Moroi dad was Turkish. That genetic combination had given me skin the same color as the inside of an almond, along with what I liked to think were semi-exotic desert-princess features: big dark eyes and hair so deep brown that it usually looked black. I wouldn't have minded inheriting the red hair, but we take what we get.

Kirova threw her hands up in exasperation and turned to him. "You see? Completely undisciplined! All the psychic bonds and *very* raw potential in the world can't make up for that. A guardian without discipline is worse than no guardian."

"So teach her discipline. Classes just started. Put her back in and get her training again."

"Impossible. She'll still be hopelessly behind her peers."

"No, I won't," I argued. No one listened to me.

"Then give her extra training sessions," he said.

They continued on while the rest of us watched the exchange like it was a Ping-Pong game. My pride was still hurt over the ease with which Dimitri had tricked us, but it occurred to me that he might very well keep me here with Lissa. Better to stay at this hellhole than be without her. Through our bond, I could feel her trickle of hope.

"Who's going to put in the extra time?" demanded Kirova. "You?"

Dimitri's argument came to an abrupt stop. "Well, that's not what I—"

Kirova crossed her arms with satisfaction. "Yes. That's what I thought."

Clearly at a loss, he frowned. His eyes flicked toward Lissa and me, and I wondered what he saw. Two pathetic girls, looking at him with big, pleading eyes? Or two runaways who'd broken out of a high-security school and swiped half of Lissa's inheritance?

"Yes," he said finally. "I can mentor Rose. I'll give her extra sessions along with her normal ones."

"And then what?" retorted Kirova angrily. "She goes unpunished?"

"Find some other way to punish her," answered Dimitri. "Guardian numbers have gone down too much to risk losing another. A girl, in particular."

His unspoken words made me shudder, reminding me of my earlier statement about "blood whores." Few dhampir girls became guardians anymore.

Victor suddenly spoke up from his corner. "I'm inclined to agree with Guardian Belikov. Sending Rose away would be a shame, a waste of talent."

Ms. Kirova stared out her window. It was completely black outside. With the Academy's nocturnal schedule, *morning* and *afternoon* were relative terms. That, and they kept the windows tinted to block out excess light.

When she turned back around, Lissa met her eyes. "Please, Ms. Kirova. Let Rose stay."

Oh, Lissa, I thought. *Be careful.* Using compulsion on another Moroi was dangerous—particularly in front of witnesses. But Lissa was only using a tiny bit, and we needed all the help we could get. Fortunately, no one seemed to realize what was happening.

I don't even know if the compulsion made a difference, but finally, Kirova sighed.

"If Miss Hathaway stays, here's how it will be." She turned to me. "Your continued enrollment at St. Vladimir's is strictly probationary. Step out of line *once*, and you're gone. You will attend all classes and required trainings for novices your age. You will also train with Guardian Belikov in every spare moment you have—before *and* after classes. Other than that, you are banned from all social activities, except meals, and will stay in your dorm. Fail to comply with any of this, and you will be sent . . . away."

I gave a harsh laugh. "Banned from all social activities? Are you trying to keep us apart?" I nodded toward Lissa. "Afraid we'll run away again?"

"I'm taking precautions. As I'm sure you recall, you were never properly punished for destroying school property. You have a lot to make up for." Her thin lips tightened into a straight line. "You are being offered a very generous deal. I suggest you don't let your attitude endanger it."

I started to say it wasn't generous at all, but then I caught Dimitri's gaze. It was hard to read. He might have been telling me he believed in me. He might have been telling me I was an idiot to keep fighting with Kirova. I didn't know.

Looking away from him for the second time during the meeting, I stared at the floor, conscious of Lissa beside me and her own encouragement burning in our bond. At long last, I exhaled and glanced back up at the headmistress.

"Fine. I accept."

THREE

Sending us straight to class after our meeting seemed beyond cruel, but that's exactly what Kirova did. Lissa was led away, and I watched her go, glad the bond would allow me to keep reading her emotional temperature.

They actually sent me to one of the guidance counselors first. He was an ancient Moroi guy, one I remembered from before I'd left. I honestly couldn't believe he was still around. The guy was so freaking old, he should have retired. Or died.

The visit took all of five minutes. He said nothing about my return and asked a few questions about what classes I'd taken in Chicago and Portland. He compared those against my old file and hastily scrawled out a new schedule. I took it sullenly and headed out to my first class.

1st Period	*Advanced Guardian Combat Techniques*
2nd Period	*Bodyguard Theory and Personal Protection 3*
3rd Period	*Weight Training and Conditioning*
4th Period	*Senior Language Arts (Novices)*
	—Lunch—
5th Period	*Animal Behavior and Physiology*
6th Period	*Precalculus*

7th Period   *Moroi Culture 4*
8th Period   *Slavic Art*

Ugh. I'd forgotten how long the Academy's school day was. Novices and Moroi took separate classes during the first half of the day, which meant I wouldn't see Lissa until after lunch—if we had any afternoon classes together. Most of them were standard senior classes, so I felt my odds were pretty good. Slavic art struck me as the kind of elective no one signed up for, so hopefully they'd stuck her in there too.

Dimitri and Alberta escorted me to the guardians' gym for first period, neither one acknowledging my existence. Walking behind them, I saw how Alberta wore her hair in a short, pixie cut that showed her promise mark and *molnija* marks. A lot of female guardians did this. It didn't matter so much for me now, since my neck had no tattoos yet, but I didn't want to ever cut my hair.

She and Dimitri didn't say anything and walked along almost like it was any other day. When we arrived, the reactions of my peers indicated it was anything but. They were in the middle of setting up when we entered the gym, and just like in the commons, all eyes fell on me. I couldn't decide if I felt like a rock star or a circus freak.

All right, then. If I was going to be stuck here for a while, I wasn't going to act afraid of them all anymore. Lissa and I had once held this school's respect, and it was time to remind everyone of that. Scanning the staring, openmouthed novices, I looked for a familiar face. Most of them were guys. One caught my eye, and I could barely hold back my grin.

"Hey Mason, wipe the drool off your face. If you're going to think about me naked, do it on your own time."

A few snorts and snickers broke the awed silence, and Mason Ashford snapped out of his haze, giving me a lopsided smile. With red hair that stuck up everywhere and a smattering of freckles, he was nice-looking, though not exactly hot. He was also one of the funniest guys I knew. We'd been good friends back in the day.

"This *is* my time, Hathaway. I'm leading today's session."

"Oh yeah?" I retorted. "Huh. Well, I guess this is a good time to think about me naked, then."

"It's *always* a good a time to think about you naked," added someone nearby, breaking the tension further. Eddie Castile. Another friend of mine.

Dimitri shook his head and walked off, muttering something in Russian that didn't sound complimentary. But as for me . . . well, just like that, I was one of the novices again. They were an easygoing bunch, less focused on pedigree and politics than the Moroi students.

The class engulfed me, and I found myself laughing and seeing those I'd nearly forgotten about. Everyone wanted to know where we'd been; apparently Lissa and I had become legends. I couldn't tell them why we'd left, of course, so I offered up a lot of taunts and wouldn't-you-like-to-knows that served just as well.

The happy reunion lasted a few more minutes before the adult guardian who oversaw the training came over and scolded Mason for neglecting his duties. Still grinning, he barked out orders to everyone, explaining what exercises to start with. Uneasily, I realized I didn't know most of them.

"Come on, Hathaway," he said, taking my arm. "You can be my partner. Let's see what you've been doing all this time."

An hour later, he had his answer.

"Not practicing, huh?"

"Ow," I groaned, momentarily incapable of normal speech.

He extended a hand and helped me up from the mat he'd knocked me down on—about fifty times.

"I hate you," I told him, rubbing a spot on my thigh that was going to have a wicked bruise tomorrow.

"You'd hate me more if I held back."

"Yeah, that's true," I agreed, staggering along as the class put the equipment back.

"You actually did okay."

"What? I just had my ass handed to me."

"Well, of course you did. It's been two years. But hey, you're still walking. That's something." He grinned mockingly.

"Did I mention I hate you?"

He flashed me another smile, which quickly faded to something more serious. "Don't take this the wrong way. . . . I mean, you really are a scrapper, but there's no way you'll be able to take your trials in the spring—"

"They're making me take extra practice sessions," I explained. Not that it mattered. I planned on getting Lissa and me out of here before these practices really became an issue. "I'll be ready."

"Extra sessions with who?"

"That tall guy. Dimitri."

Mason stopped walking and stared at me. "You're putting in extra time with Belikov?"

"Yeah, so what?"

"So the man is a *god*."

"Exaggerate much?" I asked.

"No, I'm serious. I mean, he's all quiet and antisocial usually, but when he fights . . . wow. If you think you're hurting now, you're going to be dead when he's done with you."

Great. Something else to improve my day.

I elbowed him and went on to second period. That class covered the essentials of being a bodyguard and was required for all seniors. Actually, it was the third in a series that had started junior year. That meant I was behind in this class too, but I hoped protecting Lissa in the real world had given me some insight.

Our instructor was Stan Alto, whom we referred to simply as "Stan" behind his back and "Guardian Alto" in formal settings. He was a little older than Dimitri, but not nearly as tall, and he always looked pissed off. Today, that look intensified when he walked into the classroom and saw me sitting there. His eyes widened in mock surprise as he circled the room and came to stand beside my desk.

"What's this? No one told me we had a guest speaker here today. Rose Hathaway. What a privilege! How very *generous* of you to take time out of your busy schedule and share your knowledge with us."

I felt my cheeks burning, but in a great show of self-control, I stopped myself from telling him to fuck off. I'm pretty sure my face must have delivered that message, however, because his sneer increased. He gestured for me to stand up.

"Well, come on, come on. Don't sit there! Come up to the front so you can help me lecture the class."

I sank into my seat. "You don't really mean—"

The taunting smile dried up. "I mean *exactly* what I say, Hathaway. Go to the front of the class."

A thick silence enveloped the room. Stan was a scary instructor, and most of the class was too awed to laugh at my disgrace quite yet. Refusing to crack, I strode up to the front of the room and turned to face the class. I gave them a bold look and tossed my hair over my shoulders, earning a few sympathetic smiles from my friends. I then noticed I had a larger audience than expected. A few guardians—including Dimitri—lingered in the back of the room. Outside the Academy, guardians focused on one-on-one protection. Here, guardians had a lot more people to protect *and* they had to train the novices. So rather than follow any one person around, they worked shifts guarding the school as a whole and monitoring classes.

"So, Hathaway," said Stan cheerfully, strolling back up to the front with me. "Enlighten us about your protective techniques."

"My . . . techniques?"

"Of course. Because presumably you must have had some sort of plan the rest of us couldn't understand when you took an underage Moroi royal out of the Academy and exposed her to constant Strigoi threats."

It was the Kirova lecture all over again, except with more witnesses.

"We never ran into any Strigoi," I replied stiffly.

"Obviously," he said with a snicker. "I already figured that out, seeing as how you're still alive."

I wanted to shout that maybe I could have defeated a Strigoi, but after getting beat up in the last class, I now suspected I couldn't have survived an attack by Mason, let alone an actual Strigoi.

When I didn't say anything, Stan started pacing in front of the class.

"So what'd you do? How'd you make sure she stayed safe? Did you avoid going out at night?"

"Sometimes." That was true—especially when we'd first run away. We'd relaxed a little after months went by with no attacks.

"*Sometimes*," he repeated in a high-pitched voice, making my answer sound incredibly stupid. "Well then, I suppose you slept during the day and stayed on guard at night."

"Er . . . no."

"No? But that's one of the first things mentioned in the chapter on solo guarding. Oh wait, you wouldn't know that because *you weren't here.*"

I swallowed back more swear words. "I watched the area whenever we went out," I said, needing to defend myself.

"Oh? Well that's something. Did you use Carnegie's Quadrant Surveillance Method or the Rotational Survey?"

I didn't say anything.

"Ah. I'm guessing you used the Hathaway Glance-Around-When-You-Remember-To Method."

"No!" I exclaimed angrily. "That's not true. I watched her. She's still alive, isn't she?"

He walked back up to me and leaned toward my face. "Because you got *lucky.*"

"Strigoi aren't lurking around every corner out there," I shot back. "It's not like what we've been taught. It's safer than you guys make it sound."

"Safer? *Safer?* We are at war with the Strigoi!" he yelled. I could smell coffee on his breath, he was so close. "One of them could walk right up to you and snap your pretty little neck before you even noticed him—and he'd barely break a sweat doing it. You might have more speed and strength than a Moroi or a human, but you are nothing, *nothing*, compared to a Strigoi. They are deadly, and they are powerful. And do you know what makes them more powerful?"

No way was I going to let this jerk make me cry. Looking

away from him, I tried to focus on something else. My eyes rested on Dimitri and the other guardians. They were watching my humiliation, stone-faced.

"Moroi blood," I whispered.

"What was that?" asked Stan loudly. "I didn't catch it."

I spun back around to face him. "Moroi blood! Moroi blood makes them stronger."

He nodded in satisfaction and took a few steps back. "Yes. It does. It makes them stronger and harder to destroy. They'll kill and drink from a human or dhampir, but they want Moroi blood more than anything else. They seek it. They've turned to the dark side to gain immortality, and they want to do whatever they can to keep that immortality. Desperate Strigoi have attacked Moroi in public. Groups of Strigoi have raided academies exactly like this one. There are Strigoi who have lived for thousands of years and fed off generations of Moroi. They're almost impossible to kill. And *that* is why Moroi numbers are dropping. They aren't strong enough—even with guardians—to protect themselves. Some Moroi don't even see the point of running anymore and are simply turning Strigoi by choice. And as the Moroi disappear . . ."

". . . so do the dhampirs," I finished.

"Well," he said, licking sprayed spit off his lips. "It looks like you learned something after all. Now we'll have to see if you can learn enough to pass this class and qualify for your field experience next semester."

Ouch. I spent the rest of that horrible class—in my seat,

thankfully—replaying those last words in my mind. The senior-year field experience was the best part of a novice's education. We'd have no classes for half a semester. Instead, we'd each be assigned a Moroi student to guard and follow around. The adult guardians would monitor us and test us with staged attacks and other threats. How a novice passed that field experience was almost as important as all the rest of her grades combined. It could influence which Moroi she got assigned to after graduation.

And me? There was only one Moroi I wanted.

Two classes later, I finally earned my lunch escape. As I stumbled across campus toward the commons, Dimitri fell into step beside me, not looking particularly godlike—unless you counted his godly good looks.

"I suppose you saw what happened in Stan's class?" I asked, not bothering with titles.

"Yes."

"And you don't think that was unfair?"

"Was he right? Do you think you were fully prepared to protect Vasilisa?"

I looked down at the ground. "I kept her alive," I mumbled.

"How did you do fighting against your classmates today?"

The question was mean. I didn't answer and knew I didn't need to. I'd had another training class after Stan's, and no doubt Dimitri had watched me get beat up there too.

"If you can't fight *them*—"

"Yeah, yeah, I know," I snapped.

He slowed his long stride to match my pain-filled one. "You're strong and fast by nature. You just need to keep yourself trained. Didn't you play any sports while you were gone?"

"Sure," I shrugged. "Now and then."

"You didn't join any teams?"

"Too much work. If I'd wanted to practice that much, I'd have stayed here."

He gave me an exasperated look. "You'll never be able to really protect the princess if you don't hone your skills. You'll always be lacking."

"I'll be able to protect her," I said fiercely.

"You have no guarantees of being assigned to her, you know—for your field experience *or* after you graduate." Dimitri's voice was low and unapologetic. They hadn't given me a warm and fuzzy mentor. "No one wants to waste the bond— but no one's going to give her an inadequate guardian either. If you want to be with her, then you need to work for it. You have your lessons. You have me. Use us or don't. You're an ideal choice to guard Vasilisa when you both graduate—if you can prove you're worthy. I hope you will."

"Lissa, call her Lissa," I corrected. She hated her full name, much preferring the Americanized nickname.

He walked away, and suddenly, I didn't feel like such a badass anymore.

By now, I'd burned up a lot of time leaving class. Most everyone else had long since sprinted inside the commons for lunch, eager to maximize their social time. I'd almost made it back there myself when a voice under the door's overhang called to me.

"Rose?"

Peering in the voice's direction, I caught sight of Victor Dashkov, his kind face smiling at me as he leaned on a cane near the building's wall. His two guardians stood nearby at a polite distance.

"Mr. Dash—er, Your Highness. Hi."

I caught myself just in time, having nearly forgotten Moroi royal terms. I hadn't used them while living among humans. The Moroi chose their rulers from among twelve royal families. The eldest in the family got the title of "prince" or "princess." Lissa had gotten hers because she was the only one left in her line.

"How was your first day?" he asked.

"Not over yet." I tried to think of something conversational. "Are you visiting here for a while?"

"I'll be leaving this afternoon after I say hello to Natalie. When I heard Vasilisa—and you—had returned, I simply had to come see you."

I nodded, not sure what else to say. He was more Lissa's friend than mine.

"I wanted to tell you . . ." He spoke hesitantly. "I understand the gravity of what you did, but I think Headmistress

Kirova failed to acknowledge something. You *did* keep Vasilisa safe all this time. That is impressive."

"Well, it's not like I faced down Strigoi or anything," I said.

"But you faced down some things?"

"Sure. The school sent psi-hounds once."

"Remarkable."

"Not really. Avoiding them was pretty easy."

He laughed. "I've hunted with them before. They aren't *that* easy to evade, not with their powers and intelligence." It was true. Psi-hounds were one of many types of magical creatures that wandered the world, creatures that humans never knew about or else didn't believe they'd really seen. The hounds traveled in packs and shared a sort of psychic communication that made them particularly deadly to their prey—as did the fact that they resembled mutant wolves. "Did you face anything else?"

I shrugged. "Little things here and there."

"Remarkable," he repeated.

"Lucky, I think. It turns out I'm really behind in all this guardian stuff." I sounded just like Stan now.

"You're a smart girl. You'll catch up. And you also have your bond."

I looked away. My ability to "feel" Lissa had been such a secret for so long, it felt weird to have others know about it.

"The histories are full of stories of guardians who could feel when their charges were in danger," Victor continued.

"I've made a hobby of studying up on it and some of the ancient ways. I've heard it's a tremendous asset."

"I guess." I shrugged. *What a boring hobby,* I thought, imagining him poring over prehistoric histories in some dank library covered in spiderwebs.

Victor tilted his head, curiosity all over his face. Kirova and the others had had the same look when we'd mentioned our connection, like we were lab rats. "What is it like—if you don't mind me asking?"

"It's . . . I don't know. I just sort of always have this hum of how she feels. Usually it's just emotions. We can't send messages or anything." I didn't tell him about slipping into her head. That part of it was hard even for me to understand.

"But it doesn't work the other way? She doesn't sense you?"

I shook my head.

His face shone with wonder. "How did it happen?"

"I don't know," I said, still glancing away. "Just started two years ago."

He frowned. "Near the time of the accident?"

Hesitantly, I nodded. The accident was *not* something I wanted to talk about, that was for sure. Lissa's memories were bad enough without my own mixing into them. Twisted metal. A sensation of hot, then cold, then hot again. Lissa screaming over me, screaming for me to wake up, screaming for her parents and her brother to wake up. None of them had, only me.

And the doctors said that was a miracle in itself. They said I shouldn't have survived.

Apparently sensing my discomfort, Victor let the moment go and returned to his earlier excitement.

"I can still barely believe this. It's been so long since this has happened. If it did happen more often . . . just think what it could do for the safety of all Moroi. If only others could experience this too. I'll have to do more research and see if we can replicate it with others."

"Yeah." I was getting impatient, despite how much I liked him. Natalie rambled a lot, and it was pretty clear which parent she'd inherited *that* quality from. Lunch was ticking down, and although Moroi and novices shared afternoon classes, Lissa and I wouldn't have much time to talk.

"Perhaps we could—" He started coughing, a great, seizing fit that made his whole body shake. His disease, Sandovsky's Syndrome, took the lungs down with it while dragging the body toward death. I cast an anxious look at his guardians, and one of them stepped forward. "Your Highness," he said politely, "you need to go inside. It's too cold out here."

Victor nodded. "Yes, yes. And I'm sure Rose here wants to eat." He turned to me. "Thank you for speaking to me. I can't emphasize how much it means to me that Vasilisa is safe— and that you helped with that. I'd promised her father I'd look after her if anything happened to him, and I felt like quite the failure when you left."

A sinking sensation filled my stomach as I imagined him wracked with guilt and worry over our disappearance. Until now, I hadn't really thought about how others might have felt about us leaving.

We made our goodbyes, and I finally arrived inside the school. As I did, I felt Lissa's anxiety spike. Ignoring the pain in my legs, I picked up my pace into the commons.

And nearly ran right into her.

She didn't see me, though. Neither did the people standing with her: Aaron and that little doll girl. I stopped and listened, just catching the end of the conversation. The girl leaned toward Lissa, who seemed more stunned than anything else.

"It looks to *me* like it came from a garage sale. I thought a precious Dragomir would have standards." Scorn dripped off the word *Dragomir*.

Grabbing Doll Girl by the shoulder, I jerked her away. She was so light, she stumbled three feet and nearly fell.

"She does have standards," I said, "which is why you're done talking to her."

FOUR

We didn't have the entire commons' attention this time, thank God, but a few passing people had stopped to stare.

"What the hell do you think you're doing?" asked Doll Girl, blue eyes wide and sparkling with fury. Up close now, I was able to get a better look at her. She had the same slim build as most Moroi but not the usual height, which was partly what made her look so young. The tiny purple dress she wore was gorgeous—reminding me that I was indeed dressed in thrift-shop wear—but closer inspection led me to think it was a designer knockoff .

I crossed my arms across my chest. "Are you lost, little girl? The elementary school's over on west campus."

A pink flush spread over her cheeks. "Don't you ever touch me again. You screw with me, and I'll screw you right back."

Oh man, what an opening that was. Only a head shake from Lissa stopped me from unleashing any number of hilarious comebacks. Instead, I opted for simple brute force, so to speak.

"And if you mess with either of us again, I'll break you in half. If you don't believe me, go ask Dawn Yarrow about what I did to her arm in ninth grade. You were probably at nap time when it happened."

The incident with Dawn hadn't been one of my finer moments. I honestly hadn't expected to break any bones when I shoved her into a tree. Still, the incident had given me a dangerous reputation, in addition to my smartass one. The story had gained legendary status, and I liked to imagine that it was still being told around campfires late at night. Judging from the look on this girl's face, it was.

One of the patrolling staff members strolled by right then, casting suspicious eyes at our little meeting. Doll Girl backed off, taking Aaron's arm. "Come on," she said.

"Hey, Aaron," I said cheerfully, remembering he was there. "Nice to see you again."

He gave me a quick nod and an uneasy smile, just as the girl dragged him off. Same old Aaron. He might be nice and cute, but aggressive he was not.

I turned to Lissa. "You okay?" She nodded. "Any idea who I just threatened to beat up?"

"Not a clue." I started to lead her toward the lunch line, but she shook her head at me. "Gotta go see the feeders."

A funny feeling settled over me. I'd gotten so used to being her primary blood source that the thought of returning to the Moroi's normal routine seemed strange. In fact, it almost bothered me. It shouldn't have. Daily feedings were part of a Moroi's life, something I hadn't been able to offer her while living on our own. It had been an inconvenient situation, one that left me weak on feeding days and her weak on the days in between. I should have been happy she would get some normality.

I forced a smile. "Sure."

We walked into the feeding room, which sat adjacent to the cafeteria. It was set up with small cubicles, dividing the room's space in an effort to offer privacy. A dark-haired Moroi woman greeted us at the entrance and glanced down at her clipboard, flipping through the pages. Finding what she needed, she made a few notes and then gestured for Lissa to follow. Me she gave a puzzled look, but she didn't stop me from entering.

She led us to one of the cubicles where a plump, middle-aged woman sat leafing through a magazine. She looked up at our approach and smiled. In her eyes, I could see the dreamy, glazed-over look most feeders had. She'd probably neared her quota for the day, judging from how high she appeared to be.

Recognizing Lissa, her smile grew. "Welcome back, Princess."

The greeter left us, and Lissa sat down in the chair beside the woman. I sensed a feeling of discomfort in her, a little different from my own. This was weird for her too; it had been a long time. The feeder, however, had no such reservations. An eager look crossed her face—the look of a junkie about to get her next fix.

Disgust poured into me. It was an old instinct, one that had been drilled in over the years. Feeders were essential to Moroi life. They were humans who willingly volunteered to be a regular blood source, humans from the fringes of society who gave their lives over to the secret world of the Moroi. They were well cared for and given all the comforts they could need. But at the heart of it, they were drug users, addicts to Moroi saliva and the rush it offered with each bite. The Moroi—and guardians—looked down on this dependency, even though the Moroi couldn't have survived otherwise unless they took victims by force. Hypocrisy at its finest.

The feeder tilted her head, giving Lissa full access to her neck. Her skin there was marked with scars from years of daily bites. The infrequent feedings Lissa and I had done had kept my neck clear; my bite marks never lasted more than a day or so.

Lissa leaned forward, fangs biting into the feeder's yielding flesh. The woman closed her eyes, making a soft sound of pleasure. I swallowed, watching Lissa drink. I couldn't see any blood, but I could imagine it. A surge of emotion grew in my chest: longing. Jealousy. I averted my eyes, staring at the floor. Mentally, I scolded myself.

What's wrong with you? Why should you miss it? You only did it once every day. You aren't addicted, not like this. And you don't want to be.

But I couldn't help myself, couldn't help the way I felt as I recalled the bliss and rush of a vampire's bite.

Lissa finished and we returned to the commons, moving toward the lunch line. It was short, since we only had fifteen minutes left, and I strolled up and began to load my plate with french fries and some rounded, bite-size objects that looked vaguely like chicken nuggets. Lissa only grabbed a yogurt. Moroi needed food, as dhampirs and humans did, but rarely had an appetite after drinking blood.

"So how'd classes go?" I asked.

She shrugged. Her face was bright with color and life now. "Okay. Lots of stares. A *lot* of stares. Lots of questions about where we were. Whispering."

"Same here," I said. The attendant checked us out, and we walked toward the tables. I gave Lissa a sidelong glance. "You okay with that? They aren't bothering you, are they?"

"No—it's fine." The emotions coming through the bond contradicted her words. Knowing I could feel that, she tried to change the subject by handing me her class schedule. I looked it over.

1st *Period*	*Russian 2*
2nd *Period*	*American Colonial Literature*
3rd *Period*	*Basics of Elemental Control*
4th *Period*	*Ancient Poetry*
	—Lunch—
5th *Period*	*Animal Behavior and Physiology*
6th *Period*	*Advanced Calculus*
7th *Period*	*Moroi Culture 4*
8th *Period*	*Slavic Art*

"Nerd," I said. "If you were in Stupid Math like me, we'd have the same afternoon schedule." I stopped walking. "Why are you in elemental basics? That's a sophomore class."

She eyed me. "Because seniors take specialized classes."

We fell silent at that. All Moroi wielded elemental magic. It was one of the things that differentiated living vampires from Strigoi, the dead vampires. Moroi viewed magic as a gift. It was part of their souls and connected them to the world.

A long time ago, they had used their magic openly, averting natural disasters and helping with things like food and water production. They didn't need to do that as much anymore, but the magic was still in their blood. It burned in them and made them want to reach out to the earth and wield their power. Academies like this existed to help Moroi control the magic and learn how to do increasingly complex things with it. Students also had to learn the rules that surrounded magic, rules that had been in place for centuries and were strictly enforced.

All Moroi had a small ability in each element. When they got to be around our age, students "specialized" when one element grew stronger than the others: earth, water, fire, or air. Not specializing was like not going through puberty.

And Lissa . . . well, Lissa hadn't specialized yet.

"Is Ms. Carmack still teaching that? What she'd say?"

"She says she's not worried. She thinks it'll come."

"Did you—did you tell her about—"

Lissa shook her head. "No. Of course not."

We let the subject drop. It was one we thought about a lot but rarely spoke of.

We started moving again, scanning the tables as we

decided where to sit. A few pairs of eyes looked up at us with blatant curiosity.

"Lissa!" came a nearby voice. Glancing over, we saw Natalie waving at us. Lissa and I exchanged looks. Natalie was sort of Lissa's cousin in the way Victor was sort of her uncle, but we'd never hung out with her all that much.

Lissa shrugged and headed in that direction. "Why not?"

I followed reluctantly. Natalie was nice but also one of the most uninteresting people I knew. Most royals at the school enjoyed a kind of celebrity status, but Natalie had never fit in with that crowd. She was too plain, too uninterested in the politics of the Academy, and too clueless to really navigate them anyway.

Natalie's friends eyed us with a quiet curiosity, but she didn't hold back. She threw her arms around us. Like Lissa, she had jade-green eyes, but her hair was jet black, like Victor's had been before his disease grayed it.

"You're back! I knew you would be! Everyone said you were gone forever, but I never believed that. I knew you couldn't stay away. Why'd you go? There are so many stories about why you left!" Lissa and I exchanged glances as Natalie prattled on. "Camille said one of you got pregnant and went off to have an abortion, but I knew that couldn't be true. Someone else said you went off to hang out with Rose's mom, but I figured Ms. Kirova and Daddy wouldn't have been so upset if you'd turned up there. Did you know we might get to be roommates? I was talking to . . ."

On and on she chatted, flashing her fangs as she spoke. I

smiled politely, letting Lissa deal with the onslaught until Natalie asked a dangerous question.

"What'd you do for blood, Lissa?"

The table regarded us questioningly. Lissa froze, but I immediately jumped in, the lie coming effortlessly to my lips.

"Oh, it's easy. There are a lot of humans who want to do it."

"Really?" asked one of Natalie's friends, wide-eyed.

"Yup. You find 'em at parties and stuff. They're all looking for a fix from something, and they don't really get that a vampire's doing it: most are already so wasted they don't remember anyway." My already vague details dried up, so I simply shrugged in as cool and confident a way as I could manage. It wasn't like any of them knew any better. "Like I said, it's easy. Almost easier than with our own feeders."

Natalie accepted this and than launched into some other topic. Lissa shot me a grateful look.

Ignoring the conversation again, I took in the old faces, trying to figure out who was hanging out with whom and how power had shifted within the school. Mason, sitting with a group of novices, caught my eye, and I smiled. Near him, a group of Moroi royals sat, laughing over something. Aaron and the blond girl sat there too.

"Hey, Natalie," I said, turning around and cutting her off. She didn't seem to notice or mind. "Who's Aaron's new girlfriend?"

"Huh? Oh. Mia Rinaldi." Seeing my blank look, she asked, "Don't you remember her?"

"Should I? Was she here when we left?"

"She's always been here," said Natalie. "She's only a year younger than us."

I shot a questioning look at Lissa, who only shrugged.

"Why is she so pissed off at us?" I asked. "Neither of us know her."

"I don't know," answered Natalie. "Maybe she's jealous about Aaron. She wasn't much of anybody when you guys left. She got *really* popular *really* fast. She isn't royal or anything, but once she started dating Aaron, she—"

"Okay, thanks," I interrupted. "It doesn't really—"

My eyes lifted up from Natalie's face to Jesse Zeklos's, just as he passed by our table. Ah, Jesse. I'd forgotten about him. I liked flirting with Mason and some of the other novices, but Jesse was in an entirely different category. You flirted with the other guys simply for the sake of flirting. You flirted with Jesse in the hopes of getting semi-naked with him. He was a royal Moroi, and he was so hot, he should have worn a WARNING: FLAMMABLE sign. He met my eyes and grinned.

"Hey Rose, welcome back. You still breaking hearts?"

"Are you volunteering?"

His grin widened. "Let's hang out sometime and find out. If you ever get parole."

He kept walking, and I watched him admiringly. Natalie and her friends stared at me in awe. I might not be a god in the Dimitri sense, but with this group, Lissa and I *were* gods— or at least former gods—of another nature.

"Oh my gawd," exclaimed one girl. I didn't remember her

name. "That was *Jesse*."

"Yes," I said, smiling. "It certainly was."

"I wish I looked like you," she added with a sigh.

Their eyes fell on me. Technically, I was half-Moroi, but my looks were human. I'd blended in well with humans during our time away, so much so that I'd barely thought about my appearance at all. Here, among the slim and small-chested Moroi girls, certain features—meaning my larger breasts and more defined hips—stood out. I knew I was pretty, but to Moroi boys, my body was more than just pretty: it was sexy in a risqué way. Dhampirs were an exotic conquest, a novelty all Moroi guys wanted to "try."

It was ironic that dhampirs had such an allure here, because slender Moroi girls looked very much like the super-skinny runway models so popular in the human world. Most humans could never reach that "ideal" skinniness, just as Moroi girls could never look like me. Everyone wanted what she couldn't have.

Lissa and I got to sit together in our shared afternoon classes but didn't do much talking. The stares she'd mentioned certainly did follow us, but I found that the more I talked to people, the more they warmed up. Slowly, gradually, they seemed to remember who we were, and the novelty—though not the intrigue—of our crazy stunt wore off.

Or maybe I should say, they remembered who *I* was.

Because I was the only one talking. Lissa stared straight ahead, listening but neither acknowledging nor participating in my attempts at conversation. I could feel anxiety and sadness pouring out of her.

"All right," I told her when classes finally ended. We stood outside the school, and I was fully aware that in doing so, I was already breaking the terms of my agreement with Kirova. "We're not staying here," I told her, looking around the campus uneasily. "I'm going to find a way to get us out."

"You think we could really do it a second time?" Lissa asked quietly.

"Absolutely." I spoke with certainty, again relieved she couldn't read my feelings. Escaping the first time had been tricky enough. Doing it again would be a real bitch, not that I couldn't still find a way.

"You really would, wouldn't you?" She smiled, more to herself than to me, like she'd thought of something funny. "Of course you would. It's just, well . . ." She sighed. "I don't know if we should go. Maybe—maybe we should stay."

I blinked in astonishment. "What?" Not one of my more eloquent answers, but the best I could manage. I'd never expected this from her.

"I saw you, Rose. I saw you talking to the other novices during class, talking about practice. You miss that."

"It's not worth it," I argued. "Not if . . . not if *you* . . ." I couldn't finish, but she was right. She'd read me. I *had* missed the other novices. Even some of the Moroi. But there was more to it than just that. The weight of my inexperience, how much I'd fallen behind, had been growing all day.

"It might be better," she countered. "I haven't had as many . . . you know, things happening in a while. I haven't felt like anyone was following or watching us."

I didn't say anything to that. Before we'd left the Academy, she'd always felt like someone was following her, like she was being hunted. I'd never seen evidence to support that, but I had once heard one of our teachers go on and on about the same sort of thing. Ms. Karp. She'd been a pretty Moroi, with deep auburn air and high cheekbones. And I was pretty sure she'd been crazy.

"You never know who's watching," she used to say, walking briskly around the classroom as she shut all the blinds. "Or who's following you. Best to be safe. Best to *always* be safe." We'd snickered amongst ourselves because that's what students do around eccentric and paranoid teachers. The thought of Lissa acting like her bothered me.

"What's wrong?" Lissa asked, noticing that I was lost in thought.

"Huh? Nothing. Just thinking." I sighed, trying to balance my own wants with what was best for her. "Liss, we can stay, I guess . . . but there are a few conditions."

This made her laugh. "A Rose ultimatum, huh?"

"I'm serious." Words I didn't say very much. "I want you to stay away from the royals. Not like Natalie or anything, but you know, the others. The power players. Camille. Carly. That group."

Her amusement turned to astonishment. "Are you serious?"

"Sure. You never liked them anyway."

"*You* did."

"No. Not really. I liked what they could offer. All the parties and stuff."

"And you can go without that now?" She looked skeptical.

"Sure. We did in Portland."

"Yeah, but that was different." Her eyes stared off, not really focused on any one thing. "Here . . . *here* I've got to be a part of that. I can't avoid it."

"The hell you do. Natalie stays out of that stuff."

"Natalie isn't going to inherit her family's title," she retorted. "I've already got it. I've got to be involved, start making connections. Andre—"

"Liss," I groaned. "You *aren't* Andre." I couldn't believe she was still comparing herself to her brother.

"He was always involved in all that stuff."

"Yeah, well," I snapped back, "he's *dead* now."

Her face hardened. "You know, sometimes you aren't very nice."

"You don't keep me around to be nice. You want nice, there are a dozen sheep in there who would rip each other's throats to get in good with the Dragomir princess. You keep me around to tell you the truth, and here it is: Andre's dead. You're the heir now, and you're going to deal with it however you can. But for now, that means staying away from the other royals. We'll just lie low. Coast through the middle. Get involved in that stuff again, Liss, and you'll drive yourself . . ."

"*Crazy?*" she supplied when I didn't finish.

Now I looked away. "I didn't mean . . ."

"It's okay," she said, after a moment. She sighed and touched my arm. "Fine. We'll stay, and we'll keep out of all that stuff. We'll 'coast through the middle' like you want. Hang out with Natalie, I guess."

To be perfectly honest, I didn't want any of that. I wanted to go to all the royal parties and wild drunken festivities like we'd done before. We'd kept out of that life for years until Lissa's parents and brother died. Andre should have been the one to inherit her family's title, and he'd certainly acted like it. Handsome and outgoing, he'd charmed everyone he knew and had been a leader in all the royal cliques and clubs that existed on campus. After his death, Lissa had felt it was her family duty to take his place.

I'd gotten to join that world with her. It was easy for me, because I didn't really have to deal with the politics of it. I was a pretty dhampir, one who didn't mind getting into trouble and pulling crazy stunts. I became a novelty; they liked having me around for the fun of it.

Lissa had to deal with other matters. The Dragomirs were one of the twelve ruling families. She'd have a very powerful place in Moroi society, and the other young royals wanted to get in good with her. Fake friends tried to schmooze her and get her to team up against other people. The royals could bribe and backstab in the same breath—and that was just with *each other*. To dhampirs and non-royals, they were completely unpredictable.

That cruel culture had eventually taken its toll on Lissa. She had an open, kind nature, one that I loved, and I hated to see her upset and stressed by royal games. She'd grown fragile since the accident, and all the parties in the world weren't worth seeing her hurt.

"All right then," I said finally. "We'll see how this goes. If anything goes wrong—anything at all—we leave. No arguments."

She nodded.

"Rose?"

We both looked up at Dimitri's looming form. I hoped he hadn't heard the part about us leaving.

"You're late for practice," he said evenly. Seeing Lissa, he gave a polite nod. "Princess."

As he and I walked away, I worried about Lissa and wondered if staying here was the right thing to do. I felt nothing alarming through the bond, but her emotions spiked all over the place. Confusion. Nostalgia. Fear. Anticipation. Strong and powerful, they flooded into me.

I felt the pull just before it happened. It was exactly like what had happened on the plane: her emotions grew so strong that they "sucked" me into her head before I could stop them. I could now see and feel what she did.

She walked slowly around the commons, toward the small Russian Orthodox chapel that served most of the school's religious needs. Lissa had always attended mass regularly. Not me. I had a standing arrangement with God: I'd agree to believe in him—barely—so long as he let me sleep in on Sundays.

But as she went inside, I could feel that she wasn't there to pray. She had another purpose, one I didn't know about. Glancing around, she verified that neither the priest nor any worshippers were close by. The place was empty.

Slipping through a doorway in the back of the chapel, she climbed a narrow set of creaky stairs up into the attic. Here it was dark and dusty. The only light came through a large stained-glass window that fractured the faint glow of sunrise into tiny, multicolored gems across the floor.

I hadn't known until that moment that this room was a regular retreat for Lissa. But now I could feel it, feel her memories of how she used to escape here to be alone and to think. The anxiety in her ebbed away ever so slightly as she took in the familiar surroundings. She climbed up into the window seat and leaned her head back against its side, momentarily entranced by the silence and the light.

Moroi could stand some sunlight, unlike the Strigoi, but they had to limit their exposure. Sitting here, she could almost pretend she was in the sun, protected by the glass's dilution of the rays.

Breathe, just breathe, she told herself. *It'll be okay. Rose will take care of everything.*

She believed that passionately, like always, and relaxed further.

Then a low voice spoke from the darkness.

"You can have the Academy but not the window seat."

She sprang up, heart pounding. I shared her anxiety, and my own pulse quickened. "Who's there?"

A moment later, a shape rose from behind a stack of crates, just outside her field of vision. The figure stepped forward, and in the poor lighting, familiar features materialized. Messy black hair. Pale blue eyes. A perpetually sardonic smirk.

Christian Ozera.

"Don't worry," he said. "I won't bite. Well, at least not in the way you're afraid of." He chuckled at his own joke.

She didn't find it funny. She had completely forgotten about Christian. So had I.

No matter what happened in our world, a few basic truths about vampires remained the same. Moroi were alive; Strigoi were undead. Moroi were mortal; Strigoi were immortal. Moroi were born; Strigoi were *made.*

And there were two ways to make a Strigoi. Strigoi could forcibly turn humans, dhampirs, or Moroi with a single bite. Moroi tempted by the promise of immortality could become Strigoi by choice if they purposely killed another person while feeding. Doing that was considered dark and twisted, the greatest of all sins, both against the Moroi way of life and nature itself. Moroi who chose this dark path lost their ability to connect with elemental magic and other powers of the world. That was why they could no longer go into the sun.

This is what had happened to Christian's parents. They were Strigoi.

FIVE

Or rather, they *had* been Strigoi. A regiment of guardians had hunted them down and killed them. If rumors were true, Christian had witnessed it all when he was very young. And although he wasn't Strigoi himself, some people thought he wasn't far off, with the way he always wore black and kept to himself.

Strigoi or not, I didn't trust him. He was a jerk, and I silently screamed at Lissa to get out of there—not that my screaming did much good. Stupid one-way bond.

"What are you doing here?" she asked.

"Taking in the sights, of course. That chair with the tarp on it is particularly lovely this time of year. Over there, we have an old box full of the writings of the blessed and crazy St. Vladimir. And let's not forget that beautiful table with no legs in the corner."

"Whatever." She rolled her eyes and moved toward the door, wanting to leave, but he blocked her way.

"Well, what about *you*?" he taunted. "Why are you up here? Don't you have parties to go to or lives to destroy?"

Some of Lissa's old spark returned. "Wow, that's hilarious. Am I like a rite of passage now? Go and see if you can piss off Lissa to prove how cool you are? Some girl I don't even know yelled at me today, and now I've got to deal with you? What does it take to be left alone?"

"Oh. So that's why you're up here. For a pity party."

"This isn't a joke. I'm serious." I could tell Lissa was getting angry. It was trumping her earlier distress.

He shrugged and leaned casually against the sloping wall. "So am I. I love pity parties. I wish I'd brought the hats. What do you want to mope about first? How it's going to take you a whole day to be popular and loved again? How you'll have to wait a couple weeks before Hollister can ship out some new clothes? If you spring for rush shipping, it might not be so long."

"Let me leave," she said angrily, this time pushing him aside.

"Wait," he said, as she reached the door. The sarcasm disappeared from his voice. "What . . . um, what was it like?"

"What was *what* like?" she snapped.

"Being out there. Away from the Academy."

She hesitated for a moment before answering, caught off guard by what seemed like a genuine attempt at conversation. "It was great. No one knew who I was. I was just another face. Not Moroi. Not royal. Not anything." She looked down at the floor. "Everyone here thinks they know who I am."

"Yeah. It's kind of hard to outlive your past," he said bitterly.

It occurred to Lissa at that moment—and me to by default—just how hard it might be to be Christian. Most of the time, people treated him like he didn't exist. Like he was a ghost. They didn't talk to or about him. They just didn't notice him. The stigma of his parents' crime was too strong, casting its shadow onto the entire Ozera family.

Still, he'd pissed her off, and she wasn't about to feel sorry for him.

"Wait—is this your pity party now?"

He laughed, almost approvingly. "This room has been my pity party for a year now."

"Sorry," said Lissa snarkily. "I was coming here before I left. I've got a longer claim."

"Squatters' rights. Besides, I have to make sure I stay near the chapel as much as possible so people know I haven't gone Strigoi . . . yet." Again, the bitter tone rang out.

"I used to always see you at mass. Is that the only reason you go? To look good?" Strigoi couldn't enter holy ground. More of that sinning-against-the-world thing.

"Sure," he said. "Why else go? For the good of your *soul*?"

"Whatever," said Lissa, who clearly had a different opinion. "I'll leave you alone then."

"Wait," he said again. He didn't seem to want her to go. "I'll make you a deal. You can hang out here too if you tell me one thing."

"What?" She glanced back at him.

He leaned forward. "Of all the rumors I heard about you today—and believe me, I heard plenty, even if no one actually told them to me—there was one that didn't come up very much.

They dissected everything else: why you left, what you did out there, why you came back, the specialization, what Rose said to Mia, blah, blah, blah. And in all of that, no one, no one ever questioned that stupid story that Rose told about there being all sorts of fringe humans who let you take blood."

She looked away, and I could feel her cheeks starting to burn. "It's not stupid. Or a story."

He laughed softly. "I've lived with humans. My aunt and I stayed away after my parents . . . died. It's not that easy to find blood." When she didn't answer, he laughed again. "It was Rose, wasn't it? She fed you."

A renewed fear shot through both her and me. No one at school could know about that. Kirova and the guardians on the scene knew, but they'd kept that knowledge to themselves.

"Well. If that's not friendship, I don't know what it is," he said.

"You can't tell anyone," she blurted out.

This was all we needed. As I'd just been reminded, feeders were vampire-bite addicts. We accepted that as part of life but still looked down on them for it. For anyone else—*especially* a dhampir—letting a Moroi take blood from you was almost, well, dirty. In fact, one of the kinkiest, practically pornographic things a dhampir could do was let a Moroi drink blood during sex.

Lissa and I hadn't had sex, of course, but we'd both known what others would think of me feeding her.

"Don't tell anyone," Lissa repeated.

He stuffed his hands in his coat pockets and sat down on one of the crates. "Who am I going to tell? Look, go grab the window seat. You can have it today and hang out for a while. If you're not still afraid of me."

She hesitated, studying him. He looked dark and surly, lips curled in a sort of I'm-such-a-rebel smirk. But he didn't look too dangerous. He didn't look Strigoi. Gingerly, she sat back down in the window seat, unconsciously rubbing her arms against the cold.

Christian watched her, and a moment later, the air warmed up considerably.

Lissa met Christian's eyes and smiled, surprised she'd never noticed how icy blue they were before. "You specialized in fire?"

He nodded and pulled up a broken chair. "Now we have luxury accommodations."

I snapped out of the vision.

"Rose? Rose?"

Blinking, I focused on Dimitri's face. He was leaning toward me, his hands gripping my shoulders. I'd stopped walking; we stood in the middle of the quad separating the upper school buildings.

"Are you all right?"

"I . . . yeah. I was . . . I was with Lissa. . . ." I put a hand to my forehead. I'd never had such a long or clear experience like that. "I was in her head."

"Her . . . head?"

"Yeah. It's part of the bond." I didn't really feel like elaborating.

"Is she all right?"

"Yeah, she's . . ." I hesitated. *Was* she all right? Christian Ozera had just invited her to hang out with him. Not good. There was "coasting through the middle," and then there was turning to the dark side. But the feelings humming through our bond were no longer scared or upset. She was almost content, though still a little nervous. "She's not in danger," I finally said. I hoped.

"Can you keep going?"

The hard, stoic warrior I'd met earlier was gone—just for a moment—and he actually looked concerned. Truly concerned. Feeling his eyes on me like that made something flutter inside of me—which was stupid, of course. I had no reason to get all goofy, just because the man was too good-looking for his own good. After all, he was an antisocial god, according to Mason. One who was supposedly going to leave me in all sorts of pain.

"Yeah. I'm fine."

I went into the gym's dressing room and changed into the workout clothes someone had finally thought to give me after a day of practicing in jeans and a T-shirt. Gross. Lissa hanging out with Christian troubled me, but I shoved that thought away for later as my muscles informed me they did not want to go through any more exercise today.

So I suggested to Dimitri that maybe he should let me off this time.

He laughed, and I was pretty sure it was *at* me and not *with* me.

"Why is that funny?"

"Oh," he said, his smile dropping. "You were serious."

"Of course I was! Look, I've technically been awake for *two* days. Why do we have to start this training now? Let me go to bed," I whined. "It's just one hour."

He crossed his arms and looked down at me. His earlier concern was gone. He was all business now. Tough love. "How do you feel right now? After the training you've done so far?"

"I hurt like hell."

"You'll feel worse tomorrow."

"So?"

"So, better to jump in now while you still feel . . . not as bad."

"What kind of logic is that?" I retorted.

But I didn't argue anymore as he led me into the weight room. He showed me the weights and reps he wanted me to do, then sprawled in a corner with a battered Western novel. Some god.

When I finished, he stood beside me and demonstrated a few cool-down stretches.

"How'd you end up as Lissa's guardian?" I asked. "You weren't here a few years ago. Were you even trained at this school?"

He didn't answer right away. I got the feeling he didn't talk about himself very often. "No. I attended the one in Siberia."

"Whoa. That's got to be the only place worse than Montana."

A glint of something—maybe amusement—sparked in his eyes, but he didn't acknowledge the joke. "After I graduated, I was a guardian for a Zeklos lord. He was killed recently." His smile dropped, his face grew dark. "They sent me here because they needed extras on campus. When the princess turned up, they assigned me to her, since I'd already be around. Not that it matters until she leaves campus."

I thought about what he'd said before. Some Strigoi killed the guy he was supposed to have been guarding? "Did this lord die on your watch?"

"No. He was with his other guardian. I was away."

He fell silent, his mind obviously somewhere else. The Moroi expected a lot from us, but they did recognize that the guardians were—more or less—only human. So, guardians got pay and time off like you'd get in any other job. Some hard-core guardians—like my mom—refused vacations, vowing never to leave their Moroi's sides. Looking at Dimitri now, I had a feeling he might very well turn into one of those. If he'd been away on legitimate leave, he could hardly blame himself for what happened to that guy. Still, he probably did anyway. I'd blame myself too if something happened to Lissa.

"Hey," I said, suddenly wanting to cheer him up, "did you

help come up with the plan to get us back? Because it was pretty good. Brute force and all that."

He arched an eyebrow curiously. Cool. I'd always wished I could do that. "You're complimenting me on that?"

"Well, it was a hell of a lot better than the last one they tried."

"Last one?"

"Yeah. In Chicago. With the pack of psi-hounds."

"This was the first time we found you. In Portland."

I sat up from my stretches and crossed my legs. "Um, I don't think I imagined psi-hounds. Who else could have sent them? They only answer to Moroi. Maybe no one told you about it."

"Maybe," he said dismissively. I could tell by his face he didn't believe that.

I returned to the novices' dorm after that. The Moroi students lived on the other side of the quad, closer to the commons. The living arrangements were partly based on convenience. Being here kept us novices closer to the gym and training grounds. But we also lived separately to accommodate the differences in Moroi and dhampir lifestyles. Their dorm had almost no windows, aside from tinted ones that dimmed sunlight. They also had a special section where feeders always stayed on hand. The novices' dorm was built in a more open way, allowing for more light.

I had my own room because there were so few novices, let alone girls. The room they'd given me was small and plain, with a twin bed and a desk with a computer. My few belongings had been spirited out of Portland and now sat in boxes around the room. I rummaged through them, pulling out a T-shirt to sleep in. I found a couple of pictures as I did, one of Lissa and me at a football game in Portland and another taken when I'd gone on vacation with her family, a year before the accident.

I set them on my desk and booted up the computer. Someone from tech support had helpfully given me a sheet with instructions for renewing my e-mail account and setting up a password. I did both, happy to discover no one had realized that this would serve as a way for me to communicate with Lissa. Too tired to write to her now, I was about to turn everything off when I noticed I already had a message. From Janine Hathaway. It was short:

I'm glad you're back. What you did was inexcusable.

"Love you too, Mom," I muttered, shutting it all down.

When I went to bed afterward, I passed out before even hitting the pillow, and just as Dimitri had predicted, I felt ten times worse when I woke up the next morning. Lying there in bed, I reconsidered the perks of running away. Then I remembered getting my ass kicked and figured the only way to prevent that from happening again was to go endure some more of it this morning.

My soreness made it all that much worse, but I survived the before-school practice with Dimitri and my subsequent classes without passing out or fainting.

At lunch, I dragged Lissa away from Natalie's table early and gave her a Kirova-worthy lecture about Christian—particularly chastising her for letting him know about our blood arrangement. If that got out, it'd kill both of us socially, and I didn't trust him not to tell.

Lissa had other concerns.

"You were in my head again?" she exclaimed. "For *that* long?"

"I didn't do it on purpose," I argued. "It just happened. And that's not the point. How long did you hang out with him afterward?"

"Not that long. It was kind of . . . fun."

"Well, you can't do it again. If people find out you're hanging out with him, they'll crucify you." I eyed her warily. "You aren't, like, into him, are you?"

She scoffed. "No. Of course not.

"Good. Because if you're going to go after a guy, steal Aaron back." He was boring, yes, but safe. Just like Natalie. How come all the harmless people were so lame? Maybe that was the definition of safe.

She laughed. "Mia would claw my eyes out."

"We can take her. Besides, he deserves someone who doesn't shop at Gap Kids."

"Rose, you've got to stop saying things like that."

"I'm just saying what you won't."

"She's only a year younger," said Lissa. She laughed. "I can't believe you think *I'm* the one who's going to get us in trouble."

Smiling as we strolled toward class, I gave her a sidelong glance. "Aaron does look pretty good though, huh?"

She smiled back and avoided my eyes. "Yeah. Pretty good."

"Ooh. You see? You should go after him."

"Whatever. I'm fine being friends now."

"Friends who used to stick their tongues down each other's throats."

She rolled her eyes.

"Fine." I let my teasing go. "Let Aaron stay in the nursery school. Just so long as you stay away from Christian. He's dangerous."

"You're overreacting. He's not going Strigoi."

"He's a bad influence."

She laughed. "You think *I'm* in danger of going Strigoi?"

She didn't wait for my answer, instead pushing ahead to open the door to our science class. Standing there, I uneasily replayed her words and then followed a moment later. When I did, I got to see royal power in action. A few guys—with giggling, watching girls—were messing with a gangly-looking Moroi. I didn't know him very well, but I knew he was poor and certainly not royal. A couple of his tormentors were air-magic users, and they'd blown the papers off his desk and were pushing them around the room on currents of air while the guy tried to catch them.

My instincts urged me to do something, maybe go smack one of the air users. But I couldn't pick a fight with everyone who annoyed me, and certainly not a group of royals—especially when Lissa needed to stay off their radar. So I could only give them a look of disgust as I walked to my desk. As I did, a hand caught my arm. Jesse.

"Hey," I said jokingly. Fortunately, he didn't appear to be participating in the torture session. "Hands off the merchandise."

He flashed me a smile but kept his hand on me. "Rose, tell Paul about the time you started the fight in Ms. Karp's class."

I cocked my head toward him, giving him a playful smile. "I started a lot of fights in her class."

"The one with the hermit crab. And the gerbil."

I laughed, recalling it. "Oh yeah. It was a hamster, I think. I just dropped it into the crab's tank, and they were both worked up from being so close to me, so they went at it."

Paul, a guy sitting nearby whom I didn't really know, chuckled too. He'd transferred last year, apparently, and hadn't heard of this. "Who won?"

I looked at Jesse quizzically. "I don't remember. Do you?"

"No. I just remember Karp freaking out." He turned toward Paul. "Man, you should have seen this messed-up teacher we used to have. Used to think people were after her and would go off on stuff that didn't make any sense. She was nuts. Used to wander campus while everyone was asleep."

I smiled tightly, like I thought it was funny. Instead, I thought back to Ms. Karp again, surprised to be thinking about her for the second time in two days. Jesse was right—

she *had* wandered campus a lot when she still worked here. It was pretty creepy. I'd run into her once—unexpectedly.

I'd been climbing out of my dorm window to go hang out with some people. It was after hours, and we were all supposed to be in our rooms, fast asleep. Such escape tactics were a regular practice for me. I was good at them.

But I fell that time. I had a second-floor room, and I lost my grip about halfway down. Sensing the ground rush up toward me, I tried desperately to grab hold of something and slow my fall. The building's rough stone tore into my skin, causing cuts I was too preoccupied to feel. I slammed into the grassy earth, back first, getting the wind knocked out of me.

"Bad form, Rosemarie. You should be more careful. Your instructors would be disappointed."

Peering through the tangle of my hair, I saw Ms. Karp looking down at me, a bemused look on her face. Pain, in the meantime, shot through every part of my body.

Ignoring it as best I could, I clambered to my feet. Being in class with Crazy Karp while surrounded by other students was one thing. Standing outside alone with her was an entirely different matter. She always had an eerie, distracted gleam in her eye that made my skin break out in goose bumps.

There was also now a high likelihood she'd drag me off to Kirova for a detention. Scarier still.

Instead, she just smiled and reached for my hands. I flinched but let her take them. She *tsk*ed when she saw the scrapes. Tightening her grip on them, she frowned slightly. A tingle burned my skin, laced with a sort of pleasant buzz, and then the wounds closed up. I had a brief sense of dizziness. My temperature spiked. The blood disappeared, as did the pain in my hip and leg.

Gasping, I jerked my hands away. I'd seen a lot of Moroi magic, but never anything like that.

"What . . . what did you do?"

She gave me that weird smile again. "Go back to your dorm, Rose. There are bad things out here. You never know what's following you."

I was still staring at my hands. "But . . ."

I looked back up at her and for the first time noticed scars on the sides of her forehead. Like nails had dug into them. She winked. "I won't tell on you if you don't tell on me."

I jumped back to the present, unsettled by the memory of that bizarre night. Jesse, in the meantime, was telling me about a party.

"You've got to slip your leash tonight. We're going up to that spot in the woods around eight thirty. Mark got some weed."

I sighed wistfully, regret replacing the chill I'd felt over the memory of Ms. Karp. "Can't slip that leash. I'm with my Russian jailer."

He let go of my arm, looking disappointed, and ran a hand through his bronze-colored hair. Yeah. Not being able to hang out with him was a damned shame. I really would have to fix that someday. "Can't you ever get off for good behavior?" he joked.

I gave him what I hoped was a seductive smile as I found my seat. "Sure," I called over my shoulder. "If I was ever good."

SIX

As much as Lissa and Christian's meeting bothered me, it gave me an idea the next day.

"Hey, Kirova—er, Ms. Kirova." I stood in the doorway of her office, not having bothered to make an appointment. She raised her eyes from some paperwork, clearly annoyed to see me.

"Yes, Miss Hathaway?"

"Does my house arrest mean I can't go to church?"

"I beg your pardon?"

"You said that whenever I'm not in class or practice, I have to stay in the dorm. But what about church on Sundays? I don't think it's really fair to keep me away from my religious . . . um, needs." Or deprive me of another chance—no matter how short and boring—to hang out with Lissa.

She pushed her glasses up the bridge of her nose. "I wasn't aware you had any religious needs."

"I found Jesus while I was gone."

"Isn't your mother an atheist?" she asked skeptically.

"And my dad's probably Muslim. But I've moved on to my own path. You shouldn't keep me from it."

She made a noise that sort of sounded like a snicker. "No, Miss Hathaway, I should not. Very well. You may attend services on Sundays."

The victory was short-lived, however, because church was every bit as lame as I remembered when I attended a few days later. I did get to sit next to Lissa, though, which made me feel like I was getting away with something. Mostly I just people-watched. Church was optional for students, but with so many Eastern European families, a lot of students were Eastern Orthodox Christians and attended either because they believed or because their parents made them.

Christian sat on the opposite side of the aisle, pretending to be just as holy as he'd said. As much as I didn't like him, his fake faith still made me smile. Dimitri sat in the back, face lined with shadows, and, like me, didn't take communion. As thoughtful as he looked, I wondered if he even listened to the service. I tuned in and out.

"Following God's path is never easy," the priest was saying. "Even St. Vladimir, this school's own patron saint, had a difficult time. He was so filled with spirit that people often flocked around him, enthralled just to listen and be in his presence. So great was his spirit, the old texts say, that he could heal the sick. Yet despite these gifts, many did not respect him. They mocked him, claiming he was misguided and confused."

Which was a nice way of saying Vladimir was insane. Everyone knew it. He was one of a handful of Moroi saints, so the priest liked to talk about him a lot. I'd heard all about him, many times over, before we left. Great. It looked like I had an eternity of Sundays to hear his story over and over again.

". . . and so it was with shadow-kissed Anna."

I jerked my head up. I had no idea what the priest was talking about now, because I hadn't been listening for some time. But those words burned into me. *Shadow-kissed*. It had been a while since I heard them, but I'd never forgotten them. I waited, hoping he'd continue, but he'd already moved on to the next part of the service. The sermon was over.

Church concluded, and as Lissa turned to go, I shook my head at her. "Wait for me. I'll be right there."

I pushed my way through the crowd, up to the front, where the priest was speaking with a few people. I waited impatiently while he finished. Natalie was there, asking him about volunteer work she could do. Ugh. When she finished, she left, greeting me as she passed.

The priest raised his eyebrows when he saw me. "Hello, Rose. It's nice to see you again."

"Yeah . . . you too," I said. "I heard you talking about Anna. About how she was 'shadow-kissed.' What does that mean?"

He frowned. "I'm not entirely sure. She lived a very long time ago. It was often common to refer to people by titles that reflected some of their traits. It might have been given to make her sound fierce."

I tried to hide my disappointment. "Oh. So who was she?"

This time his frown was disapproving rather than thoughtful. "I mentioned it a number of times."

"Oh. I must have, um, missed that."

His disapproval grew, and he turned around. "Wait just a moment."

He disappeared through the door near the altar, the one Lissa had taken to the attic. I considered fleeing but thought God might strike me down for that. Less than a minute later, the priest returned with a book. He handed it to me. *Moroi Saints.*

"You can learn about her in here. The next time I see you, I'd like to hear what you've learned."

I scowled as I walked away. Great. Homework from the priest.

In the chapel's entryway, I found Lissa talking to Aaron. She smiled as she spoke, and the feelings coming off her were happy, though certainly not infatuated.

"You're kidding," she exclaimed.

He shook his head. "Nope."

Seeing me stroll over, she turned to me. "Rose, you're never going to believe this. "You know Abby Badica? And Xander? Their guardian wants to resign. And marry *another* guardian."

Now *this* was exciting gossip. A scandal, actually. "Seriously? Are they, like, going to run off together?"

She nodded. "They're getting a house. Going to get jobs with humans, I guess."

I glanced at Aaron, who had suddenly turned shy with me there. "How are Abby and Xander dealing with that?"

"Okay. Embarrassed. They think it's stupid." Then he realized who he was speaking to. "Oh. I didn't mean—"

"Whatever." I gave him a tight smile. "It *is* stupid."

Wow. I was stunned. The rebellious part of me loved any

story where people "fought the system." Only, in this case, they were fighting *my* system, the one I'd been trained to believe in my entire life.

Dhampirs and Moroi had a strange arrangement. Dhampirs had originally been born from Moroi mixing with humans. Unfortunately, dhampirs couldn't reproduce with each other—or with humans. It was a weird genetic thing. Mules were the same way, I'd been told, though that wasn't a comparison I really liked hearing. Dhampirs and full Moroi *could* have children together, and, through another genetic oddity, their kids came out as standard dhampirs, with half human genes, half vampire genes.

With Moroi being the only ones with whom dhampirs could reproduce, we had to stay close to them and intermingle with them. Likewise, it became important to us that the Moroi simply *survived*. Without them, we were done. And with the way Strigoi loved picking off Moroi, their survival became a legitimate concern for us.

That was how the guardian system developed. Dhampirs couldn't work magic, but we made great warriors. We'd inherited enhanced senses and reflexes from our vampire genes and better strength and endurance from our human genes. We also weren't limited by a need for blood or trouble with sunlight. Sure, we weren't as powerful as the Strigoi, but we trained hard, and guardians did a kick-ass job at keeping Moroi safe. Most dhampirs felt it was worth risking their own lives to make sure our kind could still keep having children.

Since Moroi usually wanted to have and raise Moroi children, you didn't find a lot of long-term Moroi-dhampir romances. You especially didn't find a lot of Moroi women hooking up with dhampir guys. But plenty of young Moroi men liked fooling around with dhampir women, although those guys usually went on to marry Moroi women. That left a lot of single dhampir mothers, but we were tough and could handle it.

However, many dhampir mothers chose not to become guardians in order to raise their children. These women sometimes worked "regular" jobs with Moroi or humans; some of them lived together in communities. These communities had a bad reputation. I don't know how much of it was true, but rumors said Moroi men visited *all the time* for sex. and that some dhampir women let them drink blood while doing it. Blood whores.

Regardless, almost all guardians were men, which meant there were a lot more Moroi than guardians. Most dhampir guys accepted that they wouldn't have kids. They knew it was their job to protect Moroi while their sisters and cousins had babies.

Some dhampir women, like my mother, still felt it was their duty to become guardians—even if it meant not raising their own kids. After I'd been born, she'd handed me over to be raised by Moroi. Moroi and dhampirs start school pretty young, and the Academy had essentially taken over as my parent by the time I was four.

Between her example and my life at the Academy, I believed wholeheartedly that it was a dhampir's job to protect Moroi. It was part of our heritage, *and* it was the only way we'd keep going. It was that simple.

And that was what made what the Badicas' guardian had done so shocking. He'd abandoned his Moroi and run off with another guardian, which meant she'd abandoned *her* Moroi. They couldn't even have children together, and now two families were unprotected. What was the point? No one cared if teenage dhampirs dated or if adult dhampirs had flings. But a long-term relationship? Particularly one that involved them running away? A complete waste. And a disgrace.

After a little more speculation on the Badicas, Lissa and I left Aaron. As we stepped outside, I heard a funny shifting sound and then something sliding. Too late, I realized what was happening, just as a pile of slush slid off the chapel's roof and onto us. It was early October, and we'd had early snow last night that had started melting almost immediately. As a result, the stuff that fell on us was very wet and very cold.

Lissa took the brunt of it, but I still yelped as icy water landed on my hair and neck. A few others squealed nearby too, having caught the edge of the mini-avalanche.

"You okay?" I asked her. Her coat was drenched, and her platinum hair clung to the sides of her face.

"Y-yeah," she said through chattering teeth.

I pulled off my coat and handed it to her. It had a slick surface and had repelled most of the water. "Take yours off."

"But you'll be—"

"Take this."

She did, and as she slipped on my coat, I finally tuned into the laughter that always follows these situations. I avoided the eyes, instead focusing on holding Lissa's wet jacket while she changed.

"Wish you hadn't been wearing a coat, Rose," said Ralf Sarcozy, an unusually bulky and plump Moroi. I hated him. "That shirt would have looked good wet."

"That shirt's so ugly it should be burned. Did you get that from a homeless person?"

I glanced up as Mia walked over and looped her arm through Aaron's. Her blond curls were arranged perfectly, and she had on an awesome pair of black heels that would have looked much better on me. At least they made her look taller, I'd give her that. Aaron had been a few steps behind us but had miraculously avoided being nailed by the slush. Seeing how smug she looked, I decided there'd been no miracles involved.

"I suppose you want to offer to burn it, huh?" I asked, refusing to let her know how much that insult bugged me. I knew perfectly well my fashion sense had slipped over the last two years. "Oh, wait—fire isn't your element, is it? You work with water. What a coincidence that a bunch just fell on us."

Mia looked as if she'd been insulted, but the gleam in her eyes showed that she was enjoying this way too much to be an innocent bystander. "What's that supposed to mean?"

"Nothing to me. But Ms. Kirova will probably have something to say when she finds out you used magic against another student."

"That wasn't an attack," she scoffed. "And it wasn't me. It was an act of God."

A few others laughed, much to her delight. In my imagination, I responded with, *So is this*, and then slammed her into the side of the church. In real life, Lissa simply nudged me and said, "Let's go."

She and I walked off toward our respective dorms, leaving behind laughter and jokes about our wet states and how Lissa wouldn't know anything about specialization. Inside, I seethed. I had to do something about Mia, I realized. In addition to the general irritation of Mia's bitchiness, I didn't want Lissa to have to deal with any more stress than she had to. We'd been okay this first week, and I wanted to keep it that way.

"You know," I said, "I'm thinking more and more that you stealing Aaron back is a good thing. It'll teach Bitch Doll a lesson. I bet it'd be easy, too. He's still crazy about you."

"I don't want to teach anyone a lesson," said Lissa. "And *I'm* not crazy about him."

"Come on, she picks fights and talks about us behind our backs. She accused me of getting jeans from the Salvation Army yesterday."

"Your jeans *are* from the Salvation Army."

"Well, yeah," I snorted, "but she has no right making fun of them when she's wearing stuff from Target."

"Hey, there's nothing wrong with Target. I like Target."

"So do I. That's not the point. She's trying to pass her stuff off like it's freaking Stella McCartney."

"And that's a crime?"

I affected a solemn face. "Absolutely. You've gotta take revenge."

"I told you, I'm not interested in revenge." Lissa cut me a sidelong look. "And you shouldn't be either."

I smiled as innocently as I could, and when we parted ways, I felt relieved again that she couldn't read my thoughts.

"So when's the big catfight going to happen?"

Mason was waiting for me outside our dorm after I'd parted ways with Lissa. He looked lazy and cute, leaning against the wall with crossed arms as he watched me.

"I'm sure I don't know what you mean."

He unfolded himself and walked with me into the building, handing me his coat, since I'd let Lissa go off with my dry one. "I saw you guys sparring outside the chapel. Have you no respect for the house of God?"

I snorted. "You've got about as much respect for it as I do, you heathen. You didn't even go. Besides, as you said, we were *outside*."

"And you still didn't answer the question."

I just grinned and slipped on his coat.

We stood in the common area of our dorm, a well-supervised

lounge and study area where male and female students could mingle, along with Moroi guests. Being Sunday, it was pretty crowded with those cramming for last-minute assignments due tomorrow. Spying a small, empty table, I grabbed Mason's arm and pulled him toward it.

"Aren't you supposed to go straight to your room?"

I hunkered down in my seat, glancing around warily. "There are so many people here today, it'll take them a while to notice me. God, I'm so sick of being locked away. And it's only been a week."

"I'm sick of it too. We missed you last night. A bunch of us went and shot pool in the rec room. Eddie was on fire."

I groaned. "Don't tell me that. I don't want to hear about your glamorous social life."

"All right." He propped his elbow up on the table and rested his chin in his hand. "Then tell me about Mia. You're just going to turn around and punch her one day, aren't you? I think I remember you doing that at least ten times with people that pissed you off."

"I'm a new, reformed Rose," I said, doing my best impression of demure. Which wasn't very good. He emitted a choking sort of laugh. "Besides, if I do that, I'll have broken my probation with Kirova. Gotta walk the straight and narrow."

"In other words, find some way to get back at Mia that you won't get in trouble for."

I felt a smile tug at the corners of my lips. "You know what I like about you, Mase? You think just like I do."

"Frightening concept," he replied drily. "So tell me what you think of this: I might know something about her, but I probably shouldn't tell you. . . ."

I leaned forward. "Oh, you already tipped me off. You've *got* to tell me now."

"It'd be wrong," he teased. "How do I know you'd use this knowledge for good instead of evil?"

I batted my eyelashes. "Can you resist this face?"

He took a moment to study me. "No. I can't, actually. Okay, here you go: Mia isn't royal."

I slouched back in my chair. "No kidding. I already knew that. I've known who's royal since I was two."

"Yeah, but there's more than just that. Her parents work for one of the Drozdov lords." I waved my hand impatiently. A lot of Moroi worked out in the human world, but Moroi society had plenty of jobs for its own kind too. Someone had to fill them. "Cleaning stuff. Practically servants. Her dad cuts grass, and her mom's a maid."

I actually had a healthy respect for anyone who pulled a full day's work, regardless of the job. People everywhere had to do crappy stuff to make a living. But, much like with Target, it became another matter altogether when someone was trying to pass herself off as something else. And in the week that I'd been here, I'd picked up on how desperately Mia wanted to fit in with the school elite.

"No one knows," I said thoughtfully.

"And she doesn't want them to. You know how the royals

are." He paused. "Well, except for Lissa, of course. They'd give Mia a hard time over it."

"How do you know all this?"

"My uncle's a guardian for the Drozdovs."

"And you've just been sitting on this secret, huh?"

"Until you broke me. So which path will you choose: good or evil?"

"I think I'll give her a grace—"

"Miss Hathaway, you know you aren't supposed to be here."

One of the dorm matrons stood over us, disapproval all over her face.

I hadn't been joking when I said Mason thought like me. He could bullshit as well as I could. "We have a group project to do for our humanities class. How are we supposed to do it if Rose is in isolation?"

The matron narrowed her eyes. "You don't look like you're doing work."

I slid over the priest's book and opened it at random. I'd placed it on the table when we sat down. "We're, um, working on this."

She still looked suspicious. "One hour. I'll give you one more hour down here, and I'd better actually see you working."

"Yes, ma'am," said Mason straight-faced. "Absolutely."

She wandered off, still eyeing us. "My hero," I declared.

He pointed at the book. "What is this?"

"Something the priest gave me. I had a question about the service."

He stared at me, astonished.

"Oh, stop it and look interested." I skimmed the index. "I'm trying to find some woman named Anna."

Mason slid his chair over so that he was sitting right beside me. "All right. Let's 'study.'"

I found a page number, and it took me to the section on St. Vladimir, not surprisingly. We read through the chapter, scanning for Anna's name. When we found it, the author didn't have much to say about her. He did include an excerpt written by some guy who had apparently lived at the same time as St. Vladimir:

And with Vladimir always is Anna, the daughter of Fyodor. Their love is as chaste and pure as that of brother and sister, and many times has she defended him from Strigoi who would seek to destroy him and his holiness. Likewise, it is she who comforts him when the spirit becomes too much to bear, and Satan's darkness tries to smother him and weaken his own health and body. This too she defends against, for they have been bound together ever since he saved her life as a child. It is a sign of God's love that He has sent the blessed Vladimir a guardian such as her, one who is shadow-kissed and always knows what is in his heart and mind.

"There you go," Mason said. "She was his guardian."

"It doesn't say what 'shadow-kissed' means."

"Probably doesn't mean anything."

Something in me didn't believe that. I read it again, trying to make sense of the old-fashioned language. Mason watched me curiously, looking like he very much wanted to help.

"Maybe they were hooking up," he suggested.

I laughed. "He was a *saint*."

"So? Saints probably like sex too. That 'brother and sister' stuff is probably a cover." He pointed to one of the lines. "See? They were 'bound' together." He winked. "It's code."

Bound. It was a weird word choice, but that didn't necessarily mean Anna and Vladimir were ripping each other's clothes off.

"I don't think so. They're just close. Guys and girls can just be friends." I said it pointedly, and he gave me a dry look.

"Yeah? *We're* friends, and I don't know what's in your 'heart and mind.'" Mason put on a fake philosopher's look. "Of course, some might argue that one can never know what's in the heart of a woman—"

"Oh, shut up," I groaned, punching him in the arm.

"For they are strange and mysterious creatures," he continued in his scholarly voice, "and a man must be a mind reader if he ever wishes to make them happy."

I started giggling uncontrollably and knew I'd probably get in trouble again. "Well, try to read my mind and stop being such a—"

I stopped laughing and looked back down at the book.

Bound together and *always knows what is in his heart and mind.*

They had a bond, I realized. I would have bet everything I owned—which wasn't much—on it. The revelation was astonishing. There were lots of vague stories and myths about how guardians and Moroi 'used to have bonds.' But this was the first I'd ever heard of anyone specific that it had happened to.

Mason had noticed my startled reaction. "You okay? You look kind of weird."

I shrugged it off. "Yeah. Fine."

SEVEN

A couple weeks passed after that, and I soon forgot about the Anna thing as life at the Academy wrapped around me. The shock of our return had worn off a little, and we began to fall into a semi-comfortable routine. My days revolved around church, lunch with Lissa, and whatever sort of social life I could scrape together outside of that. Denied any real free time, I didn't have too hard a time staying out of the spotlight, although I did manage to steal a little attention here and there, despite my noble speech to her about 'coasting through the middle.' I couldn't help it. I liked flirting, I liked groups, and I liked making smartass comments in class.

Her new, incognito role attracted attention simply because it was so different than before we'd left, back when she'd been so active with the royals. Most people soon let that go, accepting that the Dragomir princess was fading off the social radar and content to run with Natalie and her group. Natalie's rambling still made me want to beat my head against a wall sometimes, but she was really nice—nicer than almost any of the other royals—and I enjoyed hanging around her most of the time.

And, just as Kirova had warned, I was indeed training and working out all the time. But as more time passed, my body stopped hating me. My muscles grew tougher, and my stamina increased. I still got my ass kicked in practice but not quite as badly as I used to, which was something. The biggest toll now seemed to be on my skin. Being outside in the cold so much was chapping my face, and only Lissa's constant supply of skin-care lotions kept me from aging before my time. She couldn't do much for the blisters on my hands and feet.

A routine also developed with Dimitri and me. Mason had been right about him being antisocial. Dimitri didn't hang out much with the other guardians, though it was clear they all respected him. And the more I worked with him, the more I respected him too, though I didn't really understand his training methods. They didn't seem very badass. We always started by stretching in the gym, and lately he'd been sending me outside to run, braving the increasingly cold Montana autumn.

Three weeks after my return to the Academy, I walked into the gym before school one day and found him sprawled on a mat, reading a Louis L'Amour book. Someone had brought in a portable CD player, and while that cheered me up at first, the song coming from it did not: "When Doves Cry" by Prince. It was embarrassing to know the title, but one of our former housemates had been obsessed with the '80s.

"Whoa, Dimitri," I said, tossing my bag on the floor. "I realize this is actually a current hit in Eastern Europe right now, but do you think we could maybe listen to something that wasn't recorded before I was born?"

Only his eyes flicked toward me; the rest of his posture

remained the same. "What does it matter to you? I'm the one who's going to be listening to it. You'll be outside running."

I made a face as I set my foot up on one of the bars and stretched my hamstrings. All things considered, Dimitri had a good-natured tolerance for my snarkiness. So long as I didn't slack in my training, he didn't mind my running commentary.

"Hey," I asked, moving on to the next set of stretches, "what's with all the running, anyway? I mean, I realize the importance of stamina and all that, but shouldn't I be moving on to something with a little hitting? They're still killing me in group practice."

"Maybe you should hit harder," he replied drily.

"I'm serious."

"Hard to tell the difference." He set the book down but didn't move from his sprawl. "My job is to get you ready to defend the princess and fight dark creatures, right?"

"Yup."

"So tell me this: suppose you manage to kidnap her again and take her off to the mall. While you're there, a Strigoi comes at you. What will you do?"

"Depends on what store we're in."

He looked at me.

"Fine. I'll stab him with a silver stake."

Dimitri sat up now, crossing his long legs in one fluid motion. I still couldn't figure out how someone so tall could be so graceful. "Oh?" He raised his dark eyebrows. "Do you have a silver stake? Do you even know how to use one?"

I dragged my eyes away from his body and scowled. Made with elemental magic, silver stakes were a guardian's deadliest weapon. Stabbing a Strigoi through the heart with one meant instant death. The blades were also lethal to Moroi, so they weren't given out lightly to novices. My classmates had just started learning how to use them. I'd trained with a gun before, but no one would let me near a stake yet. Fortunately, there were two other ways to kill a Strigoi.

"Okay. I'll cut his head off."

"Ignoring the fact that you don't have a weapon to do that, how will you compensate for the fact that he may be a foot taller than you?"

I straightened up from touching my toes, annoyed. "Fine, then I'll set him on fire."

"Again, with what?"

"All right, I give up. You've already got the answer. You're just messing with me. I'm at the mall and I see a Strigoi. What do I do?"

He looked at me and didn't blink. "You run."

I repressed the urge to throw something at him. When I finished my stretches, he told me he'd run with me. That was a first. Maybe running would give me some insight into his killer reputation.

We set out into the chilly October evening. Being back on a vampiric schedule still felt weird to me. With school about to start in an hour, I expected the sun to be coming up, not down. But it was sinking on the western horizon, lighting up the snow-capped mountains with an orange glow. It didn't really warm things up, and I soon felt the cold pierce my lungs as my need for oxygen deepened. We didn't speak. He slowed his pace to match mine, so we stayed together.

Something about that bothered me; I suddenly very much wanted his approval. So I picked up my own pace, working my lungs and muscles harder. Twelve laps around the track made three miles; we had nine more to go.

When we reached the third-to-last loop, a couple of other novices passed by, preparing to go to the group practice I'd soon be at as well. Seeing me, Mason cheered. "Good form, Rose!"

I smiled and waved back.

"You're slowing down," Dimitri snapped, jerking my gaze from the boys. The harshness in his voice startled me. "Is this why your times aren't getting any faster? You're easily distracted?"

Embarrassed, I increased my speed once more, despite the fact that my body started screaming obscenities at me. We finished the twelve laps, and when he checked, he found we'd shaved two minutes off my best time.

"Not bad, huh?" I crowed when we headed back inside for cool-down stretches. "Looks like I could get as far as the Limited before the Strigoi got me at the mall. Not sure how Lissa would do."

"If she was with you, she'd be okay."

I looked up in surprise. It was the first real compliment

he'd paid me since I started training with him. His brown eyes watched me, both approving and amused.

And that's when it happened.

I felt like someone had shot me. Sharp and biting, terror exploded in my body and in my head. Small razors of pain. My vision blurred, and for a moment, I wasn't standing there. I was running down a flight of stairs, scared and desperate, needing to get out of there, needing to find . . . me.

My vision cleared, leaving me back on the track and out of Lissa's head. Without a word to Dimitri, I tore off, running as fast as I could toward the Moroi dorm. It didn't matter that I'd just put my legs through a mini-marathon. They ran hard and fast, like they were shiny and new. Distantly, I was aware of Dimitri catching up to me, asking me what was wrong. But I couldn't answer him. I had one task and one alone: get to the dorm.

Its looming, ivy-covered form was just coming into view when Lissa met up with us, her face streaked with tears. I came to a jarring stop, my lungs ready to burst.

"What's wrong? What happened?" I demanded, clutching her arms, forcing her to look into my eyes.

But she couldn't answer. She just flung her arms around me, sobbing into my chest. I held her there, stroking her sleek, silky hair while I told her it was going to be all right—whatever 'it' was. And honestly, I didn't care what it was just then. She was here, and she was safe, which was all that mattered. Dimitri hovered over us, alert and ready for any threat, his body coiled to attack. I felt safe with him beside us.

A half hour later, we were crammed inside Lissa's dorm room with three other guardians, Ms. Kirova, and the hall matron. This was the first time I'd seen Lissa's room. Natalie had indeed managed to get her as a roommate, and the two sides of the room were a study in contrasts. Natalie's looked lived in, with pictures on the wall and a frilly bedspread that wasn't dorm-issue. Lissa had as few possessions as I did, making her half noticeably bare. She did have one picture taped to the wall, a picture taken from last Halloween, when we'd dressed up like fairies, complete with wings and glittery makeup. Seeing that picture and remembering how things used to be made a dull pain form in my chest.

With all the excitement, no one seemed to remember that I wasn't supposed to be in there. Outside in the hall, other Moroi girls crowded together, trying to figure out what was going on. Natalie pushed her way through them, wondering what the commotion in her room was. When she discovered it, she came to a screeching halt.

Shock and disgust showed on almost everyone's faces as we stared at Lissa's bed. There was a fox on the pillow. Its coat was reddish-orange, tinged in white. It looked so soft and cuddly that it could have been a pet, perhaps a cat, something you'd hold in your arms and snuggle with.

Aside from the fact that its throat had been slit.

The inside of the throat looked pink and jellylike. Blood stained that soft coat and had run down onto the yellow bedspread, forming a dark pool that spread across the fabric. The fox's eyes stared upward, glazed, over with a sort of shocked look about them, like the fox couldn't believe this was happening.

Nausea built up in my stomach, but I forced myself to keep looking. I couldn't afford to be squeamish. I'd be killing Strigoi someday. If I couldn't handle a fox, I'd never survive major kills.

What had happened to the fox was sick and twisted, obviously done by someone too fucked up for words. Lissa stared at it, her face death-pale, and took a few steps toward it, hand involuntarily reaching out. This gross act hit her hard, I knew, digging at her love of animals. She loved them, they loved her. While on our own, she'd often begged me for a pet, but I'd always refused and reminded her we couldn't take care of one when we might have to flee at a moment's notice. Plus, they hated me. So she'd contented herself with helping and patching up strays she found and making friends with other people's pets, like Oscar the cat.

She couldn't patch this fox up, though. There was no coming back for it, but I saw in her face she wanted to help it, like she helped everything. I took her hand and steered her away, suddenly recalling a conversation from two years ago.

"What is that? Is it a crow?"

"Too big. It's a raven."

"Is it dead?"

"Yeah. Definitely dead. Don't touch it."

She hadn't listened to me back then. I hoped she would now.

"It was still alive when I got back," Lissa whispered to me, clutching my arm. "Barely. Oh God, it was twitching. It must have suffered so much."

I felt bile rise in my throat now. Under no circumstances would I throw up. "Did you—?"

"No. I wanted to. . . . I started to. . . ."

"Then forget about it," I said sharply. "It's stupid. Somebody's stupid joke. They'll clean it up. Probably even give you a new room if you want."

She turned to me, eyes almost wild. "Rose . . . do you remember . . . that one time. . . ."

"Stop it," I said. "Forget about it. This isn't the same thing."

"What if someone saw? What if someone knows? . . ."

I tightened my grip on her arm, digging my nails in to get her attention. She flinched. "No. It's not the same. It has nothing to do with that. Do you hear me?" I could feel both Natalie and Dimitri's eyes on us. "It's going to be okay. Everything's going to be okay."

Not looking like she believed me at all, Lissa nodded.

"Get this cleaned up," Kirova snapped to the matron. "And find out if anyone saw anything."

Someone finally realized I was there and ordered Dimitri to take me away, no matter how much I begged them to let me stay with Lissa. He walked me back to the novices' dorm. He didn't speak until we were almost there. "You know something. Something about what happened. Is this what you meant when you told Headmistress Kirova that Lissa was in danger?"

"I don't know anything. It's just some sick joke."

"Do you have any idea who'd do it? Or why?"

I considered this. Before we'd left, it could have been any number of people. That was the way it was when you were popular. People loved you, people hated you. But now? Lissa had faded off to a certain extent. The only person who really and truly despised her was Mia, but Mia seemed to fight her battles with words, not actions. And even if she did decide to do something more aggressive, why do this? She didn't seem like the type. There were a million other ways to get back at a person.

"No," I told him. "No clue."

"Rose, if you know something, tell me. We're on the same side. We both want to protect her. This is serious."

I spun around, taking my anger over the fox out on him. "Yeah, it *is* serious. It's all serious. And you have me doing laps every day when I should be learning to fight and defend her! If you want to help her, then teach me something! *Teach me how to fight*. I already know how to run away."

I didn't realize until that moment how badly I did want to learn, how I wanted to prove myself to him, to Lissa, and to everyone else. The fox incident had made me feel powerless, and I didn't like that. I wanted to do something, *anything*.

Dimitri watched my outburst calmly, with no change in his expression. When I finished, he simply beckoned me forward like I hadn't said anything. "Come on. You're late for practice."

EIGHT

Burning with anger, I fought harder and better that day than I ever had in any of my classes with the novices. So much so that I finally won my first hand-to-hand pairing, annihilating Shane Reyes. We'd always gotten along, and he took it good-naturedly, applauding my performance, as did a few others.

"The comeback's starting," observed Mason after class.

"So it would seem."

He gently touched my arm. "How's Lissa?"

It didn't surprise me that he knew. Gossip spread so fast around here sometimes, it felt like everyone had a psychic bond.

"Okay. Coping." I didn't elaborate on how I knew that. Our bond was a secret from the student body. "Mase, you claim to know about Mia. You think she might have done that?"

"Whoa, hey, I'm not an expert on her or anything. But honestly? No. Mia won't even do dissections in biology. I can't picture her actually catching a fox, let alone, um, killing it."

"Any friends who might do it for her?"

He shook his head. "Not really. They're not really the types to get their hands dirty either. But who knows?"

Lissa was still shaken when I met her for lunch later, her

mood made worse when Natalie and her crew wouldn't shut up about the fox. Apparently Natalie had overcome her disgust enough to enjoy the attention the spectacle had brought her. Maybe she wasn't as content with her fringe status as I'd always believed.

"And it was just *there*," she explained, waving her hands for emphasis. "Right in the middle of the bed. There was blood *everywhere*."

Lissa looked as green as the sweater she wore, and I pulled her away before I even finished my food and immediately launched into a string of obscenities about Natalie's social skills.

"She's nice," Lissa said automatically. "You were just telling me the other day how much you liked her."

"I do like her, but she's just incompetent about certain things."

We stood outside our animal behavior class, and I noticed people giving us curious looks and whispering as they passed. I sighed.

"How are you doing with all this?"

A half-smile crossed her face. "Can't you already feel it?"

"Yeah, but I want to hear it from you."

"I don't know. I'll be okay. I wish everyone wouldn't keep staring at me like I'm some kind of freak."

My anger exploded again. The fox was bad. People upsetting her made it worse, but at least I could do something about them. "Who's bothering you?"

"Rose, you can't beat up everyone we have a problem with."

"Mia?" I guessed.

"And others," she said evasively. "Look, it doesn't matter. What I want to know is how this could have . . . that is, I can't stop thinking about that time—"

"Don't," I warned.

"Why do you keep pretending that didn't happen? You of all people. You made fun of Natalie for going on and on, but it's not like you've got a good grip on your control switch. You'll normally talk about anything."

"But not *that*. We need to forget about it. It was a long time ago. We don't even really know what happened."

She stared at me with those big green eyes, calculating her next argument.

"Hey, Rose."

Our conversation dropped as Jesse strolled up to us. I turned on my best smile.

"Hey."

He nodded cordially to Lissa. "So hey, I'm going to be in your dorm tonight for a study group. You think . . . maybe . . ."

Momentarily forgetting Lissa, I focused my full attention on Jesse. Suddenly, I *so* needed to do something wild and bad. Too much had happened today. "Sure."

He told me when he'd be there, and I told him I'd meet him in one of the common areas with "further instructions."

Lissa stared at me when he left. "You're under house arrest. They won't let you hang out and talk to him."

"I don't really want to 'talk' to him. We'll slip away."

She groaned. "I just don't know about you sometimes."

"That's because you're the cautious one, and I'm the reckless one."

Once animal behavior started, I pondered the likelihood of Mia being responsible. From the smug look on her psychoangel face, she certainly seemed to be enjoying the sensation caused by the bloody fox. But that didn't mean she was the culprit, and after observing her over the last couple of weeks, I knew she'd enjoy anything that upset Lissa and me. She didn't need to be the one who had done it.

"Wolves, like many other species, differentiate their packs into alpha males and alpha females whom the others defer to. Alphas are almost always the strongest physically, though many times, confrontations turn out to be more a matter of willpower and personality. When an alpha is challenged and replaced, that wolf may find himself ostracized from the group or even attacked."

I looked up from my daydreams and focused on Ms. Meissner.

"Most challenges are likely to occur during mating season," she continued. This, naturally, brought snickers from the class. "In most packs, the alpha pair are the *only* ones who mate. If the alpha male is an older, seasoned wolf, a younger competitor may think he has a shot. Whether that is true works on a case-by-case basis. The young often don't realize how seriously outclassed they are by the more experienced."

The old-and-young-wolf thing notwithstanding, I thought the rest was pretty relevant. Certainly in the Academy's social structure, I decided bitterly, there seemed to be a lot of alphas and challenges.

Mia raised her hand. "What about foxes? Do *they* have alphas too?"

There was a collective intake of breath from the class, followed by a few nervous giggles. No one could believe Mia had gone there.

Ms. Meissner flushed with what I suspected was anger. "We're discussing wolves today, Miss Rinaldi."

Mia didn't seem to mind the subtle chastising, and when the class paired off to work on an assignment, she spent more time looking over at us and giggling. Through the bond, I could feel Lissa growing more and more upset as images of the fox kept flashing through her mind.

"Don't worry," I told her. "I've got a way—"

"Hey, Lissa," someone interrupted.

We both looked up as Ralf Sarcozy stopped by our desks. He wore his trademark stupid grin, and I had a feeling he'd come over here on a dare from his friends.

"So, admit it," he said. "You killed the fox. You're trying to convince Kirova you're crazy so that you can get out of here again."

"Screw you," I told him in a low voice.

"Are you offering?"

"From what I've heard, there isn't much to screw," I shot back.

"Wow," he said mockingly. "You *have* changed. Last I remembered, you weren't too picky about who you got naked with."

"And the last *I* remember, the only people you ever saw naked were on the Internet."

He cocked his head in an overly dramatic fashion. "Hey, I just got it: it was you, wasn't it?" He looked at Lissa, the back at me. "She got *you* to kill the fox, didn't she? Some weird kind of lesbian voo—ahhh!"

Ralf burst into flames.

I jumped up and pushed Lissa out of the way—not easy to do, since we were sitting at our desks. We both ended up on the floor as screams—Ralf's in particular—filled the classroom and Ms. Meissner sprinted for the fire extinguisher.

And then, just like that, the flames disappeared. Ralf was still screaming and patting himself down, but he didn't have a single singe mark on him. The only indication of what had happened was the lingering smell of smoke in the air.

For several seconds, the entire classroom froze. Then, slowly, everyone put the pieces together. Moroi magical specializations were well known, and after scanning the room, I deduced three fire users: Ralf, his friend Jacob, and—

Christian Ozera.

Since neither Jacob nor Ralf would have set Ralf on fire, it sort of made the culprit obvious. The fact that Christian was laughing hysterically sort of gave it away too.

Ms. Meissner changed from red to deep purple. "Mr. Ozera!" she screamed. "How dare you—do you have any idea—report to Headmistress Kirova's office now!"

Christian, completely unfazed, stood up and slung his backpack over one shoulder. That smirk stayed on his face. "Sure thing, Ms. Meissner."

He went out of his way to walk past Ralf, who quickly backed away as he passed. The rest of the class stared, open-mouthed.

After that, Ms. Meissner attempted to return the class to normal, but it was a lost cause. No one could stop talking about what had happened. It was shocking on a few different levels. First, no one had ever seen that kind of spell: a massive fire that didn't actually burn anything. Second, Christian had used it offensively. He had attacked another person. Moroi never did that. They believed magic was meant to take care of the earth, to help people live better lives. It was never, ever used as a weapon. Magic instructors never taught those kinds of spells; I don't think they even knew any. Finally, craziest of all, *Christian* had done it. Christian, whom no one ever noticed or gave a damn about. Well, they'd noticed him now.

It appeared someone still knew offensive spells after all, and as much as I had enjoyed the look of terror on Ralf's face, it suddenly occurred to me that Christian might really and truly be a psycho.

"Liss," I said as we walked out of class, "please tell me you haven't hung out with him again."

The guilt that flickered through the bond told me more than any explanation could.

"Liss!" I grabbed her arm.

"Not that much," she said uneasily. "He's really okay—"

"Okay? *Okay?*" People in the hall stared at us. I realized I was practically shouting. "He's out of his mind. *He set Ralf on fire.* I thought we decided you weren't going to see him anymore."

"You decided, Rose. Not me." There was an edge in her voice I hadn't heard in a while.

"What's going on here? Are you guys . . . you know? . . ."

"No!" she insisted. "I told you that already. God." She shot me a look of disgust. "Not everyone thinks—and acts—like you."

I flinched at the words. Then we noticed that Mia was passing by. She hadn't heard the conversation but had caught the tone. A snide smile spread over her face. "Trouble in paradise?"

"Go find your pacifier, and shut the hell up," I told her, not waiting to hear her response. Her mouth dropped open, then tightened into a scowl.

Lissa and I walked on in silence, and then Lissa burst out laughing. Like that, our fight diffused.

"Rose . . ." Her tone was softer now.

"Lissa, he's dangerous. I don't like him. Please be careful."

She touched my arm. "I am. I'm the cautious one, remember? You're the reckless one."

I hoped that was still true.

But later, after school, I had my doubts. I was in my room doing homework when I felt a trickle of what could only be called sneakiness coming from Lissa. Losing track of my work, I stared off into space, trying to get a more detailed understanding of what was happening to her. If ever there was a time for me to slip into her mind, it was now, but I didn't know how to control that.

Frowning, I tried to think what normally made that connection occur. Usually she was experiencing some strong emotion, an emotion so powerful it tried to blast into my mind. I had to work hard to fight against that; I always sort of kept a mental wall up.

Focusing on her now, I tried to remove the wall. I steadied my breathing and cleared my mind. My thoughts didn't matter, only hers did. I needed to open myself to her and let us connect.

I'd never done anything like this before; I didn't have the patience for meditation. My need was so strong, however, that I forced myself into an intense, focused relaxation. I needed to know what was going on with her, and after a few more moments, my effort paid off.

I was in.

NINE

I snapped into her mind, once again seeing and directly experiencing what went on around her.

She was sneaking into the chapel's attic again, confirming my worst fears. Like last time, she met no resistance. *Good God*, I thought, *could that priest be any worse about securing his own chapel?*

Sunrise lit up the stained-glass window, and Christian's silhouette was framed against it: he was sitting in the window seat.

"You're late," he told her. "Been waiting a while."

Lissa pulled up one of the rickety chairs, brushing dust off it. "I figured you'd be tied up with Headmistress Kirova."

He shook his head. "Not much to it. They suspended me for a week, that's all. Not like it's hard to sneak out." He waved his hands around. "As you can see."

"I'm surprised you didn't get more time."

A patch of sunlight lit up his crystal-blue eyes. "Disappointed?"

She looked shocked. "You set someone on fire!"

"No, I didn't. Did you see any burns on him?"

"He was covered in flames."

"I had them under control. I kept them off of him."

She sighed. "You shouldn't have done that."

Straightening out of his lounging position, he sat up and leaned toward her. "I did it for you."

"You attacked someone for me?"

"Sure. He was giving you and Rose a hard time. She was doing an okay job against him, I guess, but I figured she could use the backup. Besides, this'll shut anyone else up about the whole fox thing, too."

"You shouldn't have done that," she repeated, looking away. She didn't know how to feel about this "generosity." "And don't act like it was all for me. You *liked* doing it. Part of you wanted to—just because."

Christian's smug expression dropped, replaced by one of uncharacteristic surprise. Lissa might not be psychic, but she had a startling ability to read people.

Seeing him off guard, she continued. "Attacking someone else with magic is forbidden—and that's *exactly* why you wanted to do it. You got a thrill out of it."

"Those rules are stupid. If we used magic as a weapon instead of just for warm and fuzzy shit, Strigoi wouldn't keep killing so many of us."

"It's wrong," she said firmly. "Magic is a gift. It's peaceful."

"Only because they say it is. You're repeating the party line we've been fed our whole lives." He stood up and paced the small space of the attic. "It wasn't always that way, you know. We used to fight, right along with the guardians—centuries ago. Then people started getting scared and stopped. Figured it was safer to just hide. They forgot the attack spells."

"Then how did you know that one?"

He crooked her a smile. "Not everyone forgot."

"Like your family? Like your parents?"

The smile disappeared. "You don't know anything about my parents."

His face darkened, his eyes grew hard. To most people, he might have appeared scary and intimidating, but as Lissa studied and admired his features, he suddenly seemed very, very vulnerable.

"You're right," she admitted softly, after a moment. "I don't. I'm sorry."

For the second time in this meeting, Christian looked astonished. Probably no one apologized to him that often. Hell, no one even talked to him that often. Certainly no one ever listened. Like usual, he quickly turned into his cocky self.

"Forget it." Abruptly, he stopped pacing and knelt in front of her so they could look each other in the eye. Feeling him so close made her hold her breath. A dangerous smile curled his lips. "And really, I don't get why *you* of all people should act so outraged that I used 'forbidden' magic."

"Me 'of all people'? What's that supposed to mean?"

"You can play all innocent if you want—and you do a pretty good job—but I know the truth."

"What truth is that?" She couldn't hide her uneasiness from me or Christian.

He leaned even closer. "That you use compulsion. All the time."

"No, I don't," she said immediately.

"Of course you do. I've been lying awake at night, trying to figure out how in the world you two were able to rent out a place and go to high school without anyone ever wanting to meet your parents. Then I figured it out. You had to be using compulsion. That's probably how you broke out of here in the first place."

"I see. You just figured it out. Without any proof."

"I've got all the proof I need, just from watching you."

"You've been watching me—spying on me—to prove I'm using compulsion?"

He shrugged. "No. Actually, I've been watching you just because I like it. The compulsion thing was a bonus. I saw you use it the other day to get an extension on that math assignment. And you used it on Ms. Carmack when she wanted to make you go through more testing."

"So you assume it's compulsion? Maybe I'm just really good at convincing people." There was a defiant note in her voice: understandable, considering her fear and anger. Only she delivered it with a toss of her hair which—if I didn't know any better—might have been considered flirtatious. And I did know better . . . right? Suddenly, I wasn't sure.

He went on, but something in his eyes told me he'd noticed the hair, that he always noticed everything about her. "People get these goofy looks on their faces when you talk to them. And not just any people—you're able to do it to Moroi. Probably dhampirs, too. Now *that's* crazy. I didn't even know that was possible. You're some kind of superstar. Some kind of evil, compulsion-abusing superstar." It was an accusation, but his tone and presence radiated the same flirtatiousness she had.

Lissa didn't know what to say. He was right. Everything he'd said was right. Her compulsion was what had allowed us to dodge authority and get along in the world without adult help. It was what had allowed us to convince the bank to let her tap into her inheritance.

And it was considered every bit as wrong as using magic as a weapon. Why not? It *was* a weapon. A powerful one, one that could be abused very easily. Moroi children had it drilled into them from an early age that compulsion was very, very wrong. No one was taught to use it, though every Moroi technically had the ability. Lissa had just sort of stumbled into it— deeply—and, as Christian had pointed out, she could wield it over Moroi, as well as humans and dhampirs.

"What are you going to do then?" she asked. "You going to turn me in?"

He shook his head and smiled. "No. I think it's hot."

She stared, eyes widening and heart racing. Something about the shape of his lips intrigued her. "Rose thinks you're dangerous," she blurted out nervously. "She thinks you might have killed the fox."

I didn't know how I felt about being dragged into this

bizarre conversation. Some people were scared of me. Maybe he was too.

Judging from the amusement in his voice when he spoke, it appeared he wasn't. "People think I'm unstable, but I tell you, Rose is ten times worse. Of course, that makes it harder for people to fuck with *you*, so I'm all for it." Leaning back on his heels, he finally broke the intimate space between them. "And I sure as hell didn't do *that*. Find out who did, though . . . and what I did to Ralf won't seem like anything."

His gallant offer of creepy vengeance didn't exactly reassure Lissa . . . but it did thrill her a little. "I don't want you doing anything like that. And I still don't know who did it."

He leaned back toward her and caught her wrists in his hands. He started to say something, then stopped and looked down in surprise, running his thumbs over faint, barely there scars. Looking back up at her, he had a strange—for him— kindness in his face.

"You might not know who did it. But you know something. Something you aren't talking about."

She stared at him, a swirl of emotions playing in her chest. "You can't know all my secrets," she murmured.

He glanced back down at her wrists and then released them, that dry smile of his back on his face. "No. I guess not."

A feeling of peace settled over her, a feeling I thought only I could bring. Returning to my own head and my room, I sat on the floor staring at my math book. Then, for reasons I didn't really get, I slammed it shut and threw it against the wall.

I spent the rest of the night brooding until the time I was supposed to meet Jesse came around. Slipping downstairs, I went into the kitchen—a place I could visit so long as I kept things brief—and caught his eye when I cut through the main visiting area.

Moving past him, I paused and whispered, "There's a lounge on the fourth floor that nobody uses. Take the stairs on the other side of the bathrooms and meet me there in five minutes. The lock on the door is broken."

He complied to the second, and we found the lounge dark, dusty, and deserted. The drop in guardian numbers over the years meant a lot of the dorm stayed empty, a sad sign for Moroi society but terribly convenient right now.

He sat down on the couch, and I lay back on it, putting my feet in his lap. I was still annoyed after Lissa and Christian's bizarre attic romance and wanted nothing more than to forget about it for a while.

"You really here to study, or was it just an excuse?" I asked.

"No. It was real. Had to do an assignment with Meredith." The tone in his voice indicated he wasn't happy about that.

"Oooh," I teased. "Is working with a dhampir beneath your royal blood? Should I be offended?"

He smiled, showing a mouth full of perfect white teeth and fangs. "You're a lot hotter than she is."

"Glad I make the cut." There was a sort of a heat in his eyes that was turning me on, as was his hand sliding up my leg. But I needed to do something first. It was time for some vengeance. "Mia must too, since you guys let her hang out with you. She's not royal."

His finger playfully poked me in the calf. "She's with Aaron. And I've got lots of friends who aren't royal. And friends who are dhamps. I'm not a total asshole."

"Yeah, but did you know her parents are practically custodians for the Drozdovs?"

The hand on my leg stopped. I'd exaggerated, but he was a sucker for gossip—and he was notorious for spreading it.

"Seriously?"

"Yeah. Scrubbing floors and stuff like that."

"Huh."

I could see the wheels turning in his dark blue eyes and had to hide a smile. The seed was planted.

Sitting up, I moved closer to him and draped a leg over his lap. I wrapped my arms around him, and without further delay, thoughts of Mia disappeared as his testosterone kicked in. He kissed me eagerly—sloppily, even—pushing me against the back of the couch, and I relaxed into what had to be the first enjoyable physical activity I'd had in weeks.

We kissed like that for a long time, and I didn't stop him when he pulled off my shirt.

"I'm not having sex," I warned between kisses. I had no intention of losing my virginity on a couch in a lounge.

He paused, thinking about this, and finally decided not to push it. "Okay."

But he pushed me onto the couch, lying over me, still kissing with that same fierceness. His lips traveled down to my neck, and when the sharp points of his fangs brushed against my skin, I couldn't help an excited gasp.

He raised himself up, looking into my face with open surprise. For a moment, I could barely breathe, recalling that rush of pleasure that a vampire bite could fill me with, wondering what it'd be like to feel that while making out. Then the old taboos kicked in. Even if we didn't have sex, giving blood while we did *this* was still wrong, still dirty.

"Don't," I warned.

"You want to." His voice held excited wonder. "I can tell."

"No, I don't."

His eyes lit up. "You do. How—hey, have you done it before?"

"No," I scoffed. "Of course not."

Those gorgeous blue eyes watched me, and I could see the wheels spinning behind them. Jesse might flirt a lot and have a big mouth, but he wasn't stupid.

"You act like you have. You got excited when I was by your neck."

"You're a good kisser," I countered, though it wasn't entirely true. He drooled a little more than I would have preferred. "Don't you think everyone would know if I was giving blood?"

The realization seized him. "Unless you weren't doing it before you left. You did it while you were gone, didn't you? You fed Lissa."

"Of course not," I repeated.

But he was on to something, and he knew it. "It was the only way. You didn't have feeders. Oh, man."

"She found some," I lied. It was the same line we'd fed Natalie, the one she'd spread around and that no one—except Christian—had ever questioned. "Plenty of humans are into it."

"Sure," he said with a smile. He leaned his mouth back to my neck.

"I'm not a blood whore," I snapped, pulling away from him.

"But you *want* to. You like it. All you dhamp girls do." His teeth were on my skin again. Sharp. Wonderful.

I had a feeling hostility would only make things worse, so I defused the situation with teasing. "Stop it," I said gently, running a fingertip over his lips. "I told you, I'm not like that. But if you want something to do with your mouth, I can give you some ideas."

That peaked his interest. "Yeah? Like wha—?"

And that was when the door opened.

We sprang apart. I was ready to handle a fellow student or even possibly the matron. What I was not ready for was Dimitri.

He burst in the door like he'd expected to find us, and in

that horrible moment, with him raging like a storm, I knew why Mason had called him a god. In the blink of an eye, he crossed the room and jerked Jesse up by his shirt, nearly holding the Moroi off the ground.

"What's your name?" barked Dimitri.

"J-Jesse, sir. Jesse Zeklos, sir."

"Mr. Zeklos, do you have permission to be in this part of the dorm?"

"No, sir."

"Do you know the rules about male and female interactions around here?"

"Yes, sir."

"Then I suggest you get out of here as fast as you can before I turn you over to someone who will punish you accordingly. If I ever see you like this again"—Dimitri pointed to where I cowered, half-dressed, on the couch—"*I* will be the one to punish you. And it will hurt. A lot. Do you understand?"

Jesse swallowed, eyes wide. None of the bravado he usually showed was there. I guess there was "usually" and then there was being held in the grip of a really ripped, really tall, and really pissed-off Russian guy. "Yes, sir!"

"Then *go*." Dimitri released him, and, if possible, Jesse got out of there faster than Dimitri had burst in. My mentor then turned to me, a dangerous glint in his eyes. He didn't say anything, but the angry, disapproving message came through loud and clear.

And then it shifted.

It was almost like he'd been taken by surprise, like he'd never noticed me before. Had it been any other guy, I would have said he was checking me out. As it was, he was definitely studying me. Studying my face, my body. And I suddenly realized I was only in jeans and a bra—a black bra at that. I knew perfectly well that there weren't a lot of girls at this school who looked as good in a bra as I did. Even a guy like Dimitri, one who seemed so focused on duty and training and all of that, had to appreciate that.

And, finally, I noticed that a hot flush was spreading over me, and that the look in his eyes was doing more to me than Jesse's kisses had. Dimitri was quiet and distant sometimes, but he also had a dedication and an intensity that I'd never seen in any other person. I wondered how that kind of power and strength translated into . . . well, sex. I wondered what it'd be like for him to touch me and—shit!

What was I thinking? Was I out of my mind? Embarrassed, I covered my feelings with attitude.

"You see something you like?" I asked.

"Get dressed."

The set of his mouth hardened, and whatever he'd just felt was gone. That fierceness sobered me up and made me forget about my own troubling reaction. I immediately pulled my shirt back on, uneasy at seeing his badass side.

"How'd you find me? You following me to make sure I don't run away?"

"Be quiet," he snapped, leaning down so that we were at

eye level. "A janitor saw you and reported it. Do you have any idea how stupid this was?"

"I know, I know, the whole probation thing, right?"

"Not just that. I'm talking about the stupidity of getting in *that* kind of situation in the first place."

"I get in *that* kind of situation all the time, Comrade. It's not a big deal." Anger replaced my fear. I didn't like being treated like a child.

"Stop calling me that. You don't know even know what you're talking about."

"Sure I do. I had to do a report on Russia and the R.S.S.R. last year."

"*U*.S.S.R. And it *is* a big deal for a Moroi to be with a dhampir girl. They like to brag."

"So?"

"*So*?" he looked disgusted. "So don't you have any respect? Think about Lissa. You make yourself look cheap. You live up to what a lot of people already think about dhampir girls, and it reflects back on her. And me."

"Oh, I see. Is that what this is about? Am I hurting your big, bad male pride? Are you afraid I'll ruin your reputation?"

"My reputation is already made, Rose. I set my standards and lived up to them long ago. What you do with yours remains to be seen." His voice hardened again. "Now get back to your room—if you can manage it without throwing yourself at someone else."

"Is that your subtle way of calling me a slut?"

"I hear the stories you guys tell. I've heard stories about you."

Ouch. I wanted to yell back that it was none of his business what I did with my body, but something about the anger and disappointment on his face made me falter. I didn't know what it was. "Disappointing" someone like Kirova was a non-event, but Dimitri? . . . I remembered how proud I'd felt when he praised me the last few times in our practices. Seeing that disappear from him . . . well, it suddenly made me feel as cheap as he'd implied I was.

Something broke inside of me. Blinking back tears, I said, "Why is it wrong to . . . I don't know, have fun? I'm seventeen, you know. I should be able to enjoy it."

"You're seventeen, and in less than a year, someone's life and death will be in your hands." His voice still sounded firm, but there was a gentleness there too. "If you were human or Moroi, you could have fun. You could do things other girls could."

"But you're saying I can't."

He glanced away, and his dark eyes went unfocused. He was thinking about something far away from here. "When I was seventeen, I met Ivan Zeklos. We weren't like you and Lissa, but we became friends, and he requested me as his guardian when I graduated. I was the top student in my school. I paid attention to everything in my classes, but in the end, it wasn't enough. That's how it is in this life. One slip, one distraction . . . " He sighed. "And it's too late."

A lump formed in my throat as I thought about one slip or one distraction costing Lissa her life.

"Jesse's a Zeklos," I said, suddenly realizing Dimitri had just thrown around a relative of his former friend and charge.

"I know."

"Does it bother you? Does he remind you of Ivan?"

"It doesn't matter how I feel. It doesn't matter how any of us feel."

"But it does bother you." It suddenly became very obvious to me. I could read his pain, though he clearly worked hard to hide it. "You hurt. Every day. Don't you? You miss him."

Dimitri looked surprised, like he didn't want me to know that, like I'd uncovered some secret part of him. I'd been thinking he was some aloof, antisocial tough guy, but maybe he kept himself apart from other people so he wouldn't get hurt if he lost them. Ivan's death had clearly left a permanent mark.

I wondered if Dimitri was lonely.

The surprised look vanished, and his standard serious one returned. "It doesn't matter how I feel. *They* come first. Protecting them."

I thought about Lissa again. "Yeah. They do."

A long silence fell before he spoke again.

"You told me you want to fight, to *really* fight. Is that still true?"

"Yes. Absolutely."

"Rose . . . I can teach you, but I have to believe you're

dedicated. Really dedicated. I can't have you distracted by things like this." He gestured around the lounge. "Can I trust you?"

Again, I felt like crying under that gaze, under the seriousness of what he asked. I didn't get how he could have such a powerful effect on me. I'd never cared so much about what one person thought. "Yes. I promise."

"All right. I'll teach you, but I need you strong. I know you hate the running, but it really is necessary. You have no idea what Strigoi are like. The school tries to prepare you, but until you've seen how strong they are and how fast . . . well, you can't even imagine. So I can't stop the running and the conditioning. If you want to learn more about fighting, we need to add more trainings. It'll take up more of your time. You won't have much left for your homework or anything else. You'll be tired. A lot."

I thought about it, about him, and about Lissa. "It doesn't matter. If you tell me to do it, I'll do it."

He studied me hard, like he was still trying to decide if he could believe me. Finally satisfied, he gave me a sharp nod. "We'll start tomorrow."

TEN

"Excuse me, Mr. Nagy? I can't really concentrate with Lissa and Rose passing notes over there."

Mia was attempting to distract attention from herself—as well as from her inability to answer Mr. Nagy's question—and it was ruining what had otherwise been a promising day. A few of the fox rumors still circulated, but most people wanted to talk about Christian attacking Ralf. I still hadn't cleared Christian of the fox incident—I was pretty sure he was psycho enough to have done it as some crazy sign of affection for Lissa—but whatever his motives, he had shifted the attention off her, just as he'd said.

Mr. Nagy, legendary for his ability to humiliate students by reading notes aloud, homed in on us like a missile. He snatched the note away, and the excited class settled in for a full reading. I swallowed my groan, trying to look as blank and unconcerned as possible. Beside me, Lissa looked like she wanted to die.

"My, my," he said, looking the note over. "If only students would write this much in their essays. One of you has considerably worse writing than the other, so forgive me if I get anything wrong here." He cleared his throat. "'So, I saw J last night,' begins the person with bad handwriting, to which the response is, 'What happened,' followed by no fewer than five question marks. Understandable, since sometimes one—let alone four—just won't get the point across, eh?" The class laughed, and I noticed Mia throwing me a particularly mean smile. "The first speaker responds: 'What do you think happened? We hooked up in one of the empty lounges.'"

Mr. Nagy glanced up after hearing some more giggles in the room. His British accent only added to the hilarity.

"May I assume by this reaction that the use of 'hook up' pertains to the more recent, shall we say, carnal application of the term than the tamer one I grew up with?"

More snickers ensued. Straightening up, I said boldly, "Yes, sir, Mr. Nagy. That would be correct, sir." A number of people in the class laughed outright.

"Thank you for that confirmation, Miss Hathaway. Now, where was I? Ah yes, the other speaker then asks, 'How was it?' The response is, 'Good,' punctuated with a smiley face to confirm said adjective. Well. I suppose kudos are in order for the mysterious J, hmmm? 'So, like, how far did you guys go?' Uh, ladies," said Mr. Nagy, "I do hope this doesn't surpass a PG rating. 'Not very. We got caught.' And again, we are shown the severity of the situation, this time through the use of a not-smiling face. 'What happened?' 'Dimitri showed up. He threw Jesse out and then bitched me out.'"

The class lost it, both from hearing Mr. Nagy say "bitched" and from finally getting some participants named.

"Why, Mr. Zeklos, are you the aforementioned J? The one

who earned a smiley face from the sloppy writer?" Jesse's face turned beet red, but he didn't look entirely displeased at having his exploits made known in front of his friends. He'd kept what had happened a secret thus far—including the blood talk—because I suspected Dimitri had scared the hell out of him. "Well, while I applaud a good misadventure as much as the next teacher whose time is utterly wasted, do remind your 'friends' in the future that my class is not a chat room." He tossed the paper back on to Lissa's desk. "Miss Hathaway, it seems there's no feasible way to punish you, since you're already maxed out on penalties around here. Ergo, you, Miss Dragomir, will serve two detentions instead of one on behalf of your friend. Stay here when the bell rings, please."

After class, Jesse found me, an uneasy look on his face. "Hey, um, about that note . . . you know I didn't have anything to do with that. If Belikov finds out about it . . . you'll tell him? I mean, you'll let him know I didn't—"

"Yeah, yeah," I interrupted him. "Don't worry, you're safe."

Standing with me, Lissa watched him walk out of the room. Thinking of how easily Dimitri had thrown him around—and of his apparent cowardice—I couldn't help but remark, "You know, Jesse's suddenly not as hot as I used to think."

She only laughed. "You'd better go. I've got desks to wash."

I left her, heading back for my dorm. As I did, I passed

a number of students gathered in small clusters outside the building. I regarded them wistfully, wishing I had the free time to socialize.

"No, it's true," I heard a confident voice say. Camille Conta. Beautiful and popular, from one of the most prestigious families in the Conta clan. She and Lissa had sort of been friends before we left, in the uneasy way two powerful forces keep an eye on each other. "They, like, clean toilets or something."

"Oh my God," her friend said. "I'd die if I was Mia."

I smiled. Apparently Jesse had spread some of the stories I'd told him last night. Unfortunately, the next overheard conversation shattered my victory.

"—heard it was still *alive*. Like, twitching on her bed."

"That is so gross. Why would they just leave it there?"

"I don't know. Why kill it in the first place?"

"You think Ralf was right? That she and Rose did it to get kicked—"

They saw me and shut up.

Scowling, I skulked off across the quadrangle. *Still alive, still alive.*

I'd refused to let Lissa talk about the similarities between the fox and what had happened two years ago. I didn't want to believe they were connected, and I certainly didn't want her to either.

But I hadn't been able to stop thinking about that incident, not only because it was chilling, but because it really did remind me of what had just happened in her room.

We had been out in the woods near campus one evening, having skipped out on our last class. I'd traded a pair of cute, rhinestone-studded sandals to Abby Badica for a bottle of peach schnapps—desperate, yes, but you did what you had to in Montana—which she'd somehow gotten hold of. Lissa had shaken her head in disapproval when I suggested cutting class to go put the bottle out of its misery, but she'd come along anyway. Like always.

We found an old log to sit on near a scummy green marsh. A half-moon cast a tiny sliver of light on us, but it was more than enough for vampires and half-vampires to see by. Passing the bottle back and forth, I grilled her on Aaron. She'd fessed up that the two of them had had sex the weekend before, and I felt a surge of jealousy that she'd been the one to have sex first.

"So what was it like?"

She shrugged and took another drink. "I don't know. It wasn't anything."

"What do you mean it wasn't anything? Didn't the earth move or the planets align or something?"

"No," she said, smothering a laugh. "Of course not."

I didn't really get why that should be funny, but I could tell she didn't want to talk about it. This was around the time the bond had begun forming, and her emotions were starting to creep into me now and then. I held up the bottle and glared at it.

"I don't think this stuff is working."

"That's because there's barely any alcohol in—"

The sound of something moving in the brush came from nearby. I immediately shot up, putting my body between her and the noise.

"It's some animal," she said when a minute went by in silence.

That didn't mean it wasn't dangerous. The school's wards kept out Strigoi, but wild animals often wandered into the outskirts of campus, posing their own threats. Bears. Cougars.

"Come on," I told her. "Let's head back."

We hadn't gone very far when I heard something moving again, and someone stepped out into our path. "Ladies."

Ms. Karp.

We froze, and whatever quick reactions I'd shown back by the marsh disappeared as I delayed a few moments in hiding the bottle behind my back.

A half-smile crossed her face, and she held out her hand.

Sheepishly, I gave the bottle to her, and she tucked it under her arm. She turned without another word, and we followed, knowing there would be consequences to deal with.

"You think no one notices when half a class is gone?" she asked after a little while.

"Half a class?"

"A few of you apparently chose today to skip. Must be the nice weather. Spring fever."

Lissa and I trudged along. I'd never been comfortable around Ms. Karp since the time she'd healed my hands. Her weird, paranoid behavior had taken on a strange quality to me—a lot stranger than before. Scary, even. And lately I couldn't look at her without seeing those marks by her forehead. Her deep red hair usually covered them but not always. Sometimes there were new marks; sometimes the old ones faded to nothing.

A weird fluttering noise sounded to my right. We all stopped.

"One of your classmates, I imagine," murmured Ms. Karp, turning toward the sound.

But when we reached the spot, we found a large black bird lying on the on the ground. Birds—and most animals—didn't do anything for me, but even I had to admire its sleek feathers and fierce beak. It could probably peck someone's eyes out in thirty seconds—if it weren't obviously dying. With a last, half-hearted shake, the bird finally went still.

"What is that? Is it a crow?" I asked.

"Too big," said Ms. Karp. "It's a raven."

"Is it dead?" asked Lissa.

I peered at it. "Yeah. Definitely dead. Don't touch it."

"Probably attacked by another bird," observed Ms. Karp. "They fight over territory and resources sometimes."

Lissa knelt down, compassion on her face. I wasn't surprised, since she'd always had a thing for animals. She'd lectured me for days after I'd instigated the infamous hamster-and-hermit-crab fight. I'd viewed the fight as a testing of worthy opponents. She'd seen it as animal cruelty.

Transfixed, she reached toward the raven.

"Liss!" I exclaimed, horrified. "It's probably got a disease."

But her hand moved out like she hadn't even heard me. Ms. Karp stood there like a statue, her white face looking like a ghost's. Lissa's fingers stroked the raven's wings.

"Liss," I repeated, starting to move toward her, to pull her back. Suddenly, a strange sensation flooded through my head, a sweetness that was beautiful and full of life. The feeling was so intense, it stopped me in my tracks.

Then the raven moved.

Lissa gave a small scream and snatched her hand back. We both stared wide-eyed.

The raven flapped its wings, slowly trying to right itself and stand up. When it managed to do so, it turned toward us, fixing Lissa with a look that seemed too intelligent for a bird. Its eyes held hers, and I couldn't read her reaction through the bond. At long last, the raven broke the gaze and lifted into the air, strong wings carrying it away.

Wind stirring the leaves was the only sound left.

"Oh my God," breathed Lissa. "What just happened?"

"Hell if I know," I said, hiding my stark terror.

Ms. Karp strode forward and grabbed Lissa's arm, forcefully turning her so that they faced each other. I was there in a flash, ready to take action if Crazy Karp tried anything, though even I had qualms about taking down a teacher.

"Nothing happened," said Ms. Karp in an urgent voice, her eyes wild-looking. "Do you hear me? Nothing. And you can't tell anyone—*anyone*—about what you saw. Both of you. Promise me. Promise me you won't ever talk about this again."

Lissa and I exchanged uneasy glances. "Okay," she croaked out.

Ms. Karp's grip relaxed a little. "And don't ever do it again. If you do, they'll find out. They'll try to find you." She turned to me. "You can't let her do it. Not ever again."

On the quad, outside my dorm, someone was saying my name.

"Hey, Rose? I've called you, like, a hundred times."

I forgot about Ms. Karp and the raven and glanced over at Mason, who had apparently started walking with me toward the dorm while I was off in la-la land.

"Sorry," I mumbled. "I'm out of it. Just . . . um, tired."

"Too much excitement last night?"

I gave him a narrow-eyed look. "Nothing I couldn't handle."

"I guess," he laughed, though he didn't exactly sound amused. "Sounds like Jesse couldn't handle it."

"He did okay."

"If you say so. But personally, I think you've got bad taste."

I stopped walking. "And *I* don't think it's any of your business."

He looked away angrily. "You made it the whole class's business."

"Hey, I didn't do that on purpose."

"Would've happened anyway. Jesse's got a big mouth."

"He wouldn't have told."

"Yeah," said Mason. "Because he's so cute and has such an important family."

"Stop being an idiot," I snapped. "And why do you even care? Jealous I'm not doing it with you?"

His flush grew, going all the way to the roots of his red hair. "I just don't like hearing people talk shit about you, that's all. There are a lot of nasty jokes going around. They're calling you a slut."

"I don't care what they call me."

"Oh, yeah. You're really tough. You don't need anyone."

I stopped. "I don't. I'm one of the best novices in this fucking place. I don't need you acting all gallant and coming to my defense. Don't treat me like I'm some helpless girl."

I turned around and kept walking, but he caught up to me easily. The woes of being five-seven.

"Look . . . I didn't mean to upset you. I'm just worried about you."

I gave a harsh laugh.

"I'm serious. Wait . . ." he began. "I, uh, did something for you. Sort of. I went to the library last night and tried to look up St. Vladimir."

I stopped again. "You did?"

"Yeah, but there wasn't much on Anna. All the books were kind of generic. Just talked about him healing people, bringing them back from the edge of death."

That last part hit a nerve.

"Was . . . was there anything else?" I stammered.

He shook his head. "No. You probably need some primary sources, but we don't have any here."

"Primary what?"

He scoffed, a smile breaking over his face. "Do you do anything but pass notes? We just talked about them the other day in Andrews' class. They're books from the actual time period you want to study. Secondary ones are written by people living today. You'll get better information if you find something written by the guy himself. Or someone who actually knew him."

"Huh. Okay. What are you, like, a boy genius now?"

Mason gave me a light punch in the arm. "I pay attention, that's all. You're so oblivious. You miss all sorts of things." He smiled nervously. "And look . . . I really am sorry about what I said. I was just—"

Jealous, I realized. I could see it in his eyes. How had I never noticed this before? He was crazy about me. I guess I really was oblivious.

"It's all right, Mase. Forget about it." I smiled. "And thanks for looking that stuff up."

He smiled back, and I went inside, sad that I didn't feel the same way about him.

ELEVEN

"You need something to wear?" Lissa asked.

"Hmm?"

I glanced over at her. We were waiting for Mr. Nagy's Slavic art class to start, and I was preoccupied with listening to Mia adamantly deny the claims about her parents to one of her friends.

"It's not like they're servants or anything," she exclaimed, clearly flustered. Straightening her face, she tried for haughtiness. "They're practically advisors. The Drozdovs don't decide *anything* without them."

I choked on a laugh, and Lissa shook her head.

"You're enjoying this way too much."

"Because it's awesome. What'd you just ask me?" I dug through my bag, messily looking for my lip gloss. I made a face when I found it. It was almost empty; I didn't know where I was going to score some more.

"I asked if you need something to wear tonight," she said.

"Well, *yeah*, of course I do. But none of your stuff fits me."

"What are you going to do?"

I shrugged my shoulders. "Improvise, like always. I don't really care anyway. I'm just glad Kirova's letting me go."

We had an assembly tonight. It was November 1, All Saints'

Day—which also meant we'd been back almost a month now. A royal group was visiting the school, including Queen Tatiana herself. Honestly, that wasn't what excited me. She'd visited the Academy before. It was pretty common and a lot less cool than it sounded. Besides, after living among humans and elected leaders, I didn't think much of stiff royals. Still, I'd gotten permission to go because everyone else would be there. It was a chance to hang out with actual people for a change and not stay locked in my dorm room. A little freedom was definitely worth the pain of sitting through a few boring speeches.

I didn't stay to chat with Lissa after school like I usually did. Dimitri had stuck to his promise about extra trainings, and I was trying to stick to mine. I now had two additional hours of practice with him, one before *and* one after school. The more I watched him in action, the more I understood the badass-god reputation. He clearly knew a lot—his six *molnija* marks proved as much—and I burned to have him teach me what he knew.

When I arrived at the gym, I noticed he was wearing a T-shirt and loose running pants, as opposed to his usual jeans. It was a good look for him. Really good. *Stop looking,* I immediately told myself.

He positioned me so that we stood facing each other on the mat and crossed his arms. "What's the first problem you'll run into when facing a Strigoi?"

"They're immortal?"

"Think of something more basic."

More basic than that? I considered. "They could be bigger than me. And stronger."

Most Strigoi—unless they'd been human first—had the same height as their Moroi cousins. Strigoi also had better strength, reflexes, and senses than dhampirs. That's why guardians trained so hard; we had a "learning curve" to compensate for.

Dimitri nodded. "That makes it difficult but not impossible. You can usually use a person's extra height and weight against them."

He turned and demonstrated several maneuvers, pointing out where to move and how to strike someone. Going through the motions with him, I gained some insight into why I took such a regular beating in group practice. I absorbed his techniques quickly and couldn't wait to actually use them. Near the end of our time together, he let me try.

"Go ahead," he said. "Try to hit me."

I didn't need to be told twice. Lunging forward, I tried to land a blow and was promptly blocked and knocked down onto the mat. Pain surged through my body, but I refused to give in to it. I jumped up again, hoping to catch him off guard. I didn't.

After several more failed attempts, I stood up and held out my hands in a gesture of truce. "Okay, what am I doing wrong?"

"Nothing."

I wasn't as convinced. "If I wasn't doing anything wrong, I'd have rendered you unconscious by now."

"Unlikely. Your moves are all correct, but this is the first time you've really tried. I've done it for years."

I shook my head and rolled my eyes at his older-and-wiser manner. He'd once told me he was twenty-four. "Whatever you say, Grandpa. Can we try it again?"

"We're out of time. Don't you want to get ready?"

I looked at the dusty clock on the wall and perked up. Almost time for the banquet. The thought made me giddy. I felt like Cinderella, but without the clothes.

"Hell, yeah, I do."

He walked off ahead of me. Studying him carefully, I realized I couldn't let the opportunity go by. I leapt at his back, positioning myself exactly the way he'd taught me. I had the element of surprise. Everything was perfect, and he wouldn't even see me coming.

Before I could make contact, he spun around at a ridiculously high speed. In one deft motion, he grabbed me like I weighed nothing and threw me to the ground, pinning me there.

I groaned. "I didn't do anything wrong!"

His eyes looked levelly into mine as he held my wrists, but he didn't look as serious as he had during the lesson. He seemed to find this funny. "The battle cry sort of gave you away. Try not to yell next time."

"Would it have really made a difference if I'd been quiet?"

He thought about it. "No. Probably not."

I sighed loudly, still in too much of a good mood to really let this disappointment get me down. There were some advantages to having such a kick-ass mentor—one who also happened to have a foot of height on me and outweighed me considerably. And that wasn't even considering his strength. He wasn't bulky, but his body had a lot of hard, lean muscle. If I could ever beat *him*, I could beat anyone.

All of a sudden, it occurred to me that he was still holding me down. The skin on his fingers was warm as he clutched my wrists. His face hovered inches from my own, and his legs and torso were actually pressing against mine. Some of his long brown hair hung around his face, and he appeared to be noticing me too, almost like he had that night in the lounge. And oh *God*, did he smell good. Breathing became difficult for me, and it had nothing to do with the workout or my lungs being crushed.

I would have given anything to be able to read his mind right then. Ever since that night in the lounge, I'd noticed him watching me with this same, studious expression. He never actually did it during the trainings themselves—those were *business*. But before and after, he would sometimes lighten up just a little, and I'd see him look at me in a way that was almost admiring. And sometimes, if I was really, really lucky, he'd smile at me. A real smile, too—not the dry one that accompanied the sarcasm we tossed around so often. I didn't want to admit it to anyone—not to Lissa, not even to myself—

but some days, I lived for those smiles. They lit up his face. "Gorgeous" no longer adequately described him.

Hoping to appear calm, I tried to think of something professional and guardian-related to say. Instead, I said, "So um . . . you got any other moves to show me?"

His lips twitched, and for a moment, I thought I was going to get one of those smiles. My heart leapt. Then, with visible effort, he pushed the smile back and once more became my tough-love mentor. He shifted off me, leaned back on his heels, and rose. "Come on. We should go."

I scrambled to my own feet and followed him out of the gym. He didn't look back as he walked, and I mentally kicked myself on the way back to my room.

I was crushing on my mentor. Crushing on my *older* mentor. I had to be out of my mind. He was seven years older than me. Old enough to be my . . . well, okay, nothing. But still older than me. Seven years was a lot. He'd been learning to write when I was born. When I'd been learning to write and throw books at my teachers, he'd probably been kissing girls. Probably lots of girls, considering how he looked.

I *so* did not need this complication in my life right now.

I found a passable sweater back in my room and after a quick shower, I headed off across campus to the reception.

Despite the looming stone walls, fancy statues, and turrets on the outsides of the buildings, the Academy's insides were quite modern. We had Wi-Fi, fluorescent lights, and just about anything else technological you could imagine. The commons in particular looked pretty much like the cafeterias I'd eaten in while in Portland and Chicago, with simple rectangular tables, soothing taupe walls, and a little room off to the side where our dubiously prepared meals were served. Someone had at least hung framed black-and-white photos along the walls in an effort to decorate it, but I didn't really consider pictures of vases and leafless trees "art."

Tonight, however, someone had managed to transform the normally boring commons into a bona fide dining room. Vases spilling over with crimson roses and delicate white lilies. Glowing candles. Tablecloths made of—wait for it—bloodred linen. The effect was gorgeous. It was hard to believe this was the same place I usually ate chicken patty sandwiches in. It looked fit for, well, a queen.

The tables had been arranged in straight lines, creating an aisle down the middle of the room. We had assigned seating, and naturally, I couldn't sit anywhere near Lissa. She sat in the front with the other Moroi; I was in the back with the novices. But she did catch my eye when I entered and flashed me a smile. She'd borrowed a dress from Natalie— blue, silky, and strapless—that looked amazing with her pale features. Who'd known Natalie owned anything so good? It made my sweater lose a few cool points.

They always conducted these formal banquets in the same way. A head table sat on a dais at the front of the room, where we could all ooh and ahh and watch Queen Tatiana and other

royals eat dinner. Guardians lined the walls, as stiff and formal as statues. Dimitri stood among them, and a weird feeling
twisted my stomach as I recalled what had happened in the
gym. His eyes stared straight ahead, as if focusing on nothing
and everything in the room at once.

When the time came for the royals' entrance, we all stood
up respectfully and watched as they walked down the aisle.
I recognized a few, mostly those who had children attending the Academy. Victor Dashkov was among them, walking slowly and with a cane. While I was happy to see him, I
cringed to watch each agonizing step he took toward the front
of the room.

Once that group had passed, four solemn guardians with
red-and-black-pin-striped jackets entered the commons.
Everyone but the guardians along the walls sank to our knees
in a silly show of loyalty.

What a lot of ceremony and posturing, I thought wearily.
Moroi monarchs were chosen by the previous monarch from
within the royal families. The king or queen couldn't choose
one of his or her own direct descendents, and a council from
the noble and royal families could dispute the choice with
enough cause. That almost never happened, though.

Queen Tatiana followed her guards, wearing a red silk
dress and matching jacket. She was in her early sixties and
had dark gray hair bobbed to her chin and crowned with a
Miss America–type tiara. She moved into the room slowly,
like she was taking a stroll, four more guardians at her back.

She moved through the novices' section fairly quickly, though she did nod and smile here and there. Dhampirs might just be the half-human, illegitimate children of the Moroi, but we trained and dedicated our lives to serving and protecting them. The likelihood was strong that many of us gathered here would die young, and the queen had to show her respect for that.

When she got to the Moroi section, she paused longer and actually spoke to a few students. It was a big deal to be acknowledged, mostly a sign that someone's parents had gotten in good with her. Naturally, the royals got the most attention. She didn't really say much to them that was all that interesting, mostly just a lot of fancy words.

"Vasilisa Dragomir."

My head shot up. Alarm coursed through the bond at the sound of her name. Breaking protocol, I pushed out of my position and wiggled over to get a better view, knowing no one would notice me when the queen herself had personally singled out the last of the Dragomirs. Everyone was eager to see what the monarch had to say to Lissa the runaway princess.

"We heard you had returned. We are glad to have the Dragomirs back, even though only one remains. We deeply regret the loss of your parents and your brother; they were among the finest of the Moroi, their deaths a true tragedy."

I'd never really understood the royal "we" thing, but otherwise, everything sounded okay.

"You have an interesting name," she continued. "Many heroines in Russian fairy tales are named Vasilisa. Vasilisa the Brave, Vasilisa the Beautiful. They are different young women, all having the same name and the same excellent qualities: strength, intelligence, discipline, and virtue. All accomplish great things, triumphing over their adversaries.

"Likewise, the Dragomir name commands its own respect. Dragomir kings and queens have ruled wisely and justly in our history. They have used their powers for miraculous ends. They have slain Strigoi, fighting right alongside their guardians. They are *royal* for a reason."

She waited a moment, letting the weight of her words sink in. I could feel the mood changing in the room, as well as the surprise and shy pleasure creeping out from Lissa. This would shake the social balance. We could probably expect a few wannabes trying to get in good with Lissa tomorrow.

"Yes," Tatiana continued, "you are doubly named with power. Your names represent the finest qualities people have to offer and hearken back in time to deeds of greatness and valor." She paused a moment. "But, as you have demonstrated, names do *not* make a person. Nor do they have any bearing on how that person turns out."

And with that verbal slap in the face, she turned away and continued her procession.

A collective shock filled the room. I briefly contemplated and then dismissed any attempts at jumping into the aisle and tackling the queen. Half a dozen guardians would have me down on the floor before I'd even taken five steps. So I sat impatiently through dinner, all the while feeling Lissa's absolute mortification.

When the post-dinner reception followed, Lissa made a beeline for the doors leading out to the courtyard. I followed, but got delayed having to weave around and avoid the mingling, socializing people.

She'd wandered outside to an adjacent courtyard, one that matched the Academy's grand external style. A roof of carved, twisting wood covered the garden, with little holes here and there to let in some light, but not enough to cause damage to Moroi. Trees, leaves now gone for the winter, lined the area and guarded paths leading out to other gardens, courtyards, and the main quadrangle. A pond, also emptied for the winter, lay in a corner, and standing over it was an imposing statue of St. Vladimir himself. Carved of gray rock, he wore long robes and had a beard and mustache.

Rounding a corner, I stopped when I saw Natalie had beaten me to Lissa. I considered interrupting but stepped back before they could see me. Spying might be bad, but I was suddenly very curious to hear what Natalie had to say to Lissa.

"She shouldn't have said that," Natalie said. She wore a yellow dress similar in cut to Lissa's, but somehow lacked the grace and poise to make it look as good. Yellow was also a terrible color on her. It clashed with her black hair, which she'd put up into an off-center bun. "It wasn't right," she went on. "Don't let it bother you."

"Kind of late for that." Lissa's eyes were locked firmly on the stone walkway below.

"She was wrong."

"She's *right*," Lissa exclaimed. "My parents . . . and Andre . . . they would have hated me for what I did."

"No, they wouldn't have." Natalie spoke in a gentle voice.

"It was stupid to run away. Irresponsible."

"So what? You made a mistake. I make mistakes all the time. The other day, I was doing this assignment in science, and it was for chapter ten, and I'd actually read chapter elev—" Natalie stopped herself and, in a remarkable show of restraint, got herself back on track. "People change. We're always changing, right? You aren't the same as you were then. I'm not the same as I was then."

Actually, Natalie seemed *exactly* the same to me, but that didn't bother me so much anymore. She'd grown on me.

"Besides," she added, "was running away really a mistake? You must have done it for a reason. You must have gotten something out of it, right? There was a lot of bad stuff going on with you, wasn't there? With your parents and your brother. I mean, maybe it was the right thing to do."

Lissa hid a smile. Both of us were pretty sure Natalie was trying to find out why we had left—just like everyone else in the school. She sort of sucked at being sneaky.

"I don't know if it was, no," Lissa answered. "I was weak.

Andre wouldn't have run away. He was so good. Good at everything. Good at getting along with people and all that royal crap."

"You're good at that too."

"I guess. But I don't like it. I mean, I like people . . . but most of what they do is so fake. That's what I don't like."

"Then don't feel bad about not getting involved," Natalie said. "I don't hang out with all those people either, and look at *me*. I'm just fine. Daddy says he doesn't care if I hang out with the royals or not. He just wants me to be happy."

"And that," I said, finally making my appearance, "is why *he* should be ruling instead of that bitch of a queen. He got robbed."

Natalie nearly jumped ten feet. I felt pretty confident her vocabulary of swear words mostly consisted of "golly" and "darn."

"I wondered where you were," said Lissa.

Natalie looked back and forth between us, suddenly seeming a little embarrassed to be right between the best-friends dream team. She shifted uncomfortably and tucked some messy hair behind her ear. "Well . . . I should go find Daddy. I'll see you back in the room."

"See you," said Lissa. "And thanks."

Natalie hurried off.

"Does she really call him '*Daddy*'?"

Lissa cut me a look. "Leave her alone. She's nice."

"She is, actually. I heard what she said, and as much as I

hate to admit it, there was nothing there I could really make fun of. It was all true." I paused. "I'll kill her, you know. The queen, not Natalie. Screw the guardians. I'll do it. She can't get away with that."

"God, Rose! Don't say that. They'll arrest you for treason. Just let it go."

"Let it go? After what she said to you? In front of everyone?"

She didn't answer or even look at me. Instead, she toyed absentmindedly with the branches of a scraggly bush that had gone dormant for the winter. There was a vulnerable look about her that I recognized—and feared.

"Hey." I lowered my voice. "Don't look like that. She doesn't know what she's talking about, okay? Don't let this get you down. Don't do anything you shouldn't."

She glanced back up at me. "It's going to happen again, isn't it?" she whispered. Her hand, still clutching the tree, began to tremble.

"Not if you don't let it." I tried to look at her wrists without being too obvious. "You haven't? . . ."

"No." She shook her head and blinked back tears. "I haven't wanted to. I was upset after the fox, but it's been okay. I like the coasting thing. I miss seeing you, but everything's been all right. I like . . ." She paused.

I could hear the word forming in her mind.

"Christian."

"I wish you couldn't do that. Or wouldn't."

"Sorry. Do I need to give you the Christian's-a-psycho-pathic-loser talk again?"

"I think I've got it memorized after the last ten times," she muttered.

I started to launch into number eleven when I heard the sound of laughter and the clatter of high heels on stone. Mia walked toward us with a few friends in tow but no Aaron. Immediately, my defenses snapped on.

Internally, Lissa was still shaken over the queen's comments. Sorrow and humiliation were swirling inside of her. She felt embarrassed over what others must think of her now and kept thinking about how her family would have hated her for running away. I didn't believe that, but it felt real to her, and her dark emotions churned and churned. She was *not* okay, no matter how casual she'd just tried to act, and I was worried she might do something reckless. Mia was the last person she needed to see right now.

"What do you want?" I demanded.

Mia smiled haughtily at Lissa and ignored me, taking a few steps forward. "Just wanted to know what it's like to be *so* important and *so* royal. You must be so excited that the queen talked to you." Giggles surfaced from the gathering group.

"You're standing too close." I stepped between them, and Mia flinched a little, possibly still worried I might break her arm. "And hey, at least the queen knew her name, which is more than I can say for you and your wannabe-royal act. *Or* your parents."

I could see the pain that caused her. Man, she wanted to be royal so badly. "At least I *see* my parents," she retorted. "At least I know who they both are. God only knows who your father is. And your mom's one of the most famous guardians around, but she couldn't care less about you either. Everyone knows she never visits. Probably was glad when you were gone. If she even *noticed*."

That hurt. I clenched my teeth. "Yeah, well, at least she's famous. She really does advise royals and nobles. She doesn't clean up after them."

I heard one of her friends snicker behind her. Mia opened her mouth, no doubt to unleash one of the many retorts she'd had to accumulate since the story started going around, when the lightbulb suddenly went off in her head.

"It was *you*," she said, eyes wide. "Someone told me Jesse'd started it, but he couldn't have known anything about me. He got it from you. When you *slept* with him."

Now she was really starting to piss me off. "I didn't sleep with him."

Mia pointed at Lissa and glared back at me. "So that's it, huh? You do her dirty work because she's too pathetic to do it herself. You aren't always going to be able to protect her," she warned. "*You* aren't safe either."

Empty threats. I leaned forward, making my voice as menacing as possible. In my current mood, it wasn't difficult. "Yeah? Try and touch me now and find out."

I hoped she would. I wanted her to. We didn't need her

messed-up vendetta in our lives just now. She was a distraction—one I very much wanted to punch right now.

Looking past her, I saw Dimitri move out into the garden, eyes searching for something—or someone. I had a pretty good idea who it was. When he saw me, he strode forward, shifting his attention when he noticed the crowd gathered around us. Guardians can smell a fight a mile away. Of course, a six-year-old could have smelled this fight.

Dimitri stood beside me and crossed his arms. "Everything all right?"

"Sure thing, Guardian Belikov." I smiled as I said it, but I was furious. Raging, even. This whole Mia confrontation had only made Lissa feel worse. "We were just swapping family stories. Ever heard Mia's? It's *fascinating*."

"Come on," said Mia to her followers. She led them off, but not before she'd given me one last, chilling look. I didn't need to read her mind to know what it said. This wasn't over. She was going to try to get one or both of us back. Fine. Bring it on, Mia.

"I'm supposed to take you back to your dorm," Dimitri told me drily. "You weren't about to just start a fight, were you?"

"Of course not," I said, my eyes still staring at the empty doorway Mia had disappeared through. "I don't start fights where people can see them."

"Rose," groaned Lissa.

"Let's go. Good night, Princess."

He turned, but I didn't move. "You going to be okay, Liss?"

She nodded. "I'm fine."

It was such a lie, I couldn't believe she had the nerve to try to put it past me. I didn't need the bond to see tears shining in her eyes. We should never have come back to this place, I realized bleakly.

"Liss . . ."

She gave me a small, sad smile and nodded in Dimitri's direction. "I told you, I'm fine. You've got to go."

Reluctantly, I followed him. He led me out toward the other side of the garden. "We may need to add an extra training on self-control," he noted.

"I have plenty of self contr—hey!"

I stopped talking as I saw Christian slip past us, moving down the path we'd just come from. I hadn't seen him at the reception, but if Kirova had released me to come tonight, I suppose she would have done the same for him.

"You going to see Lissa?" I demanded, shifting my Mia rage to him.

He stuffed his hands into his pockets and gave me that look of bad-boy indifference. "What if I am?"

"Rose, this isn't the time," said Dimitri.

But it was *so* the time. Lissa had ignored my warnings about Christian for weeks. It was time to go to the source and stop their ridiculous flirtation once and for all.

"Why don't you just leave her alone? Are you so messed

up and desperate for attention that you can't tell when someone doesn't like you?" He scowled. "You're some crazy stalker,
and she knows it. She's told me all about your weird obses-
sion—how you're always hanging out in the attic together,
how you set Ralf on fire to impress her. She thinks you're a
freak, but she's too nice to say anything."

His face had paled, and something dark churned in his
eyes. "But *you* aren't too nice?"

"No. Not when I feel sorry for someone."

"Enough," said Dimitri, steering me away.

"Thanks for 'helping,' then," snapped Christian, his voice
dripping with animosity.

"No problem," I called back over my shoulder.

When we'd gone a little ways, I stole a glance behind me
and saw Christian standing just outside the garden. He'd
stopped walking and now stood staring down the path that
led to Lissa in the courtyard. Shadows covered his face as he
thought, and then, after a few moments, he turned around
and headed back toward the Moroi dorms.

TWELVE

Sleep came reluctantly that night, and I tossed and turned for a long time before finally going under.

An hour or so later, I sat up in bed, trying to relax and sort out the emotions coming to me. Lissa. Scared and upset. Unstable. The night's events suddenly came rushing back to me as I went through what could be bothering her. The queen humiliating her. Mia. Maybe even Christian—he could have found her for all I knew.

Yet . . . none of those was the problem right now. Buried within her, there was something else. Something terribly wrong.

I climbed out of bed, dressed hastily, and considered my options. I had a third-floor room now—way too high to climb down from, particularly since I had no Ms. Karp to patch me up this time. I would never be able to sneak out of the main hall. That only left going through the "appropriate" channels.

"Where do you think you're going?"

One of the matrons who supervised my hall looked up from her chair. She sat stationed at the end of the hall, near the stairs going down. During the day, that stairwell had loose supervision. At night, we might as well have been in jail.

I crossed my arms. "I need to see Dim—Guardian Belikov."

"It's late."

"It's an emergency."

She looked me up and down. "You seem okay to me."

"You're going to be in so much trouble tomorrow when everyone finds out you stopped me from reporting what I know."

"Tell me."

"It's private guardian stuff."

I gave her as hard a stare as I could manage. It must have worked, because she finally stood up and pulled out a cell phone. She called someone—Dimitri, I hoped—but murmured too low for me to hear. We waited several minutes, and then the door leading to the stairs opened. Dimitri appeared, fully dressed and alert, though I felt pretty sure we'd pulled him out of bed.

He took one look at me. "Lissa."

I nodded.

Without another word, he turned around and started back down the stairs. I followed. We walked across the quad in silence, toward the imposing Moroi dorm. It was "night" for the vampires, which meant it was daytime for the rest of the world. Mid-afternoon sun shone with a cold, golden light on us. The human genes in me welcomed it and always sort of regretted how Moroi light sensitivity forced us to live in darkness most of the time.

Lissa's hall matron gaped when we appeared, but Dimitri was too intimidating to oppose. "She's in the bathroom,"

I told them. When the matron started to follow me inside, I wouldn't let her. "She's too upset. Let me talk to her alone first."

Dimitri considered. "Yes. Give them a minute."

I pushed the door open.

"Liss?"

A soft sound, like a sob, came from within. I walked down five stalls and found the only one closed. I knocked softly.

"Let me in," I said, hoping I sounded calm and strong.

I heard a sniffle, and a few moments later, the door unlatched. I wasn't prepared for what I saw. Lissa stood before me . . .

. . . covered in blood.

Horrified, I squelched a scream and almost called for help. Looking more closely, I saw that a lot of the blood wasn't actually coming from her. It was smeared on her, like it had been on her hands and she'd rubbed her face. She sank to the floor, and I followed, kneeling before her.

"Are you okay?" I whispered. "What happened?"

She only shook her head, but I saw her face crumple as more tears spilled from her eyes. I took her hands.

"Come on. Let's get you cleaned—"

I stopped. She *was* bleeding after all. Perfect lines crossed her wrists, not near any crucial veins, but enough to leave wet, red tracks across her skin. She hadn't hit her veins when she did this; death hadn't been her goal. She met my eyes.

"I'm sorry. . . . I didn't mean . . . Please don't let them

know . . ." she sobbed. "When I saw *it*, I freaked out." She nodded toward her wrists. "This just happened before I could stop. I was upset. . . ."

"It's okay," I said automatically, wondering what "it" was. "Come on."

I heard a knock on the door. "Rose?"

"Just a sec," I called back.

I took her to the sink and rinsed the blood off her wrists. Grabbing the first-aid kit, I hastily put some Band-Aids on the cuts. The bleeding had already slowed.

"We're coming in," the matron called.

I jerked off my hoodie sweatshirt and quickly handed it to Lissa. She had just pulled it on when Dimitri and the matron entered. He raced to our sides in an instant, and I realized that in hiding Lissa's wrists, I'd forgotten the blood on her face.

"It's not mine," she said quickly, seeing his expression. "It . . . it's the rabbit. . . ."

Dimitri assessed her, and I hoped he wouldn't look at her wrists. When he seemed satisfied she had no gaping wounds, he asked, "What rabbit?" I was wondering the same thing.

With shaking hands, she pointed at the trash can. "I cleaned it up. So Natalie wouldn't see."

Dimitri and I both walked over and peered into the can. I pulled myself away immediately, swallowing back my stomach's need to throw up. I don't know how Lissa knew it was a rabbit. All I could see was blood. Blood and blood-soaked paper towels. Globs of gore I couldn't identify. The smell was horrible.

Dimitri shifted closer to Lissa, bending down until they were at eye level. "Tell me what happened." He handed her several tissues.

"I came back about an hour ago. And it was there. Right there in the middle of the floor. Torn apart. It was like it had . . . exploded." She sniffed. "I didn't want Natalie to find it, didn't want to scare her . . . so I—I cleaned it up. Then I just couldn't . . . I couldn't go back. . . ." She began to cry, and her shoulders shook.

I could figure out the rest, the part she didn't tell Dimitri. She'd found the rabbit, cleaned up, and freaked out. Then she'd cut herself, but it was the weird way she coped with things that upset her.

"No one should be able to get into those rooms!" exclaimed the matron. "How is this happening?"

"Do you know who did it?" Dimitri's voice was gentle.

Lissa reached into her pajama pocket and pulled out a crumpled piece of paper. It had so much blood soaked into it, I could barely read it as he held it and smoothed it out.

I know what you are. You won't survive being here. I'll make sure of it. Leave now. It's the only way you might live through this.

The matron's shock transformed into something more determined, and she headed for the door. "I'm getting Ellen." It took me a second to remember that was Kirova's first name.

"Tell her we'll be at the clinic," said Dimitri. When she left, he turned to Lissa. "You should lie down."

When she didn't move, I linked my arm through hers. "Come on, Liss. Let's get you out of here."

Slowly, she put one foot in front of the other and let us lead her to the Academy's medical clinic. It was normally staffed by a couple of doctors, but at this time of night, only a nurse stayed on duty. She offered to wake one of the doctors, but Dimitri declined. "She just needs to rest."

Lissa had no sooner stretched out on a narrow bed than Kirova and a few others showed up and started questioning her.

I thrust myself in front of them, blocking her. "Leave her alone! Can't you see she doesn't want to talk about it? Let her get some sleep first!"

"Miss Hathaway," declared Kirova, "you're out of line as usual. I don't even know what you're doing here."

Dimitri asked if he could speak with her privately and led her into the hall. I heard angry whispers from her, calm and firm ones from him. When they returned, she said stiffly, "You may stay with her for a little while. We'll have janitors do further cleaning and investigation in the bathroom and your room, Miss Dragomir, and then discuss the situation in detail in the morning."

"Don't wake Natalie," whispered Lissa. "I don't want to scare her. I cleaned up everything in the room anyway."

Kirova looked doubtful. The group retreated but not before the nurse asked if Lissa wanted anything to eat or drink. She declined. Once we were alone, I lay down beside her and put my arm around her.

"I won't let them find out," I told her, sensing her worry about her wrists. "But I wish you'd told me before I left the reception. You'd said you'd always come to me first."

"I wasn't going to do it then," she said, her eyes staring blankly off. "I swear, I wasn't going to. I mean, I was upset . . . but I thought . . . I thought I could handle it. I was trying so hard . . . really, Rose. I was. But then I got back to my room, and I saw *it*, and I . . . just lost it. It was like the last straw, you know? And I knew I had to clean it up. Had to clean it up before they saw, before they found out, but there was so much blood . . . and afterward, after it was done, it was too much, and I felt like I was going to . . . I don't know . . . explode, and it was just too much, I had to let it out, you know? I had to—"

I interrupted her hysteria. "It's okay, I understand."

That was a lie. I didn't get her cutting at all. She'd done it sporadically, ever since the accident, and it scared me each time. She'd try to explain it to me, how she didn't want to die—she just needed to get *it* out somehow. She felt so much emotionally, she would say, that a physical outlet—physical pain—was the only way to make the internal pain go away. It was the only way she could control it.

"Why is this happening?" she cried into her pillow. "Why am I a freak?"

"You aren't a freak."

"No one else has this happen to them. No one else does magic like I can."

"Did you try to do magic?" No answer. "Liss? Did you try to heal the rabbit?"

"I reached out, just to see if I could maybe fix it, but there was just too much blood. . . . I couldn't."

The more she uses it, the worse it'll get. Stop her, Rose.

Lissa was right. Moroi magic could conjure fire and water, move rocks and other pieces of earth. But no one could heal or bring animals back from the dead. No one except Ms. Karp.

Stop her before they notice, before they notice and take her away too. Get her out of here.

I hated carrying this secret, mostly because I didn't know what to do about it. I didn't like feeling powerless. I needed to protect her from this—and from herself. And yet, at the same time, I needed to protect her from *them*, too.

"We should go," I said abruptly. "We're going to leave."

"Rose—"

"It's happening again. And it's worse. Worse than last time."

"You're afraid of the note."

"I'm not afraid of any note. But this place isn't safe."

I suddenly longed for Portland again. It might be dirtier and more crowded than the rugged Montana landscape, but at least you knew what to expect—not like here. Here at the Academy, past and present warred with each other. It might have its beautiful old walls and gardens, but inside, modern things were creeping in. People didn't know how to handle that. It was just like the Moroi themselves. Their archaic royal families still held the power on the surface, but people were growing discontent. Dhampirs who wanted more to their lives. Moroi like Christian who wanted to fight the Strigoi. The royals still clung to their traditions, still touted their power over everyone else, just as the Academy's elaborate iron gates put on a show of tradition and invincibility.

And, oh, the lies and secrets. They ran through the halls and hid in the corners. Someone here hated Lissa, someone who was probably smiling right to her face and pretending to be her friend. I couldn't let them destroy her.

"You need to get some sleep," I told her.

"I can't sleep."

"Yes, you can. I'm right here. You won't be alone."

Anxiety and fear and other troubled emotions coursed through her. But in the end, her body's needs won out. After a while, I saw her eyes close. Her breathing became even, and the bond grew quiet.

I watched her sleep, too keyed up with adrenaline to allow myself any rest. I think maybe an hour had passed when the nurse returned and told me I had to leave.

"I can't go," I said. "I promised her she wouldn't be alone."

The nurse was tall, even for a Moroi, with kind brown eyes. "She won't be. I'll stay with her."

I regarded her skeptically.

"I promise."

Back in my room, I had my own crash. The fear and excitement had worn me out too, and for an instant, I wished I could have a normal life and a normal best friend. Immediately, I cast that thought out. No one was normal, not really. And I'd never have a better friend than Lissa . . . but man, it was so hard sometimes.

I slept heavily until morning. I went to my first class tentatively, nervous that word about last night had gotten around. As it turned out, people *were* talking about last night, but their attention was still focused on the queen and the reception. They knew nothing about the rabbit. As hard as it was to believe, I'd nearly forgotten about that other stuff. Still, it suddenly seemed like a small thing compared to someone causing a bloody explosion in Lissa's room.

Yet, as the day went on, I noticed something weird. People stopped looking at Lissa so much. The started looking at *me*. Whatever. Ignoring them, I hunted around and found Lissa finishing up with a feeder. That funny feeling I always got came over me as I watched her mouth work against the feeder's neck, drinking his blood. A trickle of it ran down his throat, standing out against his pale skin. Feeders, though human, were nearly as pale as Moroi from all the blood loss. He didn't seem to notice; he was long gone on the high of the bite. Drowning in jealousy, I decided I needed therapy.

"You okay?" I asked her later, on our way to class. She wore long sleeves, purposefully obscuring her wrists.

"Yeah . . . I still can't stop thinking about that rabbit. . . . It was so horrible. I keep seeing it in my head. And then what I did." She squeezed her eyes shut, just for a moment, and then opened them again. "People are talking about us."

"I know. Ignore them."

"I *hate* it," she said angrily. A surge of darkness shot up into her and through the bond. It made me cringe. My best friend was lighthearted and kind. She didn't have feelings like that. "I hate all the gossip. It's so stupid. How can they all be so shallow?"

"Ignore them," I repeated soothingly. "You were smart not to hang out with them anymore."

Ignoring them grew harder and harder, though. The whispers and looks increased. In animal behavior, it became so bad, I couldn't even concentrate on my now-favorite subject. Ms. Meissner had started talking about evolution and survival of the fittest and how animals sought mates with good genes. It fascinated me, but even she had a hard time staying on task, since she had to keep yelling at people to quiet down and pay attention.

"Something's going on," I told Lissa between classes. "I don't know what, but they're all over something new."

"Something else? Other than the queen hating me? What more could there be?"

"Wish I knew."

Things finally came to a head in our last class of the day, Slavic art. It started when a guy I barely knew made a very explicit and nearly obscene suggestion to me while we all worked on individual projects. I replied in kind, letting him know exactly what he could do with his request.

He only laughed. "Come on, Rose. I *bleed* for you."

Loud giggles ensued, and Mia cut us a taunting look. "Wait, it's Rose who does the bleeding, right?"

More laughter. Understanding slapped me in the face. I jerked Lissa away. "They know."

"Know what?"

"About us. About how you . . . you know, how I fed you while we were gone."

She gaped. "How?"

"How do you think? Your 'friend' Christian."

"No," she said adamantly. "He wouldn't have."

"Who else knew?"

Faith in Christian flashed in her eyes and in our bond. But she didn't know what I knew. She didn't know how I'd bitched him out last night, how I'd made him think she hated him. The guy was unstable. Spreading our biggest secret—well, one of them—would be an adequate revenge. Maybe he'd killed the rabbit, too. After all, it had died only a couple hours after I'd told him off.

Not waiting around to hear her protests, I stalked off to the other side of the room where Christian was working by himself, as usual. Lissa followed in my wake. Not caring if people saw us, I leaned across the table toward him, putting my face inches from his.

"I'm going to kill you."

His eyes darted to Lissa, the faintest glimmer of longing in them, and then a scowl spread over his face. "Why? Is it like guardian extra credit?"

"Stop with the attitude," I warned, pitching my voice low. "You told. You told how Lissa had to feed off me."

"Tell her," said Lissa desperately. "Tell her she's wrong."

Christian dragged his eyes from me to her, and as they regarded each other, I felt such a powerful wave of attraction, it was a wonder it didn't knock me over. Her heart was in her eyes. It was obvious to me he felt the same way about her, but she couldn't see it, particularly since he was still glaring at her.

"You can stop it, you know," he said. "You don't have to pretend anymore."

Lissa's giddy attraction vanished, replaced by hurt and shock over his tone. "I . . . what? Pretend what? . . ."

"You *know* what. Just stop. Stop with the act."

Lissa stared at him, her eyes wide and wounded. She had no clue I'd gone off on him last night. She had no clue that he believed she hated him.

"Get over feeling sorry for yourself, and tell us what's going on," I snapped at him. "Did you or didn't you tell them?"

He fixed me with a defiant look. "No. I didn't."

"I don't believe you."

"I do," said Lissa.

"I know it's impossible to believe a *freak* like me could keep his mouth shut—especially since neither of you can—but I have better things to do than spread stupid rumors. You want someone to blame? Blame your golden boy over there."

I followed his gaze to where Jesse was laughing about something with that idiot Ralf.

"Jesse doesn't know," said Lissa defiantly.

Christian's eyes were glued to me. "He *does*, though. Doesn't he, Rose? He knows."

My stomach sank out of me. Yes. Jesse did know. He'd figured it out that night in the lounge. "I didn't think . . . I didn't think he'd tell. He was too afraid of Dimitri."

"You *told* him?" exclaimed Lissa.

"No, he guessed." I was starting to feel sick.

"He apparently did more than guess," muttered Christian.

I turned on him. "What's that supposed to mean?"

"Oh. You don't know."

"I swear to God, Christian, I'm going to break your neck after class."

"Man, you really are unstable." He said it almost happily, but his next words were more serious. He still wore that sneer, still glowed with anger, but when he spoke, I could hear the faintest uneasiness in his voice. "He sort of elaborated on what was in your note. Got into a little more detail."

"Oh, I get it. He said we had sex." I didn't need to mince words. Christian nodded. So. Jesse was trying to boost his own reputation. Okay. That I could deal with. Not like my reputation was that stellar to begin with. Everyone already believed I had sex all the time.

"And uh, Ralf too. That you and he—"

Ralf? No amount of alcohol or any illegal substance would

make me touch him. "I—what? That I had sex with Ralf too?"

Christian nodded.

"That asshole! I'm going to—"

"There's more."

"How? Did I sleep with the basketball team?"

"He said—they both said—you let them . . . well, you let them drink your blood."

That stopped even me. Drinking blood during sex. The dirtiest of the dirty. Sleazy. Beyond being easy or a slut. A gazillion times worse than Lissa drinking from me for survival. Blood-whore territory.

"That's crazy!" Lissa cried. "Rose would never—Rose?"

But I wasn't listening anymore. I was in my own world, a world that took me across the classroom to where Jesse and Ralf sat. They both looked up, faces half smug and half . . . nervous, if I had to guess. Not unexpected, since they were both lying through their teeth.

The entire class came to a standstill. Apparently they'd been expecting some type of showdown. My unstable reputation in action.

"What the hell do you think you're doing?" I asked in a low, dangerous voice.

Jesse's nervous look turned to one of terror. He might have been taller than me, but we both knew who would win if I turned violent. Ralf, however, gave me a cocky smile.

"We didn't do anything you didn't want us to do." His smiled turned cruel. "And don't even think about laying a hand on us. You start a fight, and Kirova'll kick you out to go live with the other blood whores."

The rest of the students were holding their breaths, waiting to see what we'd do. I don't know how Mr. Nagy could have been oblivious to the drama occurring in his class.

I wanted to punch both of them, hit them so hard that it'd make Dimitri's brawl with Jesse look like a pat on the back. I wanted to wipe that smirk off Ralf's face.

But asshole or not, he was right. If I touched them, Kirova would expel me in the blink of an eye. And if I got kicked out, Lissa would be alone. Taking a deep breath, I made one of the hardest decisions of my life.

I walked away.

The rest of the day was miserable. In backing down from the fight, I opened myself up to mockery from everyone else. The rumors and whispers grew louder. People stared at me openly. People laughed. Lissa kept trying to talk to me, to console me, but I ignored even her. I went through the rest of my classes like a zombie, and then I headed off to practice with Dimitri as fast I could. He gave me a puzzled look but didn't ask any questions.

Alone in my room later on, I cried for the first time in years.

Once I got that out of my system, I was about to put on my pajamas when I heard a knock at my door. Dimitri. He studied my face and then glanced away, obviously aware I'd been crying. I could tell, too, that the rumors had finally reached him. He knew.

"Are you okay?"

"It doesn't matter if I am, remember?" I looked up at him. "Is Lissa okay? This'll be hard on her."

A funny look crossed his face. I think it astonished him that I'd still be worried about her at a time like this. He beckoned me to follow and led me out to a back stairwell, one that usually stayed locked to students. But it was open tonight, and he gestured me outside. "Five minutes," he warned.

More curious than ever, I stepped outside. Lissa stood there. I should have sensed she was close, but my own out-of-control feelings had obscured hers. Without a word, she put her arms around me and held me for several moments. I had to hold back more tears. When we broke apart, she looked at me with calm, level eyes.

"I'm sorry," she said.

"Not your fault. It'll pass."

She clearly doubted that. So did I.

"It *is* my fault," she said. "She did it to get back at me."

"She?"

"Mia. Jesse and Ralf aren't smart enough to think of something like that on their own. You said it yourself: Jesse was too scared of Dimitri to talk much about what happened. And why wait until now? It happened a while ago. If he'd wanted to spread stuff around, he would have done it back then. Mia's doing this as retaliation for you talking about her parents. I don't know how she managed it, but she's the one who got them to say those things."

In my gut, I realized Lissa was right. Jesse and Ralf were the tools; Mia had been the mastermind.

"Nothing to be done now," I sighed.

"Rose—"

"Forget it, Liss. It's done, okay?"

She studied me quietly for a few seconds. "I haven't seen you cry in a long time."

"I wasn't crying."

A feeling of heartache and sympathy beat through to me from the bond.

"She can't do this to you," she argued.

I laughed bitterly, half surprised at my own hopelessness. "She already did. She said she'd get back at me, that I wouldn't be able to protect you. She did it. When I go back to classes . . ." A sickening feeling settled in my stomach. I thought about the friends and respect I'd managed to eke out, despite our low profile. That would be gone. You couldn't come back from something like this. Not among the Moroi. Once a blood whore, always a blood whore. What made it worse was that some dark, secret part of me did like being bitten.

"You shouldn't have to keep protecting me," she said.

I laughed. "That's my job. I'm going to be your guardian."

"I know, but I meant like this. You shouldn't suffer because of me. You shouldn't always have to look after me. And yet you always do. You got me out of here. You took care of everything when we were on our own. Even since coming back . . . you've always been the one who does all the work. Every time I break down—like last night—you're always there. Me, I'm *weak*. I'm not like you."

I shook my head. "That doesn't matter. It's what I do. I don't mind."

"Yeah, but look what happened. I'm the one she really has a grudge against—even though I still don't know why. Whatever. It's going to stop. I'm going to protect *you* from now on."

There was a determination in her expression, a wonderful confidence radiating off of her that reminded me of the Lissa I'd known before the accident. At the same time, I could feel something else in her—something darker, a sense of deeply buried anger. I'd seen this side of her before too, and I didn't like it. I didn't want her tapping into it. I just wanted her to be safe.

"Lissa, you can't protect me."

"I can," she said fiercely. "There's one thing Mia wants more than to destroy you and me. She wants to be accepted. She wants to hang out with the royals and feel like she's one of them. I can take that away from her." She smiled. "I can turn them against her."

"How?"

"By *telling* them." Her eyes flashed.

My mind was moving too slowly tonight. It took me a while to catch on. "Liss—no. You can't use compulsion. Not around here."

"I might as well get some use out of these stupid powers."

The more she uses it, the worse it'll get. Stop her, Rose. Stop her before they notice, before they notice and take her away too. Get her out of here.

"Liss, if you get caught—"

Dimitri stuck his head out. "You've got to get back inside, Rose, before someone finds you."

I shot a panicked look at Lissa, but she was already retreating. "I'll take care of everything this time, Rose. *Everything.*"

THIRTEEN

The aftermath of Jesse and Ralf's lies was about as horrible as I'd expected. The only way I survived was by putting blinders on, by ignoring everyone and everything. It kept me sane—barely—but I hated it. I felt like crying all the time. I lost my appetite and didn't sleep well.

Yet, no matter how bad it got for me, I didn't worry about myself as much as I did Lissa. She stood by her promise to change things. It was slow at first, but gradually, I would see a royal or two come up to her at lunch or in class and say hello. She'd turn on a brilliant smile, laughing and talking to them like they were all best friends.

At first, I didn't understand how she was pulling it off. She'd told me she would use compulsion to win the other royals over and turn them against Mia. But I didn't *see* it happening. It was possible, of course, that she was winning people over without compulsion. After all, she was funny, smart, and nice. Anyone would like her. Something told me she wasn't winning friends the old-fashioned way, and I finally figured it out.

She was using compulsion when I wasn't around. I only saw her for a small part of the day, and since she knew I didn't approve, she only worked her power when I was away.

After a few days of this secret compulsion, I knew what I needed to do: I had to get back in her head again. By choice. I'd done it before; I could do it again.

At least, that's what I told myself, sitting and spacing out in Stan's class one day. But it wasn't as easy as I'd thought it would be, partly because I felt too keyed up to relax and open myself to her thoughts. I also had trouble because I picked a time when she felt relatively calm. She came through the "loudest" when her emotions were running strong.

Still, I tried to do what I'd done before, back when I'd spied on her and Christian. The meditation thing. Slow breathing. Eyes closed. Mental focus like that still wasn't easy for me, but at long last I managed the transition, slipping into her head and experiencing the world as hers. She stood in her American lit class, during project-work time, but, like most of the students, she wasn't working. She and Camille Conta leaned against a wall on the far side of the room, talking in hushed voices.

"It's gross," said Camille firmly, a frown crossing her pretty face. She had on a blue skirt made of velvetlike fabric, short enough to show off her long legs and possibly raise eyes about the dress code. "If you guys were doing it, I'm not surprised she got addicted and did it with Jesse."

"She *didn't* do it with Jesse," insisted Lissa. "And it's not like we had *sex*. We just didn't have any feeders, that's all." Lissa focused her full attention on Camille and smiled. "It's no big deal. Everyone's overreacting."

Camille looked like she seriously doubted this, and then,

the more she stared at Lissa, the more unfocused her eyes became. A blank look fell over her.

"Right?" asked Lissa, voice like silk. "It's not a big deal."

The frown returned. Camille tried to shake the compulsion. That fact that it'd even gotten this far was incredible. As Christian had observed, using it on Moroi was unheard of.

Camille, although strong-willed, lost the battle. "Yeah," she said slowly. "It's really not that big a deal."

"And Jesse's lying."

She nodded. "Definitely lying."

A mental strain burned inside of Lissa as she held onto the compulsion. It took a lot of effort, and she wasn't finished.

"What are you guys doing tonight?"

"Carly and I are going to study for Mattheson's test in her room."

"Invite me."

Camille thought about it. "Hey, you want to study with us?"

"Sure," said Lissa, smiling at her. Camille smiled back.

Lissa dropped the compulsion, and a wave of dizziness swept over her. She felt weak. Camille glanced around, momentarily surprised, then shook off the weirdness. "See you after dinner then."

"See you," murmured Lissa, watching her walk away. When Camille was gone, Lissa reached up to tie her hair up in a ponytail. Her fingers couldn't quite get all the hair through, and suddenly, another pair of hands caught hold and helped her. She spun around and found herself staring into Christian's ice-blue eyes. She jerked away from him.

"Don't do that!" she exclaimed, shivering at the realization that it had been *his* fingers touching her.

He gave her his lazy, slightly twisted smile and brushed a few pieces of unruly black hair out of his face. "Are you asking me or *ordering* me?"

"Shut up." She glanced around, both to avoid his eyes and make sure no one saw them together.

"What's the matter? Worried about what your slaves'll think if they see you talking to me?"

"They're my *friends*," she retorted.

"Oh. Right. Of course they are. I mean, from what I saw, Camille would probably *do anything* for you, right? Friends till the end." He crossed his arms over his chest, and in spite of her anger, she couldn't help but notice how the silvery gray of his shirt set off his black hair and blue eyes.

"At least she isn't like you. She doesn't pretend to be my friend one day and then ignore me for no reason."

An uncertain look flickered across his features. Tension and anger had built up between them in the last week, ever since I'd yelled at Christian after the royal reception. Believing what I'd told him, Christian had stopped talking to her and had treated her rudely every time she'd tried to start a conversation. Now, hurt and confused, she'd given up attempts at being nice. The situation just kept getting worse and worse.

Looking out through Lissa's eyes, I could see that he still

cared about her and still wanted her. His pride had been hurt, however, and he wasn't about to show weakness.

"Yeah?" he said in a low, cruel voice. "I thought that was the way all royals were supposed to act. You certainly seem to be doing a good job with it. Or maybe you're just using compulsion on me to make me think you're a two-faced bitch. Maybe you really aren't. But I doubt it."

Lissa flushed at the word *compulsion*—and cast another worried look around—but decided not to give him the satisfaction of arguing anymore. She simply gave him one last glare before storming off to join a group of royals huddled over an assignment

Returning to myself, I stared blankly around the classroom, processing what I'd seen. Some tiny, tiny part of me was starting to feel sorry for Christian. It was only a tiny part, though, and very easy to ignore.

At the beginning of the next day, I headed out to meet Dimitri. These practices were my favorite part of the day now, partly because of my stupid crush on him and partly because I didn't have to be around the others.

He and I started with running as usual, and he ran with me, quiet and almost gentle in his instructions, probably worried about causing some sort of breakdown. He knew about the rumors somehow, but he never mentioned them.

When we finished, he led me through an offensive exercise where I could use any makeshift weapons I could find to attack him. To my surprise, I managed to land a few blows on him, although they seemed to do me more damage than him. The impacts always made *me* stagger back, but he never budged. It still didn't stop me from attacking and attacking, fighting with an almost blind rage. I didn't know who I really fought in those moments: Mia or Jesse or Ralf. Maybe all of them.

Dimitri finally called a break. We carried the equipment we'd used on the field and returned everything to the supply room. While putting it away, he glanced at me and did a double take.

"Your hands." He swore in Russian. I could recognize it by now, but he refused to teach me what any of it meant. "Where are your gloves?"

I looked down at my hands. They'd suffered for weeks, and today had only made them worse. The cold had turned the skin raw and chapped, and some parts were actually bleeding a little. My blisters swelled. "Don't have any. Never needed them in Portland."

He swore again and beckoned me to a chair while he retrieved a first-aid kit. Wiping away the blood with a wet cloth, he told me gruffly, "We'll get you some."

I looked down at my destroyed hands as he worked. "This is only the start, isn't it?"

"Of what?"

"Me. Turning into Alberta. Her . . . and all the other female guardians. They're all leathery and stuff. Fighting and train-ing and always being outdoors—they aren't pretty anymore." I paused. "This . . . this life. It destroys them. Their looks, I mean."

He hesitated for a moment and looked up from my hands. Those warm brown eyes surveyed me, and something tightened in my chest. Damn it. I had to stop feeling this way around him. "It won't happen to *you*. You're too . . ." He groped for the right word, and I mentally substituted all sorts of possibilities. *Goddesslike. Scorchingly sexy.* Giving up, he simply said, "It won't happen to you."

He turned his attention back to my hands. Did he . . . did he think I was *pretty*? I never doubted the reaction I caused among guys my own age, but with him, I didn't know. The tightening in my chest increased.

"It happened to my mom. She used to be beautiful. I guess she still is, sort of. But not the way she used to be." Bitterly, I added, "Haven't seen her in a while. She could look completely different for all I know."

"You don't like your mother," he observed.

"You noticed that, huh?"

"You barely know her."

"That's the point. She abandoned me. She left me to be raised by the Academy."

When he finished cleaning my open wounds, he found a jar of salve and began rubbing it into the rough parts of my skin. I sort of got lost in the feel of his hands massaging mine.

"You say that . . . but what else should she have done? I know you want to be a guardian. I know how much it means to you. Do you think she feels any differently? Do you think she should have quit to raise you when you'd spend most of your life here anyway?"

I didn't like having reasonable arguments thrown at me. "Are you saying I'm a hypocrite?"

"I'm just saying maybe you shouldn't be so hard on her. She's a very respected dhampir woman. She's set you on the path to be the same."

"It wouldn't kill her to visit more," I muttered. "But I guess you're right. A little. It could have been worse, I suppose. I could have been raised with blood whores."

Dimitri looked up. "I was raised in a dhampir commune. They aren't as bad as you think."

"Oh." I suddenly felt stupid. "I didn't mean—"

"It's all right." He focused his attention back on my hands.

"So, did you, like, have family there? Grow up with them?"

He nodded. "My mother and two sisters. I didn't see them much after I went to school, but we still keep in touch. Mostly, the communities are about family. There's a lot of love there, no matter what stories you've heard."

My bitterness returned, and I glanced down to hide my glare. Dimitri had had a happier family life with his disgraced mother and relatives than I'd had with my "respected" guardian mother. He most certainly knew his mother better than I knew mine.

"Yeah, but . . . isn't it weird? Aren't there a lot of Moroi men visiting to, you know? . . ."

His hands rubbed circles into mine. "Sometimes."

There was something dangerous in his tone, something

that told me this was an unwelcome topic. "I—I'm sorry. I didn't mean to bring up something bad. . . ."

"Actually . . . you probably wouldn't think it's bad," he said after almost a minute had passed. A tight smile formed on his lips. "You don't know your father, do you?"

I shook my head. "No. All I know he is he must have had wicked cool hair."

Dimitri glanced up, and his eyes swept me. "Yes. He must have." Returning to my hands, he said carefully, "I knew mine."

I froze. "Really? Most Moroi guys don't stay—I mean, some do, but you know, usually they just—"

"Well, he liked my mother." He didn't say "liked" in a nice way. "And he visited her a lot. He's my sisters' father too. But when he came . . . well, he didn't treat my mother very well. He did some horrible things."

"Like . . ." I hesitated. This was Dimitri's mother we were talking about. I didn't know how far I could go. "Blood-whore things?"

"Like beating-her-up kinds of things," he replied flatly.

He'd finished the bandages but was still holding my hands. I don't even know if he noticed. I certainly did. His were warm and large, with long and graceful fingers. Fingers that might have played the piano in another life.

"Oh God," I said. How horrible. I tightened my hands in his. He squeezed back. "That's horrible. And she . . . she just let it happen?"

"She did." The corner of his mouth turned up into a sly, sad smile. "But I didn't."

Excitement surged through me. "Tell me, *tell me* you beat the crap out of him."

His smile grew. "I did."

"Wow." I hadn't thought Dimitri could be any cooler, but I was wrong. "You beat up your dad. I mean, that's really horrible . . . what happened. But, *wow*. You really are a god."

He blinked. "What?"

"Uh, nothing." Hastily, I tried to change the subject. "How old were you?"

He still seemed to be puzzling out the god comment. "Thirteen."

Whoa. Definitely a god. "You beat up your dad when you were *thirteen*?"

"It wasn't that hard. I was stronger than he was, almost as tall. I couldn't let him keep doing that. He had to learn that being royal and Moroi doesn't mean you can do anything you want to other people—even blood whores."

I stared. I couldn't believe he'd just said that about his mother. "I'm sorry."

"It's all right."

Pieces clicked into place for me. "That's why you got so upset about Jesse, isn't it? He was another royal, trying to take advantage of a dhampir girl."

Dimitri averted his eyes. "I got upset over that for a lot of reasons. After all, you were breaking the rules, and . . ."

He didn't finish, but he looked back into my eyes in a way that made warmth build between us.

Thinking about Jesse soon darkened my mood, unfortunately. I looked down. "I know you heard what people are saying, that I—"

"I know it's not true," he interrupted.

His immediate, certain answer surprised me, and I stupidly found myself questioning it. "Yeah, but how do you—"

"Because I know you," he replied firmly. "I know your character. I know you're going to be a great guardian."

His confidence made that warm feeling return. "I'm glad someone does. Everyone else thinks I'm totally irresponsible."

"With the way you worry more about Lissa than yourself . . ." He shook his head. "No. You understand your responsibilities better than guardians twice your age. You'll do what you have to do to succeed."

I thought about that. "I don't know if I can do everything I have to do."

He did that cool one-eyebrow thing.

"I don't want to cut my hair," I explained.

He looked puzzled. "You don't have to cut your hair. It's not required."

"All the other guardian women do. They show off their tattoos."

Unexpectedly, he released my hands and leaned forward. Slowly, he reached out and held a lock of my hair, twisting it around one finger thoughtfully. I froze, and for a moment, there was nothing going on in the world except him touching my hair. He let my hair go, looking a little surprised—and embarrassed—at what he'd done.

"Don't cut it," he said gruffly.

Somehow, I remembered how to talk again. "But no one'll see my tattoos if I don't."

He moved toward the doorway, a small smile playing over his lips. "Wear it up."

FOURTEEN

I continued spying on Lissa over the next couple of days, feeling mildly guilty each time. She'd always hated it when I did by accident, and now I did it on purpose.

Steadily, I watched as she reintegrated herself into the royal power players one by one. She couldn't do group compulsion, but catching one person alone was just as effective, if slower. And really, a lot didn't need to be compelled to start hanging out with her again. Many weren't as shallow as they seemed; they remembered Lissa and liked her for who she was. They flocked to her, and now, a month and a half after our return to the Academy, it was like she'd never left at all. And during this rise to fame, she advocated for me and rallied against Mia and Jesse.

One morning, I tuned into her while she was getting ready for breakfast. She'd spent the last twenty minutes blow-drying and straightening her hair, something she hadn't done in a while. Natalie, sitting on the bed in their room, watched the process with curiosity. When Lissa moved on to makeup, Natalie finally spoke.

"Hey, we're going to watch a movie in Erin's room after school. You going to come?" I'd always made jokes about Natalie being boring, but her friend Erin had the personality of dry wall.

"Can't. I'm going to help Camille bleach Carly's hair."

"You sure spend a lot of time with them now."

"Yeah, I guess." Lissa dabbed mascara across her lashes, instantly making her eyes look bigger.

"I thought you didn't like them anymore."

"I changed my mind."

"They sure seem to like you a lot now. I mean, not that anyone wouldn't like you, but once you came back and didn't talk to them, they seemed okay ignoring you too. I heard them talking about you a lot. I guess that's not surprising, because they're Mia's friends too, but isn't it weird how much they like you now? Like, I hear them always waiting to see what you want to do before they make plans and stuff. And a bunch of them are defending Rose now, which is *really* crazy. Not that I believe any of that stuff about her, but I never would have thought it was possible—"

Underneath Natalie's rambling was the seed of suspicion, and Lissa picked up on it. Natalie probably never would have dreamed of compulsion, but Lissa couldn't risk innocent questions turning into something more. "You know what?" she interrupted. "Maybe I will swing by Erin's after all. I bet Carly's hair won't take that long."

The offer derailed Natalie's train of thought. "Really? Oh wow, that would be great. She was telling me how sad she was that you're not around as much anymore, and I told her . . ."

On it went. Lissa continued her compulsion and return to popularity. I watched it all quietly, always worrying, even though her efforts were starting to reduce the stares and gossip about me.

"This is going to backfire," I whispered to her in church one day. "Someone's going to start wondering and asking questions."

"Stop being so melodramatic. Power shifts all the time around here."

"Not like this."

"You don't think my winning personality could do this on its own?"

"Of course I do, but if Christian spotted *it* right away, then someone else will—"

My words were interrupted when two guys farther down the pew suddenly exploded into snickers. Glancing up, I saw them looking right at me, not even bothering to hide their smirks.

Looking away, I tried to ignore them, suddenly hoping the priest would start up soon. But Lissa returned their looks, and a sudden fierceness flashed across her face. She didn't say a word, but their smiles grew smaller under her heavy gaze.

"Tell her you're sorry," she told them. "And make sure she believes it."

A moment later, they practically fell all over themselves apologizing to me and begging for forgiveness. I couldn't believe it. She'd used compulsion in public—in church, of all places. *And* on two people at the same time.

They finally exhausted their supply of apologies, but Lissa wasn't finished.

"That's the *best* you can do?" she snapped.

Their eyes widened in alarm, both terrified that they'd angered her.

"Liss," I said quickly, touching her arm. "It's okay. I, uh, accept their apologies."

Her face still radiated disapproval, but she finally nodded. The guys slumped in relief.

Yikes. I'd never felt so relieved to have a service start. Through the bond, I felt a sort of dark satisfaction coming from Lissa. It was uncharacteristic for her, and I didn't like it.

Needing to distract myself from her troubling behavior, I studied other people as I so often did. Nearby, Christian openly watched Lissa, a troubled look on his face. When he saw me, he scowled and turned away.

Dimitri sat in the back as usual, for once not scanning every corner for danger. His attention was turned inward, his expression almost pained. I still didn't know why he came to church. He always seemed to be wrestling with something.

In the front, the priest was talking about St. Vladimir again.

"His spirit was strong, and he was truly gifted by God. When he touched them, the crippled walked, and the blind could see. Where he walked, flowers bloomed."

Man, the Moroi needed to get more saints—

Healing cripples and blind people?

I'd forgotten all about St. Vladimir. Mason had mentioned Vladimir bringing people back from the dead, and it had reminded me of Lissa at the time. Then other things had distracted me. I hadn't thought about the saint or his "shadow-kissed" guardian—and their bond—in a while. How could I have overlooked this? Ms. Karp, I realized, wasn't the only other Moroi who could heal like Lissa. Vladimir could too.

"And all the while, the masses gathered to him, loving him, eager to follow his teachings and hear him preach the word of God. . . ."

Turning, I stared at Lissa. She gave me a puzzled look. "What?"

I didn't get a chance to elaborate—I don't even know if I could have formed the words—because I was whisked back to my prison almost as soon as I stood up at the end of the service.

Back in my room, I went online to research St. Vladimir but turned up nothing useful. Damn it. Mason had skimmed the books in the library and said there was little there. What did that leave me with? I had no way of learning more about that dusty old saint.

Or did I? What had Christian said that first day with Lissa?

Over there, we have an old box full of the writings of the blessed and crazy St. Vladimir.

The storage room above the chapel. It had the writings. Christian had pointed them out. I needed to look at them, but how? I couldn't ask the priest. How would he react if he found out students were going up there? It'd put an end to Christian's lair. But maybe . . . maybe Christian himself could help.

It was Sunday, though, and I wouldn't see him until tomorrow afternoon. Even then, I didn't know if I'd get a chance to talk to him alone.

While heading out to practice later, I stopped in the dorm's kitchen to grab a granola bar. As I did, I passed a couple of novice guys, Miles and Anthony. Miles whistled when he saw me.

"How's it been going, Rose? You getting lonely? Want some company?"

Anthony laughed. "I can't bite you, but I can give you something else you want."

I had to pass through the doorway they stood in to get outside. Glaring, I pushed past, but Miles caught me around the waist, his hand sliding down to my butt.

"Get your hands off my ass before I break your face," I told him, jerking away. In doing so, I only bumped into Anthony.

"Come on," Anthony said, "I thought you didn't have a problem taking on two guys at the same time."

A new voice spoke up. "If you guys don't walk away right now, I'll take both of you on." Mason. My hero.

"You're so full of it, Ashford," said Miles. He was the bigger of the two and left me to go square off with Mason. Anthony backed off from me, more interested in whether or not there'd be a fight. There was so much testosterone in the air, I felt like I needed a gas mask.

"Are you doing her too?" Miles asked Mason. "You don't want to share?"

"Say one more word about her, and I'll rip your head off."

"Why? She's just a cheap blood—"

Mason punched him. It didn't rip Miles' head off or even cause anything to break or bleed, but it looked like it hurt. His eyes widened, and he lunged toward Mason. The sound of doors opening in the hall caused everyone to freeze. Novices got in a lot of trouble for fighting.

"Probably some guardians coming." Mason grinned. "You want them to know you were beating up on a girl?"

Miles and Anthony exchanged glances. "Come on," Anthony said. "Let's go. We don't have time for this."

Miles reluctantly followed. "I'll find you later, Ashford."

When they were gone, I turned on Mason. "'Beat up on a girl'?"

"You're welcome," he said drily.

"I didn't need your help."

"Sure. You were doing just fine on your own."

"They caught me off guard, that's all. I could have dealt with them eventually."

"Look, don't take being pissed off at them out on me."

"I just don't like being treated like . . . a girl."

"You *are* a girl. And I was just trying to help."

I looked at him and saw the earnestness on his face. He meant well. No point in being a bitch to him when I had so many other people to hate lately.

"Well . . . thanks. Sorry I snapped at you."

We talked a little bit, and I managed to get him to spill some more school gossip. He had noticed Lissa's rise in status but didn't seem to find it strange. As I talked to him, I noticed the adoring look he always got around me spread across his face. It made me sad to have him feel that way about me. Guilty, even.

How hard would it be, I wondered, to go out with him? He was nice, funny, and reasonably good-looking. We got along. Why did I get caught up in so many messes with other guys when I had a perfectly sweet one here who wanted me? Why couldn't I just return his feelings?

The answer came to me before I'd even finished asking myself the question. I couldn't be Mason's girlfriend because when I imagined someone holding me and whispering dirty things in my ear, he had a Russian accent.

Mason continued watching me admiringly, oblivious to what was going on in my head. And seeing that adoration, I suddenly realized how I could use it to my advantage.

Feeling a little guilty, I shifted my conversation to a more flirty style and watched Mason's glow increase.

I leaned beside him on the wall so our arms just touched and gave him a lazy smile. "You know, I still don't approve of your whole hero thing, but you did scare them. That was almost worth it."

"But you don't approve?"

I trailed fingers up his arm. "No. I mean, it's hot in principle but not in practice."

He laughed. "The hell it isn't." He caught hold of my hand and gave me a knowing look. "Sometimes you need to be saved.

I think you like being saved sometimes and just can't admit it."

"And I think *you* get óff on saving people and just can't admit it."

"I don't think you know what gets me off. Saving damsels like you is just the honorable thing to do," he declared loftily.

I repressed the urge to smack him over the use of *damsels*. "Then prove it. Do me a favor just because it's 'the right thing to do.'"

"Sure," he said immediately. "Name it."

"I need you to get a message to Christian Ozera."

His eagerness faltered. "What the—? You aren't serious."

"Yes. Completely."

"Rose . . . I can't talk to him. You know that."

"I thought you said you'd help. I thought you said helping 'damsels' is the honorable thing to do."

"I don't really see how honor's involved here." I gave him the most smoldering look I could manage. He caved. "What do you want me to tell him?"

"Tell him I need St. Vladimir's books. The ones in storage. He needs to sneak them to me soon. Tell him it's for Lissa. And tell him . . . tell him I lied the night of the reception." I hesitated. "Tell him I'm sorry."

"That doesn't make any sense."

"It doesn't have to. Just do it. Please?" I turned on the beauty queen smile again.

With hasty assurances that he'd see what he could do, he left for lunch, and I went off to practice.

FIFTEEN

Mason delivered.

He found me the next day before school. He was carrying a box of books.

"I got them," he said. "Hurry and take them before you get in trouble for talking to me."

He handed them over, and I grunted. They were heavy. "Christian gave you these?"

"Yeah. Managed to talk to him without anyone noticing. He's got kind of an attitude, did you ever notice that?"

"Yeah, I noticed." I rewarded Mason with a smile that he ate up. "Thanks. This means a lot."

I hauled the loot up to my room, fully aware of how weird it was that someone who hated to study as much as I did was about to get buried in dusty crap from the fourteenth century. When I opened the first book, though, I saw that these must be reprints of reprints of reprints, probably because anything that old would have long since fallen apart.

Sifting through the books, I discovered they fell into three categories: books written by people after St. Vladimir had died, books written by other people when he was still alive, and one diary of sorts written by him. What had Mason said about primary and secondary sources? Those last two groups were the ones I wanted.

Whoever had reprinted these had reworded the books enough so that I didn't have to read Ye Olde English or anything. Or rather, Russian, I supposed. St. Vladimir had lived in the old country.

Today I healed the mother of Sava who has long since suffered from sharp pains within her stomach. Her malady is now gone, but God has not allowed me to do such a thing lightly. I am weak and dizzy, and the madness is trying to leak into my head. I thank God every day for shadow-kissed Anna, for without her, I would surely not be able to endure.

Anna again. And "shadow-kissed." He talked about her a lot, among other things. Most of the time he wrote long sermons, just like what I'd hear in church. Super boring. But other times, the book read just like a diary, recapping what he did each day. And if it really wasn't just a load of crap, he healed all the time. Sick people. Injured people. Even plants. He brought dead crops back to life when people were starving. Sometimes he would make flowers bloom just for the hell of it.

Reading on, I found out that it was a good thing old Vlad had Anna around, because he was pretty messed up. The more he used his powers, the more they started to get to him. He'd get irrationally angry and sad. He blamed it on demons and stupid stuff like that, but it was obvious he suffered from depression. Once, he admitted in his diary, he tried to kill himself. Anna stopped him.

Later, browsing through the book written by the guy who knew Vladimir, I read:

And many think it miraculous too, the power the blessed Vladimir shows over others. Moroi and dhampirs flock to him and listen to his words, happy just to be near him. Some say it is madness that touches him and not spirit, but most adore him and would do anything he asked. Such is the way God marks his favorites, and if such moments are followed by hallucinations and despair, it is a small sacrifice for the amount of good and leadership he can show among the people.

It sounded a lot like what the priest had said, but I sensed more than just a "winning personality." People adored him, would do anything he asked. Yes, Vladimir had used compulsion on his followers, I was certain. A lot of Moroi had in those days, before it was banned, but they didn't use it on Moroi or dhampirs. They couldn't. Only Lissa could.

I shut the book and leaned back against my bed. Vladimir healed plants and animals. He could use compulsion on a massive scale. And by all accounts, using those sorts of powers had made him crazy and depressed.

Added into it all, making it that much weirder was that everyone kept describing his guardian as "shadow-kissed." That expression had bugged me ever since I first heard it. . . .

"You're *shadow-kissed*! You have to take care of her!"

Ms. Karp had shouted those words at me, her hands

clenching my shirt and jerking me toward her. It had happened on a night two years ago when I'd been inside the main part of the upper school to return a book. It was nearly past curfew, and the halls were empty. I'd heard a loud commotion, and then Ms. Karp had come tearing around the corner, looking frantic and wild-eyed.

She shoved me into a wall, still gripping me. "Do you understand?"

I knew enough self-defense that I could have probably pushed her away, but my shock kept me frozen. "No."

"They're coming for me. They'll come for her."

"Who?"

"Lissa. You have to protect her. The more she uses it, the worse it'll get. Stop her, Rose. Stop her before they notice, before they notice and take her away too. Get her out of here."

"I . . . what do you mean? Get her out of . . . you mean the Academy?"

"Yes! You have to leave. You're bound. It's up to you. Take her away from this place."

Her words were crazy. No one left the Academy. Yet as she held me there and stared into my eyes, I began to feel strange. A fuzzy feeling clouded my mind. What she said suddenly sounded very reasonable, like the most reasonable thing in the world. Yes. I needed to take Lissa away, take her—

Feet pounded in the hallway, and a group of guardians rounded the corner. I didn't recognize them; they weren't from the school. They pried her off of me, restraining her wild thrashing. Someone asked me if I was okay, but I could only keep staring at Ms. Karp.

"Don't let her use the power!" she screamed. "Save her. Save her from herself!"

The guardians had later explained to me that she wasn't well and had been taken to a place where she could recover. She would be safe and cared for, they assured me. She would recover.

Only she hadn't.

Back in the present, I stared at the books and tried to put it all together. Lissa. Ms. Karp. St. Vladimir.

What was I supposed to do?

Someone rapped at my door, and I jerked out of my memories. No one had visited me, not even staff, since my suspension. When I opened the door, I saw Mason in the hall.

"Twice in one day?" I asked. "And how'd you even get up here?"

He flashed his easy smile. "Someone put a lit match in one of the bathroom's garbage cans. Damn shame. The staff's kind of busy. Come on, I'm springing you."

I shook my head. Setting fires was apparently a new sign of affection. Christian had done it and now Mason. "Sorry, no saving me tonight. If I get caught—"

"Lissa's orders."

I shut up and let him smuggle me out of the building. He took me over to the Moroi dorm and miraculously got me in

and up to her room unseen. I wondered if there was a distract-
ing bathroom fire in this building too.

Inside her room, I found a party in full swing. Lissa, Camille,
Carly, Aaron, and a few other royals sat around laughing, listening to loud music, and passing around bottles of whiskey.
No Mia, no Jesse. Natalie, I noticed a few moments later, sat
apart from the group, clearly unsure how to act around all of
them. Her awkwardness was totally obvious.

Lissa stumbled to her feet, the fuzzy feelings in our bond
indicating she'd been drinking for a while. "Rose!" She turned
to Mason with a dazzling smile. "You delivered."

He swept her an over-the-top bow. "I'm at your command."

I hoped he'd done it for the thrill of it and not because of
any compulsion. Lissa slung an arm around my waist and
pulled me down with the others. "Join the festivities."

"What are we celebrating?"

"I don't know. Your escape tonight?"

A few of the others held up plastic cups, cheering and
toasting me. Xander Badica poured two more cups, handing them to Mason and me. I took mine with a smile, all the
while feeling uneasy about the night's turn of events. Not so
long ago, I would have welcomed a party like this and would
have downed my drink in thirty seconds. Too much bothered
me this time, though. Like the fact that the royals were treat-
ing Lissa like a goddess. Like how none of them seemed to
remember that I had been accused of being a blood whore.

Like how Lissa was completely unhappy despite her smiles and laughter.

"Where'd you get the whiskey?" I asked.

"Mr. Nagy," Aaron said. He sat very close to Lissa.

Everyone knew Mr. Nagy drank all the time after school and kept a stash on campus. He continually used new hiding places—and students continually found them.

Lissa leaned against Aaron's shoulder. "Aaron helped me break into his room and take them. He had them hidden in the bottom of the paint closet."

The others laughed, and Aaron gazed at her with complete and utter worship. Amusingly, I realized she hadn't had to use any compulsion on him. He was just that crazy for her. He always had been.

"Why aren't you drinking?" Mason asked me a little while later, speaking quietly into my ear.

I glanced down at my cup, half surprised to see it full. "I don't know. I guess I don't think guardians should drink around their charges."

"She's not your charge yet! You aren't on duty. You won't be for a long time. Since when did you get so responsible?"

I didn't really think I was all that responsible. But I *was* thinking about what Dimitri had said about balancing fun and obligation. It just seemed wrong to let myself go wild when Lissa was in such a vulnerable state lately. Wiggling out of my tight spot between her and Mason, I walked over and sat beside Natalie.

"Hey Nat, you're quiet tonight."

She held a cup as full as mine. "So are you."

I laughed softly. "I guess so."

She tilted her head, watching Mason and the royals like they were some sort of science experiment. They'd consumed a lot more whiskey since I'd arrived, and the silliness had shot up considerably. "Weird, huh? You used to be the center of attention. Now she is."

I blinked in surprise. I hadn't considered it like that. "I guess so."

"Hey, Rose," said Xander, nearly spilling his drink as he walked over to me. "What was it like?"

"What was what like?"

"Letting someone feed off you?"

The others fell quiet, a sort of anticipation settling over them.

"She didn't do that," said Lissa in a warning voice. "I told you."

"Yeah, yeah, I know nothing happened with Jesse and Ralf. But you guys did it, right? While you were gone?"

"Let it go," said Lissa. Compulsion worked best with direct eye contact, and his attention was focused on me, not her.

"I mean, it's cool and everything. You guys did what you had to do, right? It's not like you're a feeder. I just want to know what it was like. Danielle Szelsky let me bite her once. She said it didn't feel like anything."

There was a collective "ew" from among the girls. Sex and

blood with dhampirs was dirty; between Moroi, it was cannibalistic.

"You are such a liar," said Camille.

"No, I'm serious. It was just a small bite. She didn't get high like the feeders. Did *you*?" He put his free arm around my shoulder. "Did you like it?"

Lissa's face went still and pale. Alcohol muted the full force of her feelings, but I could read enough to know how she felt. Dark, scared thoughts trickled into me—underscored with anger. She usually had a good grip on her temper—unlike me—but I'd seen it flare up before. Once it had happened at a party very similar to this one, just a few weeks after Ms. Karp had been taken away.

Greg Dashkov—a distant cousin of Natalie's—had held the party in his room. His parents apparently knew someone who knew someone, because he had one of the biggest rooms in the dorm. He'd been friends with Lissa's brother before the accident and had been more than happy to take Andre's little sister into his social fold. Greg had also been happy to take me in, and the two of us had been all over each other that night. For a sophomore like me, being with a royal Moroi senior was a huge rush.

I drank a lot that night but still managed to keep an eye on Lissa. She always wore an edge of anxiety around this many people, but no one really noticed, because she could interact with them so well. My heavy buzz kept a lot of her feelings from me, but as long as she looked okay, I didn't worry.

Mid-kiss, Greg suddenly broke away and looked at something over my shoulder. We both sat in the same chair, with me on his lap, and I craned my neck to see. "What is it?"

He shook his head with a sort of amused exasperation. "Wade brought a feeder."

I followed his gaze to where Wade Voda stood with his arm around a frail girl about my age. She was human and pretty, with wavy blond hair and porcelain skin pale from so much blood loss. A few other guys had homed on her and stood with Wade, laughing and touching her face and hair.

"She's already fed too much today," I said, observing her coloring and complete look of confusion.

Greg slid his hand behind my neck and turned me back to him. "They won't hurt her."

We kissed a while longer and then I felt a tap on my shoulder. "Rose."

I looked up into Lissa's face. Her anxious expression startled me because I couldn't feel the emotions behind it. Too much beer for me. I climbed off of Greg's lap.

"Where are you going?" he asked.

"Be right back." I pulled Lissa aside, suddenly wishing I was sober. "What's wrong?"

"Them."

She nodded toward the guys with the feeder girl. She still had a group around her, and when she shifted to look at one of them, I saw small red wounds scattered on her neck. They were doing a sort of group feeding, taking turns biting her and making gross suggestions. High and oblivious, she let them.

"They can't do that," Lissa told me.

"She's a feeder. Nobody's going to stop them."

Lissa looked up at me with pleading eyes. Hurt, outrage, and anger filled them. "Will *you*?"

I'd always been the aggressive one, looking after her ever since we were little. Seeing her there now, so upset and looking at me to fix things, was more than I could stand. Giving her a shaky nod, I stumbled over to the group.

"You so desperate to get some that you've got to drug girls now, Wade?" I asked.

He glanced up from where he'd been running his lips over the human girl's neck. "Why? Are you done with Greg and looking for more?"

I put my hands on my hips and hoped I looked fierce. The truth was, I was actually starting to feel a little nauseous from all I'd drunk. "Aren't enough drugs in the world to get me near you," I told him. A few of his friends laughed. "But maybe you can go make out with that lamp over there. It seems to be out of it enough to make even you happy. You don't need *her* anymore." A few other people laughed.

"This isn't any of your business," he hissed. "She's just lunch." Referring to feeders as meals was about the only thing worse than calling dhampirs blood whores.

"This isn't a feeding room. Nobody wants to see this."

"Yeah," agreed a senior girl. "It's gross." A few of her friends agreed.

Wade glared at all of us, me the hardest. "Fine. None of you have to see it. Come on." He grabbed the feeder girl's arm and jerked her away. Clumsily, she stumbled along with him out of the room, making soft whimpering noises.

"Best I could do," I told Lissa.

She stared at me, shocked. "He's just going to take her to his room. He'll do even worse things to her."

"Liss, I don't like it either, but it's not like I can go chase him down or anything." I rubbed my forehead. "I could go punch him or something, but I feel like I'm going to throw up as it is."

Her face grew dark, and she bit her lip. "He can't do that."

"I'm sorry."

I returned to the chair with Greg, feeling a little bad about what had happened. I didn't want to see the feeder get taken advantage of any more than Lissa did—it reminded me too much of what a lot of Moroi guys thought they could do to dhampir girls. But I also couldn't win this battle, not tonight.

Greg had shifted me around to get a better angle on my neck when I noticed Lissa was gone a few minutes later. Practically falling, I clambered off his lap and looked around. "Where's Lissa?"

He reached for me. "Probably the bathroom."

I couldn't feel a thing through the bond. The alcohol had numbed it. Stepping out into the hallway, I breathed a sigh of relief at escaping the loud music and voices. It was quiet out here—except for a crashing sound a couple rooms down. The door was ajar, and I pushed my way inside.

The feeder girl cowered in a corner, terrified. Lissa stood with arms crossed, her face angry and terrible. She was staring at Wade intently, and he stared back, enchanted. He also held a baseball bat, and it looked like he'd used it already, because the room was trashed: bookshelves, the stereo, the mirror. . . .

"Break the window too," Lissa told him smoothly. "Come on. It doesn't matter."

Hypnotized, he walked over to the large, tinted window. I stared, my mouth nearly hitting the floor, as he pulled back and slammed the bat into the glass. It shattered, sending shards everywhere and letting in the early morning light it normally kept blocked out. He winced as it shone in his eyes, but he didn't move away.

"Lissa," I exclaimed. "Stop it. Make him stop."

"He should have stopped earlier."

I barely recognized the look on her face. I'd never seen her so upset, and I'd certainly never seen her do anything like this. I knew what it was, of course. I knew right away. Compulsion. For all I knew, she was seconds away from having him turn the bat on himself.

"Please, Lissa. Don't do it anymore. Please."

Through the fuzzy, alcoholic buzz, I felt a trickle of her emotions. They were strong enough to practically knock me over. Black. Angry. Merciless. Startling feelings to be coming from sweet and steady Lissa. I'd known her since kindergarten, but in that moment, I barely knew her.

And I was afraid.

"Please, Lissa," I repeated. "He's not worth it. Let him go."

She didn't look at me. Her stormy eyes were focused entirely on Wade. Slowly, carefully, he lifted up the bat, tilting it so that it lined up with his own skull.

"Liss," I begged. Oh God. I was going to have to tackle her or something to make her stop. "Don't do it."

"He should have stopped," Lissa said evenly. The bat quit moving. It was now at exactly the right distance to gain momentum and strike. "He shouldn't have done that to her. People can't treat other people like that—even feeders."

"But you're scaring her," I said softly. "Look at her."

Nothing happened at first, then Lissa let her gaze flick toward the feeder. The human girl still sat huddled in a corner, arms wrapped around herself protectively. Her blue eyes were enormous, and light reflected off her wet, tear-streaked face. She gave a choked, terrified sob.

Lissa's face stayed impassive. Inside her, I could feel the battle she was waging for control. Some part of her didn't want to hurt Wade, despite the blinding anger that otherwise filled her. Her face crumpled, and she squeezed her eyes shut. Her right hand reached out to her left wrist and clenched it, nails digging deep into the flesh. She flinched at the pain, but through the bond, I felt the shock of the pain distract her from Wade.

She let go of the compulsion, and he dropped the bat, suddenly looking confused. I let go of the breath I'd been holding. In the hallway, footsteps sounded. I'd left the door open, and the crash had attracted attention. A couple of dorm staff members burst into the room, freezing when they saw the destruction in front of them.

"What happened?"

The rest of us looked at each other. Wade looked completely lost. He stared at the room, at the bat, and then at Lissa and me. "I don't know. . . . I can't . . ." He turned his full attention to me and suddenly grew angry. "What the—it was you! You wouldn't let the feeder thing go."

The dorm workers looked at me questioningly, and in a few seconds, I made up my mind.

You have to protect her. The more she uses it, the worse it'll get. Stop her, Rose. Stop her before they notice, before they notice and take her away too. Get her out of here.

I could see Ms. Karp's face in my mind, pleading frantically. I gave Wade a haughty look, knowing full well no one would question a confession I made or even suspect Lissa.

"Yeah, well, if you'd let her go," I told him, "I wouldn't have had to do this."

Save her. Save her from herself.

After that night, I never drank again. I refused to let my guard down around Lissa. And two days later, while I was supposed to be suspended for "destruction of property," I took Lissa and broke out of the Academy.

Back in Lissa's room, with Xander's arm around me and her angry and upset eyes on us, I didn't know if she'd do anything drastic again. But the situation reminded me too much of that one from two years ago, and I knew I had to defuse it.

"Just a little blood," Xander was saying. "I won't take much. I just want to see what dhampir tastes like. Nobody here cares."

"Xander," growled Lissa, "leave her alone."

I slipped out from under his arm and smiled, looking for a funny retort rather than one that might start a fight. "Come on," I teased. "I had to hit the last guy who asked me that, and you're a hell of a lot prettier than Jesse. It'd be a waste."

"Pretty?" he asked. "I'm stunningly sexy but not *pretty*."

Carly laughed. "No, you're pretty. Todd told me you buy some kind of French hair gel."

Xander, distracted as so many drunk people easily are, turned around to defend his honor, forgetting me. The tension disappeared, and he took the teasing about his hair with a good attitude.

Across the room, Lissa met my eyes with relief. She smiled and gave me a small nod of thanks before she returned her attention to Aaron.

SIXTEEN

The next day, it fully hit me how much things had changed since the Jesse-and-Ralf rumors first started. For some people, I remained a nonstop source of whispers and laughter. From Lissa's converts, I received friendliness and occasional defense. Overall, I realized, our classmates actually gave me very little of their attention anymore. This became especially true when something new distracted everyone.

Lissa and Aaron.

Apparently, Mia had found about the party and had blown up when she learned that Aaron had been there without her. She'd bitched at him and told him that if he wanted to be with her, he couldn't run around and hang out with Lissa. So Aaron had decided he didn't want to be with her. He'd broken up with her that morning . . . and moved on.

Now he and Lissa were all over each other. They stood around in the hall and at lunch, arms wrapped around one another, laughing and talking. Lissa's bond feelings showed only mild interest, despite her gazing at him as though he was the most fascinating thing on the planet. Most of this was for show, unbeknownst to him. He looked as though he could have built a shrine at her feet at any moment.

And me? I felt ill.

My feelings were nothing, however, compared to Mia's. At lunch, she sat on the far side of the room from us, eyes fixed pointedly ahead, ignoring the consolations of the friends near her. She had blotchy pink patches on her pale, round cheeks, and her eyes were red-rimmed. She said nothing mean when I walked past. No smug jokes. No mocking glares. Lissa had destroyed her, just as Mia had vowed to do us.

The only person more miserable than Mia was Christian. Unlike her, he had no qualms about studying the happy couple while wearing an open look of hatred on his face. As usual, no one except me even noticed.

After watching Lissa and Aaron make out for the tenth time, I left lunch early and went to see Ms. Carmack, the teacher who taught elemental basics. I'd been wanting to ask her something for a while.

"Rose, right?" She seemed surprised to see me but not angry or annoyed like half the other teachers did lately.

"Yeah. I have a question about, um, magic."

She raised an eyebrow. Novices didn't take magic classes. "Sure. What do you want to know?"

"I was listening to the priest talk about St. Vladimir the other day. . . . Do you know what element he specialized in? Vladimir, I mean. Not the priest."

She frowned. "Odd. As famous as he is around here, I'm surprised it never comes up. I'm no expert, but in all the stories I've heard, he never did anything that I'd say connects to any one of the elements. Either that or no one ever recorded it."

"What about his healings?" I pushed further. "Is there an element that lets you perform those?"

"No, not that I know of." Her lips quirked into a small smile. "People of faith would say he healed through the power of God, not any sort of elemental magic. After all, one thing the stories are certain about is that he was 'full of spirit.'"

"Is it possible he didn't specialize?"

Her smile faded. "Rose, is this really about St. Vladimir? Or is it about Lissa?"

"Not exactly . . ." I stammered.

"I know it's hard on her—especially in front of all her classmates—but she has to be patient," she explained gently. "It will happen. It always happens."

"But sometimes it doesn't."

"Rarely. But I don't think she'll be one of those. She's got a higher-than-average aptitude in all four, even if she hasn't hit specialized levels. One of them will shoot up any day now."

That gave me an idea. "Is it possible to specialize in more than one element?"

She laughed and shook her head. "No. Too much power. No one could handle all that magic, not without losing her mind."

Oh. Great.

"Okay. Thanks." I started to leave, then thought of something else. "Hey, do you remember Ms. Karp? What did she specialize in?"

Ms. Carmack got that uncomfortable look other teachers

did whenever anyone mentioned Ms. Karp. "Actually—"

"What?"

"I almost forgot. I think she really was one of the rare ones who never specialized. She just always kept a very low control over all four."

I spent the rest of my afternoon classes thinking about Ms. Carmack's words, trying to work them into my unified Lissa-Karp-Vladimir theory. I also watched Lissa. So many people wanted to talk to her now that she barely noticed my silence. Every so often, though, I'd see her glance at me and smile, a tired look in her eyes. Laughing and gossiping all day with people she only sort of liked was taking its toll on her.

"The mission's accomplished," I told her after school. "We can stop Project Brainwash."

We sat on benches in the courtyard, and she swung her legs back and forth. "What do you mean?"

"You've done it. You stopped people from making my life horrible. You destroyed Mia. You stole Aaron. Play with him for another couple weeks, then drop him and the other royals. You'll be happier."

"You don't think I'm happy now?"

"I know you aren't. Some of the parties are fun, but you hate pretending to be friends with people you don't like—and you don't like most of them. I know how much Xander pissed you off the other night."

"He's a jerk, but I can deal with that. If I stop hanging out with them, everything'll go back to the way it was. Mia will just start up again. This way, she can't bother us."

"It's not worth it if everything else is bothering you."

"Nothing's bothering me." She sounded a little defensive.

"Yeah?" I asked meanly. "Because you're so in love with Aaron? Because you can't wait to have sex with him again?"

She glared at me. "Have I mentioned you can be a huge bitch sometimes?"

I ignored that. "I'm just saying you've got enough shit to worry about without all this. You're burning yourself out with all the compulsion you're using."

"Rose!" She glanced anxiously around. "Be quiet!"

"But it's true. Using it all the time is going to screw with your head. For real."

"Don't you think you're getting carried away?"

"What about Ms. Karp?"

Lissa's expression went very still. "What about her?"

"You. You're just like her."

"No, I'm not!" Outrage flashed in those green eyes.

"She healed too."

Hearing me talk about this shocked her. This topic had weighed us down for so long, but we'd almost never spoken about it.

"That doesn't mean anything."

"You don't think it does? Do you know anyone else who can do that? Or can use compulsion on dhampirs *and* Moroi?"

"She never used compulsion like that," she argued.

"She did. She tried to use it on me the night she left. It started to work, but then they took her away before she finished." Or had they? After all, it was only a month later that Lissa and I had run away from the Academy. I'd always thought that was my own idea, but maybe Ms. Karp's suggestion had been the true force behind it.

Lissa crossed her arms. Her face looked defiant, but her emotions felt uneasy. "Fine. So what? So she's a freak like me. That doesn't mean anything. She went crazy because . . . well, that was just the way she was. That's got nothing to do with anything else."

"But it's not just her," I said slowly. "There's someone else like you guys, too. Someone I found." I hesitated. "You know St. Vladimir. . . ."

And that's when I finally let it all out. I told her everything. I told her about how she, Ms. Karp, and St. Vladimir could all heal and use super-compulsion. Although it made her squirm, I told her how they too grew easily upset and had tried to hurt themselves.

"He tried to kill himself," I said, not meeting her eyes. "And I used to notice marks on Ms. Karp's skin—like she'd claw at her own face. She tried to hide it with her hair, but I could see the old scratches and tell when she made new ones."

"It doesn't mean *anything*," insisted Lissa. "It—it's all a coincidence."

She sounded like she wanted to believe that, and inside,

some part of her really did. But there was another part of her, a desperate part of her that had wanted for so long to know that she wasn't a freak, that she wasn't alone. Even if the news was bad, at least now she knew there were others like her.

"Is it a coincidence that neither of them seems to have specialized?"

I recounted my conversation with Ms. Carmack and explained my theory about specializing in all four elements. I also repeated Ms. Carmack's comment about how that would burn someone out.

Lissa rubbed her eyes when I finished, smudging a little of her makeup. She gave me a weak smile. "I don't know what's crazier: what you're actually telling me or the fact that you actually *read* something to find all this out."

I grinned, relieved that she'd actually mustered a joke. "Hey, I know how to read too."

"I know you do. I also know it took you a year to read *The Da Vinci Code*." She laughed.

"That wasn't my fault! And don't try to change the subject."

"I'm not." She smiled, then sighed. "I just don't know what to think about all this."

"There's nothing to think about. Just don't do stuff that'll upset you. Remember coasting through the middle? Go back to that. It's a lot easier on you."

She shook her head. "I can't do that. Not yet."

"Why not? I already told you—" I stopped, wondering

why I hadn't caught on before. "It's not just Mia. You're doing all this because you feel like you're *supposed* to. You're still trying to be Andre."

"My parents would have wanted me to—"

"Your parents would have wanted you to be happy."

"It's not that easy, Rose. I can't ignore these people forever. I'm royal too."

"Most of them suck."

"And a lot of them are going to help rule the Moroi. Andre knew that. He wasn't like the others, but he did what he had to do because he knew how important they were."

I leaned back against the bench. "Well, maybe that's the problem. We're deciding who's 'important' based on family alone, so we end up with these screwed-up people making decisions. That's why Moroi numbers are dropping and bitches like Tatiana are queen. Maybe there needs to be a new royal system."

"Come on, Rose. This is the way it is; that's the way it's been for centuries. We have to live with that." I glared. "Okay, how about this?" she continued. "You're worried about me becoming like *them*—like Ms. Karp and St. Vladimir—right? Well, she said I shouldn't use the powers, that it would make things get worse if I did. What if I just stop? Compulsion, healing, everything."

I narrowed my eyes. "You could do that?" The convenient compulsion aside, that was what I'd wanted her to do the whole time. Her depression had started at the same time the powers emerged, just after the accident. I had to believe they were connected, particularly in light of the evidence and Ms. Karp's warnings.

"Yes."

Her face was perfectly composed, her expression serious and steady. With her pale hair woven into a neat French braid and a suede blazer over her dress, she looked like she could have taken her family's place on the council right now.

"You'd have to give up everything," I warned. "No healing, no matter how cute and cuddly the animal. And no more compulsion to dazzle the royals."

She nodded seriously. "I can do it. Will that make you feel better?"

"Yeah, but I'd feel even better if you stopped magic *and* went back to hanging out with Natalie."

"I know, I know. But I can't stop, not now at least."

I couldn't get her to budge on that—*yet*—but knowing that she would avoid using her powers relieved me.

"All right," I said, picking up my backpack. I was late for practice. Again. "You can keep playing with the brat pack, so long as you keep the 'other stuff' in check." I hesitated. "And you know, you really have made your point with Aaron and Mia. You don't have to keep him around to keep hanging out with the royals."

"Why do I keep getting the feeling you don't like him anymore?"

"I like him okay—which is about as much as you like him.

And I don't think you should get hot and sweaty with people you only like 'okay.'"

Lissa widened her eyes in pretend astonishment. "Is this Rose Hathaway talking? Have you reformed? Or do *you* have someone you like 'more than okay'?"

"Hey," I said uncomfortably, "I'm just looking out for you. That, and I never noticed how boring Aaron is before."

She scoffed. "You think everyone's boring."

"Christian isn't."

It slipped out before I could stop it. She quit smiling. "He's a *jerk*. He just stopped talking to me for no reason one day." She crossed her arms. "And don't you hate him anyway?"

"I can still hate him and think he's interesting."

But I was also starting to think that I might have made a big mistake about Christian. He was creepy and dark and liked to set people on fire, true. On the other hand, he was smart and funny—in a twisted way—and somehow had a calming effect on Lissa.

But I'd messed it all up. I'd let my anger and jealousy get the best of me and ended up separating them. If I'd let him go to her in the garden that night, maybe she wouldn't have gotten upset and cut herself. Maybe they'd be together now, away from all the school politics.

Fate must have been thinking the same thing, because five minutes after I left Lissa, I passed Christian walking across the quad. Our eyes locked for a moment before we passed each other. I nearly kept walking. Nearly. Taking a deep breath, I came to a stop.

"Wait . . . Christian." I called out to him. Damn, I was so late for training. Dimitri was going to kill me.

Christian spun around to face me, hands stuffed in the pockets of his long black coat, his posture slumped and uncaring.

"Yeah?"

"Thanks for the books." He didn't say anything. "The ones you gave to Mason."

"Oh, I thought you meant the other books."

Smartass. "Aren't you going to ask what they were for?"

"Your business. Just figured you were bored being suspended."

"I'd have to be pretty bored for that."

He didn't laugh at my joke. "What do you want, Rose? I've got places to be."

I knew he was lying, but my sarcasm no longer seemed as funny as usual. "I want you to, uh, hang out with Lissa again."

"Are you *serious*?" He studied me closely, suspicion all over him. "After what you said to me?"

"Yeah, well . . . Didn't Mason tell you? . . ."

Christian's lips turned up into a sneer. "He told me something."

"And?"

"And I don't want to hear it from Mason." His sneer

cranked up when I glared. "You sent him to apologize for you. Step up and do it yourself."

"You're a jerk," I informed him.

"Yeah. And you're a liar. I want to see you eat your pride."

"I've been eating my pride for two weeks," I growled.

Shrugging, he turned around and started to walk away.

"Wait!" I called, putting my hand on his shoulder. He stopped and looked back at me. "All right, all right. I lied about how she felt. She never said any of that stuff about you, okay? She *likes* you. I made it up because *I* don't like you."

"And yet you want me to talk to her."

When the next words left my lips, I could barely believe it. "I think . . . you might be . . . good for her."

We stared at each other for several heavy moments. His smirk dried up a little. Not much surprised him. This did.

"I'm sorry. I didn't hear you. Can you repeat that?" he finally asked.

I almost punched him in the face. "Will you stop it already? I want you to hang out with her again."

"No."

"Look, I told you, I lied—"

"It's not that. It's *her*. You think I can talk to her now? She's Princess Lissa again." Venom dripped off his words. "I can't go near her, not when she's surrounded by all those royals."

"You're royal too," I said, more to myself than him. I kept forgetting the Ozeras were one of the twelve families.

"Doesn't mean much in a family full of Strigoi, huh?"

"But *you're* not—wait. That's why she connects to you," I realized with a start.

"Because I'm going to become a Strigoi?" he asked snidely.

"No . . . because you lost your parents too. Both of you saw them die."

"She saw hers die. I saw mine murdered."

I flinched. "I know. I'm sorry. it must have been . . . well, I don't have any idea what it was like."

Those crystal-blue eyes went unfocused. "It was like seeing an army of Death invade my house."

"You mean . . . your parents?"

He shook his head. "The guardians who came to kill them. I mean, my parents were scary, yeah, but they still looked like my parents—a little paler, I guess. Some red in their eyes. But they walked and talked the same way. I didn't know anything was wrong with them, but my aunt did. She was watching me when they came for me."

"Were they going to convert you?" I'd forgotten my original mission here, too caught up in the story. "You were really little."

"I think they were going to keep me until I was older, then turn me. Aunt Tasha wouldn't let them take me. They tried to reason with her, convert her too, but when she wouldn't listen, they tried to take her by force. She fought them—got really messed up—and then the guardians showed up." His eyes drifted back to me. He smiled, but there was no happiness in it. "Like I said, an army of Death. I think you're crazy,

Rose, but if you turn out like the rest of them, you're going to be able to do some serious damage one day. Even I won't mess with you."

I felt horrible. He'd had a miserable life, and I'd taken away one of the few good things in it. "Christian, I'm sorry for screwing things up between you and Lissa. It was stupid. She wanted to be with you. I think she still does now. If you could just—"

"I told you, I can't."

"I'm worried about her. She's into all this royal stuff because she thinks it's going to get back at Mia—she's doing it for me."

"And you aren't grateful?" The sarcasm returned.

"I'm worried. She can't handle playing all these catty political games. It isn't good for her, but she won't listen to me. I could . . . I could use help."

"*She* could use help. Hey, don't look so surprised—I know there's something funny going on with her. And I'm not even talking about the wrist thing."

I jumped. "Did she tell you? . . ." Why not? She'd told him everything else.

"She didn't need to," he said. "I've got eyes." I must have looked pathetic, because he sighed and ran a hand through his hair. "Look, if I catch Lissa alone . . . I'll try to talk to her. But honestly . . . if you really want to help her . . . well, I know I'm supposed to be all anti-establishment, but you might get the best help talking to somebody else. Kirova. Your guardian guy. I don't know. Someone who knows something. Someone you trust."

"Lissa wouldn't like that." I considered. "Neither would I."

"Yeah, well, we all have to do things we don't like. That's life."

My snarky switch flipped on. "What are you, an after-school special?"

A ghostly smile flickered across his face. "If you weren't so psychotic, you'd be fun to hang around."

"Funny, I feel that way about you too."

He didn't say anything else, but the smile grew, and he walked away.

SEVENTEEN

A few days later, Lissa found me outside the commons and delivered the most astonishing news.

"Uncle Victor's getting Natalie off campus this weekend to go shopping in Missoula. For the dance. They said I could come along."

I didn't say anything. She looked surprised at my silence.

"Isn't that cool?"

"For *you*, I guess. No malls or dances in my future."

She smiled excitedly. "He told Natalie she could bring two other people besides me. I convinced her to bring you and Camille."

I threw up my hands. "Well, thanks, but I'm not even supposed to go to the library after school. No one's going to let me go to Missoula."

"Uncle Victor thinks he can get Headmistress Kirova to let you go. Dimitri's trying too."

"Dimitri?"

"Yeah. He has to go with me if I leave campus." She grinned, taking my interest in Dimitri as interest in the mall. "They figured out my account finally—I got my allowance back. So we can buy other stuff along with dresses. And you know if they let you go to the mall, they'll have to let you go to the dance."

"Do we go to dances now?" I said. We never had before. School-sponsored social events? No way.

"Of course not. But you know there'll be all kinds of secret parties. We'll start at the dance and sneak off." She sighed happily. "Mia's so jealous she can barely stand it."

She went on about all the stores we'd go to, all the things we'd buy. I admit, I was kind of excited at the thought of getting some new clothes, but I doubted I'd actually get this mythical release.

"Oh hey," she said excitedly. "You should see these shoes Camille let me borrow. I never knew we wore the same size. Hang on." She opened her backpack and began rifling through it.

Suddenly, she screamed and threw it down. Books and shoes spilled out. So did a dead dove.

It was one of the pale brown mourning doves that sat on wires along the freeway and under trees on campus. It had so much blood on it that I couldn't figure out where the wound was. Who knew something so small even had that much blood? Regardless, the bird was definitely dead.

Covering her mouth, Lissa stared wordlessly, eyes wide.

"Son of a bitch," I swore. Without hesitating, I grabbed a stick and pushed the little feathered body aside. When it was out of the way, I started shoving her stuff back into the backpack, trying not to think about dead-bird germs. "Why the hell does this keep—Liss!"

I leapt over and grabbed her, pulling her away. She had

been kneeling on the ground, with her hand outstretched to the dove. I don't think she'd even realized what she was about to do. The instinct in her was so strong, it acted on its own.

"Lissa," I said, tightening my hand around hers. She was still leaning toward the bird. "Don't. Don't do it."

"I can save it."

"No, you can't. You promised, remember? Some things have to stay dead. Let this one go." Still feeling her tension, I pleaded. "Please, Liss. You promised. No more healings. You said you wouldn't. You promised me."

After a few more moments, I felt her hand relax and her body slump against mine. "I hate this, Rose. I hate all of this."

Natalie walked outside then, oblivious to the gruesome sight awaiting her.

"Hey, do you guys—oh my God!" she squealed, seeing the dove. "What is that?"

I helped Lissa as we rose to our feet. "Another, um, prank."

"Is it . . . dead?" She scrunched up her face in disgust.

"Yes," I said firmly.

Natalie, picking up on our tension, looked between the two of us. "What else is wrong?"

"Nothing." I handed Lissa her backpack. "This is just someone's stupid, sick joke, and I'm going to tell Kirova so they can clean this up."

Natalie turned away, looking a little green. "Why do people keep doing this to you? It's horrible."

Lissa and I exchanged looks.

"I have no idea," I said. Yet as I walked to Kirova's office, I started to wonder.

When we'd found the fox, Lissa had hinted that someone must know about the raven. I hadn't believed that. We'd been alone in the woods that night, and Ms. Karp wouldn't have told anyone. But what if someone actually had seen? What if someone kept doing this not to scare her, but to see if she'd heal again? What had the rabbit note said? *I know what you are.*

I didn't mention any of this to Lissa; I figured there were only so many of my conspiracy theories she could handle. Besides, when I saw her the next day, she'd practically forgotten the dove in light of other news: Kirova had given me permission to go on the trip that weekend. The prospect of shopping can brighten a lot of dark situations—even animal murder—and I put my own worries on hold.

Only, when the time came, I discovered my release came with strings attached.

"Headmistress Kirova thinks you've done well since coming back," Dimitri told me.

"Aside from starting a fight in Mr. Nagy's class?"

"She doesn't blame you for that. Not entirely. I convinced her you needed a break . . . and that you could use this as a training exercise."

"Training exercise?"

He gave me a brief explanation as we walked out to meet the others going with us. Victor Dashkov, as sickly as ever, was there with his guardians, and Natalie practically barreled into him. He smiled and gave her a careful hug, one that ended when a coughing fit took over. Natalie's eyes went wide with concern as she waited for it to pass.

He claimed he was fine to accompany us, and while I admired his resolve, I thought he'd be putting himself through a lot just to shop with a bunch of teenage girls.

We rode out the two-hour trip to Missoula in a large school van, leaving just after sunrise. Many Moroi lived separately from humans, but many also lived among them, and when shopping at their malls, you had to go during their hours. The back windows of the van had tinted glass to filter the light and keep the worst of it away from the vampires.

We had nine people in our group: Lissa, Victor, Natalie, Camille, Dimitri, me, and three other guardians. Two of the guardians, Ben and Spiridon, always traveled with Victor. The third was one of the school's guardians: Stan, the jerk who'd humiliated me on my first day back.

"Camille and Natalie don't have personal guardians yet," Dimitri explained to me. "They're both under the protection of their families' guardians. Since they are Academy students leaving campus, a school guardian accompanies them—Stan. I go because I'm Lissa's assigned guardian. Most girls her age wouldn't have a personal guardian yet, but circumstances make her unusual."

I sat in the back of the van with him and Spiridon, so they could dispense guardian wisdom to me as part of the "training exercise." Ben and Stan sat up front, while the others sat in the middle. Lissa and Victor talked to each other a lot, catching up on news. Camille, raised to be polite among older royals, smiled and nodded along. Natalie, on the other hand, looked left out and kept trying to shift her father's attention from Lissa. It didn't work. He'd apparently learned to tune out her chatter.

I turned back to Dimitri. "She's supposed to have two guardians. Princes and princesses always do."

Spiridon was Dimitri's age, with spiky blond hair and a more casual attitude. Despite his Greek name, he had a Southern drawl. "Don't worry, she'll have plenty when the time comes. Dimitri's already one of them. Odds are you'll be one too. And that's why you're here today."

"The training part," I guessed.

"Yup. You're going to be Dimitri's partner."

A moment of funny silence fell, probably not noticeable to anyone except Dimitri and me. Our eyes met.

"Guarding partner," Dimitri clarified unnecessarily, like maybe he too had been thinking of other kinds of partners.

"Yup," agreed Spiridon.

Oblivious to the tension around him, he went on to explain how guardian pairs worked. It was standard stuff, straight from my textbooks, but it meant more now that I'd be doing it in the real world. Guardians were assigned to Moroi based on importance. Two was a common grouping, one I'd probably work in a lot with Lissa. One guardian stayed close to the target; the other stood back and kept an eye on the surroundings.

Boringly, those holding these positions were called near and far guards.

"You'll probably always be near guard," Dimitri told me. "You're female and the same age as the princess. You can stay close to her without attracting any attention."

"And I can't ever take my eyes off her," I noted. "Or you."

Spiridon laughed again and elbowed Dimitri. "You've got a star student there. Did you give her a stake?"

"No. She's not ready."

"I would be if *someone* would show me how to use one," I argued. I knew every guardian in the van had a stake and a gun concealed on him.

"More to it than just using the stake," said Dimitri in his old-and-wise way. "You've still got to subdue them. And you've got to bring yourself to kill them."

"Why wouldn't I kill them?"

"Most Strigoi used to be Moroi who purposely turned. Sometimes they're Moroi or dhampirs turned by force. It doesn't matter. There's a strong chance you might know one of them. Could you kill someone you used to know?"

This trip was getting less fun by the minute.

"I guess so. I'd have to, right? If it's them or Lissa . . . "

"You might still hesitate," said Dimitri. "And that hesitation could kill you. And her."

"Then how do you make sure you don't hesitate?"

"You have to keep telling yourself that they *aren't* the same people you knew. They've become something dark and twisted. Something unnatural. You have to let go of attachments and do what's right. If they have any grain of their former selves left, they'll probably be grateful."

"Grateful for me killing them?"

"If someone turned you into a Strigoi, what would you want?" he asked.

I didn't know how to answer that, so I said nothing. Never taking his eyes off me, he kept pushing.

"What would you want if you knew you were going to be converted into a Strigoi against your will? If you knew you would lose all sense of your old morals and understanding of what's right and wrong? If you knew you'd live the rest of your life—your immortal life—killing innocent people? What would you want?"

The van had grown uncomfortably silent. Staring at Dimitri, burdened by all those questions, I suddenly understood why he and I had this weird attraction, good looks aside.

I'd never met anyone else who took being a guardian so seriously, who understand all the life-and-death consequences. Certainly no one my age did yet; Mason hadn't been able to understand why I couldn't relax and drink at the party. Dimitri had said I grasped my duty better than many older guardians, and I didn't get why—especially when they would have seen so much more death and danger. But I knew in that moment that he was right, that I had some weird sense of how life and death and good and evil worked with each other.

So did he. We might get lonely sometimes. We might have

to put our "fun" on hold. We might not be able to live the lives we wanted for ourselves. But that was the way it had to be. We understood each other, understood that we had others to protect. Our lives would never be easy.

And making decisions like this one was part of that.

"If I became Strigoi . . . I'd want someone to kill me."

"So would I," he said quietly. I could tell that he'd had the same flash of realization I'd just had, that same sense of connection between us.

"It reminds me of Mikhail hunting Sonya," murmured Victor thoughtfully.

"Who are Mikhail and Sonya?" asked Lissa.

Victor looked surprised. "Why, I thought you knew. Sonya Karp."

"Sonya Kar . . . you mean, Ms. Karp? What about her?" She looked back and forth between me and her uncle.

"She . . . became Strigoi," I said, not meeting Lissa's eyes. "By choice."

I'd known Lissa would find out some day. It was the final piece of Ms. Karp's saga, a secret I'd kept to myself. A secret that worried me constantly. Lissa's face and bond registered complete and utter shock, growing in intensity when she realized I'd known and never told.

"But I don't know who Mikhail is," I added.

"Mikhail Tanner," said Spiridon.

"Oh. Guardian Tanner. He was here before we left." I frowned. "Why is he chasing Ms. Karp?"

"To kill her," said Dimitri flatly. "They were lovers."

The entire Strigoi thing shifted into new focus for me. Running into a Strigoi I knew during the heat of battle was one thing. Purposely hunting down someone . . . someone I'd loved. Well, I didn't know if I could do that, even if it was technically the right thing.

"Perhaps it is time to talk about something else," said Victor gently. "Today isn't a day to dwell on depressing topics."

I think all of us felt relieved to get to the mall. Shifting into my bodyguard role, I stuck by Lissa's side as we wandered from store to store, looking at all the new styles that were out there. It was nice to be in public again and do to something with her that was just *fun* and didn't involve any of the dark, twisted politics of the Academy. It was almost like old times. I'd missed just hanging out. I'd missed my best friend.

Although it was only just past mid-November, the mall already had glittering holiday decorations up. I decided I had the best job ever. Admittedly, I did feel a little put out when I realized the older guardians got to stay in contact through cool little communication devices. When I protested my lack of one, Dimitri told me I'd learn better without one. If I could handle protecting Lissa the old-fashioned way, I could handle anything.

Victor and Spiridon stayed with us while Dimitri and Ben fanned out, somehow managing not to look like creepy stalker guys watching teenage girls.

"This is so you," said Lissa in Macy's, handing me a low-cut tank top embellished with lace. "I'll buy it for you."

I regarded it longingly, already picturing myself in it. Then, making my regular eye contact with Dimitri, I shook my head and handed it back. "Winter's coming. I'd get cold."

"Never stopped you before."

Shrugging, she hung it back up. She and Camille tried on a nonstop string of clothes, their massive allowances ensuring that price posed no problem. Lissa offered to buy me anything I wanted. We'd been generous with each other our whole lives, and I didn't hesitate to take her up on it. My choices surprised her.

"You've got three thermal shirts and a hoodie," she informed me, flipping through a stack of BCBG jeans. "You've gone all boring on me."

"Hey, I don't see you buying slutty tops."

"I'm not the one who wears them."

"Thanks a lot."

"You know what I mean. You're even wearing your hair up."

It was true. I'd taken Dimitri's advice and wrapped my hair up in a high bun, earning a smile when he'd seen me. If I'd had *molnija* marks, they would have shown.

Glancing around, she made sure none of the others could hear us. The feelings in the bond shifted to something more troubled.

"You knew about Ms. Karp."

"Yeah. I heard about it a month or so after she left."

Lissa tossed a pair of embroidered jeans over her arm, not looking at me. "Why didn't you tell me?"

"You didn't need to know."

"You didn't think I could handle it?"

I kept my face perfectly blank. As I stared at her, my mind was back in time, back to two years ago. I'd been on day two of my suspension for allegedly destroying Wade's room when a royal party visited the school. I'd been allowed to attend that reception too but had been under heavy guard to make sure I didn't "try anything."

Two guardians escorted me to the commons and talked quietly with each other along the way.

"She killed the doctor attending her and nearly took out half the patients and nurses on her way out."

"Do they have any idea where she went?"

"No, they're tracking her . . . but, well, you know how it is."

"I never expected her to do this. She never seemed like the type."

"Yeah, well, Sonya was crazy. Did you see how violent she was getting near the end? She was capable of anything."

I'd been trudging along miserably and jerked my head up.

"Sonya? You mean Ms. Karp?" I asked. "She killed somebody?"

The two guardians exchanged looks. Finally, one said gravely, "She became a Strigoi, Rose."

I stopped walking and stared. "Ms. Karp? No . . . she wouldn't have. . . ."

"I'm afraid so," the other one replied. "But . . . you should keep that to yourself. It's a tragedy. Don't make it school gossip."

I went through the rest of the night in a daze. Ms. Karp. Crazy Karp. She'd killed someone to become Strigoi. I couldn't believe it.

When the reception ended, I'd managed to sneak off from my guardians and steal a few precious moments with Lissa. The bond had grown strong by now, and I hadn't needed to see her face to know how miserable she was.

"What's wrong?" I asked her. We were in a corner of the hallway, just outside the commons.

Her eyes were blank. I could feel how she had a headache; its pain transferred to me. "I . . . I don't know. I just feel weird. I feel like I'm being followed, like I have to be careful, you know?"

I didn't know what to say. I didn't think she was being followed, but Ms. Karp used to say the same thing. Always paranoid. "It's probably nothing," I said lightly.

"Probably," she agreed. Her eyes suddenly narrowed. "But Wade isn't. He won't shut up about what happened. You can't believe the things he's saying about you."

I could, actually, but I didn't care. "Forget about him. He's nothing."

"I hate him," she said. Her voice was uncharacteristically sharp. "I'm on the committee with him for that fund-raiser, and I *hate* hearing him run his fat mouth every day and seeing him flirt with anything female that walks by. You shouldn't be punished for what he did. He needs to pay."

My mouth went dry. "It's okay . . . I don't care. Calm down, Liss."

"*I care,*" she snapped, turning her anger on me. "I wish there was a way I could get back at him. Some way to hurt him like he hurt you." She put her hands behind her back and paced back and forth furiously, her steps hard and purposeful.

The hatred and anger boiled within her. I could feel it in the bond. It felt like a storm, and it scared the hell out of me. Wrapped around it all was an uncertainty, an instability that said Lissa didn't know what to do but that she wanted desperately to do something. Anything. My mind flashed to the night with the baseball bat. And then I thought about Ms. Karp. *She became a Strigoi, Rose.*

It was the scariest moment of my life. Scarier than seeing her in Wade's room. Scarier than seeing her heal that raven. Scarier than my capture by the guardians would be. Because just then, I didn't know my best friend. I didn't know what she was capable of. A year earlier, I would have laughed at anyone who said she'd want to go Strigoi. But a year earlier, I also would have laughed at anyone who said she'd want to cut her wrists or make someone "pay."

In that moment, I suddenly believed she might do the impossible. And I had to make sure she didn't. *Save her. Save her from herself.*

"We're leaving," I said, taking her arm and steering her down the hall. "Right now."

Confusion momentarily replaced her anger. "What do you mean? You want to go to the woods or something?"

I didn't answer. Something in my attitude or words must

have startled her, because she didn't question me as I led us out of the commons, cutting across campus toward the parking lot where visitors came. It was filled with cars belonging to tonight's guests. One of them was a large Lincoln Town Car, and I watched as its chauffeur started it up.

"Someone's leaving early," I said, peering at him from around a cluster of bushes. I glanced behind us and saw nothing. "They'll probably be here any minute."

Lissa caught on. "When you said, 'We're leaving,' you meant . . . no. Rose, we can't leave the Academy. We'd never get through the wards and checkpoints."

"We don't have to," I said firmly. "He does."

"But how does that help us?"

I took a deep breath, regretting what I had to say but seeing it as the lesser of evils. "You know how you made Wade do those things?"

She flinched but nodded.

"I need you to do the same thing. Go up to that guy and tell him to hide us in his trunk."

Shock and fear poured out of her. She didn't understand, and she was scared. Extremely scared. She'd been scared for weeks now, ever since the healing and the moods and Wade. She was fragile and on the edge of something neither of us understood. But through all of that, she trusted me. She believed I would keep her safe.

"Okay," she said. She took a few steps toward him, then looked back at me. "Why? Why are we doing this?"

I thought about Lissa's anger, her desire to do *anything* to get back at Wade. And I thought about Ms. Karp—pretty, unstable Ms. Karp—going Strigoi. "I'm taking care of you," I said. "You don't need to know anything else."

At the mall in Missoula, standing between racks of designer clothes, Lissa asked again, "Why didn't you tell me?"

"You didn't need to know," I repeated.

She headed toward the dressing room, still whispering with me. "You're worried I'm going to lose it. Are you worried I'll go Strigoi too?"

"No. No way. That was all her. You'd never do that."

"Even if I was crazy?"

"No," I said, trying to make a joke. "You'd just shave your head and live with thirty cats."

Lissa's feelings grew darker, but she didn't say anything else. Stopping just outside the dressing room, she pulled a black dress off the rack. She brightened a little.

"This is the dress you were born for. I don't care how practical you are now."

Made of silky black material, the dress was strapless and sleek, falling about to the knees. Although it had a slight flair at the hemline, the rest looked like it would definitely manage some serious clinging action. Super sexy. Maybe even challenge-the-school-dress-code sexy.

"That is my dress," I admitted. I kept staring at it, wanting it so badly that it ached in my chest. This was the kind of dress that changed the world. The kind of dress that started religions.

Lissa pulled out my size. "Try it on."

I shook my head and started to put it back. "I can't. It would compromise you. One dress isn't worth your grisly death."

"Then we'll just get it without you trying it on." She bought the dress.

The afternoon continued, and I found myself growing tired. Always watching and being on guard suddenly became a lot less fun. When we hit our last stop, a jewelry store, I felt kind of glad.

"Here you go," said Lissa, pointing at one of the cases. "The necklace made to go with your dress."

I looked. A thin gold chain with a gold-and-diamond rose pendant. Emphasis on the diamond part.

"I hate rose stuff."

Lissa had always loved getting me rose things—just to see my reaction, I think. When she saw the necklace's price, her smile fell away.

"Oh, look at that. Even you have limits," I teased. "Your crazy spending is stopped at last."

We waited for Victor and Natalie to finish up. He was apparently buying her something, and she looked like she might grow wings and fly away with happiness. I was glad. She'd been dying for his attention. Hopefully he was buying her something extra-expensive to make up for it.

We rode home in tired silence, our sleep schedules all messed up by the daylight trip. Sitting next to Dimitri, I leaned back against the seat and yawned, very aware that our arms were touching. That feeling of closeness and connection burned between us.

"So, I can't ever try on clothes again?" I asked quietly, not wanting to wake up the others. Victor and the guardians were awake, but the girls had fallen asleep.

"When you aren't on duty, you can. You can do it during your time off."

"I don't ever want time off. I want to always take care of Lissa." I yawned again. "Did you see that dress?"

"I saw the dress."

"Did you like it?"

He didn't answer. I took that as a yes.

"Am I going to endanger my reputation if I wear it to the dance?"

When he spoke, I could barely hear him. "You'll endanger the school."

I smiled and fell asleep.

When I woke up, my head rested against his shoulder. That long coat of his—the duster—covered me like a blanket. The van had stopped; we were back at school. I pulled the duster off and climbed out after him, suddenly feeling wide awake and happy. Too bad my freedom was about to end.

"Back to prison," I sighed, walking beside Lissa toward the commons. "Maybe if you fake a heart attack, I can make a break for it."

"Without your clothes?" She handed me a bag, and I

swung it around happily. "I can't wait to see the dress."

"Me either. If they let me go. Kirova's still deciding if I've been good enough."

"Show her those boring shirts you bought. She'll go into a coma. I'm about ready to."

I laughed and hopped up onto one of the wooden benches, pacing her as I walked along it. I jumped back down when I reached the end. "They aren't *that* boring."

"I don't know what to think of this new, responsible Rose."

I hopped up onto another bench. "I'm not that responsible."

"Hey," called Spiridon. He and the rest of the group trailed behind us. "You're still on duty. No fun allowed up there."

"No fun here," I called back, hearing the laughter in his voice. "I swear—shit."

I was up on a third bench, near the end of it. My muscles tensed, ready to jump back down. Only when I tried to, my foot didn't go with me. The wood, at one moment seemingly hard and solid, gave way beneath me, almost as though made of paper. It disintegrated. My foot went through, my ankle getting caught in the hole while the rest of my body tried to go in another direction. The bench held me, swinging my body to the ground while still seizing my foot. My ankle bent in an unnatural direction. I crashed down. I heard a cracking sound that wasn't the wood. The worst pain of my life shot through my body.

And then I blacked out.

EIGHTEEN

I woke up staring at the boring white ceiling of the clinic. A filtered light—soothing to Moroi patients—shone down on me. I felt strange, kind of disoriented, but I didn't hurt.

"Rose."

The voice was like silk on my skin. Gentle. Rich. Turning my head, I met Dimitri's dark eyes. He sat in a chair beside the bed I lay on, his shoulder-length brown hair hanging forward and framing his face.

"Hey," I said, my voice coming out as a croak.

"How do you feel?"

"Weird. Kind of groggy."

"Dr. Olendzki gave you something for the pain—you seemed pretty bad when we brought you in."

"I don't remember that. . . . How long have I been out?"

"A few hours."

"Must have been strong. Must still be strong." Some of the details came back. The bench. My ankle getting caught. I couldn't remember much after that. Feeling hot and cold and then hot again. Tentatively, I tried moving the toes on my healthy foot. "I don't hurt at all."

He shook his head. "No. Because you weren't seriously injured."

The sound of my ankle cracking came back to me. "Are you sure? I remember . . . the way it bent. No. Something must be broken." I manage to sit up, so I could look at my ankle. "Or at least sprained."

He moved forward to stop me. "Be careful. Your ankle might be fine, but you're probably still a little out of it."

I carefully shifted to the edge of the bed and looked down. My jeans were rolled up. The ankle looked a little red, but I had no bruises or serious marks.

"God, I got lucky. If I'd hurt it, it would have put me out of practice for a while."

Smiling, he returned to his chair. "I know. You kept telling me that while I was carrying you. You were very upset."

"You . . . you carried me here?"

"After we broke the bench apart and freed your foot."

Man. I'd missed out on a lot. The only thing better than imagining Dimitri carrying me in his arms was imagining him shirtless while carrying me in his arms.

Then the reality of the situation hit me.

"I was taken down by a bench," I groaned.

"What?"

"I survived the whole day guarding Lissa, and you guys said I did a good job. Then, I get back here and meet my downfall in the form of a bench." Ugh. "Do you know how embarrassing it is? And all those guys saw, too."

"It wasn't your fault," he said. "No one knew the bench was rotted. It looked fine."

"Still. I should have just stuck to the sidewalk like a normal person. The other novices are going to give me shit when I get back."

His lips held back a smile. "Maybe presents will cheer you up."

I sat up straighter. "Presents?"

The smile escaped, and he handed me a small box with a piece of paper.

"This is from Prince Victor."

Surprised that Victor would have given me anything, I read the note. It was just a few lines, hastily scrawled in pen.

Rose—

I'm very happy to see you didn't suffer any serious injuries from your fall. Truly, it is a miracle. You lead a charmed life, and Vasilisa is lucky to have you.

"That's nice of him," I said, opening the box. Then I saw what was inside. "Whoa. Very nice."

It was the rose necklace, the one Lissa had wanted to get me but couldn't afford. I held it up, looping its chain over my hand so the glittering, diamond-covered rose hung free.

"This is pretty extreme for a get-well present," I noted, recalling the price.

"He actually bought it in honor of you doing so well on your first day as an official guardian. He saw you and Lissa looking at it."

"Wow." It was all I could say. "I don't think I did *that* good of a job."

"I do."

Grinning, I placed the necklace back in the box and set it on a nearby table. "You did say 'presents,' right? Like more than one?"

He laughed outright, and the sound wrapped around me like a caress. God, I loved the sound of his laugh. "This is from me."

He handed me a small, plain bag. Puzzled and excited, I opened it up. Lip gloss, the kind I liked. I'd complained to him a number of times how I was running out, but I'd never thought he was paying attention.

"How'd you manage to buy this? I saw you the whole time at the mall."

"Guardian secrets."

"What's this for? For my first day?"

"No," he said simply. "Because I thought it would make you happy."

Without even thinking about it, I leaned forward and hugged him. "Thank you."

Judging from his stiff posture, I'd clearly caught him by surprise. And yeah . . . I'd actually caught myself by surprise, too. But he relaxed a few moments later, and when he reached around and rested his hands on my lower back, I thought I was going to die.

"I'm glad you're better," he said. His mouth sounded like

it was almost in my hair, just above my ear. "When I saw you fall . . ."

"You thought, 'Wow, she's a loser.'"

"That's not what I thought."

He pulled back slightly, so he could see me better, but we didn't say anything. His eyes were so dark and deep that I wanted to dive right in. Staring at them made me feel warm all over, like they had flames inside. Slowly, carefully, those long fingers of his reached out and traced the edge of my cheekbone, moving up the side of my face. At the first touch of his skin on mine, I shivered. He wound a lock of my hair around one finger, just like he had in the gym.

Swallowing, I dragged my eyes up from his lips. I'd been contemplating what it'd be like to kiss him. The thought both excited and scared me, which was stupid. I'd kissed a lot of guys and never thought much about it. No reason another one—even an older one—should be that big of a deal. Yet the thought of him closing the distance and bringing his lips to mine made the world start spinning.

A soft knock sounded at the door, and I hastily leaned back. Dr. Olendzki stuck her head in. "I thought I heard you talking. How do you feel?"

She walked over and made me lie back down. Touching and bending my ankle, she assessed it for damage and finally shook her head when finished.

"You're lucky. With all the noise you made coming in here, I thought your foot had been amputated. Must have just been shock." She stepped back. "I'd feel better if you sat out from your normal trainings tomorrow, but otherwise, you're good to go."

I breathed a sigh of relief. I didn't remember my hysteria— and was actually kind of embarrassed that I'd thrown such a fit— but I had been right about the problems this would have caused me if I'd broken or sprained it. I couldn't afford to lose any time here; I needed to take my trials and graduate in the spring.

Dr. Olendzki gave me the okay to go and then left the room. Dimitri walked over to another chair and brought me my shoes and coat. Looking at him, I felt a warm flush sweep me as I recalled what had happened before the doctor had entered.

He watched as I slipped one of the shoes on. "You have a guardian angel."

"I don't believe in angels," I told him. "I believe in what I can do for myself."

"Well then, you have an amazing body." I glanced up at him with a questioning look. "For healing, I mean. I heard about the accident. . . ."

He didn't specify which accident it was, but it could be only one. Talking about it normally bothered me, but with him, I felt I could say anything.

"Everyone said I shouldn't have survived," I explained. "Because of where I sat and the way the car hit the tree. Lissa was really the only one in a secure spot. She and I walked away with only a few scratches."

"And you don't believe in angels or miracles."

"Nope. I—"

Truly, it is a miracle. You lead a charmed life. . . .

And just like that, a million thoughts came slamming into my head. Maybe . . . maybe I had a guardian angel after all. . . .

Dimitri immediately noticed the shift in my feelings. "What's wrong?"

Reaching out with my mind, I tried to expand the bond and shake off the lingering effects of the pain medication. Some more of Lissa's feelings came through to me. Anxious. Upset.

"Where's Lissa? Was she here?"

"I don't know where she is. She wouldn't leave your side while I brought you in. She stayed right next the bed, right up until the doctor came in. You calmed down when she sat next to you."

I closed my eyes and felt like I might faint. I had calmed down when Lissa sat next to me because she'd taken the pain away. She'd healed me. . . .

Just as she had the night of the accident.

It all made sense now. I shouldn't have survived. Everyone had said so. Who knew what kind of injuries I'd actually suffered? Internal bleeding. Broken bones. It didn't matter because Lissa had fixed it, just like she'd fixed everything else. That was why she'd been leaning over me when I woke up.

It was also probably why she'd passed out when they took her to the hospital. She'd been exhausted for days afterward.

And that was when her depression had begun. It had seemed like a normal reaction after losing her family, but now I wondered if there was more to it, if healing me had played a role.

Opening my mind again, I reached out to her, needing to find her. If she'd healed me, there was no telling what shape she could be in now. Her moods and magic were linked, and this had been a pretty intense show of magic.

The drug was almost gone from my system, and like that, I snapped into her. It was almost easy now. A tidal wave of emotions hit me, worse than when her nightmares engulfed me. I'd never felt such intensity from her before.

She sat in the chapel's attic, crying. She didn't entirely know why she was crying either. She felt happy and relieved that I'd been unharmed, that she'd been able to heal me. At the same time, she felt weak in both body and mind. She burned inside, like she'd lost part of herself. She worried I'd be mad because she'd used her powers. She dreaded going through another school day tomorrow, pretending she liked being with a crowd who had no other interests aside from spending their families' money and making fun of those less beautiful and less popular. She didn't want to go to the dance with Aaron and see him watch her so adoringly—and feel him touching her—when she felt only friendship for him.

Most of these were all normal concerns, but they hit her hard, harder than they would an ordinary person, I thought. She couldn't sort through them or figure out how to fix them.

"You okay?"

She looked up and brushed the hair away from where it stuck to her wet cheeks. Christian stood in the entrance to the attic. She hadn't even heard him come up the stairs. She'd been too lost in her own grief. A flicker of both longing and anger sparked within her.

"I'm fine," she snapped. Sniffling, she tried to stop her tears, not wanting him to see her weak.

Leaning against the wall, he crossed his arms and wore an unreadable expression. "Do . . . do you want to talk?"

"Oh . . ." She laughed harshly. "You want to talk now? After I tried so many times—"

"I didn't want that! That was Rose—"

He cut himself off and I flinched. I was totally busted.

Lissa stood up and strode toward him. "What about Rose?"

"Nothing." His mask of indifference slipped back into place. "Forget it."

"*What about Rose?*" She stepped closer. Even through her anger, she still felt that inexplicable attraction to him. And then she understood. "She *made* you, didn't she? She told you to stop talking to me?"

He stared stonily ahead. "It was probably for the best. I would have just messed things up for you. You wouldn't be where you are now."

"What's that supposed to mean?"

"What do you think it means? God. People live or die at your command now, Your Highness."

"You're being kind of melodramatic."

"Am I? All day, I hear people talking about what you're doing and what you're thinking and what you're wearing. Whether you'll approve. Who you like. Who you hate. They're your puppets."

"It's not like that. Besides, I had to do it. To get back at Mia . . ."

Rolling his eyes, he looked away from her. "You don't even know what you're getting back at her for."

Lissa's anger flared. "She set up Jesse and Ralf to say those things about Rose! I couldn't let her get away with that."

"Rose is tough. She would have gotten over it."

"You didn't see her," she replied obstinately. "She was crying."

"So? People cry. *You're* crying."

"Not Rose."

He turned back to her, a dark smile curling his lips. "I've never seen anything like you two. Always so worried about each other. I get her thing—some kind of weird guardian hang-up—but you're just the same."

"She's my friend."

"I guess it's that simple. I wouldn't know." He sighed, momentarily thoughtful, then snapped back to sarcastic mode. "Anyway. Mia. So you got back at her over what she did to Rose. But you're missing the point. *Why* did she do it?"

Lissa frowned. "Because she was jealous about me and Aaron—"

"More to it than that, Princess. What did she have to be jealous about? She already had him. She didn't need to attack you to drive that home. She could have just made a big show of being all over him. Sort of like you are now," he added wryly.

"Okay. What else is there, then? Why did she want to ruin my life? I never did anything to her—before all this, I mean."

He leaned forward, crystal-blue eyes boring into hers.

"You're right. You didn't—but your brother did."

Lissa pulled away from him. "You don't know anything about my brother."

"I know he screwed Mia over. Literally."

"Stop it, stop lying."

"I'm not. Swear to God or whoever else you want to believe in. I used to talk to Mia now and then, back when she was a freshman. She wasn't very popular, but she was smart. Still is. She used to work on a lot of committees with royals—dances and stuff. I don't know all of it. But she got to know your brother on one of those, and they sort of got together."

"They did not. I would have known. Andre would have told me."

"Nope. He didn't tell anyone. He told her not to either. He convinced her it should be some kind of romantic secret when really, he just didn't want any of his friends to find out he was getting naked with a non-royal freshman."

"If Mia told you that, she was making it up," exclaimed Lissa.

"Yeah, well, I don't think she was making it up when I saw her crying. He got tired of her after a few weeks and dumped her. Told her she was too young and that he couldn't really get serious with someone who wasn't from a good family. From what I understand, he wasn't even nice about it either—didn't even bother with the 'let's be friends' stuff."

Lissa pushed herself into Christian's face. "You didn't even *know* Andre! He would never have done that."

"*You* didn't know him. I'm sure he was nice to his baby sister; I'm sure he loved you. But in school, with his friends, he was just as much of a jerk as the rest of the royals. I saw him because I see everything. Easy when no one notices you."

She held back a sob, unsure whether to believe him or not. "So *this* is why Mia hates me?"

"Yup. She hates you because of him. That, and because you're royal and she's insecure around all royals, which is why she worked so hard to claw up the ranks and be their friend. I think it's a coincidence that she ended up with your ex-boyfriend, but now that you're back, that probably made it worse. Between stealing him and spreading those stories about her parents, you guys really picked the best ways to make her suffer. Nice work."

The smallest pang of guilt lurched inside of her. "I still think you're lying."

"I'm a lot of things, but I'm not a liar. That's your department. And Rose's."

"We don't—"

"Exaggerate stories about people's families? Say that you hate me? Pretend to be friends with people you think are stupid? Date a guy you don't like?"

"I like him."

"Like or *like*?"

"Oh, there's a difference?"

"Yes. *Like* is when you date a big, blond moron and laugh at his stupid jokes."

Then, out of nowhere, he leaned forward and kissed her. It was hot and fast and furious, an outpouring of the rage and passion and longing that Christian always kept locked inside of him. Lissa had never been kissed like that, and I felt her respond to it, respond to *him*—how he made her feel so much more alive than Aaron or anyone else could.

Christian pulled back from the kiss but still kept his face next to hers.

"That's what you do with someone you *like*."

Lissa's heart pounded with both anger and desire. "Well, I don't like or *like* you. And I think you and Mia are both lying about Andre. *Aaron* would never make up anything like that."

"That's because Aaron doesn't say anything that requires words of more than one syllable."

She pulled away. "Get out. Get away from me."

He looked around comically. "You can't throw me out. We both signed the lease."

"Get. Out!" she yelled. "I hate you!"

He bowed. "Anything you want, Your Highness." With a final dark look, he left the attic.

Lissa sank to her knees, letting out the tears she'd held back from him. I could barely make sense out of all the things hurting her. God only knew things upset me—like the Jesse incident—but they didn't attack me in the same way. They swirled within her, beating at her brain. The stories about Andre. Mia's hate. Christian's kiss. Healing me. This, I realized, was what real depression felt like. What madness felt like.

Overcome, drowning in her own pain, Lissa made the only decision she could. The only thing she could do to channel all of these emotions. She opened up her purse and found the tiny razor blade she always carried. . . .

Sickened, yet unable to break away, I felt as she cut her left arm, making perfectly even marks, watching as the blood flowed across her white skin. As always, she avoided veins, but her cuts were deeper this time. The cutting stung horribly, yet in doing it, she was able to focus on the physical pain, distract herself from the mental anguish so that she could feel like she was in control.

Drops of blood splattered onto the dusty floor, and her world began spinning. Seeing her own blood intrigued her. She had taken blood from others her entire life. Me. The feeders. Now, here it was, leaking out. With a nervous giggle, she decided it was funny. Maybe by letting it out, she was giving it back to those she'd stolen it from. Or maybe she was wasting it, wasting the sacred Dragomir blood that everyone obsessed over.

I'd forced my way into her head, and now I couldn't get out. Her emotions had ensnared me now—they were too strong and too powerful. But I had to escape—I knew it with every ounce of my being. I had to stop her. She was too weak from the healing to lose this much blood. It was time to tell someone.

Breaking out at last, I found myself back in the clinic. Dimitri's hands were on me, gently shaking me as he said my name over and over in an effort to get my attention. Dr. Olendzki stood beside him, face dark and concerned.

I stared at Dimitri, truly seeing how much he worried and cared about me. Christian had told me to get help, to go to someone I trusted about Lissa. I'd ignored the advice because I didn't trust anyone except her. But looking at Dimitri now, feeling that sense of understanding we shared, I knew that I did trust someone else.

I felt my voice crack as I spoke. "I know where she is. Lissa. We have to help her."

NINETEEN

It's hard to say what finally made me do it. I'd held on to so many secrets for so long, doing what I believed best protected Lissa. But hiding her cutting did nothing to protect her. I hadn't been able to make her stop—and really, I now wondered if it was my fault she'd ever started. None of this had happened until she healed me in the accident. What if she'd left me injured? Maybe I would have recovered. Maybe she would be all right today.

I stayed in the clinic while Dimitri went to get Alberta. He hadn't hesitated for a second when I told him where she was. I'd said she was in danger, and he'd left immediately.

Everything after that moved like some sort of slow-motion nightmare. The minutes dragged on while I waited. When he finally returned with an unconscious Lissa, a flurry arose at the clinic, one everyone wanted me kept out of. She had lost a lot of blood, and while they had a feeder on hand right away, rousing her to enough consciousness to drink proved difficult. It wasn't until the middle of the Academy's night that someone decided she was stable enough for me to visit.

"Is it true?" she asked when I walked into the room. She lay on the bed, wrists heavily bandaged. I knew they'd put a lot of blood back into her, but she still looked pale to me. "They said it was you. You told them."

"I had to," I said, afraid to get too close. "Liss . . . you cut yourself worse than you ever have. And after healing me . . . and then everything with Christian . . . you couldn't handle it. You needed help."

She closed her eyes. "Christian. You know about that. Of course you do. You know about everything."

"I'm sorry. I just wanted to help."

"What happened to what Ms. Karp said? About keeping it all secret?"

"She was talking about the other stuff. I don't think she'd want you to keep cutting yourself."

"Did you tell them about the 'other stuff'?"

I shook my head. "Not yet."

She turned toward me, eyes cold. "'Yet.' But you're going to."

"I have to. You can heal other people . . . but it's killing you."

"I healed *you*."

"I would have been okay eventually. The ankle would have healed. It's not worth what it does to you. And I think I know how it started . . . when you first healed me. . . ."

I explained my revelation about the accident and how all of her powers and depression had started after that. I also pointed out how our bond had formed after the accident too, though I didn't fully understand why yet.

"I don't know what's going on, but this is beyond us. We need someone's help."

"They'll take me away," she said flatly. "Like Ms. Karp."

"I think they'll try to help you. They were all really worried. Liss, I'm doing this for you. I just want you to be okay."

She turned away from me. "Get out, Rose."

I did.

They released her the next morning on the condition that she'd have to come back for daily visits to the counselor. Dimitri told me they also planned on putting her on some sort of medication to help with the depression. I wasn't a big fan of pills, but I'd cheer on anything that would help her.

Unfortunately, some sophomore had been in the clinic for an asthma attack. He'd seen her come in with Dimitri and Alberta. He didn't know why she'd been admitted, but that hadn't stopped him from telling people in his hall what he'd seen. They then told others at breakfast. By lunch, all the upperclassmen knew about the late-night clinic visit.

And more importantly, everyone knew she wasn't speaking to me.

Just like that, whatever social headway I'd made plummeted. She didn't outright condemn me, but her silence spoke legions, and people behaved accordingly.

The whole day, I walked around the Academy like a ghost. People watched and occasionally spoke to me, but few made much more effort than that. They followed Lissa's lead, imitating her silence. No one was openly mean to me—they probably didn't want to risk it in case she and I patched things up. Still, I heard "blood whore" whispered here and there when someone thought I wasn't listening.

Mason would have welcomed me to his lunch table, but some of his friends might not have been so nice. I didn't want to be the cause of any fights between him and them. So I chose Natalie instead.

"I heard Lissa tried to run away again, and you stopped her," Natalie said. No one had a clue why she'd been in the clinic yet. I hoped it stayed that way.

Running away? Where in the world had that come from? "Why would she do that?"

"I don't know." She lowered her voice. "Why'd she leave before? It's just what I heard."

That story raged on as the day passed, as did all sorts of rumors about why Lissa might have gone to the med clinic. Pregnancy and abortion theories were eternally popular. Some whispered she might have gotten Victor's disease. No one even came close to guessing the truth.

Leaving our last class as quickly as possible, I was astonished when Mia started walking toward me.

"What do you want?" I demanded. "I can't come out and play today, little girl."

"You sure have an attitude for someone who doesn't exist right now."

"As opposed to you?" I asked. Remembering what Christian had said, I did feel a little sorry for her. That guilt disappeared after I took one look at her face. She might have been a victim, but now she was a monster. There was a cold, cunning look about her, very different from the desperate and depressed one from the other day. She hadn't stayed beaten after what Andre had done to her—if that was even true, and I believed it was—and I doubted she would with Lissa either. Mia was a survivor.

"She got rid of you, and you're too high and mighty to admit it." Her blue eyes practically bugged out. "Don't you want to get back at her?"

"Are you more psycho than usual? She's my best friend. And why are you still following me?"

Mia *tsk*ed. "She doesn't act like it. Come on, tell me what happened at the clinic. It's something big, isn't it? She really is pregnant, right? Tell me what it is."

"Go away."

"If you tell me, I'll get Jesse and Ralf to say they made all that stuff up."

I stopped walking and spun around to face her. Scared, she took a few steps backward. She must have recalled some of my past threats of physical violence.

"I already know they made it all up, because I didn't *do* any of it. And if you try to turn me against Lissa one more time, the stories are going to be about *you* bleeding, because I'll have ripped your throat out!"

My voice grew louder with each word until I practically shouted. Mia stepped back further, clearly terrified.

"You really are crazy. No wonder she dropped you." She shrugged. "Whatever. I'll find out what's going on without you."

When the dance came that weekend, I decided I really didn't want to go. It had sounded stupid to begin with, and I'd only been interested in going to the after-parties anyway. But without Lissa, I wasn't likely to gain admission to those. Instead, I holed up in my room, trying—and failing—to do some homework. Through the bond, I felt all sorts of mixed emotions from her, particularly anxiety and excitement. It had to be hard hanging out all night with a guy you didn't really like.

About ten minutes after the dance's start time, I decided to clean up and take a shower. When I came back down the hall from the bathroom, a towel wrapped around my head, I saw Mason standing outside my door. He wasn't exactly dressed up, but he also wasn't wearing jeans. It was a start.

"There you are, party girl. I was about ready to give up."

"Did you start another fire? No guys allowed in this hall."

"Whatever. Like that makes a difference." True. The school might be able to keep Strigoi out, but they did a horrible job at keeping the rest of us away from each other. "Let me in. You've got to get ready."

It took me a minute to realize what he meant. "No. I'm not going."

"Come on," he prodded, following me inside. "'Cause you

had a fight with Lissa? You guys are going to make up soon. No reason for you to stay here all night. If you don't want to be around her, Eddie's getting a group together over in his room later."

My old, fun-loving spirit perked its head up just a bit. No Lissa. Probably no royals. "Yeah?"

Seeing that he was starting to get me, Mason grinned. Looking at his eyes, I realized again how much he liked me. And again I wondered, Why couldn't I just have a normal boyfriend? Why did I want my hot, older mentor—the mentor I'd probably end up getting fired?

"It'll just be novices," Mason continued, oblivious to my thoughts. "And I have a surprise for you when we get there."

"Is it in a bottle?" If Lissa wanted to ignore me, I had no reason to keep myself sober.

"No, that's at Eddie's. Hurry up and get dressed. I know you aren't wearing that."

I looked down at my ripped jeans and University of Oregon T-shirt. Yeah. Definitely not wearing this.

Fifteen minutes later, we cut across the quad back over to the commons, laughing as we recounted how a particularly clumsy classmate of ours had given himself a black eye in practice this week. Moving quickly over the frozen ground wasn't easy in heels, and he kept grabbing my arm to keep me from falling over, half-dragging me along. It made us laugh that much more. A happy feeling started to well up in me—I wasn't entirely rid of the ache for Lissa, but this was a start.

Maybe I didn't have her and her friends, but I had my own friends. It was also very likely that I was going to get head-over-heels drunk tonight, which, while not a great way to solve my problems, would at least be really fun. Yeah. My life could be worse.

Then we ran into Dimitri and Alberta.

They were on their way somewhere else, talking guardian business. Alberta smiled when she saw us, giving us the kind of indulgent look older people always give to younger people who appear to be having fun and acting silly. Like she thought we were cute. The nerve. We stumbled to a halt, and Mason put a hand on my arm to steady me.

"Mr. Ashford, Miss Hathaway. I'm surprised you aren't already in the commons."

Mason gave her an angelic, teacher's-pet smile. "Got delayed, Guardian Petrov. You know how it is with girls. Always got to look perfect. You especially must know all about that."

Normally I would have elbowed him for saying something so stupid, but I was staring at Dimitri and incapable of speech. Perhaps more importantly, he was staring at me too.

I had on the black dress, and it was everything I'd hoped it could be. In fact, it was a wonder Alberta didn't call me on the dress code right there and then. The fabric clung everywhere, and no Moroi girl's chest could have held this dress up. Victor's rose hung around my neck, and I'd done a hasty blow-dry of my hair, leaving it down the way I knew

Dimitri liked it. I hadn't worn tights because no one wore tights with dresses like this anymore, so my feet were freezing in the heels. All for the sake of looking good.

And I was pretty sure I looked damn good, but Dimitri's face wasn't giving anything away. He just looked at me—and looked and looked. Maybe that said something about my appearance in and of itself. Remembering how Mason sort of held my hand, I pulled away from him. He and Alberta finished up their joking remarks, and we all went our separate ways.

Music blasted inside the commons when we arrived, white Christmas lights and—ugh—a disco ball casting the only light in the otherwise darkened room. Gyrating bodies, mostly underclassmen, packed the dance floor. Those who were our age stood in too-cool clusters along the edges of the room, waiting for an opportune time to sneak off. An assortment of chaperones, guardians and Moroi teachers alike, patrolled around, breaking up those dancers who did a little too much gyrating.

When I saw Kirova in a sleeveless plaid dress, I turned to Mason and said, "Are you sure we can't hit the hard liquor yet?"

He snickered and took my hand again. "Come on, time for your surprise."

Letting him lead me, I walked across the room, cutting through a cluster of freshmen who looked way too young to be doing the kind of pelvic thrusts they were attempting.

Where were the chaperones when you needed them? Then I saw where he was leading me and came to a screeching halt.

"No," I said, not budging when he tugged my hand.

"Come on, it's going to be great."

"You're taking me to Jesse and Ralf. The only way I can *ever* be seen with them is if I've got a blunt object, and I'm aiming between their legs."

He pulled me again. "Not anymore. Come on."

Reluctant, I finally started moving: my worst fears were realized when a few pairs eyes turned our way. Great. Everything was starting all over again. Jesse and Ralf didn't notice us at first, but when they did, an amusing array of expressions played over their faces. First they saw my body and the dress. Testosterone took over as pure male lust shone out of their faces. Then they seemed to realize it was me and promptly turned terrified. Cool.

Mason gave Jesse a sharp poke in the chest with the end of his finger. "All right, Zeklos. Tell her."

Jesse didn't say anything, and Mason repeated the gesture, only harder.

"Tell her."

Not meeting my eyes, Jesse mumbled, "Rose, we know none of that stuff happened."

I almost choked on my own laughter. "*Do* you? Wow. I'm really glad to hear that. Because you see, until you said that, I'd been thinking it *had* happened. Thank God you guys are here to set me straight and tell me what the hell I have or haven't done!"

They flinched, and Mason's light expression darkened to something harder.

"She knows that," he growled. "Tell her the rest."

Jesse sighed. "We did it because Mia told us to."

"And?" prompted Mason.

"And we're sorry."

Mason turned to Ralf. "I want to hear it from you, big boy."

Ralf wouldn't meet my eyes either, but he mumbled something that sounded vaguely like an apology.

Seeing them defeated, Mason turned chipper. "You haven't heard the best part yet."

I cut him a sidelong look. "Yeah? Like the part where we rewind time and none of this ever happened?"

"Next best thing." He tapped Jesse again. "Tell her. Tell her *why* you did it."

Jesse looked up and exchanged uneasy looks with Ralf.

"Boys," warned Mason, clearly delighted about something, "you're making Hathaway and me very angry. Tell her why you did it."

Wearing the look of one who realized things couldn't get any worse, Jesse finally met my eyes. "We did it because she slept with us. Both of us."

TWENTY

My mouth dropped open. "Uh . . . wait . . . you mean *sex*?"

My astonishment prevented me from thinking of a better response. Mason thought it was hysterical. Jesse looked like he wanted to die.

"Of course I mean sex. She said she'd do it if we said that we'd . . . you know. . . ."

I made a face. "You guys didn't both, uh, do it at the same time, did you?"

"No," said Jesse in disgust. Ralf kind of looked like he wouldn't have minded.

"God," I muttered, pushing hair out of my face. "I can't believe she hates us that much."

"Hey," exclaimed Jesse, reading into my insinuation. "What's that supposed to mean? We're not that bad. And you and me—we were pretty close to—"

"No. We weren't *even* close to that." Mason laughed again, and something struck me. "If this . . . if this happened back then, though . . . she must have still been dating Aaron."

All three guys nodded.

"Oh. Whoa."

Mia *really* hated us. She'd just moved beyond poor-girl-wronged-by-girl's-brother and well into sociopath territory. She'd slept with these two and cheated on a boyfriend whom she seemed to adore.

Jesse and Ralf looked incredibly relieved when we walked away. Mason slung a lazy arm around my shoulders. "Well? What do you think? I rule, right? You can tell me. I won't mind."

I laughed. "How'd you finally find that out?"

"I called in a lot of favors. Used some threats. The fact that Mia can't retaliate helped too."

I recalled Mia accosting me the other day. I didn't think she was entirely helpless yet but didn't say so.

"They'll start telling people on Monday," he continued. "They promised. Everyone'll know by lunch."

"Why not now?" I asked sulkily. "They slept with a girl. Hurts her more than them."

"Yeah. True. They didn't want to deal with it tonight. You could start telling people if you wanted to. We could make a banner."

With as many times as Mia had called me a slut and a whore? Not a bad idea. "You got any markers and paper? . . ."

My words trailed off as I stared across the gym to where Lissa stood surrounded by admirers, Aaron's arm around her waist. She wore a sleek pink cotton sheath in a shade I never could have pulled off. Her blond hair had been pulled up in a bun that she'd used little crystal hairpins on. It almost looked like she wore a crown. Princess Vasilisa.

The same feelings as earlier hummed through to me, anxiety and excitement. She just couldn't quite enjoy herself tonight.

Watching her from the other side of the room, lurking in the darkness, was Christian. He practically blended into the shadows.

"Stop it," Mason chided me, seeing my stare. "Don't worry about her tonight."

"Hard not to."

"It makes you look all depressed. And you're too hot in that dress to look depressed. Come on, there's Eddie."

He dragged me away, but not before I cast one last glance at Lissa over my shoulder. Our eyes met briefly. Regret flashed through the bond.

But I pushed her out of my head—figuratively speaking—and managed to put on a good face when we joined a group of other novices. We earned a lot of mileage by telling them about the Mia scandal and, petty or not, seeing my name cleared and getting revenge on her felt amazingly good. And as those in our group wandered off and mingled with others, I could see the news spreading and spreading. So much for waiting until Monday.

Whatever. I didn't care. I was actually having a good time. I fell into my old role, happy to see I hadn't grown too dusty in making funny and flirty remarks. Yet, as time passed and Eddie's party grew closer, I started to feel Lissa's anxiety pick up in intensity. Frowning, I stopped talking and turned around, scanning the room for her.

There. She was still with a group of people, still the sun in her little solar system. But Aaron was leaning very close to her, saying something in her ear. A smile I recognized as fake was plastered across her face, and the annoyance and anxiety from her increased further.

Then it spiked. Mia had walked up to them.

Whatever she'd come to say, she didn't waste any time in saying it. With the eyes of Lissa's admirers on her, little Mia in her red dress gestured wildly, mouth working animatedly. I couldn't hear the words from across the room, but the feelings grew darker and darker through the bond.

"I've got to go," I told Mason.

I half walked, half ran over to Lissa's side, catching only the tail end of Mia's tirade. She was yelling at Lissa full force now and leaning into her face. From what I could tell, word must have reached her about Jesse and Ralf selling her out.

"—you and your slutty friend! I'm going to tell everyone what a psycho you are and how they had to lock you in the clinic because you're so crazy. They're putting you on medication. That's why you and Rose left before anyone else could find out you cut—"

Whoa, not good. Just like at our first meeting in the cafeteria, I grabbed her and jerked her away.

"Hey," I said. "Slutty friend here. Remember what I said about standing too close to her?"

Mia snarled, baring her fangs. As I'd noted before, I couldn't feel too sorry for her anymore. She was dangerous.

She had stooped low to get back at me. Now, somehow, she knew about Lissa and the cutting. *Really* knew, too; she wasn't just guessing. The information she had now sounded both like what the guardians on the scene had reported, as well as what I'd told them about Lissa's history. Maybe some confidential doctor's stuff too. Mia'd snagged the records somehow.

Lissa realized it too, and the look on her face—scared and fragile, no more princess—made my decision for me. It didn't matter that Kirova had spoken the other day about giving me my freedom, that I'd been having a good time, and that I could have let my worries go and partied tonight. I was going to ruin everything, right here and right now.

I'm really not good with impulse control.

I punched Mia as hard as I could—harder, I think, than I'd even hit Jesse. I heard a crunch as my fist impacted her nose, and blood spurted out. Someone screamed. Mia shrieked and flew backwards into some squealing girls who didn't want to get blood on their dresses. I swooped in after her, getting in one more good punch before somebody peeled me off her.

I didn't fight restraint as I had when they'd taken me from Mr. Nagy's classroom. I'd expected this as soon as I'd swung at her. Stopping all signs of resistance, I let two guardians lead me out of the dance while Ms. Kirova tried to bring some semblance of order. I didn't care what they did to me. Not anymore. Punish or expel. Whatever. I could handle—

Ahead of us, through the ebbing and flowing waves of students passing through the double doors, I saw a figure in pink

dart out. Lissa. My own out-of-control emotions had overrid-
den hers, but there they were, flooding back into me. Devasta-
tion. Despair. Everyone knew her secret now. She'd face more
than just idle speculation. Pieces would fall together. She
couldn't handle that.

Knowing I wasn't going anywhere, I frantically searched
for some way to help her. A dark figure caught my eye. "Christian!" I yelled. He'd been staring at Lissa's retreating figure
but glanced up at the sound of his name.

One of my escorts shushed me and took my arm. "Be
quiet."

I ignored her. "Go after her," I called to Christian. "Hurry."

He just sat there, and I suppressed a groan.

"Go, you idiot!"

My guardians snapped at me to be quiet again, but something inside of Christian woke up. Springing up from his lounging position, he tore off in the direction Lissa had traveled.

No one wanted to deal with me that night. There'd be
hell to pay tomorrow—I heard talk of suspension or possibly
even expulsion—but Kirova had her hands full with a bleeding Mia and a hysterical student body. The guardians escorted
me to my room under the watchful eye of the dorm matron
who informed me she'd check on me every hour to make sure
I stayed in my room. A couple guardians would also hang out
around the dorm's entrances. Apparently I was now a high-
security risk. I'd probably just ruined Eddie's party; he'd
never sneak a group up to his room now.

Heedless of my dress, I flounced onto the floor of my room, crossing my legs underneath me. I reached out to Lissa. She was calmer now. The events from the dance still hurt her terribly, but Christian was soothing her somehow, although whether it was through simple words or physical mojo, I couldn't say. I didn't care. So long as she felt better and wouldn't do anything stupid. I returned to myself.

Yes, things were going to get messy now. Mia and Jesse's respective accusations were going to set the school on fire. I probably would get thrown out and have to go live with a bunch of skanky dhampir women. At least Lissa might realize Aaron was boring and that she wanted to be with Christian. But even if that was the right thing, it still meant—

Christian. Christian.

Christian was hurt.

I snapped back into Lissa's body, suddenly sucked in by the terror pounding through her. She was surrounded, surrounded by men and women who had come out of nowhere, bursting up into the attic of the chapel where she and Christian had gone to talk. Christian leapt up, fire flaring from his fingers. One of the invaders hit him on the head with something hard, making his body slump to the ground.

I desperately hoped he was okay, but I couldn't waste any more energy worrying about him. All my fear was for Lissa now. I couldn't let the same thing happen to her. I couldn't let them hurt her. I needed to save her, to get her out of there. But I didn't know how. She was too far away, and I couldn't even escape her head at the moment, let alone run over there or get help.

The attackers approached her, calling her Princess and telling her not to worry, and that they were guardians. And they *did* seem like guardians. Definitely dhampirs. Moving in precise, efficient ways. But I didn't recognize them as any of the guardians from school. Neither did Lissa. Guardians wouldn't have attacked Christian. And guardians certainly wouldn't be binding and gagging her—

Something forced me out of her head, and I frowned, staring around my room. I needed to go back to her and find out what had happened. Usually the connection just faded or I closed it off, but this—this was like something had actually removed me and pulled me. Pulled me back here.

But that made no sense. What could pull me back from . . . wait.

My mind blanked.

I couldn't remember what I'd just been thinking about. It was gone. Like static in my brain. Where had I been? With Lissa? What about Lissa?

Standing up, I wrapped my arms around myself, confused, trying to figure out what was going on. Lissa. Something with Lissa.

Dimitri, a voice inside my head suddenly said. *Go to Dimitri.*

Yes. Dimitri. My body and spirit burned for him all of a sudden, and I wanted to be with him more than I ever had before. I couldn't stay away from him. He'd know what to do.

And he'd told me before I should come to him if something was wrong with Lissa. Too bad I couldn't remember what that was. Still. I knew he'd take care of everything.

Getting up to the staff wing of the dorm wasn't hard, since they wanted to keep me inside tonight. I didn't know where his room was, but it didn't matter. *Something* was pulling me to him, urging me closer. An instinct pushed me toward one of the doors, and I beat the living daylights out of it.

After a few moments, he opened it, brown eyes widening when he saw me.

"Rose?"

"Let me in. It's Lissa."

He immediately stepped aside for me. I'd apparently caught him in bed, because the covers were peeled back on one side and only a small tableside lamp shone in the darkness. Plus, he wore only cotton pajama bottoms; his chest— which I'd never seen before, and wow, did it look great—was bare. The ends of his dark hair curled near his chin and appeared damp, like he'd taken a shower not so long ago.

"What's wrong?"

The sound of his voice thrilled me, and I couldn't answer. I couldn't stop staring at him. The force that had pulled me up here pulled me to him. I wanted him to touch me so badly, so badly I could barely stand it. He was so amazing. So unbelievably gorgeous. I knew somewhere something was wrong, but it didn't seem important. Not when I was with him.

With almost a foot separating us, there was no way I could

easily kiss his lips without his help. So instead, I aimed for his chest, wanting to taste that warm, smooth skin.

"Rose!" he exclaimed, stepping back. "What are you doing?"

"What do you think?"

I moved toward him again, needing to touch him and kiss him and do so many other things.

"Are you drunk?" he asked, holding his hand out in a warding gesture.

"Don't I wish." I tried to dodge around him, then paused, momentarily uncertain. "I thought you wanted to—don't you think I'm pretty?" In all the time we'd known each other, in all the time this attraction had built, he'd never told me I was pretty. He'd hinted at it, but that wasn't the same. And despite all the assurances I had from other guys that I was hotness incarnate, I needed to hear it from the one guy I actually wanted.

"Rose, I don't know what's going on, but you need to go back to your room."

When I moved toward him again, he reached out and gripped my wrists. With that touch, an electric current shot through both of us, and I saw him forget whatever he'd just been worrying about. Something seized him too, something that made him suddenly want me as much as I wanted him.

Releasing my wrists, he moved his hands up my arms, sliding slowly along my skin. Holding me in his dark, hungry gaze, he pulled me to him, pressing me right up to his body.

One of his hands moved up the back of my neck, twining his fingers in my hair and tipping my face up to his. He brought his lips down, barely brushing them against mine.

Swallowing, I asked again, "Do you think I'm pretty?"

He regarded me with utter seriousness, like he always did. "I think you're beautiful."

"Beautiful?"

"You are so beautiful, it hurts me sometimes."

His lips moved to mine, gentle at first, and then hard and hungry. His kiss consumed me. His hands on my arms slid down, down my hips, down to the edge of my dress. He gathered up the fabric in his hands and began pushing it up my legs. I melted into that touch, into his kiss and the way it burned against my mouth. His hands kept sliding up and up, until he'd pulled the dress over my head and tossed it on the floor.

"You . . . you got rid of that dress fast," I pointed out between heavy breaths. "I thought you liked it."

"I do like it," he said. His breathing was as heavy as mine. "I love it."

And then he took me to the bed.

TWENTY-ONE

I'd never been completely naked around a guy before. It scared the hell out of me—even though it excited me, too. Lying on the covers, we clung to each other and kept kissing—and kissing and kissing and kissing. His hands and lips took possession of my body, and every touch was like fire on my skin.

After yearning for him for so long, I could barely believe this was happening. And while the physical stuff felt great, I also just liked being close to him. I liked the way he looked at me, like I was the sexiest, most wonderful thing in the world. I liked the way he would say my name in Russian, murmured like a prayer: *Roza, Roza* . . .

And somewhere, somewhere in all of this, was that same urging voice that had driven me up to his room, a voice that didn't sound like my own but that I was powerless to ignore. *Stay with him, stay with him. Don't think about anything else except him. Keep touching him. Forget about everything else.*

I listened—not that I really needed any extra convincing.

The burning in his eyes told me he wanted to do a lot more than we were, but he took things slow, maybe because he knew I was nervous. His pajama pants stayed on. At one point, I shifted so that I hovered over him, my hair hanging around him. He tilted his head slightly, and I just barely caught sight of the back of his neck. I brushed my fingertips over the six tiny marks tattooed there.

"Did you really kill six Strigoi?" He nodded. "Wow."

He brought my own neck down to his mouth and kissed me. His teeth gently grazed my skin, different from a vampire but every bit as thrilling. "Don't worry. You'll have a lot more than me someday."

"Do you feel guilty about it?"

"Hmm?"

"Killing them. You said in the van that it was the right thing to do, but it still bothers you. It's why you go to church, isn't it? I see you there, but you aren't really into the services."

He smiled, surprised and amused I'd guessed another secret about him. "How do you know these things? I'm not guilty exactly . . . just sad sometimes. All of them used to be human or dhampir or Moroi. It's a waste, that's all, but as I said before, it's something I have to do. Something we all have to do. Sometimes it bothers me, and the chapel is a good place to think about those kinds of things. Sometimes I find peace there, but not often. I find more peace with you."

He rolled me off of him and moved on top of me again. The kissing picked up once more, harder this time. More urgent. *Oh God*, I thought. *I'm finally going to do it. This is it. I can feel it.*

He must have seen the decision in my eyes. Smiling, he slid his hands behind my neck and unfastened Victor's necklace. He set it on the bedside table. As soon as the chain left his fingers, I felt like I'd been slapped in the face. I blinked in surprise.

Dimitri must have felt the same way. "What happened?" he asked.

"I—I don't know." I felt like I was trying to wake up, like I'd been asleep for two days. I needed to remember something.

Lissa. Something with Lissa.

My head felt funny. Not pain or dizziness, but . . . the voice, I realized. The voice urging me toward Dimitri was gone. That wasn't to say I didn't want him anymore because hey, seeing him there in those sexy pajama bottoms, with that brown hair spilling over the side of his face was pretty fine. But I no longer had that outside influence pushing me to him. Weird.

He frowned, no longer turned on. After several moments of thought, he reached over and picked up the necklace. The instant his fingers touched it, I saw desire sweep over him again. He slid his other hand onto my hip, and suddenly, that burning lust slammed back into me. My stomach went queasy while my skin started to prickle and grow warm again. My breathing became heavy. His lips moved toward mine again.

Some inner part of me fought through.

"Lissa," I whispered, squeezing my eyes shut. "I have to tell you something about Lissa. But I can't . . . remember . . . I feel so strange. . . ."

"I know." Still holding onto me, he rested his cheek against my forehead. "There's something . . . something here. . . ." He pulled his face away, and I opened my eyes. "This necklace. That's the one Prince Victor gave you?"

I nodded and could see the sluggish thought process trying to wake up behind his eyes. Taking a deep breath, he removed his hand from my hip and pushed himself away.

"What are you doing?" I exclaimed. "Come back. . . ."

He looked like he wanted to—very badly—but instead he climbed out of the bed. He and the necklace moved away from me. I felt like he'd ripped part of me away, but at the same time, I had that startling sensation of waking up, like I could think clearly once more without my body making all the decisions.

On the other hand, Dimitri still wore a look of animal passion on him, and it seemed to take a great deal of effort for him to walk across the room. He reached the window and managed to open it one-handed. Cold air blasted in, and I rubbed my hands over my arms for warmth.

"What are you going to—?" The answer hit me, and I sprang out of bed, just as the necklace flew out the window. "No! Do you know how much that must have—?"

The necklace disappeared, and I no longer felt like I was *waking* up. I *was* awake. Painfully, startlingly so.

I took in my surroundings. Dimitri's room. Me naked. The rumpled bed.

But all that was nothing compared to what hit me next.

"Lissa!" I gasped out. It all came back, the memories and

the emotions. And, in fact, her held-back emotions suddenly poured into me—at staggering levels. More terror. Intense terror. Those feelings wanted to suck me back into her body, but I couldn't let them. Not quite yet. I fought against her, needing to stay here. With the words coming out in a rush, I told Dimitri everything that had happened.

He was in motion before I finished, putting on clothes and looking every bit like a badass god. Ordering me to get dressed, he tossed me a sweatshirt with Cyrillic writing on it to wear over the skimpy dress.

I had a hard time following him downstairs; he made no effort to slow for me this time. Calls were made when we got there. Orders shouted. Before long, I ended up in the guardians' main office with him. Kirova and other teachers were there. Most of the campus's guardians. Everyone seemed to speak at once. All the while, I felt Lissa's fear, felt her moving farther and farther away.

I yelled at them to hurry up and do something, but no one except Dimitri would believe my story about her abduction until someone retrieved Christian from the chapel and then verified Lissa really wasn't on campus.

Christian staggered in, supported by two guardians. Dr. Olendzki appeared shortly thereafter, checking him out and wiping blood away from the back of his head.

Finally, I thought, something would happen.

"How many Strigoi were there?" one of the guardians asked me.

"How in the world did they get in?" muttered someone else.

I stared. "Wh—? There weren't any Strigoi."

Several sets of eyes stared at me. "Who else would have taken her?" asked Ms. Kirova primly. "You must have seen it wrong through the . . . vision."

"No. I'm positive. It was . . . they were . . . guardians."

"She's right," mumbled Christian, still under the doctor's ministrations. He winced as she did something to the back of his head. "Guardians."

"That's impossible," someone said.

"They weren't school guardians." I rubbed my forehead, fighting hard to keep from leaving the conversation and going back to Lissa. My irritation grew. "Will you guys get moving? She's getting farther away!"

"You're saying a group of privately retained guardians came in and kidnapped her?" The tone in Kirova's voice implied I was playing some kind of joke.

"Yes," I replied through gritted teeth. "They . . ."

Slowly, carefully, I slipped my mental restraint and flew into Lissa's body. I sat in a car, an expensive car with tinted windows to keep out most of the light. It might be "night" here, but it was full day for the rest of the world. One of the guardians from the chapel drove; another sat beside him in the front—one I recognized. Spiridon. In the back, Lissa sat with tied hands, another guardian beside her, and on the other side—

"They work for Victor Dashkov," I gasped out, focusing back on Kirova and the others. "They're his."

"Prince Victor Dashkov?" asked one of the guardians with a snort. Like there was any other freaking Victor Dashkov.

"Please," I moaned, hands clutching my head. "Do something. They're getting so far away. They're on . . ." A brief image, seen outside the car window, flared in my vision. "Eighty-three. Headed south."

"Eighty-three already? How long ago did they leave? Why didn't you come sooner?"

My eyes turned anxiously to Dimitri.

"A compulsion spell," he said slowly. "A compulsion spell put into a necklace he gave her. It made her attack me."

"No one can use that kind of compulsion," exclaimed Kirova. "No one's done that in ages."

"Well, someone did. By the time I'd restrained her and taken the necklace, a lot of time had passed," Dimitri continued, face perfectly controlled. No one questioned the story.

Finally, finally, the group moved into action. No one wanted to bring me, but Dimitri insisted when he realized I could lead them to her. Three details of guardians set out in sinister black SUVs. I rode in the first one, sitting in the passenger seat while Dimitri drove. Minutes passed. The only times we spoke was when I gave a report.

"They're still on Eighty-three . . . but their turn is coming. They aren't speeding. They don't want to get pulled over."

He nodded, not looking at me. He most definitely *was* speeding.

Giving him a sidelong glance, I replayed tonight's earlier events. In my mind's eye, I could see it all again, the way he'd looked at me and kissed me.

But what had it been? An illusion? A trick? On the way to the car, he'd told me there really had been a compulsion spell in the necklace, a lust one. I had never heard of such a thing, but when I'd asked for more information, he just said it was a type of magic earth users once practiced but never did anymore.

"They're turning," I said suddenly. "I can't see the road name, but I'll know when we're close."

Dimitri grunted in acknowledgment, and I sank further into my seat.

What had it all meant? Had it meant anything to him? It had definitely meant a lot to me.

"There," I said about twenty minutes later, indicating the rough road Victor's car had turned off on. It was unpaved gravel, and the SUV gave us an edge over his luxury car.

We drove on in silence, the only sound coming from the crunching of the gravel under the tires. Dust kicked up outside the windows, swirling around us.

"They're turning again."

Farther and farther off the main routes they went, and we followed the whole time, led by my instructions. Finally, I felt Victor's car come to a stop.

"They're outside a small cabin," I said. "They're taking her—"

"Why are you doing this? What's going on?"

Lissa. Cringing and scared. Her feelings had pulled me into her.

"Come, child," said Victor, moving into the cabin, unsteady on his cane. One of his guardians held the door open. Another pushed Lissa along and settled her into a chair near a small table inside. It was cold in here, especially in the pink dress. Victor sat across from her. When she started to get up, a guardian gave her a warning look. "Do you think I'd seriously hurt you?"

"What did you do to Christian?" she cried, ignoring the question. "Is he dead?

"The Ozera boy? I didn't mean for that to happen. We didn't expect him to be there. We'd hoped to catch you alone, to convince others you'd run away again. We'd made sure rumors already circulated about that."

We? I recalled how the stories had resurfaced this week . . . from Natalie.

"Now?" He sighed, spreading his hands wide in a help- less gesture. "I don't know. I doubt anyone will connect it to us, even if they don't believe you ran away. Rose is the biggest liability. We'd intended to . . . dispatch her, letting others think she'd run away as well. The spectacle she cre- ated at your dance made that impossible, but I had another plan in place to make sure she stays occupied for some time . . . probably until tomorrow. We will have to contend with her later."

He hadn't counted on Dimitri figuring out the spell. He'd figured we'd be too busy getting it on all night.

"Why?" asked Lissa. "Why are you doing all this?"

His green eyes widened, reminding her of her father's. They might be distant relatives, but that jade-green color ran in both the Dragomirs and the Dashkovs. "I'm surprised you even have to ask, my dear. I need you. I need you to heal me."

TWENTY-TWO

"*Heal* you?"

Heal him? My thoughts echoed hers.

"You're the only way," he said patiently. "The only way to cure this disease. I've been watching you for years, waiting until I was certain."

Lissa shook her head. "I can't . . . no. I can't do anything like that."

"Your healing powers are incredible. No one has any idea just how powerful."

"I don't know what you're talking about."

"Come now, Vasilisa. I know about the raven—Natalie saw you do it. She'd been following you. And I know how you healed Rose."

She realized the pointlessness of denying it. "That . . . was different. Rose wasn't that hurt. But you . . . I can't do anything about Sandovsky's Syndrome."

"Not *that* hurt?" he laughed. "I'm not talking about her ankle—which was still impressive. I'm talking about the car accident. Because you're right, you know. Rose didn't get 'that hurt.' She *died*."

He let the words sink in.

"That's . . . no. She lived," Lissa finally managed.

"No. Well, yes, she did. But I read all the reports. There was *no way* she should have survived—especially with so many injuries. You healed her. You brought her back." He sighed, half wistful and half weary. "I'd suspected you could do this for so long, and I tried so hard to repeat it . . . to see how much you could control. . . ."

Lissa caught on and gasped. "The *animals*. It was you."

"With Natalie's help."

"Why would you do that? How could you?"

"Because I had to know. I have only a few more weeks to live, Vasilisa. If you can truly bring back the dead, then you can cure Sandovsky's. I had to know before I took you away that you could heal at will and not just in moments of panic."

"Why take me at all?" A spark of anger flared up in her. "You're my near-uncle. If you wanted me to do this—if you really think I can . . . " Her voice and feelings showed me she didn't really entirely believe she could heal him. "Then why kidnap me? Why didn't you just ask?"

"Because it's not a onetime affair. It took a long time to figure out what you are, but I managed to acquire some of the old histories . . . scrolls kept out of Moroi museums. When I read about how wielding spirit works—"

"Wielding what?"

"Spirit. It's what you've specialized in."

"I haven't specialized in anything! You're crazy."

"Where else do you think these powers of yours have

come from? Spirit is another element, one few people have any more."

Lissa's mind was still reeling from the kidnapping and the possible truth that she'd brought me back from the dead. "That doesn't make any sense. Even if it wasn't common, I still would have heard of another element! Or of someone having it."

"No one knows about spirit anymore. It's been forgotten. When people do specialize in it, nobody realizes it. They think the person simply hasn't specialized at all."

"Look, if you're just trying to make me feel—" She abruptly cut herself off. She was angry and afraid, but behind those emotions, her higher reasoning had been processing what he'd said about spirit users and specializing. It now caught up with her. "Oh my God. Vladimir and Ms. Karp."

He gave her a knowing look. "You've known about this all along."

"No! I swear. It's just something Rose was looking into. . . . She said they were like me. . . ." Lissa was starting to change from a little scared to all scared. The news was too shocking.

"They *are* like you. The books even say Vladimir was 'full of spirit.'" Victor seemed to find that funny. Seeing that smile made me want to slap him.

"I thought . . ." Lissa still wanted him to be wrong. The idea of not specializing was safer than specializing in some freakish element. "I thought that meant, like, the Holy Spirit."

"So does everyone else, but no. It's something else entirely. An element that's within all of us. A master element that can give you indirect control over the others." Apparently my theory about her specializing in all the elements wasn't so far off.

She worked hard to get a grip on this news and her own self-control. "That doesn't answer my question. It doesn't matter if I have this spirit thing or whatever. You didn't have to kidnap me."

"Spirit, as you've seen, can heal physical injuries. Unfortunately, it's only good on acute injuries. Onetime things. Rose's ankle. The accident wounds. For something chronic— say, a genetic disease like Sandovsky's—continual healings are required. Otherwise it will keep coming back. That's what would happen to me. I need you, Vasilisa. I need you to help me fight this and keep it away. So I can live."

"That still doesn't explain why you took me," she argued. "I would have helped you if you'd asked."

"They never would have let you do it. The school. The council. Once they got over the shock of finding a spirit user, they'd get hung up on ethics. After all, how does one choose who gets to be healed? They'd say it wasn't fair. That it was like playing God. Or else they'd worry about the toll it'd take on you."

She flinched, knowing exactly what toll he referred to.

Seeing her expression, he nodded. "Yes. I won't lie to you. It will be hard. It will exhaust you—mentally and physically. But I must do it. I *am* sorry. You'll be provided with feeders and other entertainments for your services."

She leapt from the chair. Ben immediately stepped forward and pushed her back into it. "And then what? Are you going to just make me a prisoner here? Your own private nurse?"

He made that annoying open-palmed gesture again. "I'm sorry. I have no choice."

White-hot anger blasted away the fear inside of her. She spoke in a low voice. "Yes. *You* don't have the choice, because this is *me* we're talking about."

"It's better for you this way. You know how the others turned out. How Vladimir spent the last of his days stark, raving mad. How Sonya Karp had to be taken away. The trauma you've experienced since the accident comes from more than just your family's loss. It's from using spirit. The accident woke the spirit in you; your fear over seeing Rose dead made it burst out, allowing you to heal her. It forged your bond. And once it's out, you can't put it back. It's a powerful element—but it's also dangerous. Earth users get their power from the earth, air users from the air. But spirit? Where do you think that comes from?"

She glared.

"It comes from you, from your own essence. To heal another, you must give part of yourself. The more you do that, the more it will destroy you over time. You must be noticing that already. I've seen how much certain things upset you, how fragile you are."

"I'm not fragile," snapped Lissa. "And I'm not going to go

crazy. I'm going to stop using spirit before things get worse."

He smiled. "Stop using it? You might as well stop breathing. Spirit has its own agenda. . . . You'll always have the urge to help and heal. It's part of you. You resisted the animals, but you didn't think twice about helping Rose. You can't even help compulsion—which spirit also gives you special strength in. And that's how it will always be. You can't avoid spirit. Better to stay here, in isolation, away from further sources of stress. You'd either have become increasingly unstable at the Academy, or they would have put you on some pill that would have made you feel better but stunted your power."

A calm core of confidence settled inside her, one very different from what I'd observed over the last couple of years. "I love you, Uncle Victor, but *I'm* the one who has to deal with that and decide what to do. Not you. You're making me give up my life for yours. That's not fair."

"It's a matter of which life means more. I love you too. Very much. But the Moroi are falling apart. Our numbers are dropping as we let the Strigoi prey upon us. We used to actively seek them out. Now Tatiana and the other leaders hide away. They keep you and your peers isolated. In the old days, you were trained to fight alongside your guardians! You were taught to use magic as a weapon. Not any longer. We wait. We are *victims*." As he stared off, both Lissa and I could see how caught up in his passion he was. "I would have changed that if I were king. I would have brought about a revolution the likes of which neither Moroi nor Strigoi have ever seen. *I* should have been Tatiana's heir. She was ready to name me before they discovered the disease, and then she would not. If I were cured . . . if I were cured, I could take my rightful place. . . ."

His words triggered something inside of Lissa, a sudden consideration for the state of the Moroi. She'd never contemplated what he'd said, about how different it might be if Moroi and their guardians fought side by side to rid the world of the Strigoi and their evil. It reminded her of Christian and what he'd said about using magic as a weapon too. But even if she did appreciate Victor's convictions, neither of us thought it was worth what he wanted her to do.

"I'm sorry," she whispered. "I'm sorry for you. But please don't make me do this."

"I have to."

She looked him straight in the eye. "I won't do it."

He inclined his head, and someone stepped forward from the corner. Another Moroi. No one I knew. Walking around behind Lissa, he untied her hands.

"This is Kenneth." Victor held his hands out toward her free ones. "Please, Vasilisa. Take my hands. Send the magic through me just as you did with Rose."

She shook her head. "No."

His voice was less kindly when he spoke again. "Please. One way or another, you will heal me. I'd rather it be on your terms, not ours."

She shook her head again. He made a slight gesture toward Kenneth.

And that's when the pain started.

Lissa screamed. I screamed.

In the SUV, Dimitri's grip on the wheel jerked in surprise, making us veer. Casting me an alarmed look, he started to pull over.

"No, no! Keep going!" I pressed my palms to my temples. "We have to get there!"

From behind my seat, Alberta reached forward and rested a hand on my shoulder. "Rose, what's happening?"

I blinked back tears. "They're torturing her . . . with air. This guy . . . Kenneth . . . he's making it press against her . . . into her head. The pressure's insane. It feels like my—her—skull's gonna explode." I started sobbing.

Dimitri looked at me out of the corner of his eye and pressed the gas pedal down harder.

Kenneth didn't stop with just the physical force of air. He also used it to affect her breathing. Sometimes he'd smother her with it; other times he'd take it all away and leave her gasping. After enduring all that firsthand—and it was bad enough secondhand—I felt pretty confident I would have done anything they wanted.

And finally, she did.

Hurting and bleary-eyed, Lissa took Victor's hands. I'd never been in her head when she worked magic and didn't know what to expect. At first, I felt nothing. Just a sense of concentration. Then . . . it was like . . . I don't even know how to describe it. Color and light and music and life and joy and love . . . so many wonderful things, all the lovely things that make up the world and make it worth living in.

Lissa summoned up all of those things, as many as she could, and sent them into Victor. The magic flowed through both of us, brilliant and sweet. It was alive. It was her life. And as wonderful as it all felt, she was growing weaker and weaker. But as all of those elements—bound by the mysterious spirit element—flowed into Victor, he grew stronger and stronger.

The change was startling. His skin smoothed, no longer wrinkled and pocked. The gray, thinning hair filled out, turning dark and lustrous once more. The green eyes—still jadelike—sparkled again, turning alert and lively.

He'd become the Victor she remembered from her childhood.

Exhausted, Lissa passed out.

In the SUV, I tried to relate what was happening. Dimitri's face grew darker and darker, and he spat out a string of Russian swear words he *still* hadn't taught me the meanings of.

When we were a quarter mile from the cabin, Alberta made a call on her cell phone, and our whole convoy pulled over. All of the guardians—more than a dozen—got out and stood huddled, planning strategy. Someone went ahead to scout and returned with a report on the number of people inside and outside of the cabin. When the group seemed ready to disperse, I started to get out of the car. Dimitri stopped me.

"No, Roza. You stay here."

"The hell with that. I have to go help her."

He cupped my chin with his hands, fixing me with his eyes. "You have helped her. Your job is done. You did it well. But this isn't any place for you. She and I both need you to stay safe."

Only the realization that arguing would delay the rescue kept me quiet. Swallowing back any protests, I nodded. He nodded back and joined the others. All of them slipped off into the woods, blending with the trees.

Sighing, I kicked the passenger seat back and lay down. I was so tired. Even though the sun poured through the windshield, it was night for me. I'd been up for most of it, and a lot had happened in that time. Between the adrenaline of my own role and sharing Lissa's pain, I could have passed out just like she had.

Except that she was awake now.

Slowly, her perceptions dominated mine once more. She lay on a couch in the cabin. One of Victor's henchmen must have carried her there after she'd fainted. Victor himself—alive and well now, thanks to his abuse of her—stood in the kitchen with the others as they all spoke in low voices about their plans. Only one stood near Lissa, keeping watch. He'd be easy to take down when Dimitri and the Badass Team burst inside.

Lissa studied the lone guardian and then glanced at a window beside the couch. Still dizzy from the healing, she managed to sit up. The guardian turned around, watching her warily. She met his eyes and smiled.

"You're going to stay quiet no matter what I do," she told him. "You aren't going to call for help or tell anyone when I leave. Okay?"

The thrall of compulsion slid over him. He nodded in agreement.

Moving toward the window, she unlocked it and slid the glass up. As she did, a tumble of considerations played through her mind. She was weak. She didn't know how far from the Academy—from anything, really—she was. She had no clue how far she could get before someone noticed.

But she also knew she might not get another chance at escape. She had no intention of spending the rest of her life in this cabin in the woods.

At any other time, I would have cheered on her boldness, but not this time. Not when all those guardians were about to save her. She needed to stay put. Unfortunately, she couldn't hear my advice.

Lissa climbed out the window, and I swore out loud.

"What? What'd you see?" asked a voice behind me.

I jerked up from my reclining position in the car, banging my head on the ceiling. Glancing behind me, I found Christian peering up from the cargo space behind the farthest backseats.

"What are you doing here?" I asked.

"What's it look like? I'm a stowaway."

"Don't you have a concussion or something?"

He shrugged like it didn't matter. What a great pair he and Lissa were. Neither afraid to take on crazy feats while seriously injured. Still, if Kirova had made me stay behind, I would have been right beside him in the back.

"What's happening?" he asked. "Did you see something new?

Hastily, I told him. I also got out of the car as I spoke. He followed.

"She doesn't know our guys are already coming for her. I'm going to go get her before she kills herself with exhaustion."

"What about the guardians? The school's, I mean. Are you going to tell them she's gone?"

I shook my head. "They're probably already busting down the cabin's door. I'm going after her." She was somewhere off to the right side of the cabin. I could head in that direction but wouldn't be able to get very precise until I was much closer to her. Still, it didn't matter. I had to find her. Seeing Christian's face, I couldn't resist giving him a dry smile. "And yeah, I know. You're going with me."

TWENTY-THREE

I'd never had so much trouble staying out of Lissa's head before, but then, we'd never been through anything like this together either. The strength of her thoughts and feelings kept trying to pull me in as I hurried through the forest.

Running through the brush and woods, Christian and I moved farther and farther from the cabin. Man, how I wished Lissa had stayed back there. I would have loved to see the raid through her eyes. But that was behind us now, and as I ran, Dimitri's push on laps and stamina paid off. She wasn't moving very quickly, and I could feel the distance closing between us, giving me a more precise idea of her location. Likewise, Christian couldn't keep up with me. I started to slow for him but soon realized the foolishness of that.

So did he. "Go," he gasped out, waving me on.

When I reached a point close enough to her that I thought she could hear me, I called out her name, hoping to get her to turn around. Instead, what answered me was a set of howls—a soft canine baying.

Psi-hounds. Of course. Victor had said he hunted with them; he could control those beasts. I suddenly understood why no one at school recalled sending psi-hounds after

Lissa and me in Chicago. The Academy hadn't arranged that; Victor had.

A minute later, I reached a clearing where Lissa cringed, back against a tree. From her looks and bond feelings, she should have fainted long ago. Only the barest scraps of will-power kept her hanging on. Wide-eyed and pale, she stared in horror at the four psi-hounds cornering her. Noticing the full sunlight, it occurred to me that she and Christian had another obstacle to contend with out here.

"Hey," I yelled at the hounds, trying to draw them toward me. Victor must have sent them to trap her, but I hoped they'd sense and respond to another threat—especially a dhampir. Psi-hounds didn't like us any better than other animals did.

Sure enough, they turned on me, teeth bared and drool coming out of their mouths. They resembled wolves, only with brown fur and eyes that glowed like orange fire. He'd probably ordered them not to harm her, but they had no such instructions regarding me.

Wolves. Just like in science class. What had Ms. Meissner said? A lot of confrontations were all about willpower? Bearing this mind, I tried to project an alpha attitude, but I don't think they fell for it. Any one of them outweighed me. Oh yeah—they also outnumbered me. No, they didn't have anything to be scared of.

Trying to pretend this was just a free-for-all match with Dimitri, I picked up a branch from the ground that had about the same heft and weight as a baseball bat. I'd just positioned it in my hands when two of the hounds jumped me. Claws and teeth bit into me, but I held my own surprisingly well as I tried to remember everything I'd learned in the last two months about fighting bigger and stronger opponents.

I didn't like hurting them. They reminded me too much of dogs. But it was me or them, and survival instincts won out. One of them I managed to beat to the ground, dead or unconscious I didn't know. The other was still on me, still coming on fast and furious. His companions looked ready to join him, but then a new competitor burst on the scene—sort of. Christian.

"Get out of here," I yelled at him, shaking off my hound as its claws ripped into the bare skin of my leg, nearly toppling me over. I was still wearing the dress, though I'd shed the heels a while ago.

But Christian, like any lovesick guy, didn't listen. He picked up a branch as well and swung it at one of the hounds. Flames burst from the wood. The hound backed up, still compelled to follow Victor's orders, though also clearly afraid of the fire.

Its companion, the fourth hound, circled away from the torch and came up behind Christian. Smart little bastard. It sprang at Christian, hitting him back first. The branch flew from his hands, the fire immediately going out. Both hounds then leapt onto his fallen form. I finished my hound—again feeling sick over what I had to do to subdue it—and moved toward the other two, wondering if I had the strength to take on these last ones.

But I didn't have to. Rescue appeared in the form of Alberta, emerging through some trees.

With a gun in hand, she shot the hounds without hesitation. Boring as hell perhaps—and completely useless against Strigoi—but against other things? Guns were tried and true. The hounds stopped moving and slumped next to Christian's body.

And Christian's body . . .

All three of us made our way over to it—Lissa and I practically crawling. When I saw it, I had to look away. My stomach lurched, and it took a lot of effort not to throw up. He wasn't dead yet, but I didn't think he had much longer.

Lissa's eyes, wide and distraught, drank him in. Tentatively, she reached out toward him and then dropped her hand.

"I can't," she managed in a small voice. "I don't have the strength left."

Alberta, leathery face both hard and compassionate, gently tugged her arm. "Come on, Princess. We need to get out of here. We'll send help."

Turning back to Christian, I forced myself to look at him and let myself feel how much Lissa cared about him.

"Liss," I said hesitantly. She looked over at me, like she'd forgotten I was even there. Wordlessly, I brushed my hair away from my neck and tilted it toward her.

She stared for a moment, blank-faced; then understanding shone in her eyes.

Those fangs that lurked behind her pretty smile bit into my neck, and a small moan escaped my lips. I hadn't realized how much I'd missed it, that sweet, wonderful pain followed by glorious wonder. Bliss settled over me. Dizzying. Joyful. Like being in a dream.

I don't entirely remember how long Lissa drank from me. Probably not that long. She would never even consider drinking the quantities that would kill a person and make her a Strigoi. She finished, and Alberta caught me as I started to sway.

Dizzily, I watched as Lissa leaned over Christian and rested her hands on him. In the distance, I heard the other guardians crashing through the forest.

No glowing or fireworks surrounded the healing. It all took place invisibly, occurring between Lissa and Christian. Even though the bite's endorphins had numbed my connection to her, I remembered Victor's healing and the wonderful colors and music she must be bringing forth.

A miracle unfolded before my eyes, and Alberta gasped. Christian's wounds closed. The blood dried up. Color—as much as a Moroi ever had, at least—returned to his cheeks. His eyelids fluttered, and his eyes regained their life again. Focusing on Lissa, he smiled. It was like watching a Disney movie.

I must have keeled over after that, because I don't remember anything else.

Eventually, I woke up in the Academy's clinic, where they forced fluids and sugar into me for two days. Lissa stayed by my side almost the entire time, and slowly, the events of the kidnapping unfolded.

We had to tell Kirova and a few choice others about Lissa's powers, how she'd healed Victor and Christian and, well, me. The news was shocking, but the administrators agreed to keep it secret from the rest of the school. No one even considered taking Lissa away like they had Ms. Karp.

Mostly all the other students knew was that Victor Dashkov had kidnapped Lissa Dragomir. They didn't know why. Some of his guardians had died when Dimitri's band attacked—a damned shame, when guardian numbers were so low already. Victor was now being held under 24/7 guard at the school, waiting for a royal regiment of guardians to carry him away. The Moroi rulers might be a mostly symbolic government within another country's larger government, but they had systems of justice, and I'd heard about Moroi prisons. Not any place I'd want to be.

As for Natalie . . . that was trickier. She was still a minor, but she'd conspired with her father. She'd brought in the dead animals and kept an eye on Lissa's behavior—even before we left. Being an earth user like Victor, she'd also been the one to rot the bench that broke my ankle. After she'd seen me hold Lissa back from the dove, she and Victor realized that they needed to injure *me* to get to her—it was their only chance to get her to heal again. Natalie had simply waited for a good opportunity. She wasn't locked up or anything yet, and the Academy didn't know what to do with her until a royal command came.

I couldn't help but feel sorry for her. She was so awkward and self-conscious. Anyone could have manipulated her, let alone her father, whom she loved and from whom she so desperately wanted attention. She would have done anything. Rumor said she'd stood screaming outside the detention center, begging them to let her see him. They'd refused and hauled her away.

Meanwhile, Lissa and I slipped back into our friendship like nothing had happened. In the rest of her world, a lot had happened. After all that excitement and drama, she seemed to gain a new sense of what mattered to her. She broke up with Aaron. I'm sure she did it very nicely, but it still had to be hard on him. She'd dropped him twice now. The fact that his last girlfriend had cheated on him probably wasn't helping his confidence any.

And without any more hesitation, Lissa started dating Christian, not caring about the consequences to her reputation. Seeing them out in public, holding hands, made me do a double take. He didn't seem able to believe it himself. The rest of our classmates were almost too stunned to even comprehend it yet. They could barely process acknowledging his existence, let alone him being with someone like her.

My own romantic state was less rosy than hers—if you could even *call* it a romantic state. Dimitri hadn't visited me during my recovery, and our practices were indefinitely suspended. It wasn't until the fourth day after Lissa's kidnapping that I ran into him in the gym. We were alone.

I had come back for my gym bag and froze when I saw him, unable to speak. He started to walk past and then stopped.

"Rose . . ." he began after several uncomfortable moments. "You need to report what happened. With us."

I'd been waiting a long time to talk to him, but this wasn't the conversation I'd imagined.

"I can't do that. They'll fire you. Or worse."

"They should fire me. What I did was wrong."

"You couldn't help it. It was the spell. . . ."

"It doesn't matter. It was wrong. And stupid."

Wrong? Stupid? I bit my lip, and tears threatened to fill my eyes. I quickly tried to regain my composure. "Look, it's not a big deal."

"It *is* a big deal! I took advantage of you."

"No," I said evenly. "You didn't."

There must have been something telling in my voice because he met my eyes with a deep and serious intensity.

"Rose, I'm seven years older than you. In ten years, that won't mean so much, but for now, it's huge. I'm an adult. You're a child."

Ouch. I flinched. Easier if he'd just punched me.

"You didn't seem to think I was a child when you were all over me."

Now he flinched. "Just because your body . . . well, that doesn't make you an adult. We're in two very different places. I've been out in the world. I've been on my own. I've killed, Rose—*people*, not animals. And you . . . you're just starting out. Your life is about homework and clothes and dances."

"That's all you think I care about?"

"No, of course not. Not entirely. But it's all part of your world. You're still growing up and figuring out who you are and what's important. You need to keep doing that. You need to be with boys your own age."

I didn't want boys my own age. But I didn't say that. I didn't say anything.

"Even if you choose not to tell, you need to understand that *it was a mistake*. And it isn't ever going to happen again," he added.

"Because you're too old for me? Because it isn't responsible?"

His face was perfectly blank. "No. Because I'm just not interested in you in that way."

I stared. The message—the rejection—came through loud and clear. Everything from that night, everything I'd believed so beautiful and full of meaning, turned to dust before my eyes.

"It only happened because of the spell. Do you understand?"

Humiliated and angry, I refused to make a fool of

myself by arguing or begging. I just shrugged. "Yeah. Understood."

I spent the rest of the day sulking, ignoring both Lissa and Mason's attempts to draw me out of my room. It was ironic that I should want to stay inside. Kirova had been impressed enough by my performance with the rescue to end my house arrest.

Before school the next day, I made my way to where Victor was being held. The Academy had honest-to-goodness cells, complete with bars, and two guardians stood watch in the hallway nearby. It took a little bit of finagling on my part to get them to let me inside to talk to him. Even Natalie wasn't allowed in. But one of the guardians had ridden with me in the SUV and watched me undergo Lissa's torture. I told him I needed to ask Victor about what he'd done to Lissa. It was a lie, but the guardians bought it and felt sorry for me. They allowed me five minutes to speak, backing up a discrete distance down the hall where they could see but not hear.

Standing outside Victor's cell, I couldn't believe I'd once felt sorry for him. Seeing his new and healthy body enraged me. He sat cross-legged on a narrow bed, reading. When he heard me approach, he looked up.

"Why Rose, what a nice surprise. Your ingenuity never fails to impress me. I didn't think they'd allow me any visitors."

I crossed my arms, trying to put on a look of total guardian fierceness. "I want you to break the spell. Finish it off."

"What do you mean?"

"The spell you did on me and Dimitri."

"That spell is done. It burned itself out."

I shook my head. "No. I keep thinking about him. I keep wanting to . . ."

He smiled knowingly when I didn't finish. "My dear, that was already there, long before I set that up."

"It wasn't like this. Not this bad."

"Maybe not consciously. But everything else . . . the attraction—physical and mental—was already in you. And in him. It wouldn't have worked otherwise. The spell didn't really add anything new—it just removed inhibitions and strengthened the feelings you already had for each other."

"You're lying. He said he didn't feel that way about me."

"*He's* lying. I tell you, the spell wouldn't have worked otherwise, and honestly, he should have known better. He had no right to let himself feel that way. You can be forgiven for a schoolgirl's crush. But him? He should have demonstrated more control in hiding his feelings. Natalie saw it and told me. After just a few observations of my own, it was obvious to me too. It gave me the perfect chance to distract you both. I keyed the necklace's charm for each of you, and you two did the rest."

"You're a sick bastard, doing that to me and him. And to Lissa."

"I have no regrets about what I did with her," he declared,

leaning against the wall. "I'd do it again if I could. Believe what you want, I love my people. What I wanted to do was in their best interest. Now? Hard to say. They have no leader, no *real* leader. There's no one worthy, really." He cocked his head toward me, considering. "Vasilisa actually might have been such a one—if she could ever have found it within herself to believe in something and overcome the influence of spirit. It's ironic, really. Spirit can shape someone into a leader and also crush her ability to remain one. The fear, depression, and uncertainty take over, and keep her true strength buried deep within her. Still, she has the blood of the Dragomirs, which is no small thing. And of course, she has you, her shadow-kissed guardian. Who knows? She may surprise us yet."

"'Shadow-kissed'?" There it was again, the same thing Ms. Karp had called me.

"You've been kissed by shadows. You've crossed into Death, into the other side, and returned. Do you think something like that doesn't leave a mark on the soul? You have a greater sense of life and the world—far greater than even I have—even if you don't realize it. You should have stayed dead. Vasilisa brushed Death to bring you back and bound you to her forever. You were actually in its embrace, and some part of you will always remember that, always fight to cling to life and experience all it has. That's why you're so reckless in the things you do. You don't hold back your feelings, your passion, your anger. It makes you remarkable. It makes you dangerous."

I didn't know what to say to that. I was speechless, which he seemed to like.

"It's what created your bond, too. Her feelings always press out of her, onto others. Most people can't pick up on them unless she's actually directing her thoughts toward them with compulsion. You, however, have a mind sensitive to extrasensory forces—hers in particular." He sighed, almost happily, and I remembered reading that Vladimir had saved Anna from death. That must have made *their* bond, too. "Yes, this ridiculous Academy has no idea what they have in either you or her. If not for the fact that I needed to kill you, I would have made you part of my royal guard when you were older."

"You never would've had a royal guard. Don't you think people would have been weirded out by you suddenly recovering like that? Even if no one found out about Lissa, Tatiana never would have made you king."

"You may be right, but it doesn't matter. There are other ways of taking power. Sometimes it's necessary to go outside the established channels. Do you think Kenneth is the only Moroi who follows me? The greatest and most powerful revolutions often start very quietly, hidden in the shadows." He eyed me. "Remember that."

Odd sounds came from the detention center's entrance, and I glanced toward where I'd come in. The guardians who had let me in were gone. From around the corner, I heard a few grunts and thumps. I frowned and craned my head to get a better look.

Victor stood up. "Finally."

Fear spiked down my spine—at least until I saw Natalie round the corner.

Mixed sympathy and anger flitted through me, but I forced a kind smile. She probably wouldn't see her father again once they took him. Villain or no, they should be allowed to say goodbye.

"Hey," I said, watching her stride toward me. There was an unusual purpose in her movements that some part of me whispered wasn't right. "I didn't think they'd let you in." Of course, they weren't supposed to have let me in either.

She walked right up to me and—no exaggeration— *launched* me against the far wall. My body hit it hard, and black starbursts danced across my vision.

"What? . . ." I put a hand to my forehead and tried to get up.

Unconcerned about me now, Natalie unlocked Victor's cell with a set of keys I'd seen on one of the guardian's belts. Staggering to my feet, I approached her.

"What are you doing?"

She glanced up at me, and that's when I saw it. The faint ring of red around her pupils. Skin too pale, even for a Moroi. Blood smudged around her mouth. And most telling of all, the look in her eyes. A look so cold and so evil, my heart nearly came to a standstill. It was a look that said she no longer walked among the living—a look that said she was now one of the Strigoi.

TWENTY-FOUR

In spite of all the training I'd received, all the lessons on Strigoi habits and how to defend against them, I'd never ever actually seen one. It was scarier than I'd expected.

This time, when she swung at me again, I was ready. Sort of. I dodged back, slipping out of reach, wondering what chance I had. I remembered Dimitri's joke about the mall. No silver stake. Nothing to cut her head off with. No way to set her on fire. Running seemed like the best option after all, but she was blocking my way.

Feeling useless, I simply backed down the hall as she advanced on me, her movements far more graceful than they'd ever been in life.

Then, also faster than she'd ever moved in life, she leapt out, grabbed me, and slammed my head against the wall. Pain exploded in my skull, and I felt pretty sure that was blood I tasted in the back of my mouth. Frantically, I fought against her, trying to mount some kind of defense, but it was like fighting Dimitri on crack.

"My dear," murmured Victor, "try not to kill her if you don't have to. We might be able to use her later."

Natalie paused in her attack, giving me a moment to back up, but she never took her cold eyes off me. "I'll *try* not to."

There was a skeptical tone in her voice. "Get out of here now. I'll meet you there when I'm done."

"I can't believe you!" I yelled after him. "You got your own daughter to turn Strigoi?"

"A last resort. A necessary sacrifice made for the greater good. Natalie understands." He left.

"Do you?" I hoped I could stall her with talking, just like in the movies. I also hoped my questions would hide how utterly and completely terrified I was. "Do you understand? God, Natalie. You . . . you turned. Just because he told you to?"

"My father's a great man," she replied. "He's going to save the Moroi from the Strigoi."

"Are you insane?" I cried. I was backing up again and suddenly hit the wall. My nails dug into it, as though I could dig my way through. "You *are* a Strigoi."

She shrugged, almost seeming like the old Natalie. "I had to do it to get him out of here before the others came. One Strigoi to save all of the Moroi. It's worth it, worth giving up the sun and the magic."

"But you'll want to kill Moroi! You won't be able to help it."

"He'll help me stay in control. If not, then they'll have to kill me." She reached out and grabbed my shoulders, and I shuddered at how casually she talked about her own death. It was almost as casual as the way she was no doubt contemplating *my* death.

"You *are* insane. You can't love him that much. You can't really—"

She threw me into a wall again, and as my body collapsed in a heap on the floor, I had a feeling I wouldn't be getting up this time. Victor had told her not to kill me . . . but there was a look in her eyes, a look that said she wanted to. She wanted to feed off me; the hunger was there. It was the Strigoi way. I shouldn't have talked to her, I realized. I'd hesitated, just as Dimitri had warned.

And then, suddenly, he was there, charging down the hallway like Death in a cowboy duster.

Natalie spun around. She was fast, so fast. But Dimitri was fast too and avoided her attack, a look of pure power and strength on his face. With an eerie fascination, I watched them move, circling each other like partners in a deadly dance. She was stronger than him, clearly, but she was also a fresh Strigoi. Gaining superpowers doesn't mean you know how to use them.

Dimitri, however, knew how to use the ones he had. After both giving and receiving some vicious hits, he made his move. The silver stake flashed in his hand like a streak of lightning, then it snaked forward—into her heart. He yanked it out and stepped back, his face impassive as she screamed and fell to the floor. After a few horrible moments, she stopped moving.

Just as quickly, he was leaning over me, slipping his arms under my body. He stood up, carrying me like he had when I hurt my ankle.

"Hey, Comrade," I murmured, my own voice sounding sleepy. "You were right about Strigoi." The world started to darken, and my eyelids drooped.

"Rose. Roza. Open your eyes." I'd never heard his voice so strained, so frantic. "Don't go to sleep on me. Not yet."

I squinted up at him as he carried me out of the building, practically running toward the clinic. "Was he right?"

"Who?"

"Victor . . . he said it couldn't have worked. The necklace."

I started to drift off, lost in the blackness of my mind, but Dimitri prompted me back to consciousness.

"What do you mean?"

"The spell. Victor said you had to want me . . . to care about me . . . for it to work." When he didn't say anything, I tried to grip his shirt, but my fingers were too weak. "Did you? Did you want me?"

His words came out thickly. "Yes, Roza. I did want you. I still do. I wish . . . we could be together."

"Then why did you lie to me?"

We reached the clinic, and he managed to open the door while still holding me. As soon as he stepped inside, he began yelling for help.

"Why did you lie?" I murmured again.

Still holding me in his arms, he looked down at me. I could hear voices and footsteps getting closer.

"Because we can't be together."

"Because of the age thing, right?" I asked. "Because you're my mentor?"

His fingertip gently wiped away a tear that had escaped down my cheek. "That's part of it," he said. "But also . . . well, you and I will both be Lissa's guardians someday. I need to protect her at all costs. If a pack of Strigoi come, I need to throw my body between them and her."

"I know that. Of course that's what you have to do." The black sparkles were dancing in front of my eyes again. I was fading out.

"No. If I let myself love you, I won't throw myself in front of her. I'll throw myself in front of you."

The medical team arrived and took me out of his arms.

And that was how, two days after being discharged, I ended up back in the clinic. My third time in the two months we'd been back at the Academy. It had to be some kind of record. I definitely had a concussion and probably internal bleeding, but we never really found out. When your best friend is a kick-ass healer, you sort of don't have to worry about those things.

I still had to stay there for a couple of days, but Lissa—and Christian, her new sidekick—almost never left my side when they weren't in class. Through them, I learned bits and pieces about the outside world. Dimitri had realized there was a Strigoi on campus when they'd found Natalie's victim dead and drained of blood: Mr. Nagy of all people. A surprising choice, but since he was older, he'd been able to put up less of a fight.

No more Slavic art for us. The guardians in the detention center had been injured but not killed. She'd simply slammed
them around as she had me.

Victor had been found and recaptured while trying to
escape campus. I was glad, even though it meant Natalie's
sacrifice had been for nothing. Rumors said that Victor hadn't
seemed afraid at all when the royal guards came and carried
him away. He'd simply smiled the whole time, like he had
some secret they didn't know about.

Inasmuch as it could, life returned to normal after that.
Lissa did no more cutting. The doctor prescribed her something—an anti-depressant or anti-anxiety drug, I couldn't
remember which—that made her feel better. I'd never really
known anything about those kinds of pills. I thought they
made people silly and happy. But it was a pill like any other,
meant to fix something, and mostly it just kept her normal
and feeling stable.

Which was a good thing—because she had some other
issues to deal with. Like Andre. She'd finally believed Christian's story, and allowed herself to acknowledge that Andre
might not have been the hero she'd always believed him to
be. It was hard on her, but she finally reached a peaceful decision, accepting that he could have had both good and bad
sides, like we all do. What he'd done to Mia saddened her, but
it didn't change the fact that he'd been a good brother who
loved her. Most importantly, it finally freed her from feeling
like she needed to be *him* to make her family proud. She could

be herself—which she proved daily in her relationship with Christian.

The school still couldn't get over that. She didn't care. She laughed it off, ignoring the shocked looks and disdain from the royals who couldn't believe she'd date someone from a humiliated family. Not all of them felt that way, though. Some who had gotten to know her during her brief social whirlwind actually liked her for *her*, no compulsion necessary. They liked her honesty and openness, preferring it to the games most royals played.

A lot of royals ignored her, of course, and talked viciously about her behind her back. Most surprising of all, Mia— despite being utterly humiliated—managed to wiggle back into the good graces of a couple of these royals. It proved my point. She wouldn't stay down for long. And, in fact, I saw the first signs of her revenge lurking again when I walked past her one day on the way to class. She stood with a few other people and spoke loudly, clearly wanting me to hear.

"—perfect match. Both of them are from *completely* disgraced and rejected families."

I clenched my teeth and kept walking, following her gaze to where Lissa and Christian stood. They were lost in their own world and formed a gorgeous picture, she blond and fair and he blue-eyed and black-haired. I couldn't help but stare too. Mia was right. Both of their families were disgraced. Tatiana had publicly denounced Lissa, and while no one "blamed" the Ozeras for what had happened to Christian's parents, the rest of the royal Moroi families continued to keep their distance.

But Mia had been right about the other part too. In some ways, Lissa and Christian were perfect for each other. Maybe they were outcasts, but the Dragomirs and Ozeras had once been among the most powerful Moroi leaders. And in only a very short time, Lissa and Christian had started shaping one another in ways that could put them right up there with their ancestors. He was picking up some of her polish and social poise; she was learning to stand up for her passions. The more I watched them, the more I could see an energy and confidence radiating around them.

They weren't going to stay down either.

And I think that, along with Lissa's kindness, may have been what attracted people to her. Our social circle began to steadily grow. Mason joined, of course, and made no secret of his interest in me. Lissa teased me a lot about that, and I didn't yet know what to do about him. Part of me thought maybe it was time to give him a shot as a serious boyfriend, even though the rest of me yearned for Dimitri.

For the most part, Dimitri treated me just like anyone would expect of a mentor. He was efficient. Fond. Strict. Understanding. There was nothing out of the ordinary, nothing that would make anyone suspect what had passed between us—save for an occasional meeting of our eyes. And once I overcame my initial emotional reaction, I knew he was—technically—right about us. Age was a problem, yes, particularly while I was still a student at the Academy. But the other thing he'd mentioned . . . it had never entered my mind. It should have. Two guardians in a relationship could distract each other from the Moroi they were supposed to protect. We couldn't allow that to happen, couldn't risk her life for our own wants. Otherwise, we'd be no better than the Badica guardian who'd run off. I'd told Dimitri once that my own feelings didn't matter. She came first.

I just hoped I could prove it.

"It's too bad about the healing," Lissa told me.

"Hmm?" We sat in her room, pretending to study, but my mind was off thinking about Dimitri. I'd lectured her about keeping secrets, but I hadn't told her about him or about how close I'd come to losing my virginity. For some reason, I couldn't bring myself to tell.

She dropped the history book she'd been holding. "That I had to give up the healing. And the compulsion." A frown crossed her face at that last part. The healing had been regarded as a wondrous gift in need of further study; the compulsion had met with serious reprimands from Kirova and Ms. Carmack. "I mean, I'm happy now. I should have gotten help a long time ago—you were right about that. I'm glad I'm on the medication. But Victor was right too. I can't use spirit anymore. I can still sense it, though. . . . I miss being able to touch it."

I didn't entirely know what to say. I liked her better like this. Losing that threat of madness had made her whole again, confident and outgoing, just like the Lissa I'd always known and loved. Seeing her now, it was easy to believe what Victor had said about her becoming a leader. She reminded me of her parents and of Andre—how they used to inspire devotion in those who knew them.

"And that's another thing," she continued. "He said I couldn't give it up. He was right. It hurts, not having the magic. I want it so badly sometimes."

"I know," I said. I could feel that ache within her. The pills had dulled her magic, but not our bond.

"And I keep thinking about all the things I could do, all the people I could help." She looked regretful.

"You have to help yourself first," I told her fiercely. "I don't want you getting hurt again. I won't let you."

"I know. Christian says the same thing." She got that dopey smile she always did when she thought about him. If I'd known what idiots being in love would make them, I might not have been so keen to get them back together. "And I guess you guys are right. Better to want the magic and be sane than to have it and be a lunatic. There's no middle ground."

"No," I agreed. "Not with this."

Then, out of nowhere, a thought smacked me in the head. There *was* a middle ground. Natalie's words reminded me of it. *It's worth it, worth giving up the sun and the magic.*

The magic.

Ms. Karp hadn't become Strigoi simply because she'd gone crazy. She'd become Strigoi to stay sane. Becoming Strigoi cut a person completely off from magic. In doing that, she couldn't use it. She couldn't feel it. She wouldn't want it anymore. Staring at Lissa, I felt a knot of worry coil within me. What if she figured that out? Would she want to do it too? No, I quickly decided. Lissa would never do that. She was too strong a person, too moral. And so long as she stayed on the pills, her higher reasoning would keep her from doing something so drastic.

Still, the whole concept prodded me to find out one last thing. The following morning, I went to the chapel and waited in one of the pews until the priest showed up.

"Hello, Rosemarie," he said, clearly surprised. "Can I help you with something?"

I stood up. "I need to know more about St. Vladimir. I read that book you gave me and a couple others." Best not to tell him about stealing the ones in the attic. "But nobody told how he died. What happened? How did his life end? Was he, like, martyred?"

The priest's bushy eyebrows rose. "No. He died of old age. Peacefully."

"You're sure? He didn't become Strigoi or kill himself?"

"No, of course not. Why would you think that?"

"Well . . . he was holy and everything, but he was also kind of crazy, right? I read about it. I thought he might have, I don't know, given into that."

His face was serious. "It's true he fought demons—insanity—his whole life. It was a struggle, and he did want to die sometimes. But he overcame it. He didn't let it defeat him."

I stared in wonder. Vladimir wouldn't have had pills, and he'd clearly continued to use magic.

"How? How did he do that?"

"Willpower, I guess. Well . . ." He paused. "That and Anna."

"Shadow-kissed Anna," I murmured. "His guardian."

The priest nodded. "She stayed with him. When he grew weak, she was the one who held him up. She urged him to stay strong and to never give in to his madness."

I left the chapel in a daze. Anna had done it. Anna had let Vladimir walk that middle ground, helping him to work miracles in the world without meeting a horrible end. Ms. Karp hadn't been as lucky. She hadn't had a bound guardian. She hadn't had anyone to hold her up.

Lissa *did*.

Smiling, I cut across the quadrangle toward the commons. I felt better about life than I had in a very long time. We could do this, Lissa and me. We could do it together.

Just then, I saw a dark figure out of the corner of my eye. It swooped past me and landed on a nearby tree. I stopped walking. It was a raven, large and fierce-looking, with shining black feathers.

A moment later, I realized it wasn't just *a* raven; it was *the* raven. The one Lissa had healed. No other bird would land so close to a dhampir. And no other bird would be looking at me in such an intelligent, familiar way. I couldn't believe he was still around. A chill ran down my spine, and I started to back up. Then the truth hit me.

"You're bound to her too, aren't you?" I asked, fully aware that anyone who saw me would think I was crazy. "She brought you back. You're shadow-kissed."

That was actually pretty cool. I held out my arm to it, half hoping it'd come land on me in some sort of dramatic, movie-worthy gesture. All it did was look at me like I was an idiot, spread its wings, and fly off.

I glared as it flew off into the twilight. Then I turned around and headed off to find Lissa. From far away, I heard the sound of cawing, almost like laughter.

Turn the page for
never-before-released
stories featuring
ROSE, **LISSA**, **DIMITRI**,
and all your Vampire Academy faves,
straight from the author's vault!

The Turn and the Flame

Tasha Ozera didn't like dresses. Or high heels. Or meaningless conversation. Really, she didn't like anything to do with fancy parties. She knew, however, that there was a game to play, and she'd learned how to play it long ago.

"Tasha, please stop sulking. It'll give you wrinkles."

That, unsurprisingly, came from Tasha's sister-in-law, Moira. Moira Ozera—formerly Moira Szelsky—had been a celebrated beauty back in her day. She was still beautiful. Tasha could never forget Moira and Lucas's wedding and how everyone in the ballroom had held a collective breath when the two of them whirled around on the dance floor. Tasha, only seven, had stood with the other awestruck guests and felt certain that no couple could ever be more dazzling than her brother and his bride.

Tasha trudged barefoot through the living room, uncaring that the hem of her sparkling gown dragged along the floor, and flounced onto the sofa. "I'm not sulking. I'm just thinking."

Moira paused in front of an antique mirror framed in brass vines. She smoothed a wisp of chestnut hair back into place and pursed her lips to check if she should reapply her lipstick. She decided she should.

Observing, Tasha couldn't help but think that she hadn't

put even half as much care into her appearance as Moira had into hers. And Moira wasn't even going to a party. She, Lucas, and Christian were simply driving back to their country house tonight.

"Well then, little sister, I hope you're thinking about how you'll be the star of the ball tonight." That was Lucas, striding in with his easy smile. He set a suitcase down on the floor and kissed his wife's cheek. "I remember when we were at the Summer's End Ball. You wouldn't believe how many of us were desperately following Moira around, willing to do anything just for a smile. Or even a second glance."

Tasha could believe it because she'd heard this story many times, but she smiled anyway. Lucas hadn't been this upbeat in a while, and she liked the change. "I don't think that'll happen to me tonight," she replied. "But I'll try not to embarrass the family name."

Lucas winked. "That's all we can hope for."

"No," said Moira, turning from the mirror. "That is *not* all we can hope for. We should hope that she'll get engaged. Or, at the very least, that some young man from a prestigious family might visit once in a while instead of those bohemians who are always stopping by. And why aren't you wearing your shoes, Tasha?"

The family's two guardians entered the room just then, carrying the last of the luggage. Tasha didn't like seeing them relegated to bellhops, but she knew they'd both die before uttering a word of complaint.

"Everything's ready," said Nolan. "The car's out front,

and then we'll meet up with Guardian Locke and his car at the gate. Your feeder's waiting there as well."

"I don't know why we need two cars or a borrowed guardian," said Moira. "It seems like a waste."

Lucas frowned as well. "Really, we'll be fine. Send Locke somewhere else."

"We're just looking out for your safety, Lady Moira," replied Vinh in his quiet, respectful way. "A nighttime drive is dangerous, and Guardian Locke happens to have an assignment nearby. He'll remain with you at the house until Lady Tasha and I can join you tomorrow."

"You're staying here instead of Nolan?" asked Lucas, his tone mild. A very slight furrowing of his brow was the only sign of his displeasure.

Tasha stood up and quickly said, "If you're so worried about it, Moira, just wait until tomorrow. Then we can all leave together." As she'd hoped, it deflected the conversation away from Vinh.

"Driving in daylight is always safer," added Nolan diplomatically. "It wouldn't be difficult to change our plans."

"No, no," said Moira, with more insistence than Tasha thought was needed. "Nothing's changing. I want to be back home tonight. I'm tired of Court."

"Tonight it is, then." Lucas glanced around. "Where's Christian?"

Moira sighed. "Why is he always skulking away? And why can't anyone ever keep track of him?"

Vinh's face remained neutral, but Tasha could see the

amusement sparkling in his eyes. "I'll find him."

A couple minutes later, Vinh returned with Christian. At nine years old, the boy was a miniature version of his father, sporting the black hair and pale blue eyes shared by so many Ozeras, including Tasha. Normally quiet and introspective, Christian's face was alight with glee as he clung to the tall guardian's back in a piggyback ride and then was gently deposited next to his parents. Vinh immediately straightened up and became his proper self once more.

"I don't want to go out to the house," said Christian. "It's boring. I want to go back to school. Or stay here with Aunt Tasha and see the ball. They're lighting fireworks when it's done!"

Tasha grinned. "You want to be my date tonight? You'll probably be the best company there."

"Tasha, you need to be more serious about all this," Moira scolded. "Youth and beauty are fleeting. You take them for granted now, but one day you'll wish you could hold on to them forever."

Lucas put an arm around her and walked her toward the door. "Leave her alone, dear. It's not important now. The rest of us need to go—and yes, Christian, that includes you. To the country house. Not the ball."

Tasha hugged her nephew goodbye, laughing when he complained about the prickly crystals on her dress. Moira was already getting in the car, directing the guardians on where to set the luggage and ascertaining that the feeder would ride with her. Lucas wrapped Tasha in a hug and then regarded her with a look that was equal parts affection and sorrow.

"Can we talk more about St. Croix when I see you tomorrow?" she asked eagerly.

He hesitated. "Ah, sure. For now . . . try to have fun, little sister. And I hope . . . I hope when you look back on tonight, you'll remember how much I love you. How much we all love you."

"It's just another party, Luke," she said, puzzled at his shift in demeanor. But then, Lucas had been behaving strangely for the last few months, his moods often darkening without warning. Two of his old classmates had died unexpectedly, one by Strigoi and one in a skiing accident. The two deaths were completely opposite in cause, but they'd hit her brother hard. She'd often find him looking at old pictures and getting caught up in philosophical discussions about mortality. She worried about him and hoped relaxing in the country would do him some good.

When the car finally left, Tasha reluctantly put on her silver high-heeled shoes and locked the door to her family's town house. The Summer's End Ball was being held on the opposite side of Court, and even in her uncomfortable shoes, Tasha didn't mind the walk on such a warm and breezy night. She and Vinh matched each other's steps, both quiet but at ease in the other's company as they strolled along one of the many tree-lined paths that zigzagged among the buildings of the expansive Royal Court. With its venerable architecture and grassy courtyards, it resembled a university more than a sanctuary for living vampires, but that was exactly how the Moroi wanted it. It attracted less outside attention.

"I think it'll rain later," said Tasha. There were other Moroi and dhampirs out tonight, and it wouldn't do for a young royal lady to speak even remotely informally with her guardian.

Vinh glanced up and took note of the scattered clouds drifting across the stars and moon. "I think you're right, but it may hold off until the ball ends. If it doesn't, I'll come back and get an umbrella."

"You don't need to trek through the rain for me. No one's going to hold you accountable if I get a little wet. It's not going to bother me that much."

"I'd hold myself accountable if anything bothered you at all."

A rush of heat swept over her, and she fidgeted with her bracelet so she wouldn't have to respond. It happened all the time with him. Just a few words or a small look, and she became flustered in the most wonderful way. It used to embarrass her. She used to try to ignore it. After all, a Moroi of her station shouldn't think of a dhampir that way, especially now that they were out of school and in the real world. Except . . . every once in a while, she'd see him watching her in a way that made her think she wasn't the only one who had trouble letting go of their past.

The Summer's End Ball took place in the palace, a building that matched the Court's others on the outside but contained all the grandeur and decadence of the Moroi's glorious history. That was part of what made this such a big event. The queen herself hosted it, and only royals attended. Ostensibly, it was to celebrate the waning of summer and the approach of fall—meaning longer nights and shorter days. Everyone knew, though, it was a chance for young, eligible royals to be paraded around one another. Engagements often followed in subsequent weeks.

Vinh held out his hand to Tasha when they reached the steps to the palace entrance. Tasha accepted it and lifted her skirt with her other hand. That small touch of their fingers was the only contact they ever had now, but it was everything to Tasha.

"Thank you, Vinh," she said when she let go.

Inside, the ballroom had become a fantasyland of colors and flowers. Real plants and trees filled the space, and glittering, star-shaped lights on the ceiling cast rainbow patterns on the party below. The guests themselves rivaled the lavish decor, with everyone seeming to try to outdo one another. Tasha's simply cut silver-and-blue dress was one of the tamer ones.

Around the sides of the room, mixed among the tropical splendor, guardians stood at attention, unmoving and identical in black suits and white shirts. They blended in with one another and the room—as was intended. But not Vinh. Tasha knew exactly where he was no matter where she went.

A lot of the royals she'd graduated with at St. Vladimir's were here, as well as Moroi from other schools or those who'd received their education at Court. They all sized one another up, checking out both prospective mates and possible rivals.

Despite her earlier flippancy with Lucas, Tasha wasn't im-
mune to the role she played in her family. The Ozeras were one
of the twelve royal houses, with a lineage and history honored
throughout the Moroi world. No one in her family would force
her to do anything she didn't want, but she knew her friend-
ships and romances could all affect her family's standing and
how they navigated the complex battlefield of Moroi politics.
She wanted to do the right thing—truly. She worked her way
through the party, speaking to as many important people as
she could, dancing with young men who could be advanta-
geous matches. She smiled. She made all the pleasant, demure
conversations a royal young lady was expected to.

But it felt hollow. There was no one she really connected
with, and her heart wasn't in her words. It must have shown
to others because once, while passing a group of elderly Moroi
who'd come to observe the "youngsters," she overhead a man
say, "Have you seen that up-and-coming Ozera girl? David's
daughter, God rest his soul. They haven't put out a beauty like
that in years—and they're a good-looking bunch. But she's just
so . . . odd."

Tasha started to smile and then felt guilty. She needed to
try harder. She needed to stop being odd, whatever that meant.

"Tasha? Where have you been?"

Jacob Zeklos, another St. Vladimir's alum, stepped into
her path and handed her a flute of champagne.

"Tonight?" she asked.

"No. All summer. This is supposed to be our time to party
and relax before we go on to grown-up life."

"I've been here sometimes. At our estate other times." She shrugged. "Mostly, I'm just spending time with my family."

"You can hang out with them anytime. But this? The prime of our lives?" He raised his own glass high, sloshing the contents, and she wondered how much champagne he'd had tonight. "This won't last. Nobody stays young forever, and we should enjoy it. My family's going to Bucharest next month. Come with us."

Tasha's interest was momentarily piqued. Her last visit to Romania had been as a child, and she was curious to see it through more mature eyes. "Any reason? Or just taking in the galleries and castles?"

"Only one castle—we never have to leave. One of my cousins is getting married and hosting a whole week of festivities. Party after party. Old World luxury. Unspeakable decadence." He grinned, confirming rumors she'd heard about him getting his canines filed into narrower points. It looked ridiculous. "You won't believe what they get the feeders to do."

"Thank you, but I can't. I'm trying to talk Lucas into letting me go snorkeling in St. Croix next month."

"St. Croix? Like in the Caribbean?" He wrinkled his nose in disgust. "But it's so sunny there."

The sun was one of the reasons why Lucas was being obstinate, as was the fact that the group wasn't royal. They were some of Tasha's "bohemian" friends whom Moira thought were so unworthy. Tasha didn't need her brother's permission exactly, but she did need his money since he held control of their inheritance.

"It's worth it," she said. "There are some amazing reefs and sea life there."

Jacob still looked baffled. "Do you want to be a marine biologist or something?"

"No. I just want to see it."

"Why?"

"Because it's there. Because it's something in the world I haven't experienced yet." It was obvious this conversation was going nowhere, and Tasha searched for an escape. "Excuse me—I see my uncle and need to say hello. Good talking to you."

She hurried away before Jacob could stop her and waved a hand of greeting to Ronald Ozera. He wasn't actually her uncle, but he was one of the oldest and most respected members of the Ozera clan. It was an informal custom among royals to call all older relatives "aunt" or "uncle," just as peers often referred to each other as "cousin."

"Tasha." Ronald kissed her on the cheek. "You're a vision. I've been hearing your praises sung all night. Did I just see you talking to Jacob Zeklos?"

A knowing glint shone in the older man's eyes. He was as bad as Moira. "Yes."

"He's a fine-looking young fellow, isn't he? And his father's building up quite a lot of influence among the Zekloses."

"You don't need to do any matchmaking for me. I don't want to make any hasty decisions."

It was no secret in the Ozera clan—or probably in any other—that Ronald had his eye on the throne. It wasn't going to be vacant anytime soon, but he believed in building connections and alliances well in advance of the complicated selection process monarchs endured. She might only be his distant cousin, but she was still an Ozera and therefore of use. *Like a tool*, she thought.

"Of course, of course," Ronald said. "In fact, it might be a good idea for you to wait a while for marriage. Maybe . . . several years."

Tasha didn't trust the oh-so-casual tone in his voice. "Uncle, what are you suggesting?"

"Nothing at all. Just trying to help you out. But did you notice Eric Dragomir is here tonight?"

Tasha followed Ronald's nod to a cluster of people speaking with Queen Tatiana. Eric was easy to pick out. Their family, like the Ozeras, tended to have distinct features—for the Dragomirs, it was platinum hair and green eyes.

"He doesn't get out very much," she noted.

"Indeed. He keeps his family close—which is understandable."

Yes, it was. Eric and his two children were the only Dragomirs left, which was astonishing compared to the tangle of cousins in all the other houses. There were dozens and dozens of Ozeras.

"He's married," Tasha pointed out, unsure of where Ronald was going with this.

"Yes, but his son isn't."

She turned to him incredulously. "His son is twelve years old!"

"Which is why I said you should wait several years. Once he's a young man, I'm sure you'd hit it off wonderfully, and who wouldn't be charmed by your loveliness? Rhea Dragomir is half Ozera, and we've got Dragomirs in our tree—they'd love to make a match that can boost their bloodline."

Tasha shook her head in amazement and groped for a polite response. After all, an elder member of the family deserved respect. "That is . . . an interesting suggestion."

"It's a very reasonable suggestion. Eric's influence is staggering. He doesn't have to get the consensus of his house to push his opinions into the council—he *is* his house. He's their de facto council member." He paused at that and frowned. It was another well-known fact that Ronald hoped to be elected as the Ozera council representative. Currently, another family member held that position. "He'd be a powerful ally for anyone hoping to seize the throne—which, of course, we hope Queen Tatiana will remain on for a long, long time."

"Probably for the rest of our lives. She doesn't look like she's going anywhere—ever."

"Well, I hope she doesn't. Truly. But she *is* much older than me, and there's no point in wasting time while I wait out natural causes. Now, let's go over there and say hello—just so you're on Eric's radar."

Fury flared in Tasha at Ronald's presumptuous tone. Just like that, he expected her to jump at his command, to play a role in his convoluted quest for power. He could call her a vision and laud her loveliness all he wanted, but her real value was in what she could offer him. She wanted to call him out on his selfishness and very explicitly let him know how insulting she found his treatment of her, but one didn't act that way around respected elders. She took a deep breath and swallowed her anger.

"Uncle, you are . . . always thinking."

"Indeed. Can't let any opportunity slip away. Come along." He rested a hand on her shoulder. "You and I might be from far-flung branches of the family tree, but we *are* all one family. All Ozeras. We need to look out for each other."

Tasha went with him and consoled herself with the thought that this would be more entertaining than talking to any more of her classmates. She and Ronald waited politely at the edge of Tatiana's circle—all men his age or older—until the queen's eyes fell on them. They offered a proper bow and curtsy and were rewarded with a nod of acceptance.

"Your Majesty, this party is magnificent. Even grander than last year," Ronald said as he straightened up. "You of course remember Natasha, David and Blanche's daughter."

"Yes, of course." Queen Tatiana was an impressive woman, even when she wasn't decked out in a brocade gown and crown heavy with diamonds and rubies. She carried a presence that dwarfed everyone else's, and her eyes never missed anything. "I noticed your brother isn't with us tonight."

"No, Your Majesty," said Tasha. "He left with Moira and Christian for our country house tonight. I'll be joining them tomorrow."

Tatiana didn't frown, but her disapproval came through clearly. "It's strange, missing one of the biggest celebrations of the year. Surely they could have waited until tomorrow as well."

Tasha had thought so too but now felt obligated to defend Lucas. "Moira was eager to be home. I think she's been over-tired."

"Not surprising. I always remember her being a fussy little thing. Quite vain too."

Again, Tasha secretly agreed but refused to give voice to anything that would slight her family in public. Others in the circle, hoping to win the queen's favor, were quick to jump in.

"Making a trip like that at this time of night is reckless," said Nathan Ivashkov. "Especially in light of what just happened."

"A family in St. Louis was ambushed by Strigoi last week," Eric Dragomir explained for Tasha and Ronald's benefit.

"How awful," said Ronald. "Were their guardians over-powered?"

"No guardians. They weren't royal," said Eric.

"No doubt they were careless too." Nathan glanced at Tasha and Ronald, reminding everyone of Lucas Ozera's behavior. "It's unfortunate that there aren't enough guardians to go around, but that just means one has to stay extra diligent."

"It seems like there should be some extra guardians available for non-royals, though," interjected Tasha. She gestured around the room. "My family's are split tonight, but I'm sure most royals here have their full allotment just hanging around. Why hoard them? Court's already well guarded. Any royal who knows they'll be here for an extended period of time should let their guardians take on temporary assignments elsewhere. There still wouldn't be enough for every Moroi, of course, but it could help any non-royals who happened to be in potentially dangerous situations."

Everyone stared at her. Ronald looked as though he very much regretted putting her on anyone's radar.

The queen smiled, but there was no warmth to it. "Natasha, might I have a word alone with you?"

It was the kind of statement that normally preceded the speaker stepping away. Instead, everyone else in the circle immediately moved back to give Tatiana and Tasha space.

Tasha tried not to gulp. "Yes, Your Majesty?"

"I like you," Tatiana said in a tone that expressed exactly the opposite. "And I liked your parents very much. I'd like to see you do well here tonight. I'd like to see you do well in general. As queen, my love extends to all the royal families, not just the Ivashkovs. When my people are happy, I'm happy. Therefore, I'm going to give you some advice that will make both of us happier."

Tasha, petrified, gave a jerky nod.

Tatiana leaned closer. "You're only here to look pretty, dear. Not to give your opinions. See that you remember that."

There were a million possible responses to that, but there was only one that Tasha was allowed to make: "Th-thank you, Your Majesty."

No one had heard what Tatiana had said, but the others in the earlier conversation knew she'd been chastised. Tasha was more than happy to slink back into the crowd and disappear, though Ronald caught up with her later.

"What were you thinking?" he demanded.

"I'm sorry, Uncle. I was just speaking my mind."

"Sharing our guardians among non-royals is something that's on your mind?"

"Well . . ." He wasn't angry, exactly, but his disapproval unsettled her. Still, she found her courage. "Yes, actually. There are plenty of ways guardians could be better distributed without compromising protection and—"

Ronald groaned. "Tasha, stop. Not tonight. Not in polite company. You know this is a controversial topic. No royal wants to hear about spreading our guardians thin. If you want to gain favor, start coming up with ideas on how to *increase* protection for royals."

Tasha nearly suggested one then and there. She'd long thought Moroi would benefit from learning to protect themselves, but Ronald's face told her now wasn't the time. In fact, it would probably never be the time. No one wanted to hear about change. The world was marching on, but the Moroi were locked in the past. And young ladies attending the Summer's End Ball, ones who wanted to make a good impression, did not challenge the status quo.

"I'm sorry, Uncle. I hope I didn't cause you any trouble." The words left a bad taste in her mouth, but her contrite tone appeared to soften him.

"Probably not. They've all been into so much champagne no one will even remember."

It was a relief when the party wrapped up and the guests

spilled out of the ballroom and into the palace's massive court-yard to watch the fireworks. Tasha kept away from the others and found a wrought-iron bench tucked away in a corner of the old stone walls, surrounded by honeysuckles that filled the humid air with their perfume. She soon felt a familiar presence stand behind her.

"No rain yet," she said without turning around.

"No, Lady Tasha," came Vinh's quiet reply. Once he'd graduated and been assigned to her family, he'd started using her title. Even here, alone in the shadows, he never broke pro-tocol. She was Lady Ozera in public and Lady Tasha in private. Never anything more familiar. The only concession he'd made was using *Tasha* instead of *Natasha*.

She stared off at the clusters of other partygoers, laughing and drinking as they gazed skyward for the show to start. She felt like she was a million miles away from them. "I don't think I did very well tonight, Vinh."

"What was it you were trying to—"

She heard him move behind her, and then there was a rus-tle of leaves and a yelp. Tasha spun around just in time to see Vinh lift a squirming Christian out of a hydrangea bush. Tasha jumped to her feet.

"Christian! What are you doing? Are your parents here?" She glanced around, half expecting Lucas and Moira to emerge from the bush too.

Christian shook his head as Vinh set him on his feet. "N-no. They're probably at the house by now."

"And you aren't with them because . . . ?"

He obviously knew he was in trouble but still met her eyes boldly. "Mom and Dad wanted the feeder to ride with them and Nolan. I think Mom was hungry because she kept going on and on about it. Anyway, it was crowded, so I told them I'd ride in the other car, with Guardian Locke, that borrowed guardian from the Badicas. Except I told *him* I was riding in the other car with Mom and Dad. So no one knew I was gone. And here I am."

"To watch the fireworks," Tasha guessed. "You shouldn't look so pleased with yourself. Your mother's going to have a panic attack. If she hasn't already."

Before Christian could answer back, a burst of red and gold stars exploded in the dark sky overhead and rained down in a brilliant shower of sparks. Christian's eyes went wide, and Tasha gave up on scolding him. She leaned toward Vinh. "Get word to Nolan, will you? Maybe we can at least minimize Moira's outrage."

Vinh gave a curt nod and disappeared into the darkness. Tasha sat back down and beckoned Christian to join her. He leaned his head against her, and Tasha felt happier than she had all night as she put her arm around him.

"This is all fire magic?" he asked.

"This show, yes. Sometimes they'll mix it. Use conventional fireworks and then have fire users enhance it."

Enormous blue flowers glittered above them, changed to silver, and then faded into sparkles.

"Can you do that?"

"No," she said. "But then I've never tried. Maybe we

could work on it together one day."

He turned and looked up at her hopefully. "Do you think I'll be a fire user too?"

"I do. It's your best element, and the fact that it's showing so early means you'll probably be very powerful."

He settled back against her. "Maybe I can use that power to make fireworks."

"I should hope you could use it for something more," she said, but he was too transfixed to hear her.

Vinh's wordless return told her he'd reported the unexpected itinerary change. Later, as the three walked back home, he explained, "Nolan didn't pick up, but I left a message about what happened. I said we'd bring Lord Christian when we drive down tomorrow."

Christian yawned, his steps growing slow. The eastern sky was purpling. "Aunt Tasha, do you think we could practice making fireworks back at the house?"

She laughed and ruffled his hair. "Haven't you put your mother through enough tonight?"

A raindrop landed on Tasha's cheek. Then another, and another. Suddenly, the foreseen shower was on them in full force. "No time for umbrellas," she called to Vinh as she took off her shoes. "Grab him, and run for it!"

Vinh hoisted Christian onto his back, and they raced through the deluge. Vinh matched her stride, even though Tasha knew he could have easily outrun her. They reached the town house, soaked but laughing. Tasha found towels for all of them and tried to pat her silk dress dry. It stuck to her like a second skin, and mud covered the hem. A few crystals had come loose.

"We're all going to be in trouble. Hopefully, I can get a cleaner to salvage this tomorrow."

"Change," Vinh told her. "I'll take care of him."

Tasha gratefully went to her room but soon found the tiny hooks on the back of her sodden dress were impossible to grasp while wet. She peered into the hall and saw Vinh emerging from Christian's room. He put a finger to his lips and then raised an eyebrow in surprise when she beckoned him to her.

"Help me?" she asked, turning around.

Silence. Stillness. Then, carefully, his fingers brushed the back of her neck and began to work their way down her spine as he effortlessly undid the clasps. She held her breath and couldn't help but wryly recall that he'd never had trouble taking her clothes off. In the old days, he wouldn't have stopped when the clasps ended below her shoulders. He certainly wouldn't have stepped away so quickly. Tasha pressed a hand to her chest to keep the dress from falling off, not that it seemed to be going anywhere in its sticky state. As she turned back, she just barely caught sight of his eyes traveling the length of her body before politely glancing away.

"Do you need anything else, Lady Tasha?"

All sorts of things, she thought. She wondered what he'd do if she asked him to help peel the rest of the gown away. What would he do if she took it off herself and ordered him to watch?

She let out the breath she'd been holding. "No, Vinh. I'll

meet you downstairs."

Out of respect for him, she put on the most modest pajamas she owned. When she softly crept down the stairs later, she saw that he'd switched on the small credenza lamp, providing just enough light for Moroi and dhampir eyes to see by. He looked over her wardrobe choice, and Tasha couldn't tell if he felt relieved or disappointed.

"Lord Christian fell asleep before I'd even finished buttoning up his pajamas." A rare, easy smile spread over Vinh's face. "I hope it's all right that I just put him straight to bed. I didn't bother drying his hair or anything." Vinh's black hair, always cut short, was already starting to dry.

Tasha's was still lank and dripping, and she pushed it back. "No different from me. You know, someone called me an 'effortless beauty' tonight. I wonder what he'd say now. This is pretty effortless."

Vinh crossed his arms and leaned against the wall, watchful but still relaxed. "He wouldn't say a word. He'd be too enthralled at the real you, stripped of all the makeup and jewelry and glamour. Nothing to distract. Just the pure, steady flame of who you are." He could control their physical contact, but sometimes, in private, he left his words unguarded.

Tasha gave a brief smile at the warrior-turned-poet, but the heat of his earlier touch had faded now that she reflected on the evening's events. She stared off at the rain beating against the living room window. "I don't know what that flame is. Who the real me is. I keep trying to be who Natasha Ozera is supposed to be. I go to all the places I'm supposed to.

I say the things I'm supposed to—well, most of the time. I do everything I'm meant to . . . but it turns out that I'm not actually doing them right. Maybe because I don't really *feel* that they're right."

"Maybe you need a new definition of what 'right' is."

"It's hard to do anything new around here. You should have seen their faces tonight—including the queen's—when I suggested a way to reallocate guardians to serve royal *and* non-royal Moroi. And that's just the beginning! I think all Moroi should learn some basic fighting. I nearly said it. But then I backed down. I was too intimidated. The rules, the traditions, the judgment . . . no one can fight against that."

"Maybe because no one's tried."

She glanced back up and couldn't help another smile. "You're acting very rebellious tonight."

"Not me. My role is defined, and I don't mind following the rules. It suits me. But you? I think you're something different. I think your role, whatever it is, has yet to be discovered. You're more than the 'effortless beauty' who says the right things . . . that aren't actually right."

Despite the amusement in his last words, his face stayed completely, intensely serious. She felt pinned by his gaze and had no desire to break free of it. "I wouldn't even know where to start," she said.

"Start small. Don't worry about all Moroi learning to defend themselves. *You* learn it first."

Tasha laughed outright at that. "If I walked over to the guardians' office right now, do you think anyone would teach me? Would you?"

He hesitated, caught by his own words. "You don't need guardians to teach you. Go to any city, and you'll find endless options. Walk down a street and turn into the first place you find that can teach you any semblance of self-defense. A dojo. A jujitsu studio. A kickboxing class. It doesn't matter what it is. Start with something, and go from there. Go until you're unstoppable."

"You want to send me off to wander alone among humans?"

"I never said alone. I'm your family's guardian. Right now I'm assigned to you. You don't need anyone's permission to leave, and if you order me to come along and protect you, I will, and no rules will be broken."

"It's that easy, huh?" She watched the rain again and then gave him a sidelong look. "What if I command you to call me just Tasha, instead of Lady Tasha?"

"That would be breaking a rule. And I can't do that." Again, hesitation. "Even if I wanted to."

We do the right things too but don't do them right either, she mused. In the course of this brief conversation, they'd already moved closer together without either of them realizing it. It happened all the time in these rare, clandestine talks of theirs when she could finally drop the façade the rest of the world expected of her and say what was really in her heart. Well, not everything in her heart. Otherwise, she'd tell him how standing near him still made her nervous and excited, just as it had when they used to slip away together at St. Vladimir's. She'd

360

tell him how now, deprived of those stolen kisses, she lived for the brief, casual touches that were all they could share anymore. She'd tell him there was no other person who made her feel so valued. So *real*. She'd tell him that she loved how he was real too, with none of the show and ego that muddled the rest of the world. And she'd tell him she loved him, too.

Instead, she said, "I wish you weren't so good at your job."

For a few fleeting seconds, his stoic guardian face faltered, and she saw a longing that matched her own. "Me too, Lady Tasha."

She couldn't meet his eyes for long, not with that look in them. It wasn't fair that dhampirs were forced to serve Moroi at all costs. It wasn't fair that their society wouldn't legitimize relationships between Moroi and dhampirs, no matter the indiscretions that took place on the side. His own birth had come about that way when a royal vacationing in Vietnam had been smitten by Vinh's dhampir mother. He'd wooed her into a brief affair and then never spoke to her again, not even when she sent word about their son.

Tasha's eyes strayed to the window again, where the rain had slowed and was falling against the panes in long streaks, tears to match those she refused to shed.

She saw the dark figure moving outside just a heartbeat before the glass shattered. A second window met the same fate, and then three guardians burst through the front door. Tasha screamed as all five of them fanned out around her and Vinh, their hands wielding guns and silver stakes. Tasha stepped back and bumped into the wall.

"Do you know where they are?" demanded one of the guardians.

"Know where who are?" she asked. She held her hands up, even though no one had asked her to. It seemed like the thing to do.

"Did you know what they had planned? Are you going to join them?"

Vinh faced a moment of indecision, stuck between obligation to Tasha and obedience to the guardian order. He chose her. He had no weapon, not on household duty at Court, but he positioned himself fearlessly between her and the five guardians.

"What's going on?" he exclaimed. "How dare you break into this house and speak to her that way? She's a scion of House Ozera! She and her brother—"

"She has no brother," said the lead guardian bluntly. "He's gone."

"G-gone?" she stammered. "If you mean tonight, they were just driving to—"

"I mean, Lady Ozera, that he's no longer among the living."

The room began to spin around Tasha, and her knees gave out from under her. Vinh was by her side in an instant, his arm around her for support. "Lucas is . . . dead?" She could hardly hear her own voice.

"Not truly dead," said another guardian. "Turned. He and his wife are Strigoi."

"No . . . no! That's . . . no. It's impossible!" Or was it? They'd been warned of the dangers of traveling at night. Tasha leaned further into Vinh and tried to bring the room back into focus. "Where were they attacked? On the road? At our house?" Both seemed unlikely. A moving car wasn't an easy target, and heavy wards ringed the house.

"They weren't attacked," said the first guardian. "They chose to turn Strigoi."

Tasha's moment of weakness vanished, and she pulled herself upright, suddenly recharged with fury. There was no greater sin in the Moroi world than purposely choosing the dark, undead path of the Strigoi, to give up one's soul and morals in exchange for power and immortality. Suggesting it of Lucas and Moira insulted Tasha, her family, and the entire Ozera name.

She strode toward the guardians, fists clenched and fear gone. "You're lying. There's no way they would do that."

The guardian who spoke didn't flinch under her gaze. "The evidence is very clear. There's no indication of any attack by outside Strigoi. We found one of their cars abandoned on the side of the highway. One of them had drained their feeder. The other snapped Nolan Orr's neck and drained him."

Tasha heard a sharp intake of breath from Vinh. He and Nolan had become close friends in the year they'd worked together. Nolan had protected her since she was a child. "There was another guardian," she said. "Locke. One who was—"

"He's dead too, Lady Ozera. We found his body thrown into the brush nearby. The Strigoi took the second car."

There were no words to describe what Tasha felt in that moment. Nothing she could say. Nothing she could even think. She started to tremble. Seeing that the news had finally sunk in, the lead guardian asked, "Do you have any idea at all of where they'd go? Did they say anything? They're not at the house—it's still warded."

"Please, Lady Ozera," said another. "I know this must be difficult, but we need to act while we can still track them. New Strigoi are careless."

We need to act while we can still track them.

Track them to kill them. Because that was the only thing to be done at this point.

"No." The word barely came out. Tasha swallowed and tried again. "*No.* I have no idea where they'd be. All they said was that they were going home tonight. I was supposed to join them tomorrow. Today." It was dawn, after all.

She didn't know where they were, but she should have known something was up. Not this, of course . . . but something. They'd been so insistent they leave last night, despite the risk. Darkness, away from the safety of Court, was ideal for Strigoi and apparently for their creation, too. Neither had wanted the extra guardian. And Moira had wanted the feeder close, an easy victim to drain and initiate the turning.

Try to have fun, little sister. And I hope . . . I hope when you look back on tonight, you'll remember how much I love you. How much we all love you.

Tasha didn't realize she was getting dizzy again until Vinh returned to her side. "Breathe," he murmured. "Just breathe."

"I'm sorry, Lady Ozera." The lead guardian, calmer now, appeared sincere. "I believe that you didn't know anything. But we'll still have to interrogate you back in our headquarters, just in case there's some detail you don't realize is important."

Again, she had no words. How could she? Not when—

"Aunt Tasha?"

She whirled around and saw Christian peering around the bannister at the top of the stairs, his young face drawn and uneasy.

"Christian! Go back to bed. Everything . . ." Tasha could feel herself choking up. "Everything's going to be okay. . . ."

But nothing was okay. Nothing would ever be okay again.

Christian stepped out of the shadows, fully revealing himself. He looked beyond Tasha, to the group of guardians. Uncertain, he finally settled his gaze on Vinh.

"You have to hunt down my parents, don't you?"

Vinh didn't blink, but Tasha knew his heart was breaking, just as hers was. "Yes, Lord Christian."

"Because you have to kill them."

Tasha turned away and buried her face in her hands, not wanting to hear the rest. And she knew that Christian was addressing Vinh because Vinh had always treated him like an adult and would always tell him the truth.

"Yes, Lord Christian."

Word spread quickly at Court. Gossip usually did, and this was the sort of horror that people often speculated about but never expected to happen. Tasha and Christian were allowed to clean up and change, and by the time the guardians escorted the two of them away for questioning, curious onlookers had gathered outside both the town house and the guardians' office.

Except most everyone was trying very hard not to appear like an onlooker. They acted as though they were casually out and about, that they'd just happened to be strolling around at noon—when most Moroi were asleep. Some even tried to pretend that they hadn't noticed Tasha and Christian. Others had no such tact. But Tasha felt the weight of all their eyes. She saw them lean their heads together to speak covertly. She heard the whispers.

"Aunt Tasha, all these people are watching us."

Tasha tightened her hold on Christian's hand and quickened her step. "They don't matter. None of them matters to us."

It was a relief to reach the guardians' headquarters, not that interrogation proved much better. A group of guardians questioned Tasha for almost two hours, and she had a hard time answering coherently when she herself was still having trouble coming to terms with what had happened. It seemed dreamlike. Or like it was happening to another person, and she was simply watching from the outside.

They interrogated Christian next, and although they warned her not to say anything, they at least allowed her to stay in the room. As the afternoon progressed, something new occurred to her as she analyzed both the line of questioning and the gawkers' attitudes. There was more to this than just the shock of Lucas and Moira's crime.

"They think we might turn too, don't they?" she asked Vinh once it was over. "Or, at least, that I will."

He couldn't lie to her any more than he could lie to Christian. "Most Moroi who turn by choice act alone. They're mentally disturbed. Or desperate. Or too selfish to have ties to others. When pairs or groups turn . . . yes, sometimes there's a larger conspiracy of loved ones doing it together."

"And some people just think it's in the blood," she added. "That there's something inherently evil in all of us."

His silence was confirmation enough. As they were about to exit the building, Tasha caught sight of two guardians walking into a conference room. When the doors opened, she saw more guardians inside, gathered in front of a giant screen. Faces were tense. This wasn't an ordinary patrol meeting.

She came to a halt. "That's where they're planning it, isn't it? How to track Lucas and Moira down?"

Vinh gently touched her arm, but she was too distracted to experience any of the old thrill. "Lady Tasha, you should go home."

"I want to see." She pulled away. "I have a right to see, don't I?"

"Yes," he said after a moment's consideration. "I'll go with you. But not him. I'll get another guardian to take him back home."

Tasha looked down at Christian and felt the ache inside her intensify. How did someone so young even begin to make sense of this? "No. He's not going back out there without me—

not while those vultures are still circling. He can wait in the hall. . . ." But she faltered, unsure if she wanted to leave him alone here either.

"Lady Ozera? I can wait with him while you meet with the others. I'll make sure no one bothers him."

The speaker was a dhampir a little younger than her, his Russian accent thick. He stood taller even than Vinh, with the kind of face that probably made girls swoon, and every bit of him was composed and respectful. "This is Dimitri Belikov," said Vinh. "He's part of a group of novices who are visiting Court. You can trust him."

There weren't many Tasha truly believed she could trust anymore, but if Vinh trusted this novice, then she would as well. She knelt down and brushed a kiss over Christian's forehead. "I'll be right back. I need to . . . check on something."

Christian's icy-blue eyes—Lucas's eyes, her eyes—studied her without comment. He wasn't stupid. He knew what was happening.

The guardians' meeting was already in session when she and Vinh entered the room. It came to a standstill when the others noticed her, and the guardian taking charge at the podium—a short, fierce woman with red hair—cleared her throat. "Lady Ozera, we're honored at your presence, but perhaps . . . this isn't the best place for you to be right now."

The more people stared at her today, the easier it became for Tasha to ignore them. "Thank you, but this is exactly where I should be right now, Guardian . . ."

"Hathaway," Vinh murmured. "Janine Hathaway."

"Guardian Hathaway," Tasha said. "Please continue."

Janine studied Tasha a beat more and then gave a sharp nod before pointing at the screen. It displayed a map of the area south of the Poconos and Court. "Here's where the first car was found. Based on the estimated time of turning, we can accurately calculate the farthest they could have gone before sunrise. That's still a big area, but at least it's contained. For now. When nighttime comes, the radius gets larger and larger, and then it's beyond our control. Studying the highways, we can also make some educated guesses on which way they went and start sending search parties. New Strigoi usually steer clear of Moroi areas because they don't want to run into guardians. They do, however, have less control of their bloodlust than a more experienced Strigoi does. We can count on them to make at least one human kill tonight, and that'll help us pinpoint the direction they went, if not their location."

Tasha again had that strange detached feeling as she listened to more of the plan. It was all so logical, all so strategic. The guardians addressed the problem with total indifference, and Tasha could almost—*almost*—forget that it was Lucas and Moira being hunted and not some other monster.

Lucas. My big brother. Almost like a father because of the age difference, especially after our own passed. He used to spin me around until I was too dizzy to stand. He didn't tease me when I was eleven and gave myself that terrible haircut. He loved cinnamon rolls. He binge-watched old TV sitcoms and would laugh and laugh at the stupidest jokes. . . .

But Lucas hadn't laughed so much in recent days, not after

his friends died. Knowing what she knew now, Tasha kicked herself for not having realized that when he grew quiet and stared off, he wasn't reliving old memories. He was fearing for the future, and the inevitable end of his life. How could immortality not sound appealing? Especially with his vain wife constantly panicking about losing her youth and beauty . . .

"Let's go," she told Vinh when the guardians dispersed.

"I'll find a more discreet way back."

"Not to our town house." She peered around the hall and spied Dimitri speaking with Christian. The boy was smiling, but his smile had a haunted quality. "I want to leave Court, Vinh. I need to get away from here. I don't want Christian around this anymore—around their judgment. And their condemnation."

"The guardians won't want you to go far," Vinh warned. "And they'll want you to go somewhere well guarded."

"To protect me from myself, no doubt."

But she had nowhere to go. The country house was out of the question. Statistics said Lucas and Moira wouldn't return to it, but it was still suspect. Out of options, she trekked over to Ronald's Court home. His eyes went wide when he found her and Christian at his door.

"Uncle, I want to go to your estate in Poughkeepsie."

"Now, Tasha, let's not do anything that—"

"There's no time for your scheming or pandering! People saw me come here. You can't avoid that. Give us the keys, and let us stay upstate for a while until this blows over."

Some of Ronald's shock faded. "Until this blows over?

Do you realize what's been done? Tasha, this is never going to blow over! The stain of this will be with your family forever."

"*Our* family," she snapped. "Remember what you told me last night? About how all the Ozeras look after one another?"

He cringed again. Did he think she was going to turn Strigoi before his very eyes? Or was he just unprepared to have her finally stand up to him? "Tasha, please. Try to understand where I'm coming from. It's not too late for me. If I can distance myself from this . . . tragedy, my political career still has a chance."

Tasha took a step forward and saw Ronald's guardian tense in her periphery. "Your political career has a better chance if you make the council. And guess what. *I* am now the voting member of my branch of the Ozeras. And if you want to hold on to any hope of being elected to the Ozera council seat, you will give me those keys now."

An hour later, she was on the road with Vinh, Christian, and another borrowed guardian, Jonas. Officially, he'd come along so that she and Christian could each have their own protection. In reality, she knew it was to put a double watch on her. Christian was too young to drain anyone and become Strigoi, but she was still suspect. And no feeder had been allowed to come with them.

Ronald hadn't visited his other home in a while. Dust had gathered, and much of the furniture remained covered. Even still, the estate was bigger and more luxurious than Lucas's, though it hadn't been styled with Moira's eye for detail. Tasha wondered how much of a person's self vanished with the soul when becoming Strigoi. Even as a bloodthirsty creature of the night, was Moira still consumed by the latest fashions?

They arrived a couple of hours before sunset, prime time for Moroi, but their schedules were all thrown off from not sleeping the previous day. After a light dinner, Tasha let Christian run off to the house's massive home theater. Jonas, unsure of the wards' status, patrolled the house's periphery. Tasha uncovered a sofa and collapsed onto it, too exhausted to do anything else. She didn't intend to sleep, but the next thing she knew, she was yawning and blinking at the garden scene painted on Ronald's vaulted ceiling. Vinh sat across from her on another couch.

She shot upright. "Where's Christian?"

"He's fine. Hiding."

"Hiding?"

"Don't worry, I know where he is. I found him upstairs but pretended I didn't." Vinh's smile was short-lived. "He seemed like he wanted to be alone. I think . . . he has a lot to process."

"Him and me both." Tasha rubbed her eyes and noted the dark windows. "How long did I sleep?"

"Not long enough. Rest more if you want."

"I can't." She yawned again and pushed hair out of her face. "I'm afraid of what I'll see. I'm afraid that every time I close my eyes, I'll see Lucas—as one of those monsters."

"But it won't actually be him," Vinh reminded her. "He's gone."

"Is he? If he'd died—or even if he'd been forcibly turned—there would've been a line of mourners outside our door back there, offering condolences, bringing us flowers. But there was nothing. Not one word of acknowledgment. Even when they were staring at us . . . it was like we didn't exist."

"That'll change with time."

Tasha slumped forward, resting her face in her hands. "Will it, Vinh? You heard what Ronald said."

He crossed the living room and sat beside her, first placing his gun and silver stake on a nearby table. "Ronald Ozera is a petty man who can't see past his own ambition. This didn't even happen to his brother and he's ready to crumble right now. Whereas you? You'll weather this. It'll hurt, but you'll come out stronger for it. You and Lord Christian both."

"Really?" She uncovered her face and straightened again. "I don't feel like I have much of anything left in me, let alone strength."

"I can feel your strength." He placed his hand over hers. "It shines around you. I feel it every time I'm near you. I have since the moment we met, back in our freshman history class."

She looked into his eyes and saw that elusive and precious emotion that he usually kept concealed. The heat of his hand flowed into hers, and there was no obligation or utilitarian reason for that touch. When she laced her fingers in his, he didn't pull away. "Will you still follow me if I run away?"

"Lady Tasha, I . . ." His other hand grazed her cheek, and she was surprised to feel him shake. "I'll follow you anywhere."

Tasha was swimming in the darkness of his eyes, melting at the closeness of his body. Moments later, stark understanding sent a jolt through her, and euphoria gave way to bitterness. "Because you have to. Because they ordered you to."

He shook his head. "No. I was lucky when I graduated. I had a few families to choose from, and I requested yours."

"Did you? But I know . . . I know how hard it's been for you. I see it. How it tests your discipline. I always thought . . ." She cast her eyes downward. "I always thought being assigned to us, to me, was agony for you. Why would you choose it?"

"Because . . . because I can't stay away from you."

His fingers curled into her cheek, tilting her face upward as he brought his mouth to hers. She stiffened, almost wondering if she was dreaming, and then surrendered to the kiss. His lips were the same as she remembered, soft and full, but the way they moved against hers had changed. He tasted her. He devoured her. A new intensity had ignited between them, almost a desperation. They were both older now, past the stage of dares and experimentation. This was a connection to another soul.

But, so help her, it was also desire. He always said she had a flame within her, and just then, she believed him. Every caress of his lips, every bold touch of his hands against her body . . . it all set her ablaze. And suddenly, there was heat and life in a world that she'd thought would forever be filled with coldness and death. The world still felt dangerous and lonely, but if he loved her enough to finally break with the taboos that said their connection was wrong, then maybe—just maybe—there was still hope in the world. Maybe she could change it.

She wrapped herself against him, ready to let go of inhibition and fear and propriety. Her hands slid under his shirt, greedy to possess him like she used to. He'd succumbed as well and started to push the straps of her tank top down.

And then they heard the scream.

They instantly broke apart, and in a heartbeat, the lust within her was obliterated by fear. The sound had come from outside, and despite the distance, there was no mistaking the complete and almost primal terror in it. Vinh shot to his feet, the silver stake and gun back in his hands. When silence fell—almost more sinister than the scream—he scanned the living room intently, his gaze lingering longest on the windows and the doorway that led to a hall connecting to the foyer and kitchen.

He handed over the gun without looking at her. "Take this. Go upstairs."

Tasha started to tell him she didn't know how to use a gun, but when she saw her brother appear in the living room's doorway, the whole world slowed down. Her mouth couldn't form any words. Her body couldn't move. She couldn't draw breath.

Vinh moved in front of her, murmuring as he passed: "That's not your brother. *Go.*"

Tasha, still frozen, tried to truly, clearly take Lucas in. *That's not your brother.* But he looked like him. His hair was the same—her hair, Christian's hair. The features of his face were the same, down to a small mole by his left ear. Even his clothes were the same as they'd been the last time she saw him.

But the eyes . . . those weren't the Ozera eyes. They weren't her eyes or Christian's eyes. The crystalline blue was all but gone, obscured by the bloody ring of red surrounding his pupils. And he no longer had the fair skin of a Moroi. This went beyond fair, beyond pale. It went beyond life. Lucas's pallor was that of someone already in the grave.

Even if his eye and hair color hadn't changed, Tasha would've known her brother was gone simply by the way he regarded them. That malevolence, that complete detachment from any sort of compassion or empathy . . . *That's not your brother*. She was looking at some other entity wearing Lucas's skin.

Tasha felt his gaze slide over her, but Vinh, approaching with his stake, remained Lucas's main focus. "You were the lucky one," he told Vinh. Again, it was surreal. Lucas's voice . . . but not. "You got to live an extra day. An extra day in my little sister's company."

Vinh didn't speak as he strode forward, totally honed in on his foe. He was moving at an angle rather than a straight line, intentionally drawing the action away from Tasha and the stairs that offered her escape. Tension crackled through both men, every part of them poised and waiting for the other to strike. Lucas still had his slim and lean build, but she knew he now possessed a strength that surpassed all of theirs. *He snapped Nolan's neck*. Could Vinh stand against that? He'd been trained to, and new Strigoi were supposed to be less lethal than more seasoned ones—but still very, very lethal.

There's a chance, she thought. Vinh might be able to hold his own against one fresh Strigoi. He could stake him. Stake her brother.

That thing is not my brother.

The window behind them burst apart, and Moira leapt through it, landing in the living room with far more agility than she'd ever displayed in life. She paused to brush glass off her designer jacket, but if that fastidious nature really had carried over to the undead, it was one of the few things that had. Like Lucas, there was no question that this creature that looked so like Moira Ozera contained nothing but evil.

Vinh realized it was over seconds before Tasha did. Both Strigoi sprang toward him at once, and the guardian brought his stake down toward Lucas, yelling, *"Tasha, get out of here!"* And then she could hardly see him at all because Lucas and Moira had tackled him to the floor. Tasha heard his screams, could make out his legs flailing, and then she finally came back to herself.

Feeling like a traitor and a coward, she turned away from the grisly scene and raced up the stairs, only to realize she didn't know where Christian had ended up hiding. *Don't worry, I know where he is,* Vinh had said. But Vinh couldn't help her anymore. For a frantic moment, she thought maybe it was better if Christian stayed hidden, but that was foolish. If a guardian had found him, two Strigoi with enhanced senses could. He needed her.

"Christian!" she shouted, staring around at the vast hall and adjacent rooms. "Christian, where are you?"

Below, the screams had stopped, and she couldn't stand to think about what that meant. From a darkened doorway on the third floor, Christian stuck his head out, his eyes filled with terror. "What's happening? They're here, aren't they?"

Tasha shot up the rest of the stairs. She shoved him back into the room and slammed the heavy wooden door behind them before turning on the light. They were in a rec room filled with vintage arcade games and various tabletop sports. There were no true windows, only a set of French doors that opened to a balcony. Another door, closed, looked like it was probably a storage closet.

"Help me," she cried, grabbing a billiards table. She intended to buy them some time and block the door, but there was no time. There wasn't time for anything. She hadn't even gotten the table to budge when Moira and Lucas kicked through the wooden door. Tasha took hold of Christian's hand and pulled him along as she backed up toward the balcony. "Those aren't your parents," she said to Christian, just as Vinh had told her.

She'd spoken softly, but Strigoi had superior hearing. "Of course we are," said Moira. "And we want to be with our son."

Tasha shouldered open the French doors behind her. They didn't offer much of an escape, not here on the third floor of a house with oversized stories, but it still meant she could put a few more feet between them and her. "I'll die before I'll let you kill him," she said.

Lucas moved closer, an animal on the prowl. "We don't want to kill him. We want him to join us. You can too, but that's your choice. It makes no difference to us. With or without your consent, we're leaving with Christian."

"You want to turn him? Keep him nine forever?" Tasha exclaimed.

"We want to keep him," clarified Moira. "Keep him until he's of age. *Then* awaken him."

Awaken. The word Strigoi used for *turn*, making it sound like some sort of holy act. As horrifying as Christian being turned into an eternally nine-year-old Strigoi was, the thought of him being held captive by Strigoi for years until he was "of age" turned Tasha's stomach just as much.

"There's nowhere else you can go," Lucas said. He was right. Another step, and she'd be fully outside on the balcony and completely trapped. He and Moira were so close now she could see their fangs—sharper and larger than a Moroi's.

Moira knelt down and smiled at Christian. Blood gleamed on her jacket, blood that hadn't been there when she'd crashed through the window. *Vinh's blood.*

"Christian, don't you want to come with us? Don't you want us to all go to a new home together? Tell Aunt Tasha to stop being so selfish."

Tasha didn't need to remind Christian that these weren't his parents. He cringed against her, his nails digging into her palm. Tasha raised the gun she'd been holding in her other hand.

"Don't talk to him. Don't come any nearer. This might not kill you, but silver bullets hurt."

Lucas laughed. "Since when can you use a gun? You're not going to hurt anyone with the safety on."

Was it on? Tasha wasn't sure. And she certainly didn't

know how to take the safety off if it was. She threw the gun down and pulled Christian all the way outside with her until their backs hit the balcony's rail. "I'll throw us both off!" she cried. "We'll be dead before you can turn anyone."

That gave the Strigoi pause, and they stopped advancing. Christian's death was the only power she held over them because it thwarted what they'd come for. It wasn't a power she wanted, though. She didn't want Christian to die. *She* didn't want to die. But if it came down to that or letting them—

Before she could complete the thought, Lucas struck, and no matter how many stories she'd heard of Strigoi speed, even after seeing them pounce on Vinh, Tasha still wasn't prepared for how quickly it happened. Lucas shot out the door and snatched her away from Christian, forcing her to lose her hold on the boy. Without pause, Lucas bent down and sank his teeth into the side of Tasha's face. Tasha's scream was lost in blood and the press of his body on hers as he held her down in the doorway. Pain ripped through her, so maddeningly intense that she nearly lost consciousness. Another scream—Christian's—forced her to keep her grip on the present, no matter her agony. Moira had dragged him into the room.

Desperate for any weapon, Tasha sent a burst of fire magic toward Lucas. It wasn't much. She rarely practiced and was certainly no creator of fireworks. She could do all the cute parlor tricks most fire-wielding Moroi could, like lighting candles. She'd even flambéed cherries at a party once. What she did now had no real force, and certainly no precision, but it was enough. Flames licked along the edge of Lucas's sleeve, and he let go of her and staggered back inside as he tried to pull the jacket off.

Pressing a hand to her cheek, Tasha steadied herself against one of the French doors and watched as Moira let go of Christian. She hurried over to help Lucas pull his jacket off, cautious about getting too near the flames. A big enough fire could kill a Strigoi. The two of them blocked Tasha's way to the room's main exit, though Christian now had a clear path. Tasha tried to tell him to run, but her mouth and jaw no longer worked properly. Her nephew stared at her with wide eyes as she frantically gestured, and she could only imagine what the boy thought of her ghastly appearance. But then, instead of turning around and running away, he shot forward and clung to her leg.

"I won't leave you," he said fiercely.

Lucas's jacket lay on the ground now, the fire stamped out. Tasha found herself in exactly the same situation as before: stuck between the Strigoi and the balcony. Well, not exactly the same situation. Now half her face was gone. But the smoldering jacket gave her a glimmer of hope. If she could use her magic to create a bigger blaze, she might be able to destroy one of them, or at least give her and Christian one last shot at escape.

Fighting through the pain, the fear, and so much more, Tasha summoned what power she could and directed it toward Moira, striving to create the greatest fire she'd ever made. And it *was* big. It surpassed Tasha's last weak attempt, but the magic was sloppy. Tasha missed Moira and ended up setting the room's large Persian rug on fire. It ignited quickly, the blaze spreading fast and far—and Tasha didn't have the strength to control it.

She sensed a trickle of fire magic beside her, and the flames on the rug redirected slightly, settling into a barrier between the Strigoi and the balcony. Tasha looked down at Christian in surprise. "I'm sorry," he said, his face strained with panic and exhaustion. "I can't control it."

Tasha patted his shoulder with her free hand and watched Lucas's and Moira's frustration as the flames grew higher and smoke filled the room. The Strigoi couldn't get to the balcony through the fire and were going to have to cut their losses soon if they wanted to escape it themselves.

We can't get through the fire either, Tasha thought. *We'll have to jump. But at least we'll die with our souls intact.*

Christian coughed and started to cover his mouth with his hand. Suddenly, he stiffened and pointed. It was hard to make out much in the hazy room anymore, but she soon caught sight of what he'd noticed. Other people streamed into the room now. Lots of people. Guardians. Janine Hathaway led them, and they all carried silver stakes.

Lucas and Moira turned their backs to Tasha and Christian and readied for the fight. But as the guardians descended, Tasha knew there was no question of how this was going to end. She took one last look at the monster wearing her brother's face and then turned Christian away so that he wouldn't have to see his parents' second death.

They clung to each other, listening to shouts and cries and

the crackling of burning wood. The smoke stung Tasha's eyes, but she felt certain she would've been crying without it. The pain in her face was unbearable, but not as great as the pain in her heart, and she had that earlier urge to close her eyes and lie down forever.

"Lady Ozera!"

Tasha blinked her eyes open, thinking she'd imagined the voice. Christian pulled her closer to the balcony's edge, and they saw a guardian waving at them below. Farther, across the estate's vast grounds, more guardians were running from a garage used by maintenance workers—and they were carrying a massive ladder.

"Hang on," the guardian below the balcony called. "This'll all be over soon."

But it was never going to be over.

Tasha knew that then. She knew it the next day and the next week. She even knew it two months later, on the day she decided to move away from Court. So long as she woke up every morning, replaying the events of that dark night, nothing about it could ever be over.

Her title ensured she would always be welcome at Court and provided with lodging when she visited. But when a royal formally gave up permanent residence at Court, custom dictated that an official farewell be made to the monarch. So, once she'd made sure the last of the town house's possessions had either been moved or disposed of, Tasha turned the keys over to the royal land manager and trekked across the Court's vast, beautiful grounds once more.

Autumn had taken hold, and the groundskeepers couldn't keep up with the red and gold leaves that kept falling across the pathways. Gray clouds loomed overhead, but Tasha hadn't brought an umbrella. She didn't plan on going back for one either. There were no lines of spectators today. No one knew her exact plans or that she'd even be outside. But those who recognized her in passing still did a double take, staring without trying to make it look like they were staring.

The others waiting in the anteroom to be received by Tatiana stared as well, their expressions mixtures of curiosity and shock. Tasha wondered how much of their reaction still came from the speculation over whether the rest of Lucas's relatives would turn.

She caught sight of her face in a polished silver vase and met that reflection unflinchingly. After treatments and surgeries, she'd been allowed to stop wearing bandages a week ago, though one doctor had tactfully said he'd understand if she wanted to keep her cheek covered. She didn't. Angry red welts still showed in the side of her face, some from the original bite and some from reconstructive surgery. The skin covering it all was irregular—too tight or too wrinkled—and that also was a byproduct of reconstruction. It would be an ongoing process. Future surgeries could fix a lot of it, but all the doctors had reiterated that her face would never be as it was. She'd always have some sort of scar.

An effortless beauty, Tasha thought.

"Lady Natasha Ozera."

Tasha entered at the sound of her name. Queen Tatiana was receiving visitors in the throne room today, which was a rarity. The Court, no matter where it was in the world, always maintained a throne room for the acting monarch, and in older days, that room would've been the chief location for all royal receptions. In modern times, the queen often listened to callers in less luxurious—but still very dignified—sitting rooms.

Tasha had been warned this morning about the venue change, the subtle message being that she should dress appropriately. But Tasha wore the same clothes she planned on wearing to the airport in two hours: jeans, T-shirt, suede jacket. A ponytail held her long hair back from her face. Courtiers whispered as she passed through the ostentatious red-and-gold room, and she realized she couldn't even tell what particular kind of gossip she stirred up anymore.

Queen Tatiana sat atop the elaborately carved throne that had honored generations of monarchs before her. At least it was situated only slightly above ground level today. For truly formal occasions, the throne would sit high on a platform that required stairs. Even so, the queen had still very clearly dressed to impress, wearing a velvet gown in shades of red and rust that Tasha thought was better suited for something like the Summer's End Ball, rather than business meetings with one's subjects. The queen kept her expression serene, but Tasha could sense the other woman's condemnation.

Tasha bowed, unable to curtsy in jeans.

"Natasha. We are pleased to see you in the palace. You

haven't been out recently. Are you feeling better?" Tatiana, wielding the royal *we*, spoke as though Tasha were getting over a cold.

"Yes, thank you, Your Majesty. I've come to officially request your leave. I'm surrendering my family's residence and moving." The request was a formality these days; Tatiana couldn't stop her.

"Understandable. Where are you moving to?"

"Minneapolis."

Surprise crept into Tatiana's face. "There aren't any Moroi strongholds there. Just a handful of feeders."

"Correct, Your Majesty."

Moroi tended to survive by clustering together with groups of their guardians or seeking isolation (while also well guarded), as Ronald had tried with his now half-burned estate. Minneapolis met none of those criteria. That was part of the reason why Tasha had chosen it as a new home. If she'd only had to worry about herself, she actually would've run as far and as fast as she could to the other side of the world. But she had to keep close to Christian, now back at school in Montana, and to Court as well. She wasn't going to let the other royals forget her or think that they'd made her run away. She was leaving by choice.

"You'll probably want a guardian to accompany you, then."

"No, Your Majesty."

"Aren't you afraid?"

Tasha laughed, shocking everyone in the room. "Your

Majesty, my own brother turned Strigoi and killed someone I cared about right in front of me. And then he tried to kill me." She turned and pointed, making sure the queen got a good look at her cheek. "After that, I had to decide whether to burn to death with my nephew or just kill us both outright with a suicidal jump."

When Tasha said no more, Tatiana waved an expectant hand. "Your point?"

"My point, Your Majesty, is that I have little left to be afraid of. Not anymore. Other Moroi? They're afraid and endanger themselves further by choosing helplessness and depending on guardians for defense. If I'd known conventional fighting methods, if I'd had better control of my magic . . ." Tasha's resolve faltered for just a moment. Could she have helped Vinh take down Lucas and Moira if she'd known more? Would it have been enough? "Well, Your Majesty, things would've turned out differently. I won't make the mistake of ignorance again, and I'm not going to take a guardian from someone who needs one more than me. I will not rely on another for my safety. I'll take charge of my own safety. You told me once that I just needed to look pretty and keep my opinions to myself, but since it turns out neither is possible now, I'll give you my opinion on what I think should be done. I think other Moroi should start taking a stand for themselves and demand tools and training to fight Strigoi. And I think the council and the crown should be facilitating that as well."

Until that moment, Tasha had never thought much about how silence had a sound. But it did. It was heavy and loud, and it filled the room. Tatiana studied her unblinkingly, and Tasha met that steely gaze with none of the fear she'd felt at the ball. As she'd said, she had little to be afraid of anymore.

"Your opinion is noted," the queen said. "And your leave is granted. The Court will, of course, maintain a place for your nephew to return to on school holidays."

"Why would he do that?"

"Because he will need to go somewhere. He's a minor. No doubt your other family will look after—"

"*I* am his family," Tasha stated, eliciting gasps at the impudence of interrupting the queen. "And *I* will look after him. He'll either come to me in Minneapolis on breaks, or I'll go to him and stay at St. Vladimir's."

Sending Christian back to school had been one of the hardest decisions Tasha had ever had to make. She could have homeschooled him; it wasn't unheard of for Moroi in isolation. Or she could have stayed at Court and sent him to its schools, where she could keep a more watchful eye on him. Ultimately, he had made the choice.

It's okay, Aunt Tasha. I'll go back. I can handle whatever happens.

She believed him but wished it wasn't a battle he had to face. His eyes—too old for someone so young—had told her that he knew what to expect. It would be like the reaction at Court, except adults had more tact than children. Usually.

"You take a lot of risks," said Queen Tatiana. "But so be it. There are plenty of other Ozeras. If you want to throw your lives away and traipse around the world, defenseless, I won't forbid it."

"Not defenseless," Tasha replied. "The Ozeras will never be defenseless again—the real Ozeras. My nephew and me. All the others? They just share the same name."

Tatiana smiled, a thin, tight-lipped smile with all the warmth of a marble bust. "I'm sure Ronald will be very happy to hear that. And I'm sure the guardians' personnel department will be glad they won't have to reallocate guardians to you after having wasted five others on your family."

"Four, Your Majesty. Four were killed."

"Were there? I lost track. But still, it's a relief. That's one less we have to replace."

"Vinh Duy Khuc. Nolan Orr. Jonas Nowicki. Ira Locke."

Tatiana frowned. "I beg your pardon?"

"Those 'ones' you need to replace. Those are their names." Tasha returned the queen's earlier icy smile with one of her own. "I can write them down for you if it'll help you keep track."

"That won't be necessary. Is there anything else you require before leaving, Natasha?"

"No, Your Majesty."

"Then you shouldn't delay your journey. I'm sure there are many . . . who will miss you." Tatiana's tone made it clear that she was not one of those people.

"Oh, don't worry. I'll be back to visit. Like I said, I'm not going to keep my opinions to myself anymore, and I expect I'll have a lot to say. I hope that won't be a problem, Your Majesty."

"Natasha, dear, you may posture all you like, but there's

very little you could say or do that would truly be a problem for me. Go." The queen waved in dismissal, possibly even boredom. "Go off on whatever quest you think will make you feel better."

Tasha left with her head held high, smiling at the scandalized onlookers. When she reached the antechamber, a young man held the door open. She looked over and recognized the visiting Russian novice who'd stayed with Christian.

"Lady Ozera."

"Mr. Belikov."

"You remembered my name," he said in surprise. "Just like you remembered the others."

"Of course."

"You . . . you said some very brave things in there." He spoke diplomatically, cautiously—well aware of the dangers of openly supporting controversial views—but something in his brown eyes told her he agreed with her. *Just like Vinh*, she thought. *So controlled and so good at his duty. So good at sitting on his feelings.*

"I said what needed to be said, Mr. Belikov. How much longer will you be at Court?"

"Another week."

"Well, have a safe trip back. I hope we cross paths again."

He bowed his head deferentially. "Me too, Lady Ozera."

"No need for that. You don't work for me. Just call me Tasha."

Surprise flashed over him, and then the edges of his mouth turned up in amusement. "Then call me Dimitri . . . Tasha."

Not like Vinh after all. Despite all her insistence on dropping the title, Vinh had obstinately kept with protocol—up until the last words he'd ever spoken to her.

Tasha, get out of here!

Tears stung her eyes, and the wound of his loss—still raw, still bleeding—tore at her. *One moment we were in each other's arms, finally ready to cast aside all those stupid, archaic rules. And then he was gone. Just like that.* The ache of his loss followed her everywhere. It was her new companion, one that made her dream of Vinh's face when the Strigoi had attacked and the screaming had followed. Tasha couldn't imagine this hole in her heart—no, this hole in her life—would ever heal, but if by some miracle it did, she'd made a vow to herself. *I will never endure this sort of pain again. If I'm able to love someone else one day, I will do whatever it takes to hold on to him. No matter the cost.*

Realizing Dimitri was staring at her curiously, Tasha blinked a few times and tried to muster a pleasant tone and expression as she returned to the present.

"Goodbye, Dimitri."

Her flight arrived in Minneapolis far too late at night for her to do much more than go to bed and try to adjust to a human schedule. But she was up with the sun, out and about as the rest of the city opened for business and began its day. She had plans to apartment-hunt later in the afternoon, but first, she had a more important task.

Coffee in hand, Tasha stood at her hotel's main entrance

and scanned both directions of the busy downtown street before her. At random, she chose to go left and walked two blocks before finding what she sought.

You don't need guardians to teach you. Go to any city, and you'll find endless options.

"Hello?" she called as she pushed open a glass door. The empty room's interior was dark and dusty and smelled like old sweat. Punching bags and weights were arranged around the walls, and a makeshift ring took over the center. After a few moments, a middle-aged human man emerged from a backroom.

"Can I help you?" He was shorter than her, but his biceps looked bigger than her waist.

"You teach boxing?"

"That's what the sign says."

Walk down a street and turn into the first place you find that can teach you any semblance of self-defense.

"Can you teach me?" she asked.

The man tilted his head to one side and scratched his neck. "I can teach anyone. But you're a skinny thing. We'd have to spend half our time just getting you stronger. You up for that?"

Start with something, and go from there. Go until you're unstoppable.

"I'm up for anything," she said.

From the Journal of Vasilisa Dragomir

January 11

It's starting to happen more often. Rose tries to hide it from me, but it's becoming too much, even for her. After school yesterday, I found some old pictures of Andre and me. They broke me. I spent most of the night crying. Hating life. Hating that I'd survived. At breakfast the next day, Rose rushed right over and hugged me. "It's going to be okay," she said. "You survived for a reason." I broke away and demanded to know how she knew what I'd been thinking last night. She claimed she could see it in my face, how sad I was . . . but I could tell she was lying. She's in my head somehow. More and more each day. And neither of us likes it.

January 15

One month since the accident. It doesn't seem real. I keep thinking that as soon as we have our next break at school, they'll all show up for a visit. It's like they're just away somewhere, maybe traveling in Europe. No one talks about them much anymore, and why should they? No one else lost their entire family in an instant. Rose knew today was the anniversary, of course. I don't have to be in her mind to know how that night haunts her. It's in her eyes, even though she pretends like she doesn't care about much of anything. She's partying more than she used to. I try not to scold her for it. I'm not her keeper, but I'm worried.

Uncle Victor knew what today was too. He sent me a nice card telling me I was in his thoughts.

January 16

Someone said "Princess Dragomir" today, and I looked around, expecting to see Mom. Then I realized they were talking to me. I am the princess now. I am the oldest in the Dragomir family. I am the Dragomir family.

January 17

I've been feeling worse and worse. So much so that I actually stopped to talk to a counselor after classes. She said that it was normal to feel sad, especially with the accident's anniversary this week. I tried to tell her it's more than sadness. More than depression. It's like a creature living inside me that's trying to take control. Rose can feel it too—not as much as I do. I think it's more of an echo in her. Or maybe she's able to block it with all the crazy things she keeps doing. Last night she and some other novices had a party in the woods with a stolen bottle of vodka. They all started climbing high trees and daring one another to jump down. Rose made out with someone but can't remember who.

January 18

It's bad today.

January 19

I finally lost it yesterday. That awful, hungry despair inside me was just too much. I had to get it out of me, but I didn't know how. And before I realized it, I was scratching my own arms. Clawing at my own skin. The only thing that came out was blood, but this morning I feel better. And that scares me.

January 21

During all the darkness last week, I completely forgot about a paper that was due for Mr. Nagy. He isn't very forgiving about that kind of thing, not even to girls recently orphaned. I stayed after class to plead my case and at least try for partial credit . . . and he didn't chastise me at all. He smiled and nodded as I stuttered out a lame excuse about having a weeklong headache. He said he completely understood and gave me an extra week to get the paper in for full credit. He added that if I needed more time, that would be no problem. I said one week was fine and hurried out of the room. I should've been happy, but the whole incident really weirded me out.

January 27

I haven't felt much like writing. I feel like I'm going through the motions every day, pretending to live an ordinary life while I'm falling apart inside. Rose knows, but she doesn't know what to do for me, and it's driving her crazy. She isn't used to feeling helpless. She always has some plan—maybe not one that's thought out very well, but at least it's something. She watches me. She feels my emotions. She says everything will be okay—but she doesn't believe it.

January 31

Rose got caught visiting me after hours by the front desk attendant, and I managed to talk her out of trouble with hardly any effort. It was just like with Mr. Nagy and the paper, and I realize now that I compelled them. But I wasn't even trying to! I'd never do that on purpose. No one should exert their will on another person. I've seen other kids do it once in a while for minor things—things very much like getting out of trouble and homework. But none of them has ever been able to pull it off like I can.

February 9

I guess there's a Valentine's Day dance coming up. Aaron says we have to go. I asked him why, and he said, "Because." God, he's getting annoying.

February 14

I went to the dance tonight. I wore one of the new dresses I bought with Mom just before the accident. It's long and lavender and has little crystals on the bodice. Everyone kept telling me how pretty I looked. Aaron couldn't stop staring at my cleavage. And the whole time, I just kept getting madder and madder. I'm still not sure why. It was that thing in me, that building darkness rearing its ugly head again. I thought about Mom picking out the dress. I thought about how tomorrow is another anniversary. When the dance ended and Aaron said we should go to Camille's after-party, I blew up. I told him I was tired of listening to him talk about what we should do. I told him I was tired of listening to him talk, period. He looked like I'd slapped him. I went back to my room, ready to explode . . . and that was when I did it again. I let the mental pain out physically. But this time I didn't use my nails. I used a blade to cut myself. Just enough to hurt. Just enough to distract from what was going on in my head. Rose showed up right away, and she yelled at me. I don't think that's ever happened before. She kept going on and on about how I should never do that again and that I needed to come to her for help. She wasn't angry, though. She was scared. And I don't think that's ever happened before either.

February 15

Two months.

February 19

Elemental testing with Ms. Carmack today. Surprise, surprise: no sign of me specializing. What's weird is I've actually improved a little in all the elements. I can work with each of them at about the same level. My control in each of them is better than what any specialized Moroi can do with their nondominant elements, but it's still nowhere near a true specialization. Ms. Carmack was really diplomatic about it all. She gave me the old line about how it just takes time and how it's not surprising after everything I've been through. Later, I heard her telling Headmistress Kirova that she's concerned. Apparently, it's actually really weird. Welcome to my life.

February 21

I don't understand what happened today. I guess I should start at the beginning.

It's not really spring yet, but the weather warmed up a lot. Rose insisted we go outside. She's been worried about me ever since the dance and keeps going out of her way to find fun things for us to do. She got a bottle of peach schnapps from Abby Badica somehow, and we sneaked out to drink it. And actually, it was fun . . . at first. It was just the two of us, laughing and drinking. It was like the old days.

Then we got busted by Ms. Karp. She was as weird as usual but was actually pretty nice about it all and didn't report us. As we were walking back to the school, we found this raven on the ground. And it was dead. But . . . I couldn't stay away from it. I've always loved animals, but that wasn't what drew me. Maybe it was that otherness in me. Rose got worked up about how the raven was probably diseased, but I couldn't help myself. I touched it, and suddenly . . . it wasn't dead. It started moving. And it flew away.

I know that sounds crazy. I might have questioned whether it had really been dead in the first place, except when I touched it, I felt . . . amazing. Like the complete and total opposite of that darkness that drags me down. I felt energized, light. Like a goddess. Like I could do anything.

Ms. Karp freaked out. She actually grabbed me and began ranting about how nothing had happened. But at the same time, she also kept saying we couldn't tell anyone what had happened. She said they'd start looking for me, but she didn't say who "they" were. I've always thought Ms. Karp was weird, but for the first time, I think she might be insane. And yet who am I to judge? After what I saw—or think I saw—maybe I am too.

February 22
Rose and I haven't talked about the raven. I still felt high and glorious, but I also felt exhausted. I went to the feeders, even though I'd just been there before school. And then I was exhausted. I slept hard and almost missed my first class today. And I don't feel wonderful anymore. I'm back in that hole. Rose can tell and hasn't wanted to leave my side all day. She's afraid I'll hurt myself again. I am too, so I'm trying to resist it. It's a little easier with her around. She makes me feel stronger.

February 28
I feel like I'm being watched.

March 2
I'm tired of people. I'm tired of smiling and dealing with the drama and expectations surrounding me. I feel like I can't breathe at St. Vladimir's anymore. There's just too much. Too much everything.

March 5
Ms. Karp is gone, and no one will tell us why. There's a new

biology instructor, and all the other teachers act like Ms. Karp never existed.

March 8

Uncle Victor came to visit Natalie today and spent some time with me. He kept wanting to know how I was. He'd ask it in different ways—how my grades were, how Aaron was, how I was coping being the only Dragomir. I've been trying to hide how strange I feel lately, but I wonder if someone noticed and told him. It makes me feel bad. He has so many of his own problems to deal with, and I don't want him to worry about me too.

March 15

It's been three months.

March 17

I lost it again. Only this time I lost it in public. It's kind of a blur. Rose and I went to this party last night. Wade had a feeder there, and she was pretty out of it—even more than a normal feeder. And he wanted to do things to her . . . things he shouldn't have . . . and I couldn't let him. He had to stop. And I was the one who made him stop. I made him suffer. I made him break a window. I made him hurt himself. Part of me knew it was awful. I hate violence. But at the same time, I knew he deserved it. He had to be punished, and that strange exhilaration burned through me the whole time. I lost myself, and Rose had to talk me back.

Afterward, when the party had been broken up because of the commotion, no one could really explain what had happened. They'd all been drunk and probably thought they were imagining things. Rose took the blame for the damage, and I can tell something's changed in her.

March 18

Rose is frightened again, but this time it's different. She isn't trying to distract herself from it. She isn't trying to distract me. She's quiet and calculating. She doesn't joke. I can tell from her eyes that she's planning something, but she won't say what. I wish I could see into her mind.

March 19

A bunch of council members visited from Court earlier, so we got to have a special schoolwide reception in their honor. Even Rose got to come while on detention. I'm still furious that she has to pay for what Wade did. For what I did. It's been tearing me up, and after the reception, I sort of went off about it to Rose and how much I hate Wade and his smug attitude. I didn't think I was acting that weird, but the more I talked, the more Rose looked like she didn't even recognize me.

Before I knew it, she was leading me out of the school, out to the parking lot. She told me we were leaving St. Vladimir's right now. That we had to. One of the councilmember's chauffeurs was getting his car ready, and Rose had me compel him to help hide us in the trunk. We found out he works for Maisie Lazar's dad and that they were actually leaving around dawn, so Rose and I each had time to race back to our respective dorms and gather a few essentials. I'm waiting for her now near the parking lot, and I still don't really understand what's happening. When I asked her why we were leaving, she just said, "I'm taking care of you. You don't need to know anything else."

March 20

We did it. We left last night.

After I met back up again with Rose at the parking lot, I made the chauffeur let us into the trunk and then forget he'd ever seen us. I felt guilty over that compulsion, but blurring his memory was nowhere near as bad as making Wade do all of those terrible things. Mr. Lazar arrived at dawn, and we got on the road. It was a miserable trip. The trunk was hot and stuffy and smelled like gasoline. I should've demanded answers from Rose. I should've told her leaving was crazy and that we needed to go back. But I didn't because, somehow, I knew we were doing the right thing. We had to get away from St. Vladimir's.

In Missoula, Rose and I climbed out of the trunk when Mr. Lazar stopped for food. The first place we went to was the bank that's always held my family's accounts. Part of my inheritance is frozen until I'm eighteen, but I still have a huge fund I can draw from as needed. Rose told me to empty it. She'd even brought a bag specifically to carry the cash. It was like a bank heist in a movie. After that, we went straight to the bus station and got on the first bus that was leaving. "Everyone's still asleep at school," Rose kept saying. "We've got to get far away before they realize we've left. And we've got to keep changing it up."

That first bus took us to Billings. Then we took another to Rapid City. That was when Rose really got tense. "They know we're gone by now. They'll check every public transportation place in a day's radius and put out our descriptions." Now we're on an overnight bus to Milwaukee. I can hardly think anymore. I'm not really on a human or Moroi schedule, just an exhausted one. I'm going to try to get some rest. Rose looks like she can stay awake forever.

March 21

We made it to Milwaukee this morning, and Rose immediately got us a ride to Madison by hitchhiking with some college kids. She never took her eyes off them the whole time. She doesn't trust hitchhiking, but getting away from bus stations makes us harder to track. We made it to Madison without any incident. I've never been to Wisconsin before. It's very flat. Our plan is to live around large universities. It's easier to blend in, and no one questions two girls on their own—or who pay rent in cash. A lot of students are looking for roommates and sublets, and by this evening, we had a room in a house with five other people. Our room had belonged to someone who'd studied abroad in France last semester and ended up staying in Paris with an artist she'd met.

We ordered a pizza for dinner, and while we were eating, I suddenly realized that today is Rose's birthday. Sweet sixteen. I still feel horrible for forgetting. "I don't have a present for you," I told her. She responded: "You're alive. That's all I need."

March 22

We went shopping today. Our room came with bunk beds, and the rest of the house has furniture and kitchen utensils, but we don't have anything personal, like sheets or towels. Rose was paranoid the whole time we were out. She kept peeking around corners and store displays and glared at anyone who came too close to us. I found some unicorn sheets that were on clearance, but when I picked them up, she said, without even looking at me: "Don't even think about it, Liss. Just because I'm on watch for guardians doesn't mean I'm oblivious to poor retail decisions."

March 23

We cooked our first meal today. I didn't know it was possible to burn spaghetti.

March 25

It turns out you can't put aluminum foil in the microwave. We have to go shopping again to buy a new one for the house.

March 27

I think I've adjusted to a human schedule, though going to bed when it's dark will never feel normal. I don't know what kind of schedule Rose is on. She's worried about Strigoi, not just guardians, so she stays up a lot of the night and naps most of the morning away.

March 29

Rose is still paranoid, but I'm starting to relax. It's so much easier here than at St. Vladimir's. I don't have all those people watching me or expecting me to do things. I'm not constantly reminded that I'm the last in my family. I just blend in with all the other students. Rose and I make a point of getting out of the house every day so that our housemates think we're taking classes. Sometimes we do go to classes. It's easy to sneak into giant lecture halls and listen. I've found a political science class I really like. Rose usually sleeps through it. Other times, we go for walks or even leave campus to explore the city. This new life seems to be keeping the darkness at bay, but I'm tired all the time. I keep going to bed earlier and earlier.

March 30

I was so tired today that I didn't want to go out at all. I spent most of the day on the couch watching talk shows.

March 31

We're starting to believe we might have really pulled off this escape. But we have a new problem: blood. It's why I'm always so wiped out. I've never gone this long without blood, and I'm even starting to dream about it. When our housemates cooked out on the grill last night, I had them make my hamburger extra rare. Rose and I aren't sure what to do. We know feeders are recruited from the underbelly of human society, and when she planned our escape, Rose thought we'd somehow just stumble across willing volunteers. It turns out that's not how it works.

April 1

I woke up feeling so awful that I could barely get out of bed. When I did, I threw up. One of our roommates is convinced I'm pregnant. Rose finally told me I needed to drink her blood. And, of course, I told her even I'm not that crazy. Moroi can survive off dhampir blood, sure, but it's wrong to do it. Beyond wrong. I still can't even believe she would have suggested it. Dhampirs guard us. They don't feed us. And there's no way I'd risk Rose getting addicted to bites.

April 2
Still sick.

April 3

I did it. I didn't want to. I swore I wouldn't. But I was so far gone today that I barely knew my own name or where I was. And when Rose offered me her neck, I didn't hesitate. I feel so much better now, though I'm still not fully recovered after so much deprivation. I drank more from her than I should have and could have easily done more. She's sleeping it off now. Watching her, I don't know how I'm going to live with the guilt. I can't do it again. We have to find another solution.

April 4

Rose says she is our solution. She says drinking from her isn't just convenient—it helps keep our presence in Madison a secret. What if we found a feeder who also feeds other Moroi? What if that person gave out our descriptions? It seems unlikely, but Rose is dead set on this. She swears giving blood doesn't bother her and that all she needs is food and a little rest. I finally caved but haggled with her all day until we reached a compromise on how we'd manage things from now on. I'll drink from her enough to keep my strength up but much less often than I would with a normal feeder. I can handle a little lethargy. It took a while to get Rose to agree to this. She wants me to be as strong as possible, but I told her she needs to be strong too in order to keep us safe. She couldn't argue against that, so I guess this is our life now.

April 9

Rose made pancakes this morning without burning them like the last five times she tried. She strutted around all day. You would've thought she'd staked her first Strigoi.

April 15

Four months.

April 29

I can't believe I haven't written in two weeks. I still feel good. We found a children's museum looking for volunteers, and after listening to me beg for two weeks, Rose finally agreed that I could do a few hours each week. It makes me feel like I have purpose. She comes with me, of course, and always takes a walk through the building before I start my shift. Then she waits outside for me, and I'm pretty sure she never takes her eyes off the front door. I told her she should find some kind of hobby and that she shouldn't always base her life around mine. She just said: "I'm a guardian."

May 2

Rose has a hobby. Some of our housemates are on an Ultimate Frisbee team and needed an extra player yesterday. Rose subbed in, and, surprise, surprise, she's really good—so good, she had to hold back so her dhampir abilities wouldn't attract any attention. They asked her to be a regular player, and she accepted. She claims in private that it's an embarrassment for someone of her "professional status" to participate in such a silly sport, but her eyes lit up when she saw the game schedule. She's needed something like this more than she realizes. I understand why she has to be so serious and always on guard, but I miss the old, carefree Rose.

May 11

Classes are done for the term, and the attitude around campus has completely changed. There's a break this month, and then summer session starts. I'm excited. A whole bunch of new classes will be starting, and I can actually sneak in and hear them from the very beginning. After going over the summer schedule, I found the two I want. One's about ethics in politics.

The other's the history of Eastern Europe after World War II. I showed their descriptions to Rose, and she said she looked forward to having some extra time to catch up on sleep.

May 14

Our housemates have been trying to get us amped up for football, even though it doesn't start until the fall. I guess it's kind of a big deal here. I don't get it, but Rose is hooked. I think she's in withdrawal from all the punching and hitting of guardian training. One of the guys in the house is so obsessed that he records past games and analyzes them. Rose has started watching with him, and sometimes I'll hear her yelling at the TV: "What are you doing? He threw it right to you!" I'm glad we're both starting to find our way here. I think this life is going to be good for us.

May 15

Five months.

May 20

I screwed up.

June 5

I'm only writing today because Rose made me. She says unburdening myself will make me feel better. I asked how she knew, and she said she saw it on a talk show. But there isn't much to tell. I've spent the last week in bed, not because I'm tired, but because I'm worthless. I ruined everything.

June 9

I'll try again.

We're not in Madison anymore. We're just outside Chicago now, living on the campus of Northwestern University. One day when I was volunteering at the children's museum back in Madison, a Moroi man and his little daughter came by. Of course they noticed I was Moroi, but the little girl was too caught up in one of the activities to really care. Not the man. He kept trying to strike up a conversation and was saying I looked familiar, even though I very clearly acted busy. Finally, he said that I reminded him of the Dragomirs. It was more of a trivia thing for him—not like he'd been hunting me. He seemed friendly enough and was just on vacation. Probably nothing would have happened, but I freaked out. I compelled him—on purpose—to forget he'd ever seen me. I ordered him to take his daughter out for ice cream and then leave Madison and never come back. And that was exactly what he did. Well, I didn't see the ice cream or him leaving Madison, but he turned right around as soon as I released him and took his daughter out of the museum. I can't explain how I know the compulsion worked, but it did.

As soon as Rose heard what had happened, she started making plans for us to leave. We went back to the house and packed up our essentials. We left an envelope with next month's rent for one of our roommates, and then we were on a bus. Rose has had a backup plan in place for a while, so she already knew where to go.

I was numb the whole time. If I hadn't made such a big deal about wanting to volunteer and be "useful," I never would have run into that Moroi. Rose said that's stupid logic and that we could have run into him anywhere else in the city—unless we never left our room. And then our roommates might report that for being weird too. She kept assuring me I didn't do anything wrong, that the risk was small, and that it's just better to be safe.

But of course I did something wrong. We had a good thing in Madison. Both of us did. And I ruined it. Not only that, I compelled someone—majorly compelled. Giving a series of orders like that and making them stick long after they've been issued is almost impossible for a Moroi to do, especially to another Moroi. No one can do that. Except for maybe Strigoi. But I did it, and I know it worked. Rose said I shouldn't feel guilty and that I needed to do whatever I could to survive. "If he forgets you, then that's a good thing. And what's so wrong about making a guy take his kid out for ice cream? For all we know, he's one of those health food nuts and only lets her eat celery."

But no one should be able to do what I did. No one should be able to play God. The worst part is, it felt so good. I had that wonderful high rushing through me, just like when I touched the raven. But that feeling didn't last. As soon as we had a new house on a new campus in Chicago, I crashed. I sat in my room and stewed in that darkness. Rose could feel it and knew how badly I wanted to cut myself. Days and days we went like that, and this is the first one I've finally been able to do something more than just feel lost. I wish I knew what was wrong with me.

June 15

Six months.

June 21

I'm starting to feel hopeful again. The darkness has finally lifted. I feel stupid about swinging to these extremes all the time, but ruminating won't help. I need to look toward the future. We're starting to build a life here. Our room is bigger than the last place, which is nice, though Rose says she might concede to each of us getting our own room the next time we move. I was surprised to hear her talk about moving. When I told her I wouldn't screw things up again, she said that wasn't what she meant. She claims moving around regularly is simply a smart strategy. We need to stay hidden until I'm eighteen, and then no one can make me go anywhere I don't want to be. But that's almost two years away.

June 27

I've found more summer lectures to sit in on. There was another political science one I wanted to take, but then I found a class at the same time that was on weapons and warfare in ancient Greece. It's not my thing at all, but I thought Rose might be into it. And is she ever! I'm pretty sure I've never seen her pay so much attention in a history class before. Yesterday's lecture was about this Spartan spear called a dory, and now Rose is trying to figure out how she can get one of her own.

June 30

All our housemates are girls, but one of them has a brother named Jeff who's also a student. He stops by sometimes and is totally in love with Rose. He doesn't even hang around his sister anymore and is always trying to ask Rose out. I've teased her that she should accept a date and have some fun, even if he's human. She said if I could read her mind, I'd know he wasn't her type. I asked what her type was, and all she could come up with was "really, really tall."

July 4

Our house had a barbecue today, and Jeff lit off fireworks in our backyard. It was fun, but I kept thinking about that summer my family stayed by Lake Tahoe and Andre tried to smuggle in fireworks without Mom knowing. Of course she found out and told him to get rid of them. He did so by destroying them with fire magic, and it practically burned our house down. It was a pretty amazing show, even though he was grounded for a month afterward. Remembering that made me sadder and sadder, and I left the party early. In the kitchen, I ran into Jeff. He'd burned his hand. I helped him wrap it up. When his sister found out, she lectured him on safety. He swore it wasn't that bad and even unwrapped it to show her. And it actually wasn't that bad. It was practically nonexistent, compared to what I'd seen earlier. I swear, sometimes I don't think I can trust my own eyes. How much am I imagining these days?

July 10

I'm sixteen today. It's hard to believe. To celebrate, Rose and I went into downtown Chicago and broke our normal budget to go on a shopping spree. Afterward, we ate at a fancy restaurant, and Rose ordered everything on the dessert tray. Even she couldn't finish it. We had them pack it up, and now our refrigerator is full of leftover crème brûlée and tiramisu.

July 14

I've got another volunteer job, this time at a nursing home, so I'm working at the other end of the age spectrum. I was nervous about it after what had happened last time, but Rose pushed me into it and even offered to volunteer with me. She's not usually the public service type, but her job there is "entertainment," so she sits around and plays poker with the residents. They actually put money on the line when the nurses and attendants aren't looking.

July 15

Seven months since I lost them all.

July 22

There's so much going on now, and it's all good. I'm happy again. Rose is too, though she never lets down her guard. I don't know what I'd do without her. She found some people who go out to Lake Michigan to play volleyball on the weekends, so we do that now. She teases me that if she's going to do good work like I do at the nursing home, then I owe it to her to give sports a try. I honestly would, if it wasn't for the sun. I stay in the shade while she plays. She loves the sun, but as usual, she has to hold back how good she is.

July 29
I don't feel like writing as much, but it's mostly because I'm so content and distracted by other things. There's not a lot to report, and honestly? I kind of love it that way.

August 6
I've been practicing the elements in my free time. I keep hoping that Ms. Carmack was right and that it was just the stress of the accident delaying me. But nothing's changed. I have limited control of all four but nothing extraordinary. When I told Rose that, she said that I was extra, extra extraordinary and that my magic was too lame to even try to catch up.

August 16
I missed the anniversary of the accident yesterday. Rose and I spent most of the day at this film festival that was really weird but lots of fun. I was so caught up that the date slipped my mind. Rose says it means that I'm moving on with my life, but it doesn't seem fair when Mom, Dad, and Andre never got that chance.

September 13
Regular term is back in session at Northwestern, and it feels like there are a million more people on campus. Rose likes it

because it's easier for us to lose ourselves in the crowd. Also, football season is back, and Rose is just as pumped up as she was watching those old games in Madison. Everyone in the house is. Now I know what Rose must have felt like sitting through those political science lectures. One of the classes I'm listening to this term is about American drama, so I've decided Saturday games are the perfect time to catch up on reading plays. I sit with everyone else around the TV, and then I read Arthur Miller and Tennessee Williams. No one even notices, so long as I cheer at the right times.

September 14
There's a class on ancient Chinese warfare. Guess who wants to sit in on it?

September 18
I forgot the anniversary again.

September 20
Jeff finally got Rose to go out with him by offering her something she couldn't resist: tickets to a live football game. And of course, Rose going out with him meant I had to go too since she wouldn't leave me. Jeff brought a friend of his along, so it was sort of a double date. Jeff thought I'd like the guy—Cal—because he's "artsy and political and doesn't like football." It was kind of true. Neither of us paid attention to the game, but all he talked about was how everything should be made of hemp and how some indie band

he used to like is no good anymore because they sold out.

September 24

Jeff keeps wanting to go out again with Rose. None of the dates he's offered involve football tickets, so she's wondering how she can let him down easy.

October 1

We went out with some of the girls from our house to a Mexican restaurant a few nights ago. Jeff invited himself along and seemed to think he'd scored a date with Rose. He sat next to her and kept piling on the compliments. Then the food arrived, and he watched in horror as she put ketchup on her tacos. I've had years to get used to this, ever since that time the cafeteria ran out of salsa, but I guess it came as kind of a shock to him. He could barely say a word for the rest of the meal. Now he's stopped calling.

October 9

Rose has had to give up joining casual sports leagues. She was playing basketball last night and didn't check herself enough. She did this crazy maneuver, sprinting across the court and making an impossible shot. The coach of the university's women's team saw her and accosted us after the game. She thinks Rose is a student and was trying to get her name and set up a meeting. We managed to get out of there without answering any questions. Rose says it's no big deal, but I can tell she's sad to be cutting out the games. Sitting still is hard for a dhampir.

October 15

Ten months since the accident. I've been sad today—but not in the stay-in-bed-all-day way. Rose and I spent a lot of time sharing good memories about my family. It sounds like a cliché, but I really did laugh and cry. I still ache for them, but I feel like I can go on with my life now.

October 20

I have the flu. Moroi don't catch human ailments very often, but I guess being around so many has taken its toll. I've needed extra blood, and of course, Rose has stepped up to give it. The result is that we're both staying in and sleeping a lot more. Also, she's gotten more vocal about offering, so I lied today and told her I'm feeling better, even though I'm not. She's nowhere near the addiction a feeder experiences, but I recognize some of that eagerness in her eyes. I have to look after her, just like she looks after me.

October 31

Halloween. There are a ton of parties and events going on around campus, but Rose doesn't like us to stay out too late at night. So we had our own party. We stayed home and dressed up like flappers. Rose loves feather boas. We also watched a bunch of "scary" vampire movies. They were hilarious.

November 12

Allison, one of our housemates, has this creepy ex-boyfriend who keeps bothering her. She actually changed her number because he wouldn't stop calling. Last night, he showed up at our house and wouldn't leave. When he tried to push past her and get through the front door, Rose came out and punched him so hard that he went flying off the porch and landed in the yard.

November 18

Allison's boyfriend doesn't bother her anymore, and she won't stop talking about how Rose came to the rescue. Normally, Rose would eat up that kind of praise, but she hates it since we're trying to keep a low profile. Blending in is a lot of work.

November 23

All our roommates went home for Thanksgiving, so we decided to celebrate on our own and cook a turkey. It didn't end well.

November 30

One of our housemates was in a play yesterday. We went to see it, and afterward, a bunch of drunk frat guys hanging around outside started hitting on us. One of them grabbed me, and I freaked out. I can't even explain what I felt. First panic, then that darkness, then that high. And I swear, he flew backward like I'd punched him, even though I hadn't laid a hand on him. Then, Rose did actually punch one of the other guys. A whole bunch of people saw, but I don't think anyone really grasped what happened with the guy who'd touched me. I don't even grasp it, and I'm questioning my own sanity again. I've seen air users push people over without touching them, but this wasn't air magic. Maybe he was drunker than he seemed and fell on his own. Rose didn't really pay attention to that either. She's more worried about us making a scene. I asked her if she really thought anyone who attended a college play would report us to the guardians. She said no, not directly, but that people mention things to other people, who then mention things to other people. Now she has that focused, hard expression again. She's been online researching West Coast cities all day.

December 8

It's exam week. Everyone is studying, so we've been staying in and pretending to as well. Mostly we sit in our room and play board games. Rose is obsessed with Clue. She also told me that for the first time ever, she wishes she could take an exam because she's pretty sure she could ace the Chinese warfare one.

December 13

Exams are over, and most of our housemates are going home. Only Ellen is remaining on campus during break. Her boyfriend is over constantly, and they pretty much stay in her bedroom all day.

December 15

Another anniversary. But not just any anniversary. One year. One year since Mom, Dad, and Andre left me. Once year since my life stopped. Except it didn't. I can't believe how much things have changed. Rose reading my mind. The

weird mood swings. Escaping St. Vladimir's. Living with humans. It's so strange—but still not as strange as not having
my family around. I miss them so much. I miss Andre's goofy
jokes. I miss Mom braiding my hair. I miss Dad calling me
"little queen" because he always said I ruled our family. It
wasn't supposed to be this way. We're taught since birth to
fear Strigoi. That's the death that looms over everyone. Not
an icy road.

December 24

Nothing like last-minute shopping. I don't know why we
waited so long. Rose and I went downtown earlier today to
get each other Christmas presents—which was kind of difficult since we never stray too far apart. So we'd go into stores,
and then one of us would have to turn around and not look
while the other shopped. What made it especially ridiculous
was that sometimes, Rose could "see" what I was buying her
anyway with her mind.

It was later than Rose wanted when we finally left. She
was keyed up the whole time we waited for a train and was
constantly watching our surroundings. It was hard to tell
with all the people and city noise, but she swears she heard a
psi-hound. I heard a howl in the distance too, but it seemed
like an ordinary dog to me. I tried to calm her down, but now
she's in a panic. She says one of her novice classes visited a
psi-hound trainer a couple of years ago and that she recog-
nizes the call. I only know the basics about psi-hounds, like
how they were bred in Siberia by Moroi centuries ago and

will obey Moroi with strong compulsion abilities. Sometimes they're used for tracking, but it's pretty rare for guardians to use them since a Moroi has to do the controlling. Rose was probably on edge because of how late it was.

December 25

Christmas. After the Thanksgiving incident, we didn't attempt any gourmet holiday meals. Instead, we had frozen pizza and cherry pie. Rose got me a fluffy pink scarf with a unicorn embroidered on it because she claims I've always wished I could've bought those unicorn sheets back in Madison. I got her a letter opener shaped like a Spartan spear. She doesn't really have any letters to open, but she loved it. I can't help but think she's holding something back from me, though. I don't know why. Just a vibe. I asked her about it this afternoon, and she just said, "It's Christmas, Liss. It's not the time for serious thoughts."

December 26

Today apparently was the time for serious thoughts. While we were eating leftover cherry pie for breakfast, Rose told me we're moving again. She still thinks we heard psi-hounds the other night. At the very least, she says, there are Moroi in the area. At the very worst, someone's looking for us. And so we're doing it again. Packing up, moving on.

December 27

We're heading west. Rose doesn't want to push any farther

east because it's too close to Court for her comfort. So we got on a train today going to Portland, Oregon. It's a long trip, but at least it's more comfortable than a bus. Rose is a little uneasy about being only a few states away from Montana, but if we went south, it might be too sunny for me. There are no Moroi schools or notable gatherings in Portland, so we're optimistic. I know caution is best, but I'm going to miss Chicago.

December 30

Portland's a lot warmer than Chicago or Montana. Not tropical, of course. But there's no snow, and the vibe is friendly and quirky. We stayed in a hotel while we looked for a home and now have a house with some students at Portland State University. Apparently, someone else came by just before us and wanted to rent it, but I used a little compulsion to get the landlord to give the room to us. I like it here, but that darkness keeps creeping in on me. It gets wearying sometimes, thinking of how we have months and months of looking over our shoulders and moving from city to city. Sometimes I'm still not even sure why we ran in the first place.

December 31

One of our housemates has a cat named Oscar. He seems to love me, and I love him back. Rose doesn't share my affection, to put it mildly.

January 1

The start of a new year. I've swung back up again. The more

we explore Portland, the more cool things I discover. Oscar visits me all the time, and it cheers me up. Rose rolls her eyes at him, but I can tell she's happy too. We feel safe here. Rose even told me this morning: "Portland's the place, Liss. We've still got to keep watch, but something in my gut tells me we're not going anywhere for a while. No guardian would think to look for us in a hipster town like this."

The Meeting

"Dimitri!"

I turned instantly at the sound of my name, shooting a glare at the guardian approaching in the darkness. What was he thinking? Everyone out here tonight knew how essential secrecy was. It didn't matter that he was young and excited about his first big mission. We had no room for errors, not when this was the only break we'd had in over a year. Realizing his mistake, he grew apologetic, though not nearly enough.

"Sorry." He dropped his voice to a stage whisper and tapped his ear. "Headset's not working. We checked the house, and they're already gone. They must have had warning, maybe a perimeter of spies on the streets." As his excitement returned, the young guardian—Laurence—began speaking rapidly. "I was thinking about it. They probably have a whole network of people working with them! It makes sense, right? How else have they managed to stay ahead of us for so long? There's no telling how deep this conspiracy goes! We might be facing an army tonight!"

I said nothing and showed nothing as I mulled over his words. It was something of a mystery how a couple of teenage girls had managed to escape detection for two years, especially when one of them was a privileged Moroi princess and the other a delinquent dhampir with a disciplinary file so long that it broke school records. When I'd joined the teaching staff of St. Vladimir's last year and learned of the princess's case, I'd honestly been surprised the girls hadn't slipped up sooner. Being in league with others might explain how they'd remained hidden . . . and yet, in all our data collection, we'd never once had even the slightest hint that they had one accomplice, let alone "a whole network" or "an army."

My silence made Laurence nervous, and he no longer smiled. "It's irrelevant now," I told him. "And there's no point jumping to conclusions when—"

"Dimitri?" A female voice crackled in my earpiece. "We've got visuals on them. They're approaching the intersection of Brown and Boudreaux, from the north."

Without another word to Laurence, I turned and headed toward the streets indicated. I heard him running after me, but his stride was shorter, and he couldn't quite keep up. I tried to force calm as my heart rate increased, but it was difficult. This was it. This was it. We might finally have her: Vasilisa Dragomir, the missing princess, last of her line. Although I knew all guardian work was honorable—including the instruction of future guardians—part of me had longed for something more at St. Vladimir's. When I'd learned about the Dragomir princess and how she'd escaped the school, I'd made finding her a personal project, pushing leads that others had said were hopeless.

Me? I didn't believe in hopeless.

I slowed my pace as I neared the intersection, allowing Laurence to catch up. A quick scan revealed the dark shapes of other guardians lurking in shadows and behind objects. This was the spot they'd chosen for the interception. Quickly, I stepped off the road and hid in the cover of a tree, urging Laurence to do the same with a jerk of my head. We didn't have to wait long. As I peered around the tree's edge, I saw two female figures approaching, one practically dragging the other along. At first, I assumed it must be the stronger dhampir helping the princess, but as they grew closer, their heights and builds revealed that it was exactly the opposite.

I had no time to ponder this oddity. When they were about six feet from me, I quickly stepped out from the tree and blocked their path. They came to a halt, and whatever weaknesses the dhampir girl had had now vanished. She grabbed the princess roughly by the arm and jerked her back, so that the dhampir's own body served as a shield to keep me away. Around us, other guardians fanned out, taking defensive positions but not advancing without my command. The dhampir girl's dark eyes made note of them, but she kept her attention focused squarely on me.

I didn't entirely know what to expect from her, maybe that she'd try to run away or beg for her freedom. Instead, she shifted into an even more defensive position in front of the princess and spoke in a voice that was barely more than a growl: "Leave her alone. Don't touch her."

The girl was hopelessly outmatched yet still defiant, as though I were the one at a disadvantage. In moments like these, I was glad my old instructors in Russia had grilled me into concealing my feelings—because I was surprised. Very surprised. And as I took this dhampir girl in, I suddenly understood with perfect clarity how they'd eluded us for so long. A network of accomplices? An army? Laurence was a fool. The princess didn't need a network or an army, not when she had this protector.

Rose Hathaway.

There was a passion and intensity that radiated off her, almost like a palpable thing. Tension filled every part of her body as she regarded me, daring me to make a move. She possessed a fierceness I hadn't expected—that no one had expected, I realized, most likely because they couldn't see past that delinquent record of hers. But there was a look in her eyes now that said this was no joke, that she would die a thousand times over before she let anyone harm the princess at her back. She reminded me of a cornered wildcat, sleek and beautiful—but fully capable of clawing your face off if provoked.

And yes, even in the poor lighting, I could see that she was beautiful—in a deadly way—and that struck me too. Her pictures hadn't done her justice. Long, dark hair framed a face filled with the sort of hard-edged beauty a man might easily dash his heart against. Her eyes, though filled with hatred for me, still managed to be alluring—which only added to her danger. She might be unarmed, but Rose Hathaway was in possession of many weapons.

I didn't want to fight her, so I held out my hands in a placating gesture as I took a step forward. "I'm not going to—"

She attacked.

I'd seen it coming and wasn't surprised by the action itself so much as that she'd even try it with the odds stacked against her. Should I have been surprised? Probably not. As I'd observed, it was clear that Rose was willing to do anything and fight anyone to protect her friend. I admired that—I admired that a lot—but it didn't stop me from striking out to block her. The princess was still my goal tonight. And although Rose might have passion and defiance, her attack was clumsy and easy to deflect. She'd been gone too long from formal training. She recovered badly and started to fall, and I remembered how she'd stumbled earlier. Out of instinct, I reached out and caught her before she could hit the ground, keeping her steady on her feet. That long, marvelous hair fell away from her face, revealing two bloody marks on the side of her neck. Another surprise—but it explained her fatigue and pale complexion. Apparently, her devotion to the princess went beyond just defense. Noticing my scrutiny, Rose knocked some of her tangled hair forward to cover her neck. She pulled away, and I didn't stop her.

Despite the hopelessness of her situation, I could see her lithe body preparing for another attack. I tensed in response, even though I didn't want this brave, beautiful, and wild girl to be my enemy. I wanted her as . . . what? I wasn't sure. Something more than an outmatched scuffle on a Portland street. There was too much potential here. This girl could be unstoppable if her talents were properly cultivated. I wanted to help her.

But I would fight her if I had to.

Suddenly, Princess Vasilisa caught hold of her friend's

hand. "Rose. Don't."

For a moment, nothing happened, and we all stood frozen. Then, slowly, the tension and hostility eased out of Rose's body. Well, not all the hostility. There was still a dangerous glint in her eyes that kept me on guard. The rest of her body language said that although she hadn't exactly admitted defeat, she had conceded to a truce—so long as I gave her no cause for alarm.

I didn't plan to. *I also don't plan on ever underestimating you again, wild girl,* I thought, momentarily locking eyes with her. *And I'll make sure no one else ever underestimates you either.*

Satisfied that she was pacified—at least momentarily— I dragged my eyes from her dark gaze and focused on the princess. After all, runaway or not, Vasilisa Dragomir was the last of a royal line, and certain protocols had to be followed. I bowed before her.

"My name is Dimitri Belikov. I've come to take you back to St. Vladimir's Academy, Princess."

Hello, My Name Is Rose Hathaway

I knew it was going to happen. I just didn't expect it to happen so fast.

"Hey, Rose, would you like to—"

"No."

"Rose, did you see that the scav—"

"No."

"I don't know if anyone's asked you yet—"

"No."

"Rose, you're doing this with us, right?"

The last request had come from Mason Ashford, so out of respect for our friendship and his puppy dog eyes, I actually let him finish his question before I turned him down.

"No."

He fell into step with me as I continued walking toward our first guardian class of the day. "Why not? Did you already join someone else's team?"

"I didn't join anyone's team," I said. "I'm not doing it this year."

"Seriously? Why not? Have you seen what's up for grabs?"

I came to an abrupt stop in the middle of the field, pivoting so I faced him. I'd missed breakfast, and low blood sugar always made me grumpy. "No, and I don't care. How can you even think I'd do it?"

Mason looked so utterly confused that it was almost cute. "Because you've done it every other year. I mean, before you left."

"Yeah, but that was also before I was on Kirova's shit list and caught up in a deranged scheme involving a power-hungry madman who tortured my best friend and persuaded his daughter to turn Strigoi! Can you see why I'd maybe—just maybe—want to lie low for a while?"

"Yeah, but . . ." He reached into his backpack and pulled out a piece of paper that had been folded into quarters. "Look at the prizes."

I snatched it from him and read as we continued walking. "'Bootleg movies. Passcode for extra Internet time. Dark chocolate bacon truffles'? That's not even a real thing."

"You didn't read it all," he said when I handed it back. "There's wine on here too."

"What kind?"

"Parkland."

"Ugh. That's that warehouse store's crappy generic brand. I'm not going to risk getting in trouble for that."

We reached the building that held novice classes, and he pulled the door open for me. "It'll be fun. Me, you, and Eddie. So what if you don't care about the prizes? I figured you'd do it for the thrill of it. You haven't lost your edge, have you?"

I jabbed a finger in his chest. "I haven't lost anything, Ashford. I just have better things to do tonight than sneak around and risk detention. Look, I'm sorry. If I were going to do it, it'd be with you guys. Really. But I'm trying to walk the straight and narrow here. You've got to have some respect for that."

"I have plenty of respect for that," he grumbled. "I'd just also like to have some crappy boxed wine."

"It's in a box too? Come on."

Mason wasn't the last one to hit me up that day. I supposed I should've been flattered that so many people wanted me on their team, but I wasn't sure it was because they liked me so much as they thought my reputation for crazy and reckless behavior would be a good asset.

The St. Varvara's Day scavenger hunt was a tradition at our school—an unofficial one. Every year, St. Vladimir's Academy put on enormous carnivals for both the lower and upper campuses in celebration of a Moroi saint who'd allegedly battled ghosts centuries ago. These days, no one in the Moroi world really believed she'd fought against ghosts. Hardly anyone even celebrated the holiday anymore, and those who did in America had sort of ended up making it a second Halloween. It actually took place a little less than a month after Halloween, so it was a handy way to reuse decorations and costumes. If the weather was decent—which, for Montana in late November, meant less than five feet of snow—the teachers held the upper and lower school carnivals outdoors. The carnivals pretty much contained every clichéd Halloween activity you could think of: bobbing for apples, costume contests, and even pumpkin carving. It was also packed with junk food. And behind all that merriment, the scavenger hunt ran in secret on upper campus.

The students who organized the hunt changed from year to year. The group usually consisted of a mix of Moroi and dhampirs who pooled together a set of prize goods that were either hard to get at school or outright banned. Teams of three competed by scurrying around campus for two hours, gathering as much as they could from a list of illicit items. Said items varied in difficulty to obtain, but stealing any one of them would get you in big trouble if you were caught. Teachers' personal possessions were a popular choice, as were classroom supplies and hallway displays. Everything had a point value based on how much effort getting it took. The last time I'd participated, one of the list's goals had been a cafeteria tray. It wasn't a high-stakes object, and it had a low point value since there were lots of them available. That same year, Mr. Nagy's Holy Mount Athos poster had been on the list—a one-of-a-kind item. Not only was breaking into his classroom difficult, you also ran the risk of getting there and finding another team had beat you to it.

I felt like I'd turned down every novice on campus by the time I went to lunch and hoped there was no one left to bug me. So it was a total shock when Lissa sat down across from me, carting a pair of angel wings, and asked, "You're doing the scavenger hunt, right?"

For half a second, I thought maybe she'd heard about all my refusals and just wanted to tease me. Now that she regularly took meds to keep spirit in check, I couldn't see her mind as clearly as I used to. But just then, her eagerness and excitement came through loud and clear. "Why does everyone keep asking that? You of all people should understand why I need to stay out of trouble right now."

She drummed her nails against the table. "Well . . . you're only in trouble if you get caught."

"Liss, I expect this from everyone else. Not you. You're the queen of sensible thinking." I pointed to the wings. "You're even dressing up like a freaking angel tonight. You can't help yourself from being good."

"Yeah, I know. And normally I am against something like this. It's stupid. It's childish. And even though everything gets returned, I think it's wrong to steal and break into rooms. But it's just . . ."

Nervousness and resolve in the bond now. I could've probed further and discovered exactly what was driving her, but I decided to wait her out. "And?" I prompted.

"And . . ." She took a deep breath. "One of the prizes is dark chocolate bacon truffles."

Had I misheard? No. It wasn't like there was really anything you could mistake that for. "Since when do you like dark chocolate bacon truffles, Liss? Scratch that—I know the answer. You don't."

"No . . . but Christian does."

"Ugh." I tossed my sandwich down and started to stand up. "That's what this is about? I think I just lost my appetite, and amazingly, it's not just because some mad scientist decided to put bacon into truffles."

Lissa grabbed my arm and pulled me back down. "Stop being melodramatic."

"I'm not! God didn't intend for chocolate and bacon to be mixed together. But I'm zero percent surprised that if anyone would want to eat it, it'd be Christian."

"Rose, listen to me." She rested her elbows on the table and leaned forward. "He loves them. Seriously. And this brand is his favorite! Haberlin's. Imported from Switzerland."

"They have bacon in Switzerland?"

"Why wouldn't they? Look, his birthday is next week, and there's no way I could get any delivered out here in time. This is a perfect solution. Please?"

"Liss—"

"Please?" Those big jade-colored eyes met mine pleadingly. No compulsion necessary. "It's a big milestone in our relationship. The first birthday since we've been a couple. And look at everything he's been through in his life. He lost his parents in the worst way possible. He nearly got killed trying to save me from Victor. Don't you think that after all that, the universe wants to make it up to him? I mean, what are the odds that—"

"Fine, fine." I buried my face in my hands, unable to handle any more—because, truthfully, I was starting to feel bad for Christian. "If you want to do the scavenger hunt, I'll do it with you."

"Oh. Well. I can't do it."

I lifted my head. "What?"

"Christian and I volunteered to help out with the elementary kids' carnival. I'm going to paint faces, and he's going to make balloon animals."

"Someone would actually let Christian—never mind. Let me make sure I've got this straight. You want to send me off—on my own—to risk my recently salvaged reputation in order to win some disgusting abomination candy as a birthday present for your boyfriend, whom I can't stand."

"That's not true. You like him more than you'll admit. And you secretly like the risk too." A mischievous smile spread over Lissa's face. She knew she had me. "And most important, you're my best friend and a good person."

A good person? I wasn't sure about that sometimes. But I was her best friend, and it was hard for me to tell her no, especially when I could read her feelings. She was so full of hope, not to mention pure, uncomplicated affection for me— and for Christian. And who could turn down that angelic face? The wings were overkill.

"Okay. I'll win this stupid scavenger hunt for you. But I may have to do it on my own since I've pretty much blown any chance of getting a team." Eddie walked by just then, almost as though the universe really did think it owed Christian an act of kindness. "Hey!" I called. "Do you and Mason have a third yet?"

Eddie stopped and tilted his head to the right. "He's asking Charlie Hunt right now."

Sure enough, there was Mason on the other side of the room, five steps away from Charlie's table. I jumped up and sprinted across the cafeteria, nearly knocking three people over in the process. Mason had reached the table and was opening his mouth to speak when I grabbed his sleeve and jerked him away. He stumbled, and someone who wasn't a nimble dhampir would have dropped his tray.

"Mason, I need to be on your team," I blurted out.

He stared at first, dumbfounded, and then slowly began to grin. "I knew you hadn't lost your edge."

As classes wrapped up that day and the carnival neared, I had two tasks. One was not to overthink what kind of crazy things I'd have to hunt down tonight. The organizers wouldn't release the list until the carnival started, to make it harder. No one would have all day to plan strategy or even just swipe one of the classroom items while the school was still open.

My other job was to figure out a costume.

I hadn't planned on wearing one tonight, though I had intended to go to the carnival. I mean, people had said a lot of outlandish things about me over the years, but only a fool would think I'd pass up a bunch of free candy. I'd wanted to just duck in, play a few games, and then slink back to my room, but now I had to look committed. Most of the teachers would be busy chaperoning and running the carnival, but they all knew the scavenger hunt was taking place. Some would be specifically tasked with locating players, and all would be watchful. I needed to blend in with the rest of the innocent fun-seekers.

An Internet search for "half-ass costumes" turned up a solid hit in about five minutes. I donned black skinny jeans and a black turtleneck and then wavered on wearing a jacket. We were actually having unseasonably warm weather, with temperatures in the fifties and no snow. Still, my clothing choices were tight and thin. That meant more maneuverability for daring deeds, though, so I skipped a coat and moved on to assembling the rest of my costume. That involved stealing a marker and a bunch of guest name tags on my way out of the dorm. By the time I reached the central quad—where the upper school's carnival was taking place—I was covered in HELLO, MY NAME IS . . . stickers with all sorts of different names written on them.

Christian looked me over, puzzled, when I met up with him and Lissa. "What are you supposed to be?"

She had on the full angel costume now, a vision in silver and white. Christian was, unoriginally, dressed up like a devil that really liked polyester. They'd never get me to admit it, but they actually looked pretty adorable.

"I'm an identity thief," I explained, pointing to the different tags. "Get it?"

"Did you just come up with that five minutes ago?" he asked.

"It's more work than it looks like," I countered. "I had to think up a lot of names."

Christian leaned forward to read. "'Vladimir. Mitzy. Amelia Earhart. Kip. Gandhi. Mary Sue.'"

Eddie strolled up to us, dressed as Batman. A figure draped in a white sheet with cutout eyeholes walked next to him. "Geez, Mason," I said. "And here I just got accused of a last-minute costume."

Mason pulled the sheet up over his head. He too wore dark clothing underneath. "Are you kidding? I've been planning this for weeks."

Say what you wanted to about St. Vlad's, but the school sometimes did try to make up for being out in the middle of nowhere, Montana. The carnival was a pretty serious affair, and I realized I'd been a little jaded in dismissing it so easily. They'd hauled in Skee-Ball and Whac-A-Mole machines. Booths held all sorts of other games, everything from ring-toss to darts-and-balloons to archery. Mr. Colfax was guessing people's weights. Students had already lined up in front of a dunk tank, and Guardian Kolobkov climbed up its ladder with grim resignation. An entire pavilion held materials and space for pumpkin carving, and everyone who wanted to enter the costume contest had to get their pictures taken. Orange lanterns were strung around the booths, and tents cast a magical glow. Heat lamps ringed the area, boosting the mild temperatures. There was even live music—although, unfortunately, it was just from Jesse Zeklos's crap cover band, Dagger Fang. What the hell was that supposed to mean, anyway?

And the food . . . there was food everywhere. Cotton candy and funnel cake. French fries and corn dogs. Candy for prizes. Candy simply given away by passing teachers. Honestly, why would anyone even want to compete for the scavenger hunt's contraband? The carnival was packed with all sorts of goodness.

But no dark chocolate bacon truffles. Lissa watched me

intently, and the bond buzzed with her wondering if I would come through for her. I gave her a small nod and turned to the other dhampirs. "Well, we'd better get started on our pumpkin-carving entries. Right, guys?"

"And Christian and I have to go over to the lower campus," said Lissa.

I'd forgotten she was volunteering at the younger students' carnival. Some of the activities were the same. Others weren't. They couldn't have darts or bows, for example, but they did have pony rides, which I thought was totally unfair.

"Try not to corrupt anyone," I called as Lissa and Christian walked away hand in hand.

Mason turned deadly earnest as soon as they were gone. "The lists are coming out in fifteen minutes. We've got to be ready to work on strategy."

"Fifteen minutes sounds like enough time for funnel cake," I said.

Apparently, everyone else thought it was time for funnel cake too because there were twenty people in line for it. Eddie shifted restlessly from foot to foot as we waited and finally couldn't take it anymore. "I don't want to miss it. I'll go get the list from Camille and meet you back here. Save me some."

"He's pretty worked up about this," I noted. "He must want that cheap-ass wine pretty badly."

Mason laughed. "No, he wants *Raptorbot*."

"What?"

"One of the bootleg movies. I guess it came out a while

ago, but he never got to see it because . . . well, you know. Because we're here. Anyway, he wants to catch up before the sequel comes out. That one's called Rampaging-something, I think."

"Huh." The delicious scent of funnel cake was heady. Only two people stood ahead of us now. "I never took Eddie for a movie fanatic."

"I think it's one of those so-bad-it's-good things. If you want to check it out—after we win—we can set up a secret screening this week."

I caught the suggestion in his voice. "With Eddie?"

"With you and me. By the time we're done with the hunt, we'll probably have sneaked into every part of campus tonight. Finding a quiet dark room after that'll be a piece of cake."

"Oh, hey. On the topic of cake—looks like it's our turn."

I stepped ahead so I wouldn't have to see his reaction to my dodging the invitation. It wasn't the first time Mason had dropped something like that on me. He liked me and wasn't shy about it. Me? I liked him too. A lot. In fact, I liked him better than any of the other guys in my class. The problem was, when I thought about a private movie screening in a dark room, it wasn't someone from my class who I wanted to curl up with.

"Nice ghost costume, Mr. Ashford. And Miss Hatha-way . . . will you enlighten me?"

In an image I'd never be able to blot from my mind, Alberta—captain of the campus guardians—smiled at us from behind the funnel cake counter. She wore an apron and chef's hat and had smudges of powdered sugar on her face. I had to blink a few times and remind myself that this was the same deadly woman who'd faced down two psi-hounds.

"I'm an identity thief."

"Ah. I see. 'Zeus.' 'Marilyn Monroe.' Who's 'Chet'?"

"Just a random name I thought up. They can't all be celebrities." I turned around and pointed to my back. "You're on here too."

"I'm flattered. I hope identities are the only things you plan on stealing tonight."

Her smile remained, but those eyes were shrewd. She might have been assigned to funnel cake duty, but Alberta was no fool. She knew what went on during the carnival, and she also knew that dhampirs took part in the scavenger hunt much more than Moroi did. Who could blame us? We were literally trained to seek danger. For all I knew, the campus guardians had crunched all sorts of data about student personalities and analyses of past hunts to calculate the suspects most likely to participate this year. And yeah, statistically speaking, my name being at the top of that list wouldn't exactly be a surprise.

"Guardian Petrov, the only thing we plan on stealing are the hearts and minds of the costume contest judges," Mason told her.

"And a few extra helpings of funnel cake," I added. "We're getting some for our friends. Like, a whole bunch of friends."

Whether she believed that or not, Alberta loaded us up with deep-fried deliciousness. "You should go get your picture taken right now," she said as we started to walk away. "There's no line."

"Picture?" I asked.

She pointed. "For the costume contest."

"Right. Hearts and brains."

"Hearts and minds," corrected Mason. "We'll go over there right now, ma'am. Thank you for the helpful tip—and for sharing your outstanding culinary skills."

"Suck-up," I told him when we were out of earshot.

"Did you see her face? She doesn't trust us. There's probably a deep-fried tracking device under all this powdered sugar that we're about to swallow. Besides, I really do want to enter the contest."

"You think you can win with a sheet?"

"It's retro."

We let Abby Badica take our picture, and after I'd given yet another explanation about my costume, we finally headed off to a grassy patch of the quad just beyond some of the carnival games. We'd barely sat down when Eddie came jogging up to us with a piece of paper. After checking for spies, we huddled over the note to read it as we munched on the cake.

20 — ONE SET OF BOXING GLOVES

5 — CASE OF CHOCOLATE PUDDING

25 — FOYER PORTRAIT OF A PAST HEADMASTER

25 — GUARDIAN JACKET

20 — TEACHER'S FORMAL ROBE

15 — ONE VOLUME FROM THE SLAVIC CULTURE ENCYCLOPEDIA SET

35 — ONE OF MR. DWIGHT'S TIES

5 — SNORKEL MASK

50 — HEADMISTRESS KIROVA'S CAT EARRINGS*

5 — DRAMA DEPARTMENT WIG

5 — ONE MARACA

40 — ONE OF GUARDIAN BELIKOV'S CDS

30 — COPY OF MISS FEDIN'S NEXT ALGEBRA QUIZ

45 — QUEEN TATIANA'S MESSAGE OF BLESSING*

45 — GUARDIAN COJOCARU'S COLOGNE*

Eddie let out a low whistle. "They aren't messing around this year."

"Are you kidding?" I asked between bites. "Apparently, this is amateur night. We should've let Lissa and Christian take this down to the lower campus for the kids to do."

Beside me, Mason scoffed. "Okay, Captain Confidence. What's your strategy?"

"The five-pointers aren't worth our time. The earrings are impossible—I heard Kirova's home tonight—so they're off the table. The other starred one-of-a-kinds are what we want. We grab those and a couple of the mid-levels, and we're done. The headmaster portraits are around the corner from the queen's blessing, so we can get one of those on our way out. This'll be an hour, tops. We've just got to get the jump on everyone." I finished off an enormous chunk of funnel cake and wiped powdered sugar off my hands. "Then we can come back and eat some more."

Mason produced a key ring from his pocket. Veterans of this game usually tried to acquire keys and access cards in advance of the list. It usually resulted in a campus-wide lock change the next day. "The cologne might be off the table too. I've got the main building, rec building, and guardian building. Sorry, no cards."

That was unfortunate. Access cards would get us into more rooms within the buildings. "Hey, I'm impressed you got the guardian building," I said. That wasn't an easy key to steal.

"Yeah, but getting anything from there is almost as impossible as Kirova's place," Eddie pointed out. "The guardians are all in and out of there on patrol tonight."

"We don't really need any of those items anyway," I said. "I'll go back to our dorm and get the cologne. Maybe Cojocaru keeps his jacket in there too."

Mason shook his head. "How are you going to pull that off? His room's right by the front desk."

"Are you doubting my edge already? Let me worry about Cojocaru. You guys get over to the main building before everyone's there and it's too hard to sneak around. You know they'll be patrolling it. Get the blessing and a portrait and then either the quiz or tie. Whichever's fastest. I'll meet you by the chapel, and we'll see what we've got."

I jogged back across campus, over to dhampir housing. There were fewer of us on campus, and dhampir staff and students shared the same residence hall. When I entered the dorm, I found the same attendant on duty from earlier. He looked me over and narrowed his eyes.

"Did you take those name tags from here? Mine are missing."

"Nope," I lied. "This is my personal stash. A bunch of people wanted to copy my sweet costume, though, so maybe they took them."

"What is your costume?"

That voice came from behind me, and I jumped when I turned around and saw Mason. Well, it seemed like Mason at first glance, seeing as the figure standing motionless in the corner wore a white sheet with cutout eyes. But there was no way Mason had beat me back here. Also, Mason didn't have a woman's voice.

The ghostly sentinel lifted the sheet and revealed Guardian Mertens. "Just me."

"Geez," I said. "No offense, Guardian, but that's pretty creepy, just standing there like that. Are you waiting for someone?"

"Just hanging out. Taking in the costumes." She kept her tone and posture casual, but I knew better. She was on guard for scavenger hunt players, and her position put her right between the lobby and the hall containing the teachers' residences. I could even see Guardian Cojocaru's door from here—which meant she could too.

I smiled back. "Well, good luck finding one better than mine. I'm an identity thief."

"Does that tag say 'Jesus'?"

"It's Spanish." I backed up toward the stairwell. "Forgot something in my room. I'll see you around. Have fun scaring people."

I glanced back once when I reached the stairs and saw she'd put the sheet back over herself. I couldn't make out her real eyes but knew without a doubt she was watching me.

Her presence was a complication, but it didn't mean this plan was dead in the water. I'd hoped to steal a master key card from the front desk, but even if I pulled that off, I could hardly enter Guardian Cojocaru's room with Guardian Mertens right there. Ground-floor windows were pretty impervious from the outside, something I knew from past experience. I could always break the glass, but one thing the scavenger hunt usually managed was mayhem without a lot of permanent damage. If that ever changed, security would get a lot worse at future carnivals. The school might even call off the carnivals, and that'd be a damned shame since it wasn't like I was going to find funnel cake anywhere else in the middle of the wilderness.

I'd wanted to do everything quietly tonight, but it looked like quiet wasn't going to cut it.

I reached the next floor, walked to the far side of the building, and then headed down a back staircase. Around the corner from it, a door labeled EMERGENCY EXIT ONLY loomed before me. I stared back at it, did a few calculations, and then kicked it open. Immediately, the alarm blared. I stuck around only long enough to push the doorstop down before tearing back up to the second floor. As I ran to the front staircase, I could imagine Guardian Mertens sprinting in the opposite direction beneath me. I hoped the desk attendant followed. Everyone was jumpy tonight.

I took the steps down two at a time and found the lobby empty. *Rose Hathaway triumphs again*, I thought. I leapt over the front desk and peered around for likely key card locations. They'd have a supply on hand for anyone who got locked out. I poked around and found a suspiciously locked drawer, just as the alarm went quiet. Crap.

No—wait. A small set of metal keys lay near the attendant's coffee cup. The guy hadn't brought them to check out the alarm. The mystery drawer opened with the third key I tried, rewarding me with an envelope labeled MASTERS. I snatched one of the key cards from within it, put everything back to its previous state, and then raced over to Guardian Cojocaru's door. The card admitted me, and I slipped inside before anyone returned.

Even if his name hadn't been on the door, I would've known I had the right place just by the smell alone. Every guardian knew you wanted your scent as nondescript as possible when out in a situation that might pit you against Strigoi. That was a novice kindergarten lesson. And we had it on good authority that in the field, Guardian Cojocaru did not, in fact, feel the need to torture everyone with obnoxious odors. In the safety of the school, while teaching guardian theory, he apparently didn't have to adhere to normal protocols.

I followed my nose to the bathroom and found the culprit sitting right out in the middle of his counter. The cologne came in a black art deco–style bottle and was called Oblivion.

"More like 'Oblivious,'" I muttered. Honestly, how could he not know how bad this stuff smelled? Was he purposely trying to discourage any chance of ever getting a date? The cologne smelled like furniture polish and low self-esteem.

I put it in a paper bag I'd found and then poked my head into his closet. There, neatly pressed, hung his formal black jacket, the one guardians wore on special occasions and for official duty. Often, the school's laundry service stored these, but he'd hung on to his. The universe really was pulling for Christian.

With the jacket and cologne in hand, I pressed my ear to the door and could hear voices in the lobby. Fortunately, getting out was easier than getting in. I unlocked the room's window and removed the screen so I could climb out. Once outside, I nearly slid the glass back down but then decided against it. That room could use a little airing out.

After that, it was a matter of making sure no one noticed my loot as I cut over to the chapel. Laughter and music from the carnival filled the air, and I looked longingly at the glittering central quad as I passed. I couldn't smell any of the food, thanks to Oblivion. "Soon, cotton candy," I murmured. "Soon."

I found a secluded spot near the chapel, sandwiched between a statue and a tree. Settling down in the shadows, I put my back to the trunk and kept an eye out for Mason and Eddie. I hoped they'd come soon. Temperatures were cooling off as the night progressed, and I shivered in my thin getup.

As I waited, I let the bond pull me over to Lissa. The connection was weak, but I could see how she sat at a table down on the lower campus, all her attention focused on painting a butterfly on the cheek of a small Moroi girl who regarded Princess Dragomir with awe. Neither Christian nor the scavenger hunt was on Lissa's mind just then. She burned with happiness, her feelings lovingly turned toward the children before her as her small acts brought them such joy.

An angel indeed. Her contentedness echoed back into me, and I was glad I'd taken on this task for her tonight. My feelings for Christian—whom I could hear in Lissa's periphery, telling some kid it was impossible to make a manatee out of a balloon—didn't even enter into it.

I blinked back into my surroundings and saw two giggling Moroi girls dressed as witches walk by. Still no Mason or Eddie. They were starting to worry me. If everything had worked out, they should've been able to get in and out of the main building quickly. That was the whole point of arriving there before any of the other players did.

What if everything didn't work out? What if they were caught? Plenty of detentions and other punishments always followed the scavenger hunt. That was a fact of the game.

"Rose?"

I turned toward the whisper and waved. "Over here."

Mason and Eddie materialized from the shadows, their arms full of objects. At least, I thought Mason's were. He had the sheet on. "I could smell you but couldn't see you," Eddie said, crouching down. "You got it."

"I did. Is that one of the encyclopedias? That's only fifteen points. You were supposed to just snag the big items."

"Yeah, well, they weren't all ripe for the snagging," Mason said, pushing the sheet back. His red hair stuck up at odd angles. He held up a framed portrait of a wizened Moroi man with a unibrow. A small plaque identified him as Gerard Trotter, St. Vladimir's headmaster from 1977 to 1981. "We got this, but the queen's blessing was already gone."

"What? Who beat us to it?"

"Shane's team. He's got Andy Brewer with him and Charlene Conta."

"Air user," I said. "That's lucky."

"That's only part of their luck." Mason took the sheet off altogether and lay back in the grass. "We were actually ahead of them when Guardian Kier stopped to question us outside. I watched Shane and Charlene actually walk behind him and go right into the building, thanks to our distraction. When we got in, they had the blessing and their own portrait and were on their way upstairs. We figured we'd get the tie and the quiz to make up for it and pretty much followed along with them."

I glanced down. "I see a tie but no quiz."

"Miss Fedin's printer ran out of ink just as they finished printing theirs," said Eddie. "Even Shane was surprised. He actually looked sorry for us and was starting to tell us where the ink supply was when we heard a bunch of noise. One of the other teams got caught, and we had to get out before the guardians found us too. Took us a while to get a clear shot on an exit, and we detoured through the library to grab an encyclopedia. Figured we should at least get something."

I stared up at the sky and did some math. "Well, I got a jacket from Cojocaru's room, so that helps."

"Sort of. Miss Fedin's robes were in her room, so Shane got those too," said Eddie, almost apologetically. "Easy score."

"Goddamnit!" I exclaimed. "Lissa was wrong. The universe hates Christian. Let's go deliver this stuff and check the tallies. We'll figure out Plan B."

No one wanted to haul their loot around throughout the hunt, so the coordinators set up a secret drop point to collect the goods and keep track of the current team standings. It was also a way to get our finds counted, in case we couldn't make it back right at the two-hour mark. We located the drop-off out in the woods, on the outskirts of the main campus. Camille Conta took inventory of what we had and then passed them on to Otto Sterling, a novice in our grade, to transport somewhere else. They didn't want to be caught with a stash of contraband any more than we did. She turned on a small flashlight and let us look at the current standings.

Mason pulled back in disgust and began pacing around. "Figures. They grabbed an encyclopedia on their way out too."

We were in second, a full twenty-five points behind Shane's team. The next-closest team had an even bigger point gap between them and us. Other teams hadn't reported in yet, but it seemed unlikely anyone else could be a contender based on what was left.

"I think the second-place team gets a smaller box of wine," Eddie remarked.

"I don't want a smaller box of wine. I want the crappy full-size one. I'm getting those bacon truffles, and you're getting your reptile movie."

"Raptor," he corrected.

Camille, listening to us, asked, "You like those truffles? Wish I'd known. I'm the one who donated them as a prize. My grandparents sent me some from Switzerland, and I gave them all away. By the way . . . what's your costume, Rose?"

Later, as my team walked back to campus, Mason pressed a hand to his forehead and pondered our situation. "We've still got an hour. We're going to have to try to pull it out with the little scores. The next-biggest thing's in Belikov's room, and no one's going to risk getting caught by him."

I'd seen Dimitri's name right away, of course. I noticed everything that had to do with the mentor I was inconveniently in love with, whether it was a wisp of brown hair escaping his ponytail or a new Western novel for him to read on his breaks. ONE OF GUARDIAN BELIKOV'S CDs, the list had read. I'd immediately dismissed it because I also didn't want to risk getting caught by Dimitri. That item also hadn't seemed necessary in the initial version of our plan, back when we thought we'd be able to score so much from the main building.

"He doesn't keep them in his room," I said, earning astonishment from my companions.

"How do you know that?" asked Eddie.

Because I've been in his room. Naked. Making out with him in his bed.

I'd been under the influence of a lust charm at the time—not that it had been entirely necessary—but even still, I'd taken in all the details of his room and noted the absence of his infamous 1980s music collection. I'd also seen him produce CDs pretty quickly when we were in the indoor training areas, far from the residence hall.

"Because he's my mentor." I certainly wasn't going to give these two any specifics. "I'm pretty sure he keeps them near the weight room."

Mason stopped walking. "That's right by all the training supplies. By the boxing gloves."

"The exterior entrance is too secure," said Eddie. "They won't risk anyone getting into the stakes. But you can access it from the other side—by the guardian offices and meeting rooms."

"Which we have a key to," I added.

We stood there staring at one another. Cheers from the carnival made me think someone must have successfully dunked a teacher.

"The key doesn't matter," said Eddie at last. "There are too many guardians. You can't walk in there without them noticing."

My eyes fell on Mason. "Actually . . . maybe I can. Anyone else crazy enough to go for the CD will think it's in Dimitri's room like you guys did. If I can get into the training center from the guardian offices, I can get it and the boxing gloves. You guys round up what you can from the rec building, just to be safe." I didn't elaborate that "just to be safe" actually meant "in case I'm caught."

Mason regarded me with awe and affection—and also concern. "Rose, I love it when you're crazy, but this might even be beyond you."

I snatched the sheet he had draped over his arm. "Not if I have this."

Ideally, I would've spent a lot longer than five minutes studying the entrance to the guardians' building before making my move. But with the clock racing, recon time was limited. In my brief surveillance, I saw two guardians leave and one enter. All were costumed. None of them was Guardian Mertens.

Showtime, Rose.

I pulled the sheet over me and emerged from my hiding place. A cluster of students carrying cotton candy crossed my path but paid little attention to me. Throwing my shoulders back, I strode up to the building's doorway as though I worked there and entered all the time—and as if I most certainly weren't a student posing as a guardian who was hopefully still on watch back in the dorm's lobby.

I used my purloined key to unlock the door and swung it open, revealing Guardian McKay—dressed as a goblin. I froze, terrified by both his reaching toward me and his cheap rubber mask. He caught the door and gave me a friendly nod as he walked out. "Hey, Wanda."

I nodded back, not that he could probably even tell under the sheet. The sheet also at least hid the fact that I was hyperventilating, so that was a bonus. Moving forward, I tried to get my bearings. I'd been in here a couple of times and had a general sense of how the building connected over to the gym and training center. I expected there to be a hallway branching to the left at some point. This facility held offices for guardians to work and grade in, as well as meeting rooms. Those were all dark tonight. A room straight ahead, at the end of the hall I walked, held most of the action: the guardian break room.

I could see three guardians in there and heard what sounded like show tunes playing. Two of the guardians stood chatting by a coffeepot while another waited for the microwave to finish. That one nodded when he caught sight of me in the hall, and I gave another concealed nod back. Was it going to look weird if I didn't go in and have a doughnut or something? I had the height, build, and attire to pass myself off as Mertens, but once I had to speak, it would be game over.

A whiteboard hung above the coffeepot, containing a grid of all the guardians, their posts tonight, and scheduled breaks. That actually would've been incredibly useful for scavenger hunt players, but right now, it could pose another serious problem for me. Mertens had her break in fifteen minutes. If anyone questioned why she was here early, my cover would be blown. And if I was somehow still here when she showed up, my cover would also be blown.

"Hey, hold up!"

I jumped at the voice behind me. Busted already. I turned slowly toward the building's entrance, ready to face my fate. But although I was the one being addressed, I wasn't the one who'd actually been busted. Alberta came storming down the hall, with three mortified students in tow. One carried a portrait of some ancient headmistress. My night would've become a lot simpler if it had been Shane's team that had been captured, but this was a group of Moroi. No surprise they'd been caught. Moroi magic was handy in some challenges, but dhampirs were the ones who excelled in stealthy operations. Without one of us to guide them, this team had just been asking for failure.

"Emil caught them trying to sneak into the rec building." Alberta still wore her apron and had even more powdered sugar than before on her. But she smelled incredible. "Joe's supposed to be doing the processing, but I've lost him. Can you stay with them while I figure out where he went?"

"Mmm-hmm."

My muffled response wasn't questioned in her agitated state. She stomped off, and while this saved me from making conversation over coffee in the break room, I wasn't sure if being stuck on guard duty for my fellow competitors was that much better.

"We were set up, Guardian," one of the Moroi blurted out. "Honest."

"Yeah," said another. "We were, uh, just holding this for someone."

"Quiet." I changed my voice to something gravelly, deep, and—hopefully—terrifying. "You should all be ashamed of yourselves and beg Guardian Petrov for mercy. St. Vladimir's is an institute of fine education. This childish behavior is a disgrace to all it and this carnival represent."

"Doesn't the carnival represent candy and costumes?" the first one asked.

"Quiet!" I barked.

Alberta hurried back a minute later and had Guardian Cojocaru with her. He was dressed as a jester and had been pretty heavy-handed with the cologne tonight. His Oblivion completely overpowered Alberta's eau de funnel cake.

"Here they are," she said to him. "Write them up and send them on their way. They're Kirova's. She can deal with them tomorrow. And I'll take this." She snatched the portrait away. "Thank you for watching them, Wanda. Don't let me delay you from your break."

I turned toward the break room and barely heard one of the Moroi behind me saying something to Alberta about mercy. Just as I reached the break room's entrance, I made a quick check to confirm no one was watching me from inside or from the hall. I veered left, down a corridor that forked in the direction I needed. After about ten steps, I paused, waiting to hear if anyone would call back and ask why I wasn't on my way to the coffee. No one did, and I took off at a run.

Only two conference rooms flanked this walkway, but soon, as expected, it opened up to a room I recognized: the training center's office. It had two doors, one of which I'd just walked through. The other door, directly opposite me, led to the training room itself. This was the office I'd seen Dimitri disappear into when he went looking for music.

The glow shining from the hallway was all the light I needed, and I immediately set to searching the room. I found the CDs in a cardboard box labeled PROPERTY OF D.B. that had been tucked under a table. Pulling off my sheet and kneeling down, I flipped through the CDs and saw they all had D.B. on them, which would help prove I had the authentic item—not that it was probably even possible to get a B-52's or After the Fire CD anywhere else on campus. Since they were alphabetized, I left the rest undisturbed in the box and just selected one from the beginning. I'd never heard of a group called Animotion, but anyone who looked at their picture would immediately know whose CD collection this had come from. Shane couldn't match this. Now I just had to get the boxing gloves, and Christian would be eating disgusting bacon truffles in no time.

I stood up, turned around, and found myself looking right at Dimitri.

And not just any Dimitri. Dimitri dressed as a cowboy.

Now, to be fair, Dimitri always kind of dressed like a cowboy. I mean, he wore a leather duster as part of his everyday attire. The crazy thing was, he wasn't wearing it now. He had on a different coat, deep gray wool that fell to his knees and was worn open to show a black-and-gray-checked vest buttoned across a crisp white dress shirt. It was accented with a blue paisley tie and, so help me, a gold pocket watch, its chain draping over the vest. And, of course, he had a hat, because what kind of lame cowboy wouldn't? A wide-brimmed gray hat that matched the coat. I supposed he wasn't so much a cowboy who rounded up cattle on a ranch as he was a sharp-eyed sheriff who stalked the streets of lawless towns.

It was ridiculous how gorgeous he was in that getup. No one had a right to look that good in a cowboy costume. He was even wearing his hair loose! If Dimitri needed a volunteer to be lassoed or handcuffed or whatever it was swanky lawmen did, I'd be the first to step up. I might as well have been wearing a HELLO, MY NAME IS SMITTEN tag.

"Rose," he said, jolting me out of my fantasies. "Is there something you'd like to tell me?"

"Sure, lots of things. Starting with how to download music. It'd take up a lot less space, you know."

He gave me a look I knew well, a hybrid of exasperation and amusement. "Rose, you're doing the scavenger hunt, aren't you?"

"What makes you say that?" When his gaze fell on the CD in my hand, I added, "Jesse's band is terrible. Did you ever consider that maybe I wanted to change things up? Bring a new vibe to the carnival?"

"No, that's something I would never consider." He reached into an inner pocket of his coat and pulled out a piece of paper I recognized. "Also, I've seen this."

I sighed. "Damn it. Someone's always stupid enough to have it on them when they get caught. They need to burn that thing. Or eat it." Mason, Eddie, and I had made sure to memorize our copy of the list before disposing of it. Once the teachers knew what we were actually after, the hunt became all but impossible.

"This is serious." Dimitri had on his stern face, and it just went along beautifully with that suit. "I thought you'd learned your lesson about reckless stunts—that you intended to take your duty to Lissa seriously from now on."

"I am! I'm doing this for her."

"Rose, don't start—"

"No, I'm serious! One of the prizes for winning this thing is chocolate bacon truffles. Now, I know what you're thinking: disgusting."

"Actually, I wasn't thinking that."

I grimaced. "Don't say anything else. If you're into those, I don't want to know. I'd rather live in ignorance. Anyway. Christian really is into them. They're apparently, like, one of his favorite things ever. And his birthday's coming up, and Lissa really wants to give them to him as a present."

Dimitri studied me for a long moment, and it was hard to not squirm under the power of those dark brown eyes. "Do you really expect me to believe that?"

"Do you really think I'd make that up? Come on, comrade. I know you're honor bound to uphold the laws of this school and all that, but can't you cut me some slack? Think of everything Christian's been through. His parents. Victor. All he asks for in this world—aside from liberties with my best friend—is some candy that was probably created as a horrible accident." I tried my best to channel the irresistible, beseeching manner Lissa had used on me earlier. "Don't you think he deserves something good for once? Don't you think it's about time the universe gives back?"

"Rules are rules. They can't be manipulated because of one person's wants, and this isn't a small thing. This scavenger hunt is the worst kind of chaos. Theft, breaking and entering. It's a terrible tradition."

I clasped my hands in front of me and widened my eyes. "More terrible than seeing your own parents hunted down in front of you? More terrible than being mauled by psi-hounds? More terrible than finally having friends to share a birthday with after years of loneliness, only to be deprived of your favorite—"

"Enough." Dimitri turned away and stuffed his hands into his pockets. "Go. Get out of here. I won't report you, but if another guardian catches you, I can't do anything for you."

I nearly fainted in relief. "Thank you, thank you, thank you. I swear, this is a onetime thing. Just a quick throwback to the old Rose in order to serve a greater good."

"I already said yes. You don't have to keep convincing me." Despite the gruff tone, he was smiling. "But why do you need two CDs? The list says one."

I held up Animotion. "That's all I've got."

He crouched down and pulled out the box. "A-ha is missing. It should be right at the beginning."

"Maybe you didn't put them in the right order."

"I always put them in the right order. Look, you can even see the gap. One there, and one here for what you took."

A cold, awful realization crept over me. "Someone's already been here. It's impossible. There's no way to get in."

He gave me a meaningful look. "Isn't there? You did."

I held up the ghostly sheet I'd dropped on the floor earlier. "I disguised myself as Mertens. How could anyone have an idea that good?"

"It doesn't have to be that good." He straightened up and pushed the box back under the table with his foot. His boot was made of elaborately tooled leather. Where did he find this stuff? "It only has to be good enough to get in here and take my CD."

I gasped. "If they were in here, they've been in the training room!"

"Rose—"

I left him behind and took off for the door opposite the one I'd entered. The training room contained pretty much everything a novice vampire hunter needed to become even more badass. Weights, weapons, targets. Also, boxing gloves. I flung open the cabinet that contained them and found twelve hooks and eleven pairs of gloves.

"Aah!" I slammed the door and collapsed against it, sinking to the floor. "Sixty points! I sneaked in here, right under Alberta's nose, for sixty points— which now mean nothing if Shane's team was the one that got these. And considering they're kicking everyone's ass tonight, that seems pretty likely. We can't close those twenty-five points with whatever Mason and Eddie dredge up from the rec building. Maybe there's a chance to win if we can score a teacher's robe, but that's not a big margin, and it only works if Shane doesn't get anything else. And I doubt he's given up. Ugh." I leaned my head back and shook my fist at the ceiling. "Universe, you're a bitch."

Dimitri stood over me and unfolded the list. "I can't believe I'm saying this . . . but aren't there other things you can get that are worth more? The headmaster portraits are right in the school's foyer. And Mr. Dwight keeps his tie collection in plain sight in his classroom."

"Got it. Got it. And a guardian jacket. And Cojocaru's gross cologne."

"You stole his Oblivion?" Dimitri would never openly admit it, but he sounded impressed.

"The only thing that could guarantee the win for us is Kirova's cat earrings. Getting into her room's impossible under normal circumstances, and everyone knows she stayed home sick tonight. The earrings got put on the list before anyone realized that. Rose Hathaway can do a lot of things, but that might really, truly be where I have to draw the line."

I expected Dimitri to agree with me. I expected him to tell me it was just as well that I couldn't win and that there was some valuable lesson to be learned here. Instead, he walked back to the office and returned with a pen and a piece of paper. He sat down beside me, so close that our legs touched, and I momentarily forgot about my failure.

Ever since Dimitri had told me that age and shared duty to Lissa would never allow us to truly be together, we'd had minimal physical contact. We trained together, we saw each other daily . . . but always, always, we both took great care in keeping a mutually understood distance between us. Until this moment, connected with just our knees, I hadn't realized how much that distance had affected me. No matter how sound the logic about us staying apart was, no matter how much his feelings for me had changed—and I really didn't believe they had—there was something inside me that still cried out for him. And I didn't think it would ever stop.

Did he share my reaction? Hard to say. He was better at concealing his feelings than I was, but then, almost everyone was.

He leaned forward and sketched a large rectangle with a smaller square embedded in one corner, then more squares within that. "Kirova has a bigger suite than the other teachers, but they all have the same layout. Living room, bedroom, kitchen—"

"Kitchen? The Moroi teachers have their own kitchens?" I knew the dhampir instructors didn't. They had private group dining rooms but still had to eat the same food the students did.

"That's just the way it is. But look. This room right here? That's her bedroom, and the wall looks like this." He drew another line so that the wall he indicated became thicker. "That's because there's a hidden staircase in it."

I looked up from the sketch. "Since when?"

"Since always. It's part of the emergency escape system."

I'd known there were various exits and secure rooms in place, in the impossible event of a Strigoi attack, but this came as a surprise. "The headmistress—or headmaster—has their own private escape? I sure don't."

He shrugged. "The school's builders made those decisions a long time ago. Don't get caught up in the politics right now. If you came through one of the secret tunnels and up the stairs, you could slip into Kirova's bedroom and take her earrings."

"Pfft. Well, yeah. If I could go through the secret tunnels, I would've finished this scavenger hunt eons ago, comrade. We've all heard rumors about those doors. They don't even take keys, right?"

"They require a thumbprint to access. Every teacher—Moroi and dhampir—has authorization to enter."

"I'm a big fan of the James Bond stuff, but unless you're suggesting I cut off a teacher's hand, I don't really see how I'm going to get an authorized thumbprint."

Dimitri stayed silent. I felt my jaw start to drop, and I clamped it shut as I began to grasp his insinuation. "Are you . . . are you offering to help me break the rules? Rules are rules. Someone told me that once."

He gave me that trademark look again, but this time it contained a lot more exasperation than amusement. "Rose, you're making me change my mind."

"No, no," I said quickly. "I'm grateful. Really. But you've got to understand my shock. You're Dimitri Belikov. Campus badass. Defender of justice. You're even dressed like a sheriff, for God's sake! It's like Lissa being an angel. Your personalities run so deep you can't even escape them when you're in costume. You're supposed to dress up like who you want to be on Halloween and St. Varvara's Day. Not who you already are."

"You want to be an identity thief."

"Hell no," I said, impressed he'd correctly identified the costume. "I'm Rose Hathaway. Why would I want to be anyone else?"

His smile returned, and I wished I could reach out and trace the edge of his lips. I clenched my hands to prevent me from doing anything stupid.

"You're running out of time if you want to pull this off," he said. "Don't tell me it's too risky for you."

I jumped to my feet. "Why does everyone doubt me? You're just like Mason."

Except he wasn't anything like Mason. Mason made me laugh with his stupid jokes and always brought an effortless comfort when we were together. When I was with him . . . I just was. But Dimitri . . . Dimitri caused my breath to catch and my heart to do gymnastics. Around him, I wanted greatness. I pushed myself to be better, smarter, faster, sharper. And when I wasn't with him, I felt like the world was incomplete. Like I walked around with a void beside me.

"Why are you doing this?" I asked as I picked up the CD and boxing gloves. "I can't even imagine what kind of trouble a teacher would get into if you're caught."

Dimitri wouldn't meet my gaze and instead played with the chain of his pocket watch. "Well. I suppose the universe really does owe Christian. And I'd better get that CD back undamaged."

But as we walked out of the room, I knew the truth. He was doing this for me.

It wasn't surprising that the guardian facilities had multiple access points to the tunnel system. The panels that read thumbprints blended seamlessly into the doors. No wonder students knew so little about them. Once we were inside, I couldn't learn much more about this legendary labyrinth because Dimitri insisted on leaving the lights off.

"Everything about these is tracked," he explained. "Already, there's a record that I've entered tonight, but it's not the kind of thing that would catch anyone's attention. We do regular checks of the doors. But start turning on lights, using power . . . that'll raise a few questions when the logs are reviewed."

So we walked through the underground tunnels in darkness—true darkness, nothing to help dhampir eyes along. Dimitri moved effortlessly, like he knew them by heart, probably because he did. He probably studied campus blueprints for fun. After the third time I ran into a wall, he took my hand and led me along. I had a vague sense of crossing campus but lost all sense of direction. When he brought us to a stop, I stuck my foot out and hit a staircase.

"This is the Moroi staff building," he told me. "She's on the top floor."

We climbed up four flights and faced another barrier. Dimitri stood behind me and guided my hand forward to a small button. I waited for him to explain what came next, but instead, we stayed like that for several moments, our bodies close and his hand over mine. I closed my eyes and wished that I could lean back into him. That I could fade into him. This close, his scent wrapped around me. I felt like I was drunk on it. No bad cologne here. He smelled like sweat and leather and a body that could make a girl melt.

Dimitri finally took a deep breath and found his voice. "You don't need a thumbprint to get out of here, but don't push that button yet. We don't know if Kirova's in her bedroom. I'm going to get out of here and pay her a friendly visit. You're going to have to gauge the time it'll take me to get back up the main stairs before you make your move."

"I can do that." I couldn't believe how calm I sounded while standing so close to him—and while preparing to break into my headmistress's home. My pulse rate was off the charts. "But how do I get out without your thumbprint?"

"Put something in the door when you enter the room. The sensor'll stop it from closing. When you're finished, go back to the bottom of these stairs, and I'll meet you. There's a nearby exit."

"Got it."

"Good luck, Rose. Give me the rest of your goods. I'll hide them in the holly bush on the west side."

He backed away, and I heard his steps fade as he descended. My breathing returned to normal. Now that I could think clearly again, I could focus back on the task at hand. I didn't know what time it was, but I knew I didn't have much longer left. I shifted with impatience, wanting to open the door and finish this night's misadventures, but I had to err on the side of caution. I was pretty sure that walking into Kirova's bedroom with her right in it would earn me the honor of being the first St. Vladimir's student to have detention for life.

When I felt confident Dimitri must have made it to the suite's front entrance, I pushed the button and tensed. The door silently slid open, revealing an empty room. An empty room decorated with so much cat stuff that I wasn't even sure I'd be able to find the earrings. It was camouflage gone crazy. Cat-ouflage?

I stepped into the room and quickly pushed a big, fluffy cat slipper into the doorway. When the panel began to slide shut, it stopped when it reached the slipper. So, that was set. Now it was time to venture into this mess. Cat posters, cat bedding, a cat-shaped nightstand, and more cat figurines than I could count. No one would believe this. Kirova's gaudy cat earrings were a well-known fixture, but I don't think anyone had realized the extent of Kirova's Catopia. I was going to have an even harder time than usual taking her seriously.

As I poked around, I could hear voices from outside the bedroom door. It wasn't fully shut. I peeked out the small gap and saw Kirova and Dimitri. She stood with her back to me, and amazingly, her robe was plain pink, without a cat in sight. She'd pulled her gray hair into a sloppy bun, and the whole place smelled like chicken soup.

"—so nice of you to stop by, but really, I'm doing fine. It's just a cold."

"I'm glad to hear it," said Dimitri. "Everyone's been concerned. A number of students have asked about you at the carnival."

"Have they?" Kirova seemed very pleased by that, and I felt a little guilty because I wasn't sure if it was true. "Well, that's very kind too. I don't know if anyone's told you this, but you really wear a vest quite well. It's a pity you don't wear them more often. I'd have no problem with it, you know. Instructors are welcome to dress as they like, so long as school policies are adhered to."

"I think this'll be a onetime thing."

"That's too bad. I've always thought the way a man wears a vest says a lot about him. Not many can pull it off, but you've got an exceptionally well-muscled chest."

Oh my God. Was she hitting on Dimitri? Or was she really just some kind of vest aficionado? I didn't want to hear any more. I pulled back and commenced my search. I kept my own meager jewelry scattered on my room's dresser, but hers didn't have anything on its surface except cat statuary. The closet only contained clothes, most of which were the regular headmistress wear I saw her in on a daily basis. That left the drawers, and I finally found a wooden box decorated with enameled cats on the lid. Jackpot. This too mostly contained respectable jewelry, but right on top of the narrow gold chains and sensible watches lay those earrings: giant burgundy cat faces with rhinestone eyes. I pocketed them and was shutting the drawer when I heard a rustling behind me.

I spun around, and unbelievably, there was a real cat in

the room.

"Well, I'll be damned," I muttered. Kirova was violating one of the school's biggest rules. Back in my freshman year, there'd been a huge scandal when a Moroi student was busted for secretly maintaining a reptile collection. He'd claimed it was for scientific research, and it had only been discovered when one of the snakes had escaped and ended up in Keely Tarus's room. In the aftermath, we'd had a special school assembly in which Kirova had droned on about how animals had no place in an institute of exceptional academics.

The cat—a calico—sniffed at a sweater crumpled on the floor and then headed across the room. Too late, I realized it had its sights set on the opening to the tunnels. Horror at the thought of losing Kirova's cat in the underground maze shot through me, and I leapt across the room and kicked the slipper into the passage, just as the cat reached the panel. The door slid shut, and with it, my escape.

The cat glared. My heart stopped. I frantically tried to put this in perspective. Surely, after all the brushes with death I'd had, this wasn't the worst thing to happen to me, right? Being trapped in my headmistress's room, holding on to her stolen property? It wasn't like she'd kill me for that. I hoped.

I crept back to the door and listened as Kirova now complimented Dimitri's boots and how their fine tool work accented the vest so nicely. I couldn't even fully appreciate the continued weirdness, not in the throes of my current crisis. With her back to me, I was able to catch Dimitri's eye and pantomime what had happened—omitting the cat's role.

Kirova had turned to pick up a mug, and there was no mistaking the meaning of the look he gave me: *You have got to be kidding. You had one job, Rose.*

I wondered if he might be able to stage some fantastic distraction so that I could run out the front door. Maybe he could undo a few buttons of the vest? That would certainly distract me, let alone someone with an obvious vest fetish. But no. I was no damsel in distress. I'd gotten myself into this. I'd find my own way out.

I stripped the cat sheets off Kirova's bed and located an extra set in the closet. Quickly, I tied them together and created a rope of sorts with knots to serve as handholds. I shot back to the doorway and waved my ingenious creation at Dimitri so that he'd know everything was cool, and then I tied one end to the leg of her bed. A tug showed me it wouldn't go anywhere. Having learned from my earlier mistakes, I locked the calico in the closet before I opened the window. I tossed the sheet-rope down the side of the building and watched as it ended about halfway down the second floor.

Okay, everything wasn't exactly cool. But I could manage. I might not land gracefully on my feet, but this building didn't have high ceilings. I scaled down easily and was at the second floor when a stern voice below shouted, "Hey, what are you doing?"

I recognized Guardian Kier's voice. I didn't dare turn around and risk being identified. I nearly started climbing back up when I realized the screen in the window my feet rested on didn't have any glass behind it, just a screen. Who'd keep a window open in October? The smell of detergent hit me, and I realized I was right next to the laundry room. I climbed back up a little and then swung inward with as much force as I could manage. My feet ripped through the screen, and I tumbled onto the tiled floor.

I could hear more shouts outside and knew it was only a matter of time before guardians searched the building. I burst out of the laundry room and stared at the corridor before me. It had the same layout as Lissa's dorm, four intersecting halls with an elevator in the middle and staircases in the front and back wings. The back seemed safest. I raced to it and flew down the stairs, only to hear footsteps behind me. I started leaping over sets of three and four steps and then heard, "Rose?"

I spun around and saw Dimitri descending. "No time to talk, comrade."

"I thought you climbed out the window. I was going around to meet you."

"Kier's out there. I had to adjust. Also, the laundry room's screen is going to need replacing."

He groaned. "Come on, this way."

We ran down a perpendicular hallway. It was one of the ones without stairs at the end, but there was a window on the upper half of the wall. "I can fit, but you'll have to lift me."

"I know," he said. "The holly bush where I put the gloves and CD is right below. Hopefully you can grab them and go."

"More rule breaking. Tonight must be a record for you."

"I've done worse."

I hoped my shocked silence properly conveyed my thoughts.

"You're running out of time, Rose."

He held out his hands and hoisted me up, holding me by the legs. I unlatched the window and shoved it open.

"You know, I'm becoming an expert at getting in and out of—"

My hands slipped on the window frame, in turn making me lose my balance. I fell over and down, but he caught me by the waist and held on to me. I instinctively put my arms around his neck, pressing us together. I expected him to push me away, but he didn't. Just like in the corridor, he clung to the moment. Something in his eyes softened as he looked down at me with an expression that held neither exasperation nor amusement. His gaze smoldered. It hungered. It wrapped me up as fiercely as his arms did, and I became very, very aware of just how tight and thin my clothes were.

The embrace lasted only for the space of a few heartbeats, but for Dimitri—who lived for duty and discipline—that delay was an eternity. The nerves of my body buzzed with electricity, and I marveled at the odds of being able to touch him so many times tonight. Maybe the universe thought it owed me a favor too.

Dimitri ran a hand over my hair, smoothing wayward locks, and then snatched it away when we heard the distant sound of shouting from the building's lobby. Nope. The universe hated me.

Without another word, he raised me up again. I gripped

the window's edge and pulled myself out, going headfirst. I was glad no one was around to see my fantastically awful spill on the ground below, made even worse by the aforementioned holly bush. Prickly leaves and branches tore into me, and it took a lot of self-control not to yell out some very unladylike words, many of which would concern Christian and bacon truffles. I saw several long, dark brown strands of something hanging on the bush's branches and then realized that "something" was my hair. Staggering up, I dusted myself off and retrieved the items Dimitri had concealed.

What time was it? Closer to the scavenger hunt's finish than I would have liked. In the distance, I could still see the lights of the carnival, but Dagger Fang's bad covers had finally ended. Enough students moved out and about now that I could walk calmly, so long as I kept the boxing gloves close to me. As soon as I made it to the woods beyond central campus, I went tearing off through the trees. Low-hanging branches whipped me as I passed, but I was too full of adrenaline and purpose to care. If I'd impersonated a teacher, crawled through multiple windows, and touched that atrocious cologne all for nothing, I was going to be seriously pissed.

A small light shone ahead of me, and I skidded to a halt. A cluster of people stood around Camille, Otto, and the rest of this year's hunt committee. "Did I make it?" I exclaimed, setting the boxing gloves and CD on the ground. The other waiting teams crowded closer.

Camille actually had a stopwatch. "With a minute to spare."

My partners in crime pushed their way over to me. "God, Rose," exclaimed Mason. "What happened to you? Did you get in a fight with a tree while getting that CD?"

"We thought for sure you'd been caught," Eddie added.

I rubbed at a scratch on my face and winced. "You wouldn't believe me if I told you."

Otto was managing the tally now and took stock of my offerings. "Close, but not close enough. A respectable second."

Shane whooped in triumph, but I held up a hand to silence him. "Don't get too cocky yet, Reyes."

I reached into my pocket and held out the earrings with a flourish. A collective gasp sounded around me. Shane leaned forward. "No way those are real."

Otto snorted as he took the earrings from me. "You think there's anything else like that in this school? Congrats, Rose. That pushed you over the top."

I patted Shane's back. His teammates, Andy and Charlene, were still in shock. "Don't worry," I said. "You'll still get some wine for second. I mean, not as much as us, obviously. You can't half-ass your way through something like this and expect success."

"Half-ass?" exclaimed Andy. "I broke into the guardian building by hiding in a garbage can!"

I faked a yawn.

Meanwhile, Eddie and Mason regarded me with rightful worship and awe. "I need to hear this story. I'll never doubt your edge again," Mason declared.

"I never doubted it at all," said Eddie.

"We'll get everyone's prizes to you tomorrow," Camille said. "Now we've got to go smuggle this stuff back. We're going to leave it in a pile in the cafeteria."

"Be careful with those earrings," I warned. "No matter how much you think Kirova likes cats, I assure you, you are completely underestimating it."

"I really need to hear this story," Mason told me.

"I can't give away my secrets." Or fact that I'd had outside help—help from one of the very people who were supposed to be stopping us. The memory of being pressed against Dimitri's body flashed through my mind, and I had to shove it aside. Slinging my arms around my teammates, I steered us back toward the main campus. "Let's go see if there's any cotton candy left."

There was. I snagged a bag of it, plus a soft pretzel, and sat down on a bench to watch the carnival wind down. Some of the games had already closed, and Alberta had stopped cooking funnel cake. It was a good thing I'd gotten mine earlier. Eddie and Mason had wandered off, and I used my moment of tranquility to ponder the night's events, everything from my daring break-ins to those precious moments in Dimitri's arms.

"Are you okay?"

I glanced up and saw Lissa. She looked as serenely perfect as she had earlier in the night, not one platinum hair out of place.

"Great. Why?"

She crouched down and picked a leaf from my hair. "You're a mess, and you've got scratches on your face."

"Don't worry about it. It's a warrior's mark of honor for a job well done."

Lissa gasped. "Do you mean . . ."

"Yes. You ask, I deliver. The universe loves Christian after all. Who knew?"

"Oh, thank you!" The joy that radiated off her nearly knocked me over as much as her giant hug did. "You're the best. You know that, right? It doesn't matter what it is, what I need. You're always there for me."

Maybe it was exhaustion, but I couldn't come up with a snarky comeback. I gave her another tight hug and said, "And I always will be."

Still beaming, she straightened up. "I've got to get back to the lower campus and help with cleanup. I just wanted to check while Christian was busy. Thank you again, Rose. Oh, hey, Mason. Thanks for your help too."

As she walked away, Mason jogged over to me. He took my hand and pulled me up. "Come see this. You won't even believe it."

Mystified, I followed him back toward the funnel cake cart. Across from it, a group of students stood near the tent where we'd had our pictures taken. Mrs. Alders waved when she saw me. "There you are. Come over here and get your prize."

A few kids parted for me, and I approached uncertainly. "Prize for what?"

"For the costume contest. You got an honorable mention. It's very clever, you know." She pointed at my shirt. "My favorite one is Louis Armstrong. I love his music."

"Oh," I said, still stunned. "I thought he was an astronaut."

She started to show me a large cardboard box when her eyes shifted toward the crowd. "Oh. Did you give one of these to Guardian Belikov?"

I followed her gaze. Dimitri stood near the edge of the crowd, stone-faced as usual, and not at all like he'd taken part in tonight's mayhem. Mrs. Alders's question did make him raise an eyebrow, though. He looked down, and sure enough, a HELLO, MY NAME IS . . . sticker was stuck to his coat. I immediately checked my own outfit and saw an empty spot on the side of my stomach. It must have transferred over when he was either lifting me or holding me. We'd been pressed together more than I realized.

My mouth went dry, but Dimitri didn't miss a beat. He peeled the sticker off and repositioned it higher up on his coat. "Yes, she gave it to me earlier. She knows what a fan I am of Judy Blume." He glanced at me, amusement flashing in his dark eyes, and then melted back into the crowd.

I pulled off the Louis Armstrong tag and gave it to Mrs. Alders. "Yeah. And you can have this."

She accepted it with a smile and then tipped the box toward me. "We've gathered all sorts of goodies. Some were picked out especially by teachers. Some were even student donations. Go ahead and choose whichever one you want."

Curious, I peered inside at the assortment of sweets and treats. And then I started laughing.

The violation of Kirova's room resulted in another school-wide assembly about the sanctity of our rules, something I found pretty hypocritical in light of her illegal feline friend. But I kept that secret to myself and tried to appear solemn as she waxed on about "the group of miscreants" who had conspired to rob her. Kier hadn't been able to identify me on the wall, and I felt pretty smug about my escapades being mistaken for the work of a group.

"Don't feel that smug," Dimitri told me after one of our early runs. "The scavenger hunt went too far. The campus will probably be on lockdown next year."

I shrugged as we walked into the locker room. "They haven't been able to stop us before. What makes you think they can now?"

He shot me a wry smile. "Because they—we—haven't been trying as hard as we could. Sure, no one approves of all the theft and trespassing, and if you're caught, you're punished. But . . . there's always been an understanding among the guardians that trying to do the impossible is good for you—the novices, at least. Stealth and problem solving aren't bad qualities, given the jobs you'll face in the real world. Kirova doesn't feel the same about the Moroi, and after this . . . Well, like I said, some of the methods we've held back on aren't going to be held back anymore. Expect a lock change right before the carnival next year. And more patrols."

"It'll be the end of an era." I pulled my duffel bag out from a locker. "But I guess it means I'll just go down in history yet again."

"Another reason why you don't want to be anyone except Rose Hathaway, huh?"

I sat down on a bench and folded my hands in my lap as I looked away. "I know I said that . . . but sometimes . . . Well. Sometimes, I wish I could steal another identity. Someone older. Someone who isn't guarding the same Moroi who . . . who other people are guarding."

Dimitri stayed silent for a long time—so much so that I finally had to glance over at him, despite my self-consciousness. For the most part, he had on his usual cool and collected expression. But in his eyes—there it was. A flash of that warmth I saw from time to time, the warmth that made the spark that perpetually burned within me for him blaze a little brighter. There was more than heat in his gaze, though. There was wistfulness too.

"Someone like that . . . would make a few things easier," he said at last, his voice low. Strained. "But someone like that wouldn't be Rose Hathaway. And I'd rather live in a much more complicated world than in one where she wasn't around."

I had to avert my gaze again because if I kept looking at him, I was either going to cry or try to kiss him. I cleared my throat and said, "Well, lucky you, because here I am, so your world's about as complicated as it can get. But it might also get a little more delicious." I unzipped the duffel bag and dared a peek back at him. A little of that tenderness lingered in his gaze, and then he smiled and shifted back to his exasperated-mentor mode.

"Oh?"

"Ta-da." I lifted a small gold-and-blue box from the bag. "Haberlin's dark chocolate bacon truffles."

His laugh, full of genuine surprise, made me as happy as that earlier look had. "Aren't those Christian's?"

"No, Lissa has those. This is my own box. Camille gave one to Mrs. Alders too, and it ended up in the prize bin. Here. Have one." I lifted the lid and held out the box.

He glanced down at it and then back up at me. "Rose . . . if I didn't know better, I'd say you broke down and tried these."

"Quality control," I said.

"There are only two left. Out of twelve."

"Lots of quality control." I picked one up. "And I'm giving the last one to you, comrade. You should be flattered. Because even if it's complicated, I hope you realize there are perks to having Rose Hathaway in your life."

His smile grew as he picked up the chocolate. "Oh, I do, Roza. I do."

RISK EVERYTHING FOR FREEDOM.

STOP AT NOTHING FOR LOVE.

WELCOME TO THE GLITTERING COURT.

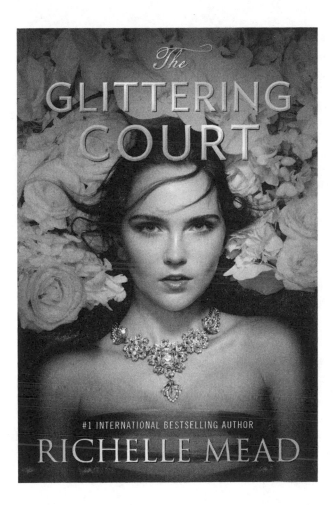

TURN THE PAGE
FOR A SNEAK PEEK!

CHAPTER 1

I'D NEVER PLANNED ON STEALING SOMEONE ELSE'S LIFE.

Really, at a glance, you wouldn't think there was anything wrong with my old life. I was young and healthy. I liked to think I was clever. I belonged to one of the noblest families in Osfrid, one that could trace its bloodline back to the country's founders. Sure, my title might have been more prestigious if my family's fortune hadn't evaporated, but that was easily fixed. All I had to do was marry well.

And that was where my problems started.

Most noblemen admired a descendant of Rupert, First Earl of Rothford, great hero of Osfrid. Centuries ago, he'd helped wrest this land from savages, thus forming the great nation we enjoyed today. But few noblemen admired my lack of resources, especially in these times. Other families were fighting their own financial crises, and a pretty face with an exalted title no longer held the appeal it once might have.

I needed a miracle, and I needed one fast.

"Darling, a miracle's happened."

I'd been staring at the ballroom's velvet-embossed wallpaper as dark thoughts swirled in my head. Blinking, I returned my attention to the noisy party and focused on my grandmother's approach. Though her face was lined and her hair pure white, people always remarked on what a handsome woman Lady Alice Witmore was. I agreed, though

I couldn't help but notice she'd seemed to age more in the years since my parents had died. But just now, her face was alight in a way I hadn't seen in some time.

"How, Grandmama?"

"We have an offer. *An offer.* He's everything we've hoped for. Young. A substantial fortune. His family line's as prestigious as yours."

That last one caught me by surprise. The blessed Rupert's line was tough to match. "Are you sure?"

"Certainly. He's your . . . cousin."

It wasn't often that words failed me. For a moment, all I could think of was my cousin Peter. He was twice my age—and married. By the rules of descent, he would be the one to inherit the Rothford title if I died without children. Whenever he was in town, he'd stop by and ask how I was feeling.

"Which one?" I asked at last, relaxing slightly. The term "cousin" was sometimes used loosely, and if you looked far enough in the family trees, half the Osfridian nobility was related to the other half. She could be referring to any number of men.

"Lionel Belshire, Baron of Ashby."

I shook my head. He was no one I knew.

She linked my arm with hers and drew me toward the opposite side of the ballroom, winding our way through some of the city's most powerful people. They were swathed in silks and velvets, adorned with pearls and gems. Above us, crystal chandeliers covered the entire ceiling, like our hosts were trying to outdo the stars. Such was life among Osfro's nobility.

"His grandmother and I were both ladies in the Duchess of Samford's coterie, back in the old days. He's only a baron." Grandmama leaned her head toward me to speak more quietly. I noted the pearl-studded cap she wore, in good shape but unfashionable for at least two years. She spent our money on clothing me. "But his blood is still good. His line comes from one of Rupert's lesser sons, though there was some scandal that Rupert might not actually have been his father. His mother was noble, though, so either way, we're covered."

I was still trying to process that when we came to a halt in front of a floor-to-ceiling window that overlooked Harlington Green. A young man stood with a woman my grandmother's age, speaking in low tones. Upon our arrival, they both looked up with keen interest.

Grandmama released my hand. "My granddaughter, the Countess of Rothford. My darling, this is Baron Belshire and his grandmother, Lady Dorothy."

Lionel bent over and kissed my hand while his grandmother curtseyed. Her deference was a show. Sharp eyes raked over every part of me. If propriety had allowed it, I think she would have examined my teeth.

I turned to Lionel as he straightened. He was the one I had to size up. "Countess, it's a pleasure to meet you. It's a shame this hasn't happened sooner, seeing as we're family. Descendants of Earl Rupert and all that."

Out of the corner of my eye, I saw Grandmama arch a skeptical eyebrow.

I gave him a demure smile, not deferential enough to diminish my superior rank but enough to make him think his charm had flustered me. His charm, of course, was yet to be assessed. At a glance, it might be all he had going for him. His face was long and pointed, his skin sallow. I would have expected at least a flush, considering how the crush of bodies had heated the room. The sagging of his narrow shoulders gave the impression he was about to cave in upon himself.

None of it mattered, though. Only the marriage logistics did. I'd never expected to marry for love.

"We're definitely overdue for a meeting," I agreed. "Really, we should all be having regular Rupert reunions, as a tribute to our progenitor. Get everyone together and have picnics on the green. We could do three-legged races, like the country folk do. I'm sure I could manage it with the skirts."

He stared at me unblinkingly and scratched his wrist. "Earl Rupert's descendants are spread out all over Osfrid. I don't think a gathering of that sort would be feasible. And it's not just unseemly for nobility to do those three-legged races; I don't allow the tenants on my estates to do such things either. The great god Uros gave us two legs, not three. To suggest otherwise is an abomination." He paused. "I don't really approve of potato-sack races either."

"You're right, of course," I said, keeping the smile fixed on my face. Beside me, Grandmama cleared her throat.

"The baron has been very successful with his barley production," she said with forced cheer. "Quite possibly the most successful in the country."

Lionel scratched his left ear. "My tenants have converted more than eighty percent of the land to barley fields. We recently bought a new estate, and those lands too now have a booming crop. Barley as far as the eye can see. Acres and acres. I even have my house servants, in both estates, eat it every morning. To boost morale."

"That's . . . a lot of barley," I said. I was starting to feel sorry for his tenants. "Well, I hope you let them splurge every once in a while. Oats. Rye, if you're feeling exotic."

That previous puzzled look returned to his face as he scratched his right ear. "Why would I do that? Barley is our livelihood. It's good for them to remember that. I hold myself to the same standard—a higher one, actually, as I make sure to include a portion of barley in *all* of my meals. It sets a good example."

"You're a man of the people," I said. I eyed the window beyond him, wondering if I could jump out of it.

An awkward silence fell, and Lady Dorothy tried to fill it. "Speaking of estates, I understand you just recently sold your *last* one." Here it was, a reminder of our financial situation. Grandmama was quick to defend our honor.

"We weren't using it." She lifted her chin. "I'm not so foolish as to waste money on an empty house and tenants who've grown lazy without supervision. Our town house here in the city is much more comfortable and keeps us close to society. We were invited to court three times this winter, you know."

"Winter, of course," said Lady Dorothy dismissively. "But surely summers in the city are dull. Especially with so much of the nobility at their own estates. When you marry Lionel, you'll live in his Northshire estate—where I live—and want for nothing. And you may plan as many social gatherings as you like. Under my close supervision, of course. It's such a lovely opportunity for you. I mean no offense—Countess, Lady Alice. You maintain yourselves so well that no one would guess your true situation. But I'm sure it'll be a relief to be settled into better circumstances."

"Better circumstances for me. A better title for him," I murmured.

As we spoke, Lionel first scratched his forehead and then his inner arm. That second bout went on for some time, and I tried not to stare. What was going on? Why was he itching so much? And why was it happening all over his whole body? I couldn't see any obvious rashes. Worse, the more I watched him, the more I suddenly wanted to scratch. I had to clasp my hands together to stop myself.

The excruciating conversation went on for several more minutes as our grandmothers made plans for the nuptials I'd only just learned about. Lionel continued to scratch. When we finally extracted ourselves, I waited all of thirty seconds before voicing my opinion to Grandmama.

"No," I said.

"Hush." She smiled at various guests we knew as we walked to the ballroom's exit and told one of our host's manservants to order our carriage around. I bit off my words until we were safely alone inside it.

"No," I repeated, sinking back into the carriage's plush seat. "Absolutely not."

"Don't be so dramatic."

"I'm not! I'm being sane. I can't believe you accepted that offer without consulting me."

"Well, it was certainly difficult choosing between that and your *many other offers*." She met my glare levelly. "Yes, dear, you're not the only one around here who can be pert. You are, however, the only one who can save us from eventual ruin."

"Now who's being dramatic? Lady Branson would take you with her into her daughter's household. You'd live very well there."

"And what happens to you while I'm living very well?"

"I don't know. I'll find someone else." I thought back to the flurry of guests I'd met at the party this evening. "What about that merchant who was there? Donald Crosby? I hear he's amassed a pretty big fortune."

"Ugh." Grandmama rubbed her temples. "Please stop talking about the nouveau riche. You know how it gives me a headache."

I scoffed. "What's wrong with him? His business is booming. And he laughed at all my jokes—which is more than can be said for Lionel."

"You know what's wrong with *Mister* Crosby. He should never have been at that party. I don't know what Lord Gilman was thinking." She paused as a particularly large pothole in the cobblestone street caused our carriage to lurch. "How do you think your exalted ancestor Rupert would feel about you mingling his line with such common blood?"

I groaned. It seemed as though, lately, we couldn't have a conversation without invoking Rupert's name. "I think someone who followed his lord across the channel to carve out an empire would place a pretty big emphasis on keeping one's self-respect. Not selling it out to a boring cousin and his tyrant grandmother. Did you count how many times she said 'under my close supervision' when we were talking about the future? I did. Five. Which is seven less times than Lionel scratched some body part."

Grandmama's expression grew weary. "Do you think you're the first girl who's had an arranged marriage? Do you think you're the first girl to resent it? Stories and songs are full of tales of woeful maidens trapped in such circumstances who escape to a glorious future. But those are stories. The reality is that most girls in your situation . . . well, endure. There's nothing else you can do. There's nowhere else you can go. It's the price we pay for this world we live in. For our rank."

"My parents would have never made me endure," I grumbled.

Her eyes hardened. "Your parents and their frivolous investments are the reason we're in this situation. We're out of money. Selling the Bentley estate has kept us living as we always have. But that's going to change. And you won't like it when it does." When my obstinate glare continued, she added, "You'll have people making choices for you your entire life. Get used to it."

Our home was located in a different—but equally fashionable— district of the city from the party. Upon our arrival, servants swarmed to attend us. They helped us out of the carriage, took our wraps and shawls. I had my own flock of maidservants who accompanied me to my suite to remove my formal attire for me. I watched as they smoothed the red velvet overdress, with its trumpet sleeves and gold embroidery. They hung it up with countless other decadent frocks, and I found myself staring at the bureau after they'd left. So much of our family's fading wealth spent on clothes that were supposed to help me achieve the opportunity to change my life for the better.

My life was certainly about to change, but for the better? That I was skeptical of.

And so, I treated it as though it wasn't real. It was how I'd dealt with my parents' deaths as well. I'd refused to believe they were gone, even when faced with the tangible proof of their graves. It wasn't possible that someone you loved so much, someone who filled up so much of your heart, could no longer exist in the world. I tried convincing myself that they would walk through my door one day. And when I couldn't make myself believe that, I simply didn't think about it all.

That was how I dealt with Lionel. I put him out of my mind and went on with my life as though nothing at that party had ever happened.

When a letter came from Lady Dorothy one day, I finally had to acknowledge his existence again. She wanted to confirm a date for the wedding, which was to be expected. What wasn't expected was her directive to cut our household staff in half and get rid of the majority of our possessions. *You won't need them when you get to Northshire,* she wrote. *The staff and items you need will be provided, under my close supervision.*

"Oh, sweet Uros," I said when I'd finished reading.

"Don't take the god's name in vain," Grandmama snapped. Despite her sharp words, I could see the strain on her. Living under someone else's thumb wasn't going to be easy for her either. "Oh. And Lionel sent you a present."

The "present" was a container of a proprietary barley cereal blend he ate each morning, with a note saying it would give me a taste of what was to come. I wanted to believe he'd intended the pun, but I sincerely doubted it.

Grandmama began fretting about how to split up the household as I walked out of the room. And I kept walking. I walked out of the town house, out through the front courtyard. I walked right out through the gate that sheltered our property from the main thoroughfare, earning a puzzled look from the servant who was manning it.

"My lady? Is there something I can help you with?"

I waved him back when he started to rise. "No," I said. He glanced around, uncertain what to do. He'd never seen me leave our property alone. No one ever had. It wasn't done.

His confusion kept him where he was, and I soon found myself swallowed up in the foot traffic moving about the street. It wasn't the gentry, of course. Servants, merchants, couriers . . . all the people whose labor helped the city's rich survive. I fell in step with them, unsure of where I was going.

Some crazy part of me thought maybe I should go make an appeal to Donald Crosby. He'd seemed to like me well enough in our minutes-long conversation. Or maybe I could seek passage somewhere. Go off to the continent and charm some Belsian noble. Or maybe I could just lose myself in the crowd, one more anonymous face to blend into the city's masses.

"Can I help you, my lady? Did you get separated from your servants?"

Apparently not so anonymous.

I'd ended up on the edge of one of the city's many commercial districts. The speaker was an older man who carried parcels on his back that looked far too heavy for his slight frame.

"How do you know I'm a lady?" I blurted out.

He grinned, showing a few missing teeth. "Ain't too many out alone dressed like you."

I glanced around and saw he was right. The violet jacquard dress I wore was a casual one for me, but it made me stand out in the sea of otherwise drab attire. There were a few others of higher classes out shopping, but they were surrounded by dutiful servants ready to shield them from any unsavory elements.

"I'm fine," I said, pushing past him. But I didn't get very far before someone else stopped me: a ruddy-faced young boy, the kind who made his living delivering messages.

"Need me to escort you home, m'lady?" he asked. "Three coppers, and I'll get you out of all this."

"No, I . . ." I let my words drop as something occurred to me. "I don't have any money. Not on me." He started to leave, and I called, "Wait. Here." I pulled off my pearl bracelet and offered it to him. "Can you take me to the Church of Glorious Vaiel?"

His eyes widened at the sight of the pearls, but he hesitated. "That's too much, m'lady. The church is only over on Cunningham Street."

I pushed the bracelet into his hand. "I have no idea where that is.

Take me."

It turned out to be only about three blocks away. I knew all the major areas of Osfro but little about how to travel between them. There'd never been any need to know.

There were no services today, but the main doors were propped slightly open, welcoming any souls in need of counsel. I walked past the elegant church, out to the graveyard. I moved through the common section, through the nicer section, and finally to the noble section. It had a wrought-iron gate surrounding it and was filled with monuments and mausoleums, rather than ordinary gravestones.

I might not know my way around Osfro streets, but I knew exactly where my family's mausoleum was in this graveyard. My guide waited near the iron gate as I walked over to the handsome stone building labeled WITMORE. It wasn't the biggest one on the property, but I thought it was one of the most beautiful. My father had loved art of all kinds, and we'd commissioned exquisite carvings of the six glorious angels on all the exterior walls.

I had no way to enter, not without prior arrangements with the church, and simply sat on the steps. I ran my fingers over the names carved amid those listed on the stone placard: LORD ROGER WITMORE, SIXTEENTH EARL OF ROTHFORD, AND LADY AMELIA ROTHFORD. Above them, my grandfather's name was listed alone: LORD AUGUSTUS WITMORE, FIFTEENTH EARL OF ROTHFORD. My grandmother's name would join his one day, and then the mausoleum would be full. "You'll have to find your own place," Grandmama had told me at my father's funeral.

My mother had died first, catching one of the many illnesses that ran rampant in the poorer parts of the city. My parents had been greatly interested in investing in charitable establishments among the less fortunate, and it had cost them their lives, my mother getting sick one summer, my father the next. Their charities fell apart. Some said my parents had been saintly. Most said they'd been foolish.

I stared up at the great stone door, which held a carving of the glorious angel Ariniel, the gatekeeper of Uros. The work was gorgeous, but I always thought Ariniel was the least interesting of the angels. All she did was open the way for others and facilitate their journeys. Was there some place she'd rather be? Something else she'd rather do? Was she content to exist so that others could achieve their goals while she stayed at a standstill? Grandmama had said I'd always have choices made for me. Was that way of both humans and angels? The scriptures had never addressed such questions. Most likely they were blasphemous.

"My lady!"

I turned from that serene face and saw a flutter of color at the gate. Three of my ladies were hurrying toward me. Far beyond them, near the church's entrance, I saw our carriage waiting. Immediately, I was swarmed.

"Oh, my lady, what were you thinking?" cried Vanessa. "Did that boy behave inappropriately?"

"You must be freezing!" Ada tossed a heavier cloak over my shoulders.

"Let me brush the dirt from your hem," said Thea.

"No, no," I said to that last one. "I'm fine. How did you find me?"

They all began talking over one another, but it basically came down to their noticing my disappearance and questioning the boy at our town house's gate and pretty much every person I'd passed in my outing. I'd apparently made an impression.

"Your grandmother doesn't know yet," said Vanessa, urging me forward. She was the cleverest of them. "Let's get back quickly."

Before I stepped away, I looked back at the angel, back at my parents' names. *"Bad things are always going to happen,"* my father had told me in his last year. *"There's no way to avoid that. Our control comes in how we face them. Do we let them crush us, making us despondent? Do we face them unflinchingly and endure the pain? Do we outsmart them?"* I'd asked him what it meant to outsmart a bad thing. *"You'll know when the time comes. And when it does, you need to act quickly."*

The maids couldn't stop fussing over me, even on the carriage ride home. "My lady, if you'd wanted to go, you should have just let us arrange a proper visit with a priest," Thea said.

"I wasn't thinking," I murmured. I wasn't about to elaborate on how the letter from Lady Dorothy had nearly given me a nervous breakdown. "I wanted the air. I decided I'd just walk over on my own."

They stared at me incredulously. "You can't do that," said Ada. "You can't do that on your own. You . . . you can't do anything on your own."

"Why not?" I snapped, feeling only a little bad when she flinched. "I'm a peeress of the realm. My family name commands respect everywhere. So why shouldn't I be free to move everywhere? To choose to do whatever I want?"

None of them spoke right away, and I wasn't surprised that it was Vanessa who finally did: "Because you're the Countess of Rothford. Someone with a name like that can't move among the nameless. And when it comes to who you are, my lady . . . well, that's something we never have a choice in."